W9-AWT-887

THE BOOK OF Q

ALSO BY JONATHAN RABB

The Overseer

THE BOOK OF Q

OF

Jonathan Rabb

A Novel

Crown Publishers
New York

Published by Crown Publishers, New York, New York.
Member of the Crown Publishing Group.

Random House, Inc. New York, Toronto, London, Sydney, Auckland
www.randomhouse.com

CROWN is a trademark and the Crown colophon is a registered trademark of Random House, Inc.

Printed in the United States of America

Design by Elina D. Nudelman

Library of Congress Cataloging-in-Publication Data
Rabb, Jonathan.
    The book of Q : a novel / Jonathan Rabb.
    1. Yugoslav War, 1991–1995—Bosnia and Hercegovina—Fiction.   2. Catholic
Church—Clergy—Fiction.   3. Bosnia and Hercegovina—Fiction.   4. Heresies,
Christian—Fiction.   5. Conspiracies—Fiction. I. Title.
PS3568.A215 B66 2001
813'.54—dc21
00-047550

ISBN 0-609-60483-X

10 9 8 7 6 5 4 3 2 1

First Edition

For Alexandra, Juliet, and Isabel

contents

 # Acknowledgments

There are always too many to thank, but I would particularly like to mention Dottore Massimo Ceresa of the Vatican Library, who opened the archives to me and was equally generous with his time and expertise; Professor Peter Brown of Princeton University, who offered insights that went far beyond the Manichaeans and Gnostics; Matt Bialer, who remains the ideal agent; Kristin Kiser, who continues to teach me the art of editing; Peter Buchi, Joanne Lessner, and Emily Stone, who provided seasoned ears for my Italian and Latin; Rob Tate, Rob Roznowski, Maya Perez, and especially Jen Smith, who gave such helpful comments on earlier drafts of the book; my family, who seem to possess an unlimited enthusiasm; and Andra Reeve, who simply makes it all worthwhile.

Language is only the instrument of science, and words are but the signs of ideas: I wish, however, that the instrument might be less apt to decay, and that signs might be permanent, like the things which they denote.

—Samuel Johnson,
Dictionary of the English Language

THE BOOK OF Q

Prologue

Earth and glass sifted through a moonless sky. A thick wall of flame some two hundred yards off pinpointed where shell had met target, seconds later a pulse of heat searing its way through an already-sweltering night.

For several moments, everything became strangely quiet. No sound of machine-gun fire, no siren song of incoming rockets, only the sharp taste of gasoline as it began to suffuse the air. A few distant shouts echoed in the open expanse, quickly drowned out by the rising pitch of the blazing school-turned-fuel-depot. It had been an age since children had inhabited the place—six, seven months at least—the entire village reduced to little more than odd mounds of stone. Prjac had never been much of a town to begin with; now it suffered a far more damning fate. Strategic importance, caught between Serbian Banja Luka and Croatian Bosanski Brod. A vital piece of turf.

For the time being.

Ian Pearse stared out into the night. He'd lost ten pounds in the past two months, his six-foot-two frame reduced to taut skin and muscle. Once clean-cropped hair now draped to near shoulder length, pulled back behind his ears, sweat and two weeks without hot water enough to keep the tangled strands in place. Yet his face remained clean-shaven. Somewhere along the way, a shipment of ten thousand safety razors had found its way to the supply dump in Slitna, a substitute for the penicillin they had been begging for. People might be dying, but at least they were well groomed.

"They're taking the bait." A whispered voice came from up ahead. "Wait for Josip to draw their fire; then go."

Prjac's church—or what was left of it—stood no more than thirty yards from him, its silhouette cast in the glow of flames, two walls, bits and pieces of roof dangling from above. Pearse clutched at the turf under his hands, listening, waiting for the peal of tommy guns. The fuel tank had been a surprise, an added bonus, far more than the diversion they had intended—blow up an old building, draw attention away from the church, away from the three boxes of black-market penicillin they had been told would be inside. A depot, however, required guards, more than they had anticipated. Which meant one or two might still be waiting.

A burst of gunfire, and Pearse leapt out, his torso crouched low as he wove his way toward the church. His legs had grown accustomed to the spongy sod of Bosnian countryside, gelatinous clumps made thick from the summer rains. He did his best to run on tiptoe, every so often his feet slipping out from under him, a quick hand to the ground to steady himself.

No more than fifteen feet from the church, he stumbled again, suddenly face-to-face with two green eyes, the outline of the fire undulating in a pair of lifeless pupils. The man's neck had been slit. Silent, efficient. Pearse placed his hand on the frozen gaze and shut the eyes. Another wave of gunfire. Somewhere up ahead, two figures darted into the church. Pearse wasted no time racing after them.

Inside, he leaned up against one of the two standing walls, to his left the remnants of Prjac's lone stained-glass window, pieces jutting out into the night, prismed blues and reds reflecting on the piles of stone scattered about. A second fuel tank ignited in the distance, another wave of stifling air. Instinctively, he pulled back and glanced around the little church; he noticed a few cots against the far wall, blankets, some straw. He wondered how many had taken refuge in the abandoned church, how many had lain here wounded or dying, praying for the trucks to come and cart them off to some imagined hospital, refugee camp—more likely, roadside grave. Muslim and Catholic lying side by side. Waiting.

It was only at moments like these that he let himself see beyond the narrow focus of survival to the real devastation. Thousands upon thousands driven from their homes by their own neighbors, friends, told to take what they could and go. Where? It didn't matter. Just go. Those lucky enough to get to the border had survived five weeks on foot for a car ride that would have taken less than six hours a month ago—forests, mountains, never the main roads for fear of paramilitaries all too ready to take potshots. And all for the dim hope of cramming themselves into sports halls, warehouses, one blanket per family. Those not so lucky were hunted down, ambushed.

Sometimes in a church.

Pearse tried not to let his mind wander. Instead, he ducked down behind one of the piles of brick and waited. He knew that to grant those thoughts more than a few seconds would have made day-to-day survival impossible; to deny them altogether, though, would have made him numb. And as much as he might still have hoped to reclaim the naïve, albeit well-intentioned, convictions that had brought him here, he knew there had to be more to it than that. His faith remained strong. Numb wasn't a possibility.

Not for someone whose future lay in the church.

His parents had been against it from the start. They were both academics, both good Catholics, but more for the sake of their own parents than for themselves; faith hadn't really been a part of the calculus.

Except for the rituals. Those, they'd always liked. It's what he and his two brothers had been brought up on, little in the way of substance, but plenty to fill the calendar. Of course, nothing that might infringe on baseball practice, but there was always something for an altar boy to do, especially for the youngest of three. When he began to notice there wasn't all that much to it, he hadn't gotten an argument. "A cultural thing," Dad had said, "to keep the family together"—which meant, of course, more time with the rituals. When he told them he'd found something even more compelling, again they'd hardly been surprised. After all, the college scouts had made it clear how good he was. Not just at the game, but in the way he played it—with a kind of delight, a wonder. Pearse was at his best when on the field, and everyone knew it. As long as he kept going to church on Sundays, no problem.

When it turned out to be faith, and not baseball, that was inspiring him, his parents had stared, stunned.

"A priest?" his father had said. "Isn't that a little . . . too Catholic?"

School had been the first compromise. Notre Dame. He'd gotten the scholarship to play; why not see it through? And, as reluctant as he was to admit it now, the status of gentleman jock had made campus life pretty nice for a while. A few big-league scouts had even come to see him play. Come and gone. Still, everyone had been duly impressed. Especially the young ladies. He hit for power. What could he say?

His major had been the second. He'd originally signed up for theology, but Mom and Dad had convinced him to broaden his horizons. Classics. Now, there was a leap. He'd laughed and acquiesced. But even he had been surprised when he'd begun to show an uncanny facility for

Latin and Greek. A special gift, he was told. The folks had been ecstatic. More so when he'd admitted just how much fun he was having in class with a collection of old fragmentary tracts. It was like a game, he said. Filling in the missing pieces of the jigsaw—the words that were never there, the scattered phrases on a parchment that he learned to turn into coherent thoughts. He'd always had a knack for puzzles. Dad had actually laughed.

Until Pearse had told him it was Saint Paul, not Horace or Aeschylus, who was providing all the fun.

"We send him to a Catholic university, and he wants to sign up for life? Where did we go wrong?" Dad had been joking, of course; his parents had never doubted his sincerity, even back in high school. But Pearse knew the jabs meant that they'd never really get it. They were far more comfortable with the intellectual detachment, debating the minutiae, reveling in the ambiguity. Not surprising. It was how they'd always dealt with their own faith, as something to be held at arm's length.

And Pearse knew that wasn't going to work for him. He'd switched to theology, spent a couple of summers working for the archdiocese in Chicago, and taken his first real steps beyond the rituals. The first steps beyond the games of scholarship, and into the trenches with the church.

And with John J.

Even now, four thousand miles away, and crouched up against a ragged pile of bricks, Pearse couldn't help but smile at the thought of Father John Joseph Blaney, rector of the Church of the Sacred Heart—that shock of white hair, those eyebrows always in need of a good clipping. The first time they'd met, Pearse had actually had trouble not staring at the wisps sitting there like spider's legs, curling to the lids, though never daring too far. It was as if even they somehow recognized Blaney's authority, hulking shoulders over an ever-thinning body, all of it an echo of the once-imposing figure.

It had been the same with the priest's flock, even among the rougher elements—no one willing to cross the sixty-five-year-old Father. Blaney had actually gone on a drug bust once, aware that several of his younger parishioners had gotten caught up in something beyond their control. Naturally, he'd brought Pearse along with him, the two of them sweating it out with three cops in a cramped basement for hours. And, in typical John J. fashion, he'd made Pearse spend the time whispering word games back and forth, a mania with the priest, a necessary passion for anyone under his tutelage. The two, it seemed, had been made for each other.

Pearse wouldn't have minded a little of that right about now.

"Faith's a puzzle," Blaney had always said. "Have to keep the mind active for it."

When the kids had finally arrived after three hours, and with what amounted to two ounces of marijuana, Pearse had nearly had to restrain one of the cops from going after John J.

"Three frickin' hours, Father, for two ounces of . . ."

Blaney had known all along what the "bust" would entail (although, of course, he'd never told Pearse). He'd also known that the sight of three undercover cops ready to explode would have a lasting effect on his twelve-year-old "dealers." Three hours for six kids. A nice trade-off, according to John J. It had taken him a little time to convince the cops of the math, but they'd eventually come around. They'd also left the offenders in John J.'s hands. The look on the boys' faces on hearing that the Father would be handling their "rehabilitation" had said it all.

Pearse had loved those summers with John J. Another kind of wonder and delight. After that, there'd really been no question.

His dad, however, had been another story.

"You're sure?" he'd asked. "I mean, absolutely sure?"

"Yeah, Pop, I'm sure." Sitting around the kitchen table that last Thanksgiving break—the two of them alone—Pearse had experienced something he never thought he'd see: his dad at a loss for words. It was the first time he'd ever felt on a par with the man.

"So I guess you were hoping I'd get sidetracked by something else."

"No. . . . Yes. I don't know."

"That's a first."

A smile. "Wiseass."

"Holy ass, I think, would be more appropriate now." He watched his father laugh. "It's what makes sense to me, Dad."

"I understand that. It's just . . . it can be a very lonely life, Ian. Priests are a different breed. I'm sure Father Blaney would be the first to tell you that."

"Is that why they get the fancy flea collar?"

"I'm being serious."

"I know. And I'm trying to tell you that I don't see it that way. Look . . . remember those summer games in the Newton league?" A nod. "Remember how I used to tell you how much I loved that feeling when there was just enough sun to see the ball but not enough to really trust it? And they'd hit one out to me, and I'd race after it, and just when

I thought I had it, I'd close my eyes and see if it would fall into my glove."

A smile. "You were a cocky son of a bitch."

Now Pearse laughed. "Yeah. Well, remember what I told you it was like when I opened my eyes and the ball was there?"

Another nod.

"It's like that, except maybe a thousand times better. You can't quite see it, but you know it's there. All the time. How can that be lonely?"

For just an instant, Pearse thought he'd seen a hint of regret in his father's eyes. Not for the son who'd "gone wrong," but for himself. A longing for a sensation he'd never know.

Even so, Dad had been the one to suggest the relief mission. Ecstatic baseball moments and summers with priests were one thing; Bosnian raids were another. Test those convictions in a place where faith seemed to be at a minimum. Before taking the plunge. It was why he had come.

Numb wasn't a possibility.

"Over here." A voice from behind one of the piles of rubble called out. "We've found them." Pearse knew the voice, Salko Mendravic, a bear of a man, who had taken Pearse under his wing within the first week of his arrival. A man who had gone to great lengths to cross himself with gusto at every opportunity during those first two days the American priests and their young entourage had stopped in the village—"Yes, Eminence, I'll make sure to take excellent care of these young men, so brave, so generous of spirit. . . ." Mendravic, an artist until the war, had been equally enthusiastic about teaching them how to dismantle and clean a Kalashnikov rifle once the priests had moved on. Not exactly the usual fare for seminary-bound young men. Six of them. The other five had lasted two weeks. For some reason, Pearse had remained.

Stronger convictions, he'd told himself.

"There's a problem." Mendravic had moved into the open, the glow from the fuel depot giving shape to his immense body. "It's Josip." He was now by Pearse's side, his voice hushed. "There was a struggle. . . ." He let the words trail off. "He won't make it. He wants a priest."

"I'm not a priest," answered Pearse.

"I know . . . but you came with the priests. And right now, he wants a priest. You're as close as he'll get. He needs absolution."

"I can't give him absolution."

The two men stared at each other for a few moments.

"Petra is with him." Mendravic tried a smile. "She's doing her best to make him comfortable."

"We'll take him with us." Pearse started to move off. "Find him a priest in Slitna."

Mendravic grabbed his arm. "It'd take two of us to carry him; even then, there's little chance he'd come through it. How many boxes are you willing to leave behind to save him, Ian?" The smile was gone, the grip powerful. "He wants to die at peace. Don't you think God will understand?"

Pearse tried to answer, but he was cut short by a sudden explosion at the church's outer wall. Mendravic pulled him to the ground, aimed his tommy gun through the onetime window, and let go with a volley. Two seconds later, they were on their feet, shadows on the far wall darting in and out to the sound of machine-gun fire. Both men dived behind a mound of wood and brick—on closer inspection, a slab of the roof now planted three feet deep in the cement floor. Bullets ricocheted behind them as they tried to catch their breath.

"Petra." Mendravic spoke in a loud whisper.

From the darkness, a woman's voice. "Here."

"How many boxes can you carry?"

"What?"

"How many boxes of the penicillin?"

There was a pause before she answered. "What are you asking? We each take one—"

"If Ian and I carry Josip, how many boxes?"

Again a pause. "Josip's dead."

For a moment, Mendravic said nothing; he then turned to Pearse. "Then we each take one."

Pearse nodded, Mendravic already pulling him by the arm, again the sound of bullets, wild shots, only a few penetrating the walls of the church—enough, though, to keep the two men as low to the ground as possible. In no time, they were with Petra; another half minute, and all three were bolting through the forty-yard corridor of grass and brick that separated the back of the church from the sanctuary of the woods, three boxes in hand.

There was no need to worry about pursuit. The soldiers at Prjac were Beli Orlovi—"White Eagles"—modern-day Chetnik thugs, eager for brutality, but not much on expending energy for something as trivial as penicillin. They would fire their guns into the night sky, happy enough to let the trees swallow up their would-be prey.

Of course, had they found Josip alive—now that would have made for an interesting evening.

▲

It was five weeks later when Pearse saw Josip again. Another night's foray—this time, two dozen eggs the prize—the chance discovery of a series of shallow graves on the outskirts of still one more nondescript town. Eight bodies, each with the identifying marks of the Beli Orlovi— mutilated faces and genitals, the latter forced into what remained of the victims' mouths. Pearse had heard of such things, been told that it was the surest sign of self-loathing, the need to disfigure an enemy who resembled oneself all too closely, but he'd never seen it. Serb, Croat, Muslim. Ethnically indistinguishable in the streets of Sarajevo two years ago. Indistinguishable now—even when the torturer stared into the face of his victim and saw himself.

The psychology and horror notwithstanding, Pearse recognized Josip from the bandanna—Notre Dame, 1992—that had been used to bind his hands. A gift the day Josip had taught him how to handle a Kalashnikov.

"I'm still not sure I could use it," Pearse had said as he'd shifted the rifle onto his shoulder, the strap pulled tightly across his chest.

"Use it?" Josip answered. "You'll be lucky if the damn thing doesn't blow up in your face. Still, it's good to have it. What do they say? 'A man who can't use a gun—' "

" 'Is no man at all.' " Petra appeared at the doorway of a nearby house—little more than two rooms, an old radio somehow connect- ing them with the other Croatian towns in the region—the com- munications center for Slitna's endless flow of refugees. She kept her hair pulled back, the ponytail struggling to keep the thick black mane out of her face. As ever, it was losing the battle. Two or three wisps across her cheeks, olive skin, the gaze of charcoal eyes.

He would find himself staring at her strange beauty amid all this, lithe body in pants, shirt, the gun at her hip dissolving easily into the long line of her legs. But always the eyes. And perhaps a smile.

He wasn't a priest yet.

"Then I guess I'm not much of one, given the way I fire this thing," he said.

A hint of a smile. "You'll get better," she said. "With practice." She stared at the rifle, at him, then walked over. She reached up and began to tug at the matted cord across his chest, slender fingers adjusting it so the rifle would hang more easily. "Are all priests this hard to fit?" She was having fun, yanking down hard on the strap, then loosening it, shifting it across his chest.

"When I become one, I'll let you know."

"Oh, that's right. I forgot." She stepped back. "You never looked like much of one anyway."

"Really?"

"Really."

For several seconds, he stood there, his own smile becoming a laugh. He reached up, pulled the strap over his head, and tossed the rifle to Josip. "Better?"

She continued to size him up. "So you think you could survive without one?"

"Maybe."

A look of mock surprise spread across her face. "You'd pray people into submission?"

"Something like that."

"Uh-huh." She unclipped her holster and let the gun drop to the ground. "So how would you make me submit?"

Pearse shot a glance over at Josip; the Croat smiled and shook his head. It was clear he was enjoying himself immensely.

"Well"—Pearse began to move toward her, picking up speed as he spoke—"there's the direct approach."

He was about to hoist her up onto his shoulder, when she suddenly reached out under his arm and twisted. Before he could react, she kicked his legs out from under him, her boot on one of his arms, her knee on his chest, fingers gripping his neck, her thumb held precariously over his Adam's apple.

"Didn't you tell me you once knocked a two-hundred-and-fifty-pound catcher unconscious?" Pearse was about to answer, but she pressed her thumb even closer. "No, no. Save your strength." The smile reappeared. "Then again, I'm not protecting someone's little ball, am I?" She pulled her thumb away and straddled his chest. "I'd learn to use the rifle if I were you. Much less dangerous than all of this."

She was on her feet, making her way back to the house, before he had a chance to recover.

"Difficult to gauge this one," said Josip as he helped Pearse up and handed him the rifle.

Pearse pulled the strap over his shoulder, all the while his eyes on Petra. "That feels about right."

"I'm not talking about the rifle." He winked and headed for the house.

"She doesn't understand why I've stayed, does she?"

Josip stopped, turned. "I don't know. It's a good question, though."

"I haven't heard any complaints."

"You haven't gotten any of us killed yet."

"Is that what worries her?"

"No." Josip looked at the gun, shook his head; he stepped over and began to fiddle with the cord. "American boy comes to deliver food, blankets, maybe a little faith to a people he's never heard of before." He pulled down on Pearse's shoulder. "Bosnians in need of help, spiritual guidance, whichever God they pray to. Simple enough for him to ease his conscience, serve his own God, and move on with the others. But he doesn't."

"That would have been too easy."

"There's nothing easy in it, at all. Difference is, you can leave whenever you want."

"But I don't."

"No, you don't." He let go of the cord. "And for that reason, you're as puzzling to us as we are to you. I'm a good Catholic, Ian, but if they weren't doing this to my home, I wouldn't be here."

"Even if you'd seen the pictures of Omarska?"

"Thousands have seen the camps. And thousands have shrugged and said how terrible that such a thing can happen in a civilized world. They're not people without conscience. But it's not their home. It's not yours. And yet you stay."

"Is that what she thinks?"

Josip laughed and shook his head. "I have no idea what she thinks. You've learned to shoot a rifle. That's good enough."

Pearse returned the smile. "I hope I never have to use it."

Josip's smile disappeared. "Then what would have been the point in learning how?"

His mangled body had already done much to feed the local wildlife. Little skin remained on the torso and legs, eyes and ears gone. The incongruity of the college bandanna, slightly bloodied, its large ND lashed across his wrists, sickened Pearse as much as the butchered flesh. For the first time, he could connect a voice, a smile, an arrogant charm to the obscenity in front of him. For the first time, he wondered how far his faith could be stretched.

"He said you were crazy for staying." Petra drew up to his side, her ponytail managing a bit better today. "But I think he admired it." The two had grown close in the last month, or at least as close as they dared. He had learned how to induce the smile, revel in the fleeting moments when she'd brush the strands from her face, talk of a past she no longer cared to recall with any accuracy.

They stood there, silently staring.

"He was so grateful when I gave it to him," Pearse finally said, his eyes on the cloth, "as if I'd handed him something irreplaceable." He shook his head.

"Maybe it was." After a moment: "We need to get going." As she moved toward Mendravic and the others, Pearse nodded, knelt down, and crossed himself.

And prayed for Josip's absolution.

▲

That night, they sat in one of the remaining houses in Slitna—few chairs, one square wooden table, beds of straw in every corner—watching as a handful of children gulped down great mounds of eggs. The mothers, in long printed skirts, solid-colored scarves around their heads, stood off to the side, beaming with each child's eager mouthful. Mendravic watched as well, smiling with the children, his empty cheeks chewing along with them in mock ecstasy, eliciting bursts of laughter from the tiny faces.

Pushing the memories of Josip aside, Pearse managed to get caught up in their delight, its novelty infectious. Petra, too. She took hold of one of the boys—only as high as her waist—and began to dance around the room with him, spinning them both, lifting his feet from the ground, wide eyes from the children as they clapped between each ravenous forkful. For a few minutes, the world beyond seemed to vanish. That fewer than half of them would make it as far as the border, and fewer still survive once there, played no part in their momentary grasp at normalcy. Enough to take what they could when they could.

Perhaps it was the sound of their own laughter, or the high-pitched screams of the exhilarated children, that muffled the telltale whistle of incoming rockets. Whatever the reason, the terrifying screech tore through the small room only seconds before the bomb struck. No time to race to the cellar, to cradle children in protective arms. The far wall was the first to go, splitting down its center as if made of paper, dust and smoke rising in great swirls. Pearse was thrown to the ground, his left shoulder landing with particular force, a jabbing pain as he tried to recover. He reached for his neck—nothing broken—the pain no less intense. Without thinking, he got to his feet and began to grab as many small bodies as he could. The children were screaming, some bloodied, some shaking frantically as he pulled four or five of them close into him. Again the whistle of artillery flooded the air, this time accompanied by a violent groan from the roof. He knew he had only seconds. Clutching the little bodies to his chest, he careened across the room, half-blinded by the dust, and leapt toward what he hoped was the door.

The appearance of stars above and a rush of fresh air told him he had found it. Only then did he feel the weight in his arms; he glanced down at the four tiny bodies still holding tightly to his waist. They were screaming, but they were alive. One of the boys tried to break away, rush back to his mother inside the now-burning building, but Pearse's grip was too strong. The boy screamed louder, began to claw at his arm—*"Molim, molim!"*—but there was nothing he could do. A second bomb exploded off to the right, the reverberation enough to dislodge the roof, a wave of wood and stone cascading into the night. Pearse dropped to his knees, trying to cover the children, the little boy still flailing away, the others trembling in abject terror. Dirt showered his head and back, a battering of pebblelike projectiles, four quivering bodies tucked under his torso as the onslaught subsided. One final explosion beyond the town's fringe, and then nothing.

The attack had been like any other—from somewhere in the hills, arbitrary, and with no real military significance. The tactic to terrorize. A drinking game for late-twentieth-century Bosnia. As quickly as it had come, it was over.

People began to appear, shouts everywhere, panic as they poured from the surrounding buildings, lucky enough to have escaped the night's target practice. Pearse tried to stand, a shooting pain in his shoulder as two of the children broke free, running haphazardly toward the house. A figure stepped out from the haze, two great arms swallowing them up. Pearse was now on his feet, his hand raised as he tried to shield his eyes from the flames and heat. It was Mendravic, thick hands pulling the two small boys from the ground, cradling them into his huge chest. He was limping, his right thigh soaked in blood, whispering to each child, soothing the small heads buried in his neck. Two women approached and took the boys; another emerged to take care of the children at Pearse's side.

"You need to stop that bleeding," Pearse said, nodding as Mendravic neared.

"You, too." The larger man pointed at Pearse, who was only now aware of the red patch growing on his shoulder. He moved the arm. Superficial. He started toward the burning house. As with the children, Mendravic pulled him back.

"There's nothing you can do in there now." His hand was like a vise. "Nothing."

A second wall collapsed, its bulk smothering a large patch of fire. Muted cries rose from within. Then silence. Instinctively, Pearse tried to break free, but Mendravic was too strong. "Petra managed to get the boy out; I took another three. I doubt more than one or two of the women made it." Simple facts not open to debate. "A crippled orphan can't survive," he said, as much to convince himself as Pearse. "Better for them to die now than alone and starving in a month, a week." Pearse had heard the rationalizations before, had almost learned to accept them. Not tonight.

"You really believe that?"

The older man said nothing, his gaze on the flames. Slowly, he let go of Pearse's arm and started to walk off. "It'll burn itself out. No need to waste the water."

Pearse stood, weightless, limbs frozen to the ground, his body suddenly trapped by the enormity of the last three months.

Better for them to die.

Each depraved moment—every detail, every image—rushed back to him in perfect clarity. And with each burst of memory, a voice cried out inside of him: What price faith? He stood apart, stunned that the question had even come to the surface. The one constant. The one certainty. Now dancing in flames in front of him.

"Walk with me." He turned, Petra by his side, only now aware of her. He had no idea how long she had been there, how long he had stood motionless. She waited, perfectly still. A black residue streaked her cheeks, tiny rivulets of blood on her neck, but Pearse saw only the eyes.

Clear, alive, and, for an instant, unable to mask the despair behind them. He nodded slowly. They began to walk.

With each step, a sense of hopelessness began to seep into the vacant space, as foreign to him as it was unnerving. Disgust, anger, even hatred had forced their way into his conscious mind in the past, but he had always found a way to diffuse them. Now he could actually feel that mechanism slipping away, in its place something far more destructive.

They moved past a second burning house, out beyond the buildings to an open field, the sound of boots on grass, two sets in perfect synchrony, the pace even, deliberate. The glow of flame receded behind them, moonlit darkness swallowing them as they continued on. Neither said a word, each finding what they needed in the plodding motion of the other. Several times, they came across large roads, sometimes taking them, sometimes not. It was always her choice, her decision. He would simply follow, happiest when back into the mindless rhythm.

When she finally spoke some two hours later—her voice barely a whisper—it seemed to echo throughout his entire body.

"It's not far from here." The sound caught him off guard, the rote motion of his legs jarred by the intrusion. He nodded and regained his pace.

Ten minutes later, she stopped. They stood at the lip of a wide patch of open land, perhaps two hundred yards in each direction, untouched as far as the eye could see. A line of shadow defined the far edge—trees, he guessed, thick wood beyond. She started out into the field, he at her side, the center of the far shadow growing taller with each step. It took him a minute to realize that there was something in the middle of the field, its outline ever clearer as they drew closer. Twenty yards from it, they stopped.

Gazing down at them was the perfect facade of a church. No dangling roof, no blown-out walls. Perfect. It was no more than three stories high, a vaulted roof with bell tower rising into the sky, its stone glistening in the moon glow. Exactly when it had been built was impossible to say. Fifty, a hundred years ago. Perhaps more. Too little had changed in the way the men of Bosnia built their churches to make an accurate guess. Weathered was the best one might do. Tucked in at the center stood two large rectangular doors, rusted iron rings on each. Petra made for the one on the right, Pearse a few steps behind her.

The inside had not fared as well. Shafts of moonlight poured in from several rows of glassless windows, enough to see that the pews had long ago been ravaged for firewood, the stone floor strewn with bits and pieces unworthy of plunder. As with anything roofed in the region, piles of straw lined the walls, vestiges of onetime tenants, though the most popular routes of escape had drifted farther and farther from the church, thus releasing it from any obligation of sanctuary. A large iron chandelier hung at center, empty sockets, glints of glass below the only remnants of long-ago-shattered bulbs. A second, smaller lamp swung above the altar at the far end, its long link chain twisting in the air from some unseen draft. Above it, segments of the phrase *"Benedictus qui venit"* were chiseled in thick block letters.

The overall structure of the church, however, remained unscathed, a few chipped pieces of brick and stone here and there, but little else in the way of damage.

"No one comes here anymore," she said, "not even the refugees." She had found something on the ground and was trying to make it out in the ivoried light.

"Incredible that it's survived." He'd begun to slide his fingers along the wall, cold, smooth stone with a hint of moisture.

"Not so incredible. Destroying it would be sacrilege."

" 'Sacrilege'?" The word seemed strangely out of place. "That didn't stop them in Prjac."

She tossed the piece back to the floor. "That was a Catholic church. Those, they take pleasure in destroying."

"And this is an Orthodox one?" he asked, pointing to the inscription above the altar. "With the Benedictus etched in stone? I don't think so."

"No, this part is Catholic." She saw the confusion on his face. "It's the foundations that are a little unusual. Underneath us is an old Orthodox church, most of it destroyed in the time of the last Turks. Enough of it survives, though, to keep it holy ground. Under that, the remains of a mosque from the time of the Bogomils, also holy. All in layers, one on top of the other. The perfect model for how we used to live. Now, destroy one, destroy them all. Sacrilege for whoever fires the rocket."

Before he could reply, she was making her way toward a small arch-way at the far left of the altar. He fell in behind her as she disappeared down a narrow set of stairs, the white stone spiraling into darkness.

The light quickly vanished. Hands against the wall, he moved cautiously down the steps, the sound of her in front of him just enough to give his groping some direction. Once or twice, the steps narrowed, breaking his rhythm. He would stop, toe his way forward for a few steps, then continue on.

"Watch your head." She was farther along than he expected, her voice a good fifteen feet beyond but only slightly below him. He guessed there were only a few steps left, and placed his hand directly in front of him. It was then that he remembered his shoulder, a momentary twinge from the tightened muscle. He had no time for it as his fingers met stone and began to trace the curve of an archway, his feet finding ground at the same instant. He ducked under his hand and continued to move slowly, his eyes growing more and more accustomed to the darkness, bits of wall and floor taking shape.

His victory was short-lived, as a bright light suddenly flooded the area in front of him, its source a flashlight in her hand.

Shielding his eyes from the glare, he noticed the walls were of a different color here, whiter, with more texture. And whereas the cut of each stone had been precise and rectangular in the church above, here they were large irregular slabs that undulated from side to side and top to bottom. The ceiling was no more than seven feet high, its smooth surface and neat brickwork a clear indication of its Catholic lineage above, an intrusion over the small Orthodox chapel in which they now stood. Nothing in the space, however, hinted at its onetime religious calling, save for a few fragments of inscription along the top of each wall, the letters Cyrillic, the words too far gone to make out. More straw, a torn blanket.

"I keep this here," she said, balancing the flashlight on a clump of stones. He said nothing. For almost a minute, neither said a word. Finally, she nodded. "Maybe I've been lucky no one takes it." It was only then that he realized they were alone. No midnight jaunts, no explosions, no fevered walks to distract. Alone. He could see she had sensed it, too.

He remained by the wall; when he didn't answer, she turned and pulled the hair from her face. "You've decided to go."

"What?" The question caught him off guard.

"To go. Back to the States."

He looked at her for several moments before answering. "I haven't decided anything."

"Time to become a priest."

Again he said nothing.

"You don't have to explain," she added, now more tender. "I'd go, too, if I could."

"Really?" His tone was dismissive. "No, you wouldn't. None of you would."

"And because of that, you think you should stay? Because we have no choice." She shook her head. "It's not a good answer."

"I've stayed because I came here for a reason."

"The *reason* you've stayed has nothing to do with why you came here." No anger, no reprimand. She watched as his gaze drifted from hers. "We both know that. Otherwise, you would have left a long time ago with all the other well-meaning boys who'd seen enough after two weeks. No, you stayed because you thought you were stronger than they were, that your . . . faith could somehow withstand more. The final test before 'taking the plunge.' Isn't that what your father called it?"

He looked over at her.

"Well, my faith lost the battle with this place a long time ago." She held his gaze. "And now, I think, you're wondering if yours has, too. Better go before it's too late."

Again, the room fell silent. He wanted to answer but couldn't. No way to defend against the truth.

After nearly a minute, he spoke: "So what do I do? Accept it?"

"No." She paused. "I don't know."

Pearse leaned his head against the wall. "That's not very helpful."

She kept her eyes on him. "You could find something else." She waited, then turned and crouched by the pile, readjusting the light on top, her back to him. "Maybe you already have." Her head tilted to one side, her hair cascading to her shoulder, neck bare, half shadow, half light.

"You know I have," he said.

She brought a few stray rocks to the top of the pile, never catching his gaze. "And that's the problem, isn't it?"

He remained by the wall. "What do you want me to say?"

She waited, then turned to him. "Does that matter?"

"Yes. Of course that matters."

"Why? We both know it won't make any difference in what you do." She waited. "Or in what I do. I *can't* leave here, Ian. You know that."

"I'm not asking you to."

"Yes, you are. It's either 'Come to the States and save me from being a priest' or 'I'm on the next plane without you.'"

"That's not fair. It's not about saving me from anything."

"Then what is it? If that's what you so desperately want, then what is this all about?" Again she waited. "Something's happened here—we both know that—and I'm sorry that everything else isn't fitting neatly into place. I'm sorry it's put a kink in your plans. I'm sorry we don't have the luxury to slip out of here and figure it out. I'm sorry about all of those things. But there's nothing I can do about them. I'm here, where I *have* to be, and you can either stay here with me or you can go. And that's your choice. I don't have one."

Pearse stared at her, more and more aware of the growing tightness in his chest as she turned back to the pile. Slowly, he pushed himself from the wall and moved toward her, all the while his eyes on her shoulders as they gently rose and fell with each breath. He sensed a slight lift in her back as he neared, a hesitation; kneeling down behind her, he eased his arms around her waist. He had never touched her like this before, never been so close as to savor the faint hint of summer rain on her cheek. They stayed motionless, neither seeming to breathe, until, slowly, his lips brushed against her neck. He tasted the residue from the explosion, his chest pressed to her, bodies arching into each other. He began to caress her shoulders, arms, her hands as eager as his own as she twisted to him, their mouths lost in a kiss.

He pulled back. He could feel her breath on his lips, see her eyes peering up at him, uncertain.

"I . . . can't stay in Bosnia," he whispered. "I can't stand back and watch all of this happen."

She stared up at him. "I know."

"No, you don't. I'm doing the one thing I promised myself I'd never do. I'm going numb. I can't let that happen. Priest or no priest, I can't lose that. . . . And I can't lose that with *you*." He waited. "Do you understand that?"

It took her a moment to answer. "No." Another moment. "Maybe." She waited, then leaned into him, as if to kiss him.

"Then why did you bring me here tonight?"

"Because I know you'll go." Their mouths were no more than an inch apart. "And this is what I want." She waited, then slowly drew him into her, a kiss, gentle at first, her hands sliding along his chest, his shoulders. She could feel him struggling to let her in, his need as great as hers, but still he held back. Softly, she slipped her fingers beneath his shirt, the touch of skin on skin enough to cloud his senses, his arms suddenly tight around her. She pulled him closer, his lips now finding her cheek, neck, hands to her thighs as he began to stand, lifting her with him, their bodies knocking against the stones, flashlight tumbling to the ground, light extinguished. Neither seemed to notice as he pulled her legs around his waist, her back up against the wall, hands free to peel away her shirt, his tongue gliding to her shoulders, her breasts. He brought her to the floor, hands untangling clothes, the sudden touch of straw beneath them.

Their bodies stripped bare—his eyes clear enough to find hers in the darkness—he guided himself inside of her. The heat between them rose up through their chests, the taste of exploration on their lips, as he lifted her legs higher, her hands swelling around his thighs, drawing him in. For a moment, they remained absolutely still, the sensation almost too much. Then slowly, they began to move with one another, fingers kneading flesh, lips lost to cheeks, chests, the ache ever more urgent. Time seemed to vanish, waves of sound driving through them, until, in an instant of perfect tension, an anguish spread across her face, eyes ever locked on his, her legs and arms no less insistent with each thrust. Every muscle within him began to tighten, claw for some unknown sanctuary, lose himself within her, as they both cried out, the climax exquisite, bodies shaking, until they released, gasping, breath once again able to subside.

A thin rivulet of sweat slid down his back, arched at his thigh, and dropped to the ground. She began to caress him, ease her fingers through the moistness of his skin. He lifted his head, a sudden burst of cold air on his chest. He stared at her, somehow even lovelier than before. And they kissed.

Burying his brow in her, they drifted off.

▲

Two hours later, he awoke, shrouded in darkness. A sound from somewhere behind him had jarred his eyes open, a scraping of stone against stone, his conscious mind trying to reorient itself. He blinked several times, slowly aware of Petra's body cradled next to him. He leaned in to kiss her but was stopped short by the repeated sound of scraping. Twisting his head round, he only now became aware of the thin beam of light emanating from the far wall. Slight as it was, it forced a momentary squint.

Petra, still lost in sleep, rolled over and tucked herself into his chest.

The light was coming from below—another set of steps leading down to the onetime mosque. *No one comes here anymore, not even the refugees.* Again the scraping, a thud, as if the stone had fallen into place. Pearse quietly disentangled himself from Petra and quickly found his pants and shirt. He put them on as the light grew stronger, bobbing, as if finding its way up the stairs. The sound of footsteps crept closer, the glare beginning to fill the far wall. Pearse remained in darkness, the shirt loose on his shoulders as light suddenly broke through, a large figure behind it. Clinging to the wall, he watched as the man headed for the stairs up to the church. He was nearly there when Petra again rolled over, the straw crinkling under her.

Light immediately flashed across the room, Pearse quick to leap from his place, his hands clearly visible in front of him, just in case the man had something more than a flashlight in his other hand. He had been caught in moments like this before; best to play the confused relief worker, hope that his size was enough of a deterrent, that the man was a Catholic, no need for alarm, no need to be seen as anything more than a harmless inconvenience.

Pearse kept his hands out as he talked, moving farther and farther from Petra.

"*Zdravo, zdravo,*" he said, continuing in Croatian. "I'm with the Catholic relief mission. . . . I was separated from my group in Slitna. . . . I'm just sleeping here for the night. I have papers."

"Stop." The light was now aimed directly at his eyes. Pearse blinked rapidly, careful not to make any sudden movements. "Your identification. Slowly."

Pearse reached into his pocket and pulled out his travel cards. They were slightly mangled but still had all the pretty stamps necessary to convince an interested party. The light fell from his eyes, several seconds before he could focus properly.

"These expired over a month ago."

The accent was not what he had expected, far too refined for one of the local black marketeers. And far too observant.

Pearse continued to pay the naif. "Yes . . . I've got the others coming, waiting for me in Zagreb." A lie, but he knew the mention of bureaucracy was the most likely way to deter further probing.

"I see."

The two stared at each other. Not only had the accent and eye for detail struck Pearse as odd; the way the man was dressed seemed even more out of place. He wore a well-tailored shirt—safari khaki—recently pressed, pants the same. His hair was cut short, tiny blond spikes in strict military fashion. On his belt hung a holster, fine leather that showed no signs of aging. And in his left hand, he carried a small satchel, also leather, also in mint condition. Most startling, though, were the boots. Pearse had seen similar ones sell for five hundred dollars in the States— hardly the type to be found anywhere within a six-hundred-mile radius of Slitna.

"You'd do well to replace them as soon as possible," the man said, now speaking English, the accent no less disquieting. Pearse thought he saw a glint of self-satisfaction in the eyes, as if the man was quite pleased with himself for displaying such facility. "There are people in this part of the world who would shoot you for such a lapse."

"Right. Of course." Pearse knew he had to placate, avoid confrontation. "My mistake." Again, the two stared at each other, neither moving, until the man slowly nodded. Even then, Pearse's eyes remained locked on the pair of steely grays less than eight inches from him. Trying to diffuse the moment, Pearse slowly began to inch his way farther out into the room.

The man stepped forward to block his path. For just an instant, the humor seemed to slip from his face, then return with added vigor. "Aren't you going to finish out the night here?" An awkward silence, the smile back on his lips. "Or have I changed those plans?" Before Pearse could answer, the man's expression shifted again. No more of the goading, no more of the playful back-and-forth. This time, a cold vacancy Pearse had never seen before.

The man's head suddenly snapped to the side as a shot rang out, his entire frame collapsing to the ground. The flashlight followed, bouncing along the floor and casting wild shadows before it rolled to a stop. Pearse stood stock-still.

"He had a knife." Petra's voice tore through him as light once again filled the space; slowly, he turned. She was standing, naked, gun in one hand, flashlight in the other. He stared at her, unable to focus. "He was going to kill you."

Pearse watched as Petra slowly placed the gun on the ground. She looked dazed, only now aware of her own nakedness.

Bending down, she began to gather her clothes. Her voice distant, she repeated, "He had a knife." She put on her shirt. "He would have killed you." Still disoriented, she slid her legs into the pants.

Pearse could do little more than nod. He had sensed it, but never been so close, never seen the instant of death. After nearly a minute, she moved to the corpse. Before she could kneel down, Pearse pulled her in close. She clutched at him as well, both of them shaking. "I've never shot someone like that," she whispered. "Waited, watched." They continued to hold each other until she suddenly pulled away. It was clear she wanted to say something. When he tried to ask, she shook her head once. She then knelt down and turned the body over, the eyes staring blankly up at her.

After several seconds, she said, "He's no refugee." She continued to pat down his pockets. Finding nothing, she moved on to the satchel. Pearse knelt at her side as she undid the leather straps.

"Thank you."

She stopped, her eyes still on the satchel. After a moment, she flipped open the front and reached inside.

"His whole face just changed," said Pearse. "I'd never seen that."

"He probably wanted you to know he was going to kill you," her voice far more animated than only moments before. "Some people find pleasure in that." She pulled a hard plastic box from inside the satchel and placed it on the ground. While she played with the clasp, he stared at the body.

The man had an athletic build, powerful arms and hands, his grip still tight around the hasp of the knife. Gazing at the small blade, Pearse realized how close he had come to the same fate. Not that the last three months hadn't forced him to confront his own mortality, but those occasions had been unspecified, bullets strafing in wild assault. The man lying in front of him was far more personal. A single knife meant for him.

The question suddenly dawned on him. "Why did he think he had to kill me?"

Petra was struggling with the box, using her own knife as a wedge. With a final dig, the top snapped open, a strange odor wafting from inside. "It's Bosnia. It doesn't take much thought."

The rationale didn't ring true. "No, you saw him. He made a choice."

Petra was too preoccupied with the contents of the box to consider an answer. Inside were three rectangular piles of parchment, each one held together by a leather string sewn into the far left edge of the stack. Held together by a primitive form of binding, the bundles lay cracked and yellowed, though virtually intact. Odd symbols filled the pages, neat rows of a language neither of them had ever seen before. Petra pulled back the first leaf of the center pile, the parchment gritty to the touch, unwilling to be moved more than an inch or two. Even so, she was able to make out similar rows below, more of the incomprehensible text.

"He was obviously protecting something," she said, trying her luck with the second and third piles. There, too, the parchment refused to budge more than a few inches. "Have you ever seen anything like this?"

Putting his own questions aside, Pearse stared hard at the three little stacks. Scanning them, he noticed a tiny mark at the top right-hand corner of each page: a triangle, one half of it darkened, the other half empty. As far as he could see, there was one on every page. He was about to point it out to Petra, when the sound of a voice crackled through the room. An amplified voice.

"*Come va?*"

The radio was strapped to the dead man's waist, silent again, waiting for an answer. When none came, a second wave of Italian erupted.

Petra shut the box, picked it up, and headed for the stairs. Pearse was right behind her, no need to be told that they had outstayed their welcome. Reaching the top, she turned off the flashlight and sped across the pewless church; they stopped at the doors, listening for anything beyond. Hearing nothing, they slipped out and crouched low, making their way across the wide expanse of field, intent on any sound, any movement around them. At the road, they found a Jeep. Empty. All was still, the eerie quiet of a 4:00 A.M. sky.

The hours they had spent with each other slipped quickly from their minds, survival once again the only thought.

▲

"Parchment, old paper . . . yes," said Mendravic, his bandaged leg up on a chair, a set of headphones to his ears. Petra and Pearse sat at a table in the new communications center, the plastic box between them. Mendravic nodded as he spoke into the microphone. "Yes, at Saint Hieronymus. . . . I would say three, four in the morning. . . . The reason is unimportant. Just tell me if you've— . . . Fine, fine. *Do videnja.*" He turned to the two at the table and shrugged. "He has no idea what they are, either. He has a contact in Zagreb. He'll call back in an hour."

They had kept most of the details from Mendravic, including the appearance of the man: the two of them had been to the church; they had found the box. End of story. Not that Mendravic was anxious for specifics. He had far more pressing matters to deal with this morning. The body count was relatively small: six children, five women. Still, they needed proper burial. A priest had to be found. A few minutes for the strange stacks of parchment were all he could afford.

Pearse stepped outside. The day was already hot, cloudless, no hint of the autumn weather they had been promised for the last two weeks. It would be oppressive by noon. Petra waited in the doorway, her eyes fixed on him.

Without turning around, he said, "Come home with me." He waited, hoping for an answer, knowing there would be none. "No. I don't suppose that's the way things work out." He turned to face her.

"Not with a priest." For some reason, she smiled.

He couldn't help but smile, as well. She stepped toward him. They started to walk. "Things change," he said.

"No, I don't think they do. I have to be here, and you . . ." She stopped and looked up at him. "You don't. We've been down this road, I think."

He nodded slowly.

"You have to go. And you have to go today." In a sudden burst of movement, she took him in her arms, her head tight to his chest. He wrapped his arms around her, pulling her in closer. They stood that way for several minutes, neither saying a word.

Finally, he whispered, "I have to know you understand," the words getting caught in his throat.

Still at his chest, she brought her hand to her face, then pulled away. Even through the half smile, he could see the moistness in her eyes.

She shook her head. "You don't get that one." She breathed in heavily, then took another step back. "You have to go today. That's what I want. Do you understand?"

Now it was Pearse who was doing all he could to stem the tears. Again, he nodded.

"I'm sure you can find a transport out of Zagreb tonight," she said. "Salko can arrange it." Without waiting for him, she turned and started back.

He was about to follow, when the sound of a helicopter rose in the distance. Pearse cleared his eyes and looked up to see the tiny bird lift above the horizon.

In his three months in Bosnia, he had never seen one, told they were too easy a target for would-be snipers, especially in broad daylight. Yet this one was flying in untouched, making for a large field just the other side of Slitna's few remaining buildings. Petra watched, as well. Mendravic was now in the doorway, his hand trying to block out the sun. As the helicopter began its descent, the older Croat limped out into the street. Making his way past Petra, he motioned for her to wait, the same for Pearse as the aircraft set down.

It took Mendravic several minutes to get within shouting distance, his hair blown wild by the slowing propellers. Petra pulled up to Pearse, both watching as two men jumped from the cockpit, each one ducking under the blades, each in sunglasses and gray suit. They approached Mendravic, the taller of the two pulling some sort of identification from his pocket. Mendravic examined the card, nodded, and began to lead them back toward town. As they drew closer, he signaled for Pearse and Petra to join him.

"These men have come about the box you found," he said, still shouting over the noise of the engines. "They're from the Vatican."

A kind of reprieve for both, they nodded and continued toward the house.

"We're eager to get it back," said the taller man as he removed his glasses, "if, of course, it turns out to be what we're looking for."

It suddenly struck Pearse that Mendravic had sent the message less than fifteen minutes ago. How had these men known to come here? "And that would be what?" he asked as they continued to walk.

The man turned to Pearse. "Pardon?"

"The pieces of parchment. What exactly are they?"

He stared at Pearse for a moment. "I take it you were the one who found them."

"Yes," he answered. "And the woman."

The man glanced at Petra. "I see." He then turned his attention back to Pearse. "You haven't looked through them, then?" They neared the house.

"We tried," Pearse replied. "None of us is familiar with the—"

"Odd symbols?" the man offered.

Pearse nodded. "Yes."

"I see."

"They're in here," said Mendravic, leading the way through the door. The man kept his eyes on Pearse until, nodding, he stepped inside.

The box sat open on the table, the shorter man quick to begin examining its contents. Pearse stayed by the door. "The Vatican," he said. "That's a long way to come. And on such short notice."

The taller man kept his eyes on the activity at the box. "Yes. Yes, it is."

"Considering we radioed less than fifteen minutes ago, I'd say remarkable."

"Yes." He paused, then turned to Pearse. "We picked up your transmission on our radio. In the helicopter." His delivery betrayed no emotion. "Quite lucky, I suppose."

"Quite," replied Pearse.

For the first time, the man smiled. No warmth, just a curling of lips. "As I said, we're eager to get it back." The practiced smile remained. "How again did you say you found the box?"

"A church," answered Pearse, his eyes locked on the man's. "Saint Hieronymus."

"Just you and the woman," he pressed, his tone suggesting he knew far more about last night than he was saying. Pearse recognized the threat.

"Yes," he answered, his eyes momentarily to Petra. She nodded.

"Church documents," the man said. When Pearse didn't answer, he added, "You asked what they were. Language, not symbols."

As much as every instinct told him to hold back, Pearse couldn't seem to let it go. "Funny that they should end up in an abandoned church in the middle of a war zone."

"Yes," the man replied, watching as his partner carefully leafed through a few of the pages. "They were stolen from the Vatican Library several months ago. We were told they had resurfaced on the black market here."

"I see." Pearse could sense Petra's gaze on him, but he chose to ignore it.

"Nasty business, the black market," the man continued. "People getting killed over a few pieces of meat." Again, he turned to Pearse. "How lucky for you that you didn't run into anyone at that church." He kept his eyes on him for another few seconds, then turned his gaze to his colleague, who nodded and shut the box. "And it looks as if you won't have to worry about it anymore." He picked up the box and moved to the door, Pearse stepping out of the way as the two men approached. "Best for everyone that way, I would guess." Another thinly veiled threat. The man stopped, looked back at the room, then at Pearse. "So much else here that demands your attention." Another smile before he followed the smaller man out into the street.

Pearse watched them as they went. A moment later, Mendravic was by his side. "You can be very stupid, Ian." Pearse now looked at his friend, whose eyes remained on the two departing figures. "I have no idea what was in that box, but you don't provoke men like that."

"I can't imagine the Vatican—"

"Neither can I, but that's not going to stop me from nodding and smiling, and giving them anything they want. How long have you been in this part of the world, that you don't understand that?" The two men reached the helicopter; Mendravic turned to Pearse. "And I won't bother asking what actually happened in that church last night." He stepped back inside, his eyes now on Petra. "I'm also grateful that no one else was there."

The helicopter lifted off, Pearse again watching as it disappeared into the sun.

▲

Five hours later, he stood beside a small van. The driver, a man originally from Tirana, had slipped across the Albanian border a few months back and was now helping others to find their way through the perilous back roads of the upper Balkans. For a price, of course. Today, he would be escorting a young American as far as Zagreb. A journalist, he had been told. The details never really mattered. Naturally, he was splitting his take with a few well-placed guards—if, in fact, one could call the apes at the border "guards"—but it was still good money. Americans always overpaid.

"You pay double if we get to the border after sundown," the man barked over the idling motor.

Pearse ignored him and continued to speak with Mendravic. "I have the address."

"He's a distant cousin," said the Croat, "but he should know I'm still alive."

Pearse nodded, tried a smile. "She won't come out, will she?"

Mendravic started to answer, then grabbed him by the shoulders and pulled him close. "Whatever brought you here is still with you. Don't ever question that." He held Pearse for some time before releasing.

"I'll try."

Mendravic smiled, nodded. "No, she won't." He reached out and cupped Pearse's cheek in his hand. "Good-bye, Ian." With that, he turned and made his way into the house.

Pearse waited a moment, then opened the door of the van. He glanced one last time at the war-torn landscape, then ducked into the seat. His Albanian seemed overly anxious.

"I'm telling you, after sundown, we don't get through. No matter how much money you have." He waited for Pearse to say something. "You *do* have the money, don't you?" Pearse nodded. The man immediately ground the van into gear, yammering away as they pulled out. It was a poor act, but at least it was entertaining. Pearse hoped it would be enough to keep him preoccupied for a few hours.

He thought of looking back, but instead, he shut his eyes.

Better that way.

Pater

one

The smell of incense hung in the air, strong and sweet within the confines of the church of San Clemente. A summer rain had caught most of the gathering unawares, dank heat compacted within the stone and marble walls, hats and hands turned to fans so as to combat the humidity. Even the mosaics above, ochered reds and greens, seemed to glisten in the heat. Usually left open, the nave was set with row after row of chairs directly behind the schola cantorum, the choir seats filled with boys in white robes. On occasion, a small hand slowly lifted to brush away a pool of perspiration; otherwise, the boys remained perfectly still as they listened to the Latin Mass for Monsignor Sebastiano Ruini. A voice rose from the altar in doleful Latin, its singular cadence lulling the crowd to sleep.

Father Ian Pearse sat on the left-hand side in the second-to-last row. He was using his program to fend off the heat, his thoughts on the multiple strands of sweat racing down his back.

Truth to tell, he hadn't really known Ruini, had seen him only once or twice at the Vatican Library—a man fascinated with fourth-century architecture, on a three-month dig somewhere in Turkey up until a few weeks ago—enough of an acquaintance, though, to merit an appearance at his funeral. It was the same with most of the congregation, fellow clergy whose time in Rome was spent less with matters of faith than with scholarship. Each might have been hard-pressed to distinguish between the two, but theirs was a different kind of service to God, one without the desire to tend a flock. It had been the perfect place to come for a young priest restless in his small Boston parish.

But perhaps restless was the wrong word. Uneasy. Uncertain. The questions in Bosnia had never really gone away. How could they have? Petra had stopped writing a couple of months after he'd gotten back—

he'd made his decision; she was making hers. All ties cut. It only made the numbness more acute. Mom and Dad had told him that he needed to go back for her, figure it all out. No ulterior motive this time. They just wanted him happy.

Instead, he'd gone down to South Bend, played the young alum, worked out with the team, put on the ten pounds he'd lost. Best shape of his life.

Still, that same emptiness.

So he'd called Jack and Andy. Little brother in need of help. Jack had been studying for orals; Andy had been three weeks into a Harvard philosophy Ph.D. They'd both dropped everything and met him out on the Cape. A week at the old summer house. Nights on the beach with more cases of beer than any of them cared to remember. And, of course, the mandatory midnight swim their last night together.

"This is fucking freezing, Padre." It was Jack's little joke. The Padres had been the one team to show any real interest in Pearse during college. Jack liked the irony. Less so the cold water. "You get on a plane and you find her. Trust me. Situation solved." Jack had a way of spelling things out for you. Ever since his two younger brothers had eclipsed his more than respectable six-foot-even, Jack had asserted his primacy in other ways. The words *trust me* were a favorite.

As ever, Pearse was trying to float on his back, his eyes locked on the stars. "Ladies and gentlemen, I give you the shriveled balls theory of resolution."

Andy let out a laugh and immediately sucked in a mouthful of water. Blessed with an Adonis-like build—six foot four, 220 pounds—he didn't have an ounce of athletic talent to go with it. He began to cough up water as he tried to stay afloat.

"You drowning on us, Lurch?" asked Pearse.

"I'll let you know."

"At least I've got some," Jack piped in.

Pearse laughed. "And this from a man who's getting a Ph.D."

"Well, it is freezing." Jack began to backstroke his way to shore. "You and Aquaman can figure it out. I'm going in."

The sound of lapping water grew more distant as Pearse let his feet drop down, only his head now above water. He could just make out Andy about ten feet from him.

"You think I should go back?" he asked.

"Maybe."

"The philosopher speaks." Pearse waited. "No, what do you really think?" He heard Andy take a few strokes to his left.

"I think it would make your life a whole lot easier if it was only about her."

"Meaning?"

"Meaning, if it was just her, you would have stayed."

Pearse didn't answer.

"So it's not just about her," said Andy. They floated silently for several minutes before he spoke again. "You should read Descartes."

"What?"

"Descartes. *Cogito ergo sum.* You should read him."

"Okay?"

"Except that's not really it. It's not the thinking that tells him he exists; it's the doubting. Because if he's doubting, then he must be thinking. So it's *dubito ergo sum* that leads him to *cogito ergo sum.*"

"How much did you have to drink?"

"You're not listening, E. Look, I'm probably the closest thing we have to an atheist in this family, but even I know faith begins with doubt. If you don't question it, what's the point in having it? So things got a little rocked over there. That was the whole reason you went, wasn't it? If you hadn't come back a little disillusioned, then you'd have a problem. I might not get it, E, but I know you do. You always have. This is the first time something's forced you to defend it. And that's what's making it so tough. Until you figure that out, she could be out here with us right now, and it wouldn't make a damn bit of difference." Pearse heard Andy duck his head underwater, then come back up. "One thing is for certain. It's fucking freezing out here." Andy started in for shore.

Pearse stayed out a few minutes longer, always happiest giving in to the isolation, his utter insignificance within a seemingly empty sea.

"Thanks, Andy."

And, somehow, the ball began to fall into his glove again.

All through seminary, he had managed to hold on to that feeling. That connection. That sense of absolute wonder. A life of cloistered contentment. The surest way to keep Petra at a distance.

And, for a time, the questions faded, even the doubt that Andy had said was so essential. Pearse preferred it that way. Pure reflection. A proximity to God felt in the shadowed recesses of an afternoon prayer.

But only for a time. Once on the outside, he began to run into even greater confusion, especially in the role of priest: too much responsibility ceded by a willing congregation; too easy a reliance on detached hierarchy. Church dogma had a way of clouding everything. And what had been so pure, so personal at the seminary came to resemble that arm's-length quality he had seen with his parents. Genuine connection no longer made sense. There was too much standing between believer and Christ to allow for it.

Not surprisingly, the emptiness from Bosnia slipped back in, threatening everything he had built for himself. He knew he needed to find another venue for his devotion, one more isolated, safer, where church structure couldn't undermine his ever-tenuous belief. And where he wouldn't allow Petra to find her way back in as a different kind of answer.

Walking alone one afternoon near Copley Square, it had suddenly dawned on him where he might find it. Or at least how. Everything had become a little too dark; he needed to lighten things up. So he'd gone back to the games, the fun of fragments and puzzles. This time, though, it wasn't Paul, whose approach had always seemed colored by a Pharisaic past, nor the writers of the Gospels, each too caught up in his own agenda, but Augustine, where the insights remained acutely personal and therefore somehow less limiting—the fun and wonder reclaimed all at once.

And so, in an act of self-salvation, he'd dived in. He found himself consumed by it, simple translations leading to the more complex world of liturgical analysis. Somewhere along the way, he even began to make a name for himself—conferences beyond the walls of the church, papers beyond the scope of personal faith—a scholar of language, everyone so surprised, no one more so than himself. Except, of course, for John J. He'd known all along. The onetime Bosnian freedom fighter caught up in a world of minutiae, intricacies of meanings—energy focused on the subtleties of belief rather than on belief itself.

So much easier to "take it and read" than to take it and know.

He was, after all, his parents' son.

Unwilling to admit that he was falling into that same trap, he'd pressed on, back to Ambrose, Augustine's mentor, inspiration for the most brilliant mind the church had ever known. The most reasoned faith it had ever known. Find clarity in that wisdom.

So, when the opportunity to sift through a sixth-century palimpsest of the letters of Saint Ambrose at the Vatican had presented itself, he'd jumped at the chance. Not just for the scholarship but also for the place itself. Maybe in Rome he'd be able to reconnect with the purity he'd somehow lost along the way. The certainty.

It had been two years since then. Two years in which to find other projects so as to keep himself busy, keep him in Rome, insulated in a world of abstract piety. The answers might not have been any easier, but at least the questions were once again more distant.

The congregation rose, Pearse with them. Communion. He moved out to take his place in the line, when he noticed a familiar face some thirty feet ahead of him, the man looking back, trying to catch his attention. Dante Cesare, brother of the monastery at San Clemente—and an avid digger in the church's storied foundations—stood by one of the half dozen vaulted archways that stretched the length of both sides of the nave. One of its few non-Irishmen, Cesare stood almost six foot five. And at no more than 180 pounds, he virtually disappeared into his robes, all thoughts of a torso lost, only scaly hands and feet protruding from the outfit. His equally elongated head bobbed above, aquiline nose stretching the skin taut around his cheekbones. An El Greco come to life.

They'd met just over a year ago in the Villa Doria Pamphili, a park just south of the Vatican, and the best place to find a pickup game on weekends. Pearse had gotten into the habit of taking a handful of kids from the American school out on Saturdays, play a couple of innings, keep himself in shape. Cesare had appeared from behind a tree one afternoon, keeping his distance, but clearly fascinated by it all. When a stray ball had rolled past him, he'd gone after it with the enthusiasm of a five-year-old. The image of those skeletal arms and legs thrashing around still brought a smile to Pearse's face. It turned out that what the monk lacked in physical ability, he more than made up for in his understanding of the game. Cesare had been a rabid Yankee fan for years, knew all the statistics, the stories. The kids loved him. Pearse handled the drills; Cesare handled everything else.

Once a week, priest and monk, two topics off-limits: Thomas Aquinas's thoughts on eternal law and Bucky Dent's affinity for the Green Monster.

The relationship had blossomed.

The Cesare who now waited beneath the archway was hardly the man Pearse had come to know over the last year. The chiseled face looked even more gaunt than usual, not all that surprising, given how close he had been to the late monsignor. Still, Pearse saw more apprehension than grief in the eyes as the monk nodded to his left—an open area just beyond the archway, frescoes and mosaics adorning the high walls. Cesare moved off, Pearse behind him.

No one seemed to notice as the two men slipped away.

"We're missing the best part," whispered Pearse.

Cesare ignored him and continued to walk. He came to a large wrought-iron gate, a key already in hand, the stairs to the lower levels of the church beyond. Without any explanation, he slid the key into the lock and pulled it open, the sound of squealing hinges drowned out by the Mass going on behind them. Cesare quickly glanced over his shoulder as he hurried Pearse through, no time for any questions. He pulled the gate shut and locked it, then moved past him to the stairs.

Pearse had ventured down only once before with his friend. Then, it had been to see a small statuette Cesare had unearthed: a fertility relic from the second-century temple of Mithras some two or three levels below—he couldn't quite remember which—one more piece in the ever-growing celebrity of San Clemente. Like so many of its counterparts around the city, the church boasted a healthy cache of archaeological finds dating back to the ancient Romans. Unlike any other, though, its lineage could be traced by descending from one floor to the next, from one church to the next—the twelfth century, the fourth, the second, each preserved in almost perfect condition. It was what made it so popular with the tourists. And why Pearse had always felt somewhat unnerved by the place. Too similar to another church. Another time.

Never quite relegated to the past.

Cesare had chosen an entrance reserved only for those involved with the excavations. He picked up a small lantern, turned it on, and handed it to Pearse; he then took one for himself and began to make his way down, still without a word. At the first landing, he again looked over his shoulder. Not knowing why, Pearse did the same; the stairwell was empty. The two continued down. Twice, Pearse tried to ask what they were doing, and twice, Cesare rebuffed him with a hand to the air.

After maneuvering their way through a series of circuitous tunnels—the sound of running water all around them—they finally arrived at the sixth-century catacombs, ragged stones hovering over narrow passageways. Cesare stopped and bent over as he turned into a small enclosure, its ceiling no more than five feet high. Pearse followed.

"This is the one," said the Italian, his words clipped. He stood hunched over in a room perhaps seven feet wide, ten feet long, the texture of the walls reminding Pearse of late-summer sandcastles on a Cape Cod beach, wet sand dripping from above, each drop threatening to undermine the entire structure. Even now, he couldn't be sure how long they both had before the brittle walls would come crumbling down.

"Another fertility god?" he asked with a smile, making it a point to stay by the doorway.

Cesare turned to him, his thoughts evidently elsewhere. "What?" A moment's recognition, and then, "No, no, nothing like that. Why are you standing at the door? Come in closer. Quickly." Pearse did as he was told and moved to the far wall.

"Never really understood that anyway," he said, the smile broader. "A monk with a fertility god."

"What?" Cesare asked distractedly. He was stooped over a small pile of rocks, busy pulling one off after another. Not waiting for an answer, he continued: "You knew Sebastiano was digging behind the Rapiza frescoes." He stopped for a moment. "What am I saying? Of course you knew he was working in the old church. It's where they found the body." He was clearly agitated; he went back to work. "Well, I don't think he was there two nights ago."

The image of the forty-five-year-old Ruini, his corpse lying in the fourth-century church—captured forever in vivid black and white by one of the local papers—flashed through Pearse's mind. "You don't think he was where they found him," Pearse echoed, his attempt at sarcasm meant to focus Cesare.

"Exactly. And I don't think our friend's heart simply gave out, as we've all been told."

Pearse kept his eyes on the Italian, nervous, jaunty movements from a man well known for his composure. "I see," he said, the ploy obviously having had no effect. "And why is that?"

Cesare stopped and looked back. "Can you help me with some of these?" He inched over so as to leave room for Pearse to kneel down next to him; again, Pearse did as he was told. Together, they removed the last few heavy stones. When they had uncovered a small hole in the wall, Cesare flattened himself on the floor and reached his arm into the crevice. A moment later, he pulled out a cylindrical metal tube; he then flipped over and sat against the wall; Pearse did the same. "Because," he continued, "three nights ago, he gave me this." He clutched the tube in his lap.

"Which is?"

"He was in an unbelievable state," Cesare continued, as if not having heard the question. "I'd never seen him like that before. He told me to hold on to it, just for a few days, and to tell no one." Cesare seemed to lose his train of thought. "He was distracted. Very distracted."

"It seems to be catching," said Pearse, trying to lighten the mood.

The comment momentarily brought Cesare back. "What?"

"Nothing. Did he tell you why he gave it to you?" he asked. When Cesare continued to stare blankly, Pearse added, "Have you looked inside?"

Cesare's eyes went wild. "Why? Why do you ask that?"

Pearse raised his hands in mock surrender, another attempt to calm his friend. "I'm just asking. I didn't mean to—"

"No, no, of course, you're just asking." Cesare placed a hand on Pearse's knee, his expression at once benign. "I'm sorry. It's just . . ." Again, he seemed to lose focus. He took in a deep breath, then slowly exhaled. Pearse waited until the monk was ready to speak again. "I took it, I put it in my rooms, and I didn't think about it anymore. And then suddenly, he's dead. Naturally I've looked inside."

"And?"

Cesare turned the tube around until he found a small handle halfway down one side; he pulled up on the metal hasp and watched as the top of the canister hissed opened—the sound of a vacuum releasing. He gently took out what looked to be a scroll of rolled vellum. "He said it was something he'd found here, behind the frescoes."

"And you have no idea what it is?" Pearse asked. Cesare shook his head quickly. "Do you know why he gave it to you?"

"To me?" It took a moment for the question to register. "No. He was frightened. We were both down here digging; he saw me . . . I don't know. He said it would be just for a few days."

Pearse nodded, more to reassure Cesare than himself. "So why did you bring the tube back here?"

The Italian let his head fall back against the stone. "Why . . . why did I bring it here?" Again, he needed a moment to collect himself. "Because the day after Sebastiano was . . . the day after he died, I went back to my rooms and discovered that someone had gone through the place."

"What?" Pearse's tone had lost all trace of humor.

"A few things were slightly out of place. I'm very particular about my things." He nodded several times for emphasis. "Anyway, I knew some-one had been there. Luckily, I have a space where I keep certain other things. They didn't find it, whoever they were. But they were there. I know that. So to be safe, I brought the tube here."

"Why not take it to the abbot, or the police?"

"You think I didn't think of that? I was in a panic. When I realized what I should have done, they'd already decided to have the funeral here. All the preparations—it's been impossible to sneak down without anyone seeing or asking. I couldn't very well have gone to the abbot or the police without this," he said, raising the scroll, then placing it back into the tube. He pulled down on the mechanism and sealed it.

"So why bring me?" It was the first time he'd thought to ask.

Cesare looked at him, his expression momentarily blank. He tried a weak smile. "I don't know. I saw you. I thought it would be better to have someone with me." He suddenly stopped, his gaze drifting to the floor. "Actually, that's not entirely true." Pearse waited for his friend to continue. "I knew you'd be here today." Cesare kept his eyes on the ground. "I knew no one would take any notice of us during the administration of Communion." He was clearly struggling with something.

Again, Pearse waited.

"Sebastiano said that the scroll . . . the writing . . ." Cesare looked up. "Well, it might have something to do with the Manichaeans." When there was no response, he continued. "You're familiar with the fourth-century heresies—Augustine's response to Mani and his followers. I thought perhaps you'd know what to do with the scroll." Now he paused. "And why someone might have been killed because of it." The last thought forced Cesare to close his eyes, drop his head back against the wall.

"The Manichaeans?" The reference caught Pearse completely by surprise, its absurdity dispelling whatever apprehension he might have been feeling. "Dante"—he smiled, trying to find the appropriate words—"I'm hardly an expert, but I do know that no one would kill anyone because of what the Manichaeans had to say. That's . . . ludicrous." He couldn't help a little laugh. "The sect died out over fifteen hundred years ago." Pearse saw his effort to console coming to naught. "Look, if that's what's in the scroll, I can tell you, you have nothing to be worried about. Nothing. Maybe you misinterpreted what Sebastiano—"

"No." The answer was tinged with anger. "I know what I saw. I know what he told me." He turned to Pearse, no less adamant. "And I know who the Manichaeans are. Of course no one kills because of an ancient heresy. I'm not stupid, Ian."

"I didn't say—"

"Sebastiano thought there was something. I find it rather strange that he's dead two days after he hands me a certain scroll, which, according to you, should give me *nothing* to worry about. My rooms are rummaged through. If you think it's something funny—"

"All right." Pearse was getting tired of sitting on the rock-hard floor. "We'll take the scroll to the abbot, or the police, or whoever you think best. And we'll see. How about that?"

Cesare waited before answering. "Fine."

"Fine," Pearse echoed. He rested his head against the wall. Sensing things were still a bit dicey, he added, "Then again, you might have reason to be worried." He kept his eyes straight ahead. He waited for Cesare to turn to him. "The Sox did pull to within four games of the Yanks last night."

It was several seconds before Cesare answered. "What?"

"The Sox. They're within four. Might be time to be getting a little nervous."

Cesare stared at Pearse. "What was the score?"

Pearse continued to gaze at the far wall. "They called it in the sixth. Ten-run rule."

Cesare couldn't hide the first hint of a smile. "I thought that was just for Little League?"

Pearse shrugged.

"Well, it's as close as they'll get," said the monk.

Now Pearse smiled. He hoisted himself up, placed a hand on Cesare's shoulder, and patted the weathered cloth. "Always the pessimist."

"It's just that you people never learn, that's all." For the first time in the last twenty minutes, he seemed to relax.

Cesare was just getting to his feet when the lights suddenly flicked on in the corridor. At once, panic, then a look of concentrated calculation fixed in his eyes. "The lights for the tourists," he said as he moved to the door. "They can only be turned on from two floors above." He scanned the corridor, then turned to Pearse, extending the tube to him. "It'll take them a few minutes to get down here. Take this and put it back in the hole."

"Dante, I'm sure—"

"Please, Ian, do as I ask. If this is nothing, you can laugh at me later. Just do this." Pearse took the tube. "Put the stones back around it, keep

your lantern off, and wait ten minutes before leaving. I'll . . . try to distract them by going now. Meet me outside the Colosseum in an hour."

Before Pearse could answer, the monk was through the door, the sound
of his feet quickly receding down the corridor. Reluctantly, Pearse did as
he was asked and turned off his lantern, the room at once pitch-black
save for a tiny patch of light bleeding in through the doorway. The area
by the stones, however, remained in complete darkness. He placed the
lantern on the floor, then knelt so as to locate the hole. Feeling his way
down the wall, he found the opening and slid the tube inside; then, one
by one, he replaced the stones. He checked his watch: 4:40. Leaning his
head back against the wall, he dropped his shoulders and closed his eyes.

The Manichaeans. Pearse couldn't help but smile. *Scourge of the true
believers.* Fifteen hundred years trapped in obscurity, and they were now
forcing him to sit in a damp cave in the basement of a church waiting
for the lights to go out. What could be more appropriate, he thought,
from the "Brothers of the Light"?

Truth be told, even Augustine had been drawn in by the Manichaean
mystique, a devoted member for a time, enticed by the sect's response
to the great question of the day: Whence comes evil? Pearse recalled
how the subject had amounted to nothing less than a mania with the
early Christians, all of whom had agreed, Not from a perfect God. But
if not from God—source of all things—then from where? The
Manichaeans, from the bits and pieces he remembered, had opted for a
rather ingenious approach: the Persian dualism—the world torn
between two combatant kingdoms of light and darkness, spirit and
nature—forcing men to rely on reason to distinguish between the two.
Suddenly, self-knowledge had held the key to salvation. Perhaps above
even faith—a step the young Augustine had ultimately refused to take.
How bitterly had he then turned on his onetime comrades, branded
them heretics, forced them underground, a nascent sect destined for
extinction. How vital it had been for him to stamp out the dangerous,
if subtle, simplicity of their teaching.

And how dramatically, Pearse thought, had all that changed in the last
fifteen hundred years. The Mass upstairs: still in the midst of Communion,
now an everyday occurrence, no need to ponder its deeper meaning, the
controversies long ago forgotten. No more battles to be won, no heresies
to be put down, nothing that might provoke any real debate.

Faith at its most docile.

Shaking the more modern doubts from his mind, Pearse tried to concentrate on Cesare. As much as he wanted to dismiss the claim that Ruini's death had been anything but natural, the intensity in the monk's plea now forced him, if only for a moment, to consider the other, far more unsettling possibility. Even then, it didn't make any sense. The newspapers had said heart failure. So, too, had the church. Why? To cover up a scroll? The Manichaeans? It was . . . absurd.

The sound of footsteps in the corridor brought his eyes open. Without thinking, he edged himself closer to the wall. It was an unnecessary precaution, as he sat shrouded in darkness, but the instinct to feel rock against his back won out over reason. He waited, certain that in a few moments a familiar face from the church above would peer through the doorway and ask him the embarrassing question: what exactly was he doing here? He tried to think of an answer as the steps drew closer, but there was something to them that stole his attention—too measured, too precise. Whoever was out there was coming slowly, as if looking for something.

Or someone.

For the first time since the strange jaunt had begun, Pearse felt uneasy. He pulled his knees into his chest and stared into the light coming from the corridor.

"He's moving to the old church." The sound of Italian echoed in the hall, the voice from a radio. "We have him." All at once, a figure ran past the doorway, too fast for Pearse to catch any features. A man of average height. Dark hair. A raincoat. A few more seconds, and the sound of his steps faded to nothing.

Pearse didn't move. The intrusion of the voice had been enough to jar him, but the words were what froze him to the ground.

We have him.

Anxiety became genuine fear, Cesare's sense of urgency now his own as Pearse tried to conceive a logical explanation for the last half minute. But he couldn't. The passionless voice over the radio coupled with the terror in the monk's eyes discounted every choice but one. *The old church.*

Without thinking, he bolted upright, his head nearly knocking into the ceiling as he moved to the door, lantern once again in hand. He inched his face out and peered along the corridor. Nothing. Running out, he ducked low, only to realize some fifteen seconds later that he had no idea how to get to the old church. Rough walls had given way to smoother ones, the roof now affording a few inches above his head, but there was no indication of which was the right way to go. He had passed a stairwell a few yards back; now he stood at the crossroads of three separate paths, each extending into distant shadows. He stopped and tried to listen for any movement up ahead, but the sound of flowing water made that all but impossible.

He chose the central alley, careful to keep his movements as quiet as possible, all the while his ears perked up for the least bit of sound up ahead. Still nothing. He reached the end of the passageway and again had a choice of two. Trying to orient himself, he closed his eyes so as to visualize the twists and turns he had made, superimposing some vague map of the church over his various meanderings. It only confused him more. He opted for the left, again picking up the pace, soon aware that he had gone much too far not to have passed the underground church. But there had been no turnoff, no other possibilities other than straight ahead. He thought about turning back, but he knew that would be equally futile.

After a maddening few minutes, he finally came to a set of stairs. Taking them two at a time, he barreled his way up, first one level, then the next, his collar soaked with perspiration as he finally emerged at a large iron gate. For a panicked moment, he remembered the key Cesare had needed. Here, however, it was only a metal pole wedged into the stone floor, enough to lift it a few inches and slide the gate back: A sign reading PRIVATO hung on the other side. He pulled the gate shut behind him and walked into a small atrium, a door at the far end, the church's cobblestoned courtyard visible through the glass.

At least now he knew where he was—the main sanctuary waited just off to his left. Better still, he remembered that the stairs to the fourth-century church lay just across the way. As unobtrusively as he could, Pearse moved out into the courtyard, his gait casual, the lantern held tightly against his leg. He pushed open the second glass door, only to be met by the hum of the Mass to his left, its monotone drowning out the sound of his steps as he hurried along to the far atrium and the stairs leading down. A token chain hung across the stairway, another sign— CHIUSO in thick red ink, the excavations closed for the funeral—little more than a high step needed to hurdle it before making his way down.

For some reason, he checked his watch: 4:55. It had been over ten minutes since the voice on the radio had told him where to find Cesare.

Ten minutes of inept fumbling. Images of the monk's eyes flashed through his mind, their panic compounded by his own sense of help- lessness. Reaching the bottom, he tried to steady his breathing, keep his strides silent as he neared the entryway to the subterranean church. Finding the Rapiza frescoes, he inched his way along the corridor, his back against the wall. Confounded by the absolute silence, he stopped at the archway, hoping for any sound, any hint of movement. Nothing. A moment later, he lunged out into the heart of the ancient church.

It stood completely empty. A series of columns lined the center of the open area, thick stone casting wide angular shadows from the overhead light. Pearse stepped farther in, his gaze moving from side to side, know- ing full well he would find nothing, yet still hoping. Coming to the far end, he turned round and repeated the mindless inspection, a small cordoned-off area marking where Ruini's body had been found, but there was no hint that anyone had been here since its discovery two days ago. He wanted to believe he had let his imagination run wild, that somehow the voice from the radio had been a bizarre coincidence, Cesare's panic a product of wild speculation. The silent room, however, only intensified his misgivings.

An eerie quiet descended on the place, conjured by the glow of fluo- rescent light on ancient stone. The high-pitched hum of the bulbs seemed to taunt him, heighten his sense of isolation. He became acutely aware of each intake of breath, the sweat creasing his neck, now sud- denly chilled by the airless space. It was impossible to think, only to move, back to the entryway, to the corridor.

He had made it halfway to the stairs when the lights suddenly flicked off. Instinct flattened him against the wall, his heart racing. He expected someone to come flying out of the darkness, something to confirm all that Cesare had said, but everything remained still. He slowly remem- bered that the switches for the lights lay one floor above. Whoever had given chase was now simply making sure to clean up after himself. There was nothing Pearse could do. He turned on his lantern and quickly started down the corridor.

Within a minute, he was once again at the top of the stairs, the sound of voices echoing nearby, people filing out of the church. The funeral was over. He placed the lantern on the second step and casually moved out into the atrium. Most were exiting by the far door, one or two opting for the courtyard, a nod here and there from a familiar face as he made his way back toward the main sanctuary. He scanned the flow of bodies, hoping to spot Cesare's unmistakable shape, a head bobbing above the rest. As he looked, Pearse suddenly realized that someone else might be doing the very same thing. Perhaps Cesare had managed to elude them. Perhaps that was why the church below had been empty. Hope was a powerful elixir. He began to broaden his sweep. He had no idea what he was looking for, but the action itself seemed to calm him.

Several minutes later, he stood by the main door. He had seen no one, nothing to draw his attention. He stepped out into Via di San Giovanni in Laterano, the rain having turned to mist. Whatever momentary peace of mind he had managed in the church now gave way to the realization that Cesare was gone.

". . . the Colosseum . . . an hour." He had no choice but to trust the monk would be there.

▲

The sound of his own footsteps trailed Stefan Kleist along the carpeted corridor. There was nothing much to distinguish him save for a pair of exceptionally broad shoulders, far wider than usual for a man his size. They gave him an unexpected power, a compact sturdiness that could very well have defined his entire personality. Elegant arms swayed at his side, muscular even through the fine material of his suit jacket, one hand now slipped casually into his pants pocket as a maid appeared from one of the rooms. She pulled the familiar cart behind her, the Bernini Bristol logo etched into the hotel's towels. Kleist smiled, a gentle lifting of his lips, pale green eyes betraying nothing but absolute contentment. The young woman nodded once, then quickly moved along in the opposite direction. The moment she had passed, Kleist's expression returned to its more accustomed steeliness, stone cold eyes, lips again a hardened flat line. Reaching the end of the corridor, he turned left and pushed through a pair of heavy leather doors toward the one remaining suite on the floor. He pressed the bell and waited.

Within a few seconds, a voice came from behind the thick double door. "Sì?"

"Stefan." A moment later, a bolt released and the door pulled back, revealing a foyer with living room beyond. Kleist stepped through, nodded to the man at the door, and proceeded into the larger room. Four others sat on various chairs and couches, each one looking over to acknowledge the recent arrival. Kleist said nothing and took a chair at the far wall, directly behind the man who was speaking.

"Probably tonight or tomorrow," the man continued, ignoring the interruption. "The end of the week the latest." Like Kleist, he was impeccably well dressed, a small handkerchief at the lapel pocket of his suit, long legs crossed delicately at the knee. Somewhere in his sixties, Erich Cardinal von Neurath had lost most of his hair, the thin ring lending his face a decided austerity. High cheekbones and sallow complexion accentuated an almost constant expression of indifference. In his usual clerical robes, it gave him an air of reflective piety. In the suit, it translated into an aristocrat's sneer.

"And there's no chance he'll miraculously recover?" asked the one woman in the room. "No act of God?" Doña Marcella de Ortas Somalo, a Castilian contessa—the one true aristocrat among them—was somewhere in her mid-fifties, and had already buried four husbands, the last a man thirty years her senior. Not one for black, she wore an Armani suit, a deep green, the skirt cut to just below the knee so as to point up her best feature. Truth to tell, all her features were her best. Delicate nose and fine cheeks highlighted two dark brown eyes, always with a gaze that said she knew exactly what everyone was thinking. And, more often than not, she did. Even the dyed blond hair tied back in a bun—which, on another woman, might have seemed an affectation, or worse—was perfect for the tone and texture of her skin. It wasn't as if she looked twenty years younger than she was. She didn't. But there wasn't a twenty-five-year-old who wouldn't have given anything to have what the contessa had. And the contessa knew it.

"No," answered von Neurath. "Even a Pope has his limitations. The doctors have no explanation for the disease's sudden appearance, but they do agree it's too far gone to help him now. As I said, the weekend the latest."

The youngest member of the quartet edged out on his seat. "Would I then . . . that is to say, will I need to—"

"Spit it out, Arturo," said von Neurath.

Arturo Ludovisi, senior analyst at the Vatican Bank, nodded once, a herky-jerky movement that made him look all the more uncomfortable. He was a little man, the crisp line of a comb etched perfectly into his well-oiled hair, shirt collar starched to the point of rigidity, a line of perspiration where neck met cloth. And yet he had a remarkably handsome face, lost in the uneasy expression that seemed always to line it. He took a breath and began again. "Do I . . . need to accelerate the number of deposits, then?"

Von Neurath looked at him. "Just manage the accounts, Arturo. No. No need to accelerate anything."

Another quick nod, Ludovisi clearly regretting his little outburst.

"And I take it I won't need to cancel any of the rites." The last of the four shifted slightly at the end of the couch. Father John Joseph Blaney, the onetime parish priest, now special envoy to the Vatican, waited for an answer.

"Not at all," answered von Neurath. "They're even more important now." He waited for the familiar Blaney nod, then continued. "So, if it's in the next few days, that means we need a confirmation on votes, and we need it quickly. There have been rumors that Peretti and I will split the conclave, leaving the papacy open for who knows who to step in."

"I can't imagine it would be that hard to apply a little pressure in various circles," said the contessa.

"Pressure, Doña, won't be a problem," interjected Kleist, still seated behind von Neurath. The two had developed a certain fondness for each other, something bordering on the maternal, without all the usual complications. A patroness for him. A confidant for her.

"It's not applying it that's the problem," said Blaney, peering past the cardinal to his minion. "I appreciate your enthusiasm, Herr Kleist, but physical intimidation—or worse—has to be a last resort. If that."

"But it is an option," said von Neurath.

Blaney hesitated. "This isn't the fifteenth century, Erich. You're no Medici prince."

"The election won't be the problem," countered the contessa, trying to move on. "We have to think of the weeks after. I thought that was why we were meeting tonight."

"Without the election," answered von Neurath, "there *are* no weeks after."

More silence. Finally, Blaney spoke. "We just need to iron out a few things."

The foursome spoke for another half an hour before Ludovisi began to gather his things. "My flight. If I'm to make the transfers . . . well, I'll need to go now." He seemed to be waiting for permission.

"Good." Von Neurath nodded. "I think we're done here."

Ludovisi stood, his relief all too apparent.

"You'll be in touch with the various cells?" asked von Neurath. "Remind them that they need to maintain absolute security now?"

Another nod from Ludovisi.

Von Neurath stood, then turned to Blaney. "Oh, by the way. Any news on that San Clemente business? Have we figured out what exactly is happening there?"

Blaney waited, then shook his head. "I really don't know. I believe Herr Kleist is looking into that." Again, he peered past von Neurath. "Isn't that right?"

The younger man was already standing. "Absolutely, Father," he answered. "I'm taking care of it."

Ludovisi headed for the door.

"Aren't you forgetting something, Arturo?" It was Blaney who spoke. "Aren't we all forgetting something?"

The contessa was the first to nod; she knelt down. Von Neurath showed a mild irritation, then followed suit. The others in the room did the same. Blaney was the last. He began to pray: "It is from the perfect light, the true ascent that I am found in those who seek me. Acquainted with me, you come to yourselves, wrapped in the light to rise to the aeons. . . ."

Five minutes later, the suite was empty.

Λ

A final surge of tourists hustled through the turnstiles, a last-minute visit before closing. Pearse sat on a bench some twenty yards from them, elbows on knees, chin on hands. He wondered why they even bothered; the light had given up on the day, too low in the sky to penetrate the thick wall of cloud, too early to be helped by the few surrounding lampposts, as yet unlit. Even so, the cameras were at the ready.

He had considered going to the police, but he knew Cesare had been right: What could he possibly say that wouldn't sound far-fetched, if not a little paranoid? After all, the scroll remained tucked away in the underbelly of San Clemente. More than that, he still believed that there was a reasonable explanation, that Cesare would arrive—a sheepish smile, a gentle shrug—the two laughing their way to a nearby café. "The Manichaeans," he would say. "What was I thinking?"

Still, the words from the catacombs continued to echo: *We have him.*

Pearse checked his watch: 6:15. He glanced around. Cesare should have been here half an hour ago. The echo grew stronger.

For perhaps the fourth time in the last fifteen minutes, he stood and stepped out into the pedestrian area, a wide swath of pavement extending some twenty yards in each direction. To his left, a small group waited at the bus stop on the Imperiali, one or two others by the coffee truck parked by the fence overlooking the Forum, but no Cesare. Another check of the watch.

It was difficult not to draw attention—a priest pacing alone, no doubt a look of concern on his face. One of the women at the coffee truck offered a nervous smile when their eyes met, Pearse awkwardly nodding, turning, hoping to see Cesare's gangly features in the distance. Nothing. He walked back, past the bench, unable to make himself sit. Nearing a section of recently added scaffolding—three tiers rising high on the amphitheater—he heard a whispered voice.

"Ian." It was Cesare, unseen, somewhere within the tangled mess of poles and boards. "Keep walking as if you're waiting for someone."

It was all Pearse could do not to spin round. He quickly checked his watch again, aware that the movement had been awkward, unconvincing.

"Move away," Cesare pressed, his voice barely audible, though insistent enough to send Pearse back toward the coffee truck. A bus pulled up, the gathering at the stop quick to file on. The driver stared down at him.

"Padre?" he asked.

It took Pearse a moment to realize the man was talking to him. The question somehow demanded more of him than he could manage. When the driver asked again, Pearse slowly shook his head. The man nodded, shut the door, and took the bus out into traffic.

Pearse turned and headed for the scaffolding. As casually as he could, he moved toward a low stone wall—no more than two feet high—one side of a grass enclosure situated between the bus stop and the Colosseum, close enough to make conversation possible. He sat, elbows again on knees. And waited.

"This was the best way I could think of talking to you," Cesare began, his voice tired, no less strained than that afternoon. Pearse nodded, his eyes now scanning the area around him, trying to be as inconspicuous as he could. "Do you have a handkerchief?" Cesare asked. Without answering, Pearse reached into his pocket and pulled one out. "If you need to answer, pretend to use it. I don't think anyone's followed me, but best to be safe."

Pearse immediately placed the handkerchief to his mouth. "What's going on?" he whispered.

"I needed to be sure you were alone."

"I looked for you in the old church. I thought someone had . . . I don't know."

There was a pause before the monk spoke. When he did, accusation laced his words. "How did you know I went to the old church?"

"Because I heard one of them over a radio, Dante." The answer firm, Pearse no longer willing to placate. He needed answers. "Who were those men?"

"A radio," he repeated. The explanation seemed to satisfy. "You have to go back for the scroll."

"What?" Confusion surged to the surface. "What are you . . . Why?"

"Because I would be followed."

"That's not what I meant." When Cesare didn't answer, Pearse prodded him. "By whom, Dante? Who were those men in the tunnels?"

"I told you. There's a link to the Manichaeans."

Pearse's frustration was building. "That's not an answer, and you know it."

"Please, Ian. All you have to do is get the scroll and—"

"No." The finality in his voice cut Cesare short. "Look," he said, his tone now softer, "just tell me what's going on. Why are you so afraid to be seen talking with me?"

For nearly half a minute, the Italian said nothing. When he did, his voice carried little of its usual insistence. "Believe me, it wasn't my intention to involve you like this."

"Involve me in what?" Pearse turned and looked directly into the scaffolding. "There's no one out here, Dante. No one's followed you." Silence. "I'm telling you, it's safe to come out."

More silence. After nearly a minute, Cesare slowly emerged from the far corner, still hidden in shadow, eyes peering about the open expanse; when he was fully satisfied, he moved out and sat next to Pearse. He kept his arms crossed at his chest, his head low. "Does this make you happier?"

"Worlds happier. Now what's going on?"

Again, the monk waited before speaking. "Two days ago, my rooms were rummaged through—"

"You've told me that," Pearse cut in.

"Yes, well, it wasn't while I was away. I walked in to find three men in the process."

"*What?*" Pearse tried to stifle his disbelief. "Why didn't you go to the police?"

Cesare continued, ignoring the question. "It was during vespers. I'd felt a bit light-headed—perhaps because I hadn't gotten much sleep the night before working with Sebastiano. I thought it best to lie down. Evidently, they thought it the perfect time to go about their business. Naturally there was an awkward moment. When I told them I was going to get the abbot, they informed me that it was the abbot who had given them permission to look through my rooms."

"The abbot—"

"Yes. That's when one of them showed me his identification: Vatican security. We both know the police remain at a distance when the Vatican is involved."

Pearse said nothing for several seconds. "So that's why you put the scroll back."

"Exactly." He nodded. "The police would have been useless. And the abbot . . . he was the one who'd let them in."

"So what did you tell them?"

"That, as far as I knew, my rooms weren't part of the Vatican. They didn't see any humor in that."

"No, they wouldn't."

"They asked if Sebastiano had given me anything the previous night. I asked them how they knew we had met. They repeated the question. I asked them if something had happened to Sebastiano. They asked again if he had given me anything. So forth and so on. I don't know why, but I told them no. There was something about them, something that told me to protect my friend. Maybe I was wrong. Maybe I should have given them what they wanted."

"I would have done the same thing," said Pearse. "Did they say anything else?"

"They wanted to know if Sebastiano had told me about anything he'd recently found in the church."

"Did they ever mention the scroll? Explain what it was?"

"No. I asked them what it was that could possibly bring Vatican security all the way out to San Clemente. They said it wasn't my concern. So it went, each of them taking turns with questions. Each time, I told them I was sorry but that I didn't know what they were looking for."

"And they believed you?"

"I have no idea. Eventually, they decided to leave."

"And that was it? Nothing else until the tunnels?"

"Nothing else?" asked Cesare somewhat surprised. "Well, not unless you consider Sebastiano's death unimportant."

Pearse turned to him. "You know that's not what I meant." He waited, then asked again. "And that's all they said?"

"Yes." Cesare started to nod, then stopped. "No." He seemed to be trying to remember something. "There was one thing." After a moment, he said, "It was when they were leaving. One of them"—his eyes were still hunting for the words—"he said, 'We're well aware of the perfect light.'" Cesare nodded to himself. "Yes, that was it, the 'perfect light.' He said, 'Don't be foolish to think you can keep it from us.'" He looked at Pearse. "That struck me as odd. Of course, I had no idea what he meant. I thought he might have been referring to the Holy Spirit or—"

"'Perfect Light'?" asked Pearse, a sudden intensity in his tone. "You're sure that's what he said?"

"I think so," Cesare replied, aware of the shift in the younger man's voice. "Yes, now that I remember it. As I said, the words were unusual." Pearse remained silent; Cesare continued. "I imagine he meant it as some sort of threat. Expected me to understand. Evidently, it was lost on me."

"It wasn't the Holy Spirit." Pearse continued to stare out. Almost to himself, he said, "He was referring to the 'Perfect Light.'"

"Yes . . ." answered the Italian, clearly puzzled by Pearse's response. "I know. That's what I just said." He waited for a response.

"'Perfect Light, True Ascent,'" Pearse added, his eyes rising to the Arch of Constantine. "Maybe it's not so absurd."

"What's not so absurd?" asked the Italian. "Ian?"

It took Pearse a moment to focus; he turned to Cesare. "'Perfect Light, True Ascent.' It's a prayer, Dante. A Manichaean prayer." Again, his gaze drifted. "It's supposed to be a collection of Jesus' sayings."

"A prayer?"

Pearse nodded. "Passed down orally. Never a written text. Or so says Augustine." He turned to the monk. "You're absolutely sure those were the words the man used?"

"Yes." Cesare took a moment. "And that's what the scroll is, this . . . 'Perfect Light'?"

Pearse shook his head. "I have no idea."

"You mean to tell me a prayer was the reason those men went through my rooms?" Cesare was suddenly more heated. "The reason they followed me to San Clemente, to the old church? A prayer is why Sebastiano was killed?" The last thought seemed to incite him further. "I don't believe that, Ian. *That* is absurd. A prayer doesn't explain what's happened."

"I realize that, but I don't have an answer for you." Cesare said nothing. "You wanted a link to the Manichaeans, well, here it is. For whatever it's worth." Restless, Pearse stood. "You're sure they were the same men who were in the tunnel?"

"Yes. Who else would they be?"

A question suddenly crossed his mind; he turned to Cesare. "How do you know, if they never caught you?"

Cesare looked up, momentarily taken aback by the question. "How do I know?" Pearse heard the defensiveness in the monk's voice. "There are plenty of ways to be seen and not be seen in those tunnels, Ian. It wasn't that hard to let them find me, and just as easy to lose them. I'm sure that by the time they reached the old church, I was already making my way here. Why is this of any importance?"

"So if you knew you'd lost them, why were you afraid that you'd been followed?"

A tinge of anger flickered over Cesare's face. "I'm not sure I understand what you're asking?"

The two men stared at each other. Finally, Pearse shook his head, sat back down on the bench. "I don't know . . . neither do I."

The monk took a moment before responding. "Look, I've put you in an uncomfortable position. I understand. Naturally you're suspicious. Maybe it's better that way."

Again silence before Pearse continued. "So what do you do now?"

"I have a few friends. They can put me up for tonight."

"And then what?"

From under the top of his tunic, Cesare pulled a bag that hung around his neck. "Is there anyone who would understand these kinds of prayers more—how can I say it?—more—"

"Better than I do?" asked Pearse with a smile. "Of course."

"Then I think that person needs to see the scroll."

"And you want me to get it."

Cesare opened the bag and pulled a piece of paper from inside. "I drew you a little map. How to get to the catacombs from the main sanctuary entrance. You could go tomorrow." He held the paper out to Pearse.

"And once I have it, does this start all over again? Am I going to be talking to someone through scaffolding two days from now?"

Cesare said nothing; he laid the paper on Pearse's lap.

"And if I say no?" Pearse asked.

"Sebastiano is dead. If I go back to San Clemente, maybe those men are there; maybe this time, it's not questions. You've told me there's a real link here to something that was supposed to have been rooted out centuries ago."

"And if it wasn't," Pearse insisted, "what possible threat could it pose now anyway? We're talking about ideology, Dante. The church has had fifteen hundred years to establish itself. I don't think an ancient heresy has any hope of undermining that authority."

"Fine. Then why have these men gone to such lengths for a prayer? Does that make any more sense to you?" Cesare waited before continuing. "Doesn't it strike you as odd that it's Vatican security who have been the ones to take such an interest? Whatever this is, it's clearly important to someone. Important enough to take a man's life."

Pearse stared into Cesare's eyes. For several moments, neither said a word. Finally, he reached down and took the paper from his lap.

"Thank you," said the monk. "And tomorrow, we'll take it to this expert of yours."

Pearse stared at the scrawled map. "You're sure you'll be okay tonight?" he asked.

"They're old friends." Cesare stood, placed a hand on the younger man's shoulder, then turned and began to walk away. About ten yards from him, he turned back. "Go in peace." The two exchanged a smile before Cesare turned again and headed off.

Sitting alone, Pearse watched as the monk made his way past the arch. *Go in peace.* If only it were that easy.

▲

Stefan Kleist sat in a small sound studio, several television screens in front of him. One of the monitors pictured a girl, perhaps seven years old, playing on the grass, other children with her, an older woman on a park bench in the distance. A typical spring afternoon. The camera zoomed in on the older woman. She had nodded off, her head tilted back, one hand having fallen from her lap to the bench. The camera again panned to the girl. Kleist spoke into a microphone, a device placed at its base to distort his voice. "I could have taken her then while the old woman slept. Your sister should be more careful with her granddaughter." The tape moved to another scene. The same girl, this time with a younger woman on a busy street, the woman staring into a shop window, unaware as the little girl ambled farther and farther off. The camera now zoomed in on the woman as she turned from the window. Panic rose on her face, her eyes scanning frantically as she realized the girl was gone. When she spotted the tiny figure two stores down, she ran after her, grabbed her arm, and berated her for wandering off. Again Kleist spoke into the microphone. "Or then, when your niece was preoccupied. So easy to have taken the girl then." Once more, the screen faded to another shot, this one through an iron fence, the girl seated on a set of stairs, her small chin resting on tiny hands as she waited in front of a convent school. The camera whipped around and lighted on a young priest making his way through the far gate. "That could be me," intoned Kleist. "Or there," he added as the camera focused on a sister coming out from one of the entrances. "What child wouldn't take the hand of a nun?" The screen now filled with myriad images of the girl—at school, with friends, the park—anywhere a seven-year-old might find herself. "So many choices. So difficult to guard against them all. And if you think the police could help you, don't. I would know before you had hung up the phone. And the girl would be gone."

The screen dissolved to black, then to an old newsreel clip. It was difficult at first to recognize the picture. The Vatican. Smoke from a chimney, thousands watching as the puffs lifted into the air. The 1920s by the look of things. White smoke. Cheering. A nondistorted voice broke through. "Pope Pius the Eleventh is elected in Rome. And the world celebrates. . . ." The voice faded, replaced by Kleist's. "When it comes time for you to make your choice, Eminence, don't forget the little girl. Don't forget what can happen even to a cardinal's grand-niece." Another picture of the girl at play, then black.

Kleist rewound the tape, ran it through once more to make sure the sound was right, then pulled it from the machine. Rudimentary but effective. *The election won't be the problem. We have to think of the weeks after.* How right the contessa had been. Still, the work now was important. Kleist checked the label—Madrid—and slid the tape into its cover. He then set it on a stack of perhaps twenty others that stood to his left:

Buenos Aires, Sydney, St. Louis—just a few of the titles. Reaching to his right, he pulled another—New York, as yet without narration—and slid it into the video recorder. Sixty or so to go.

He knew it would be a long night.

▲

Pearse had walked from the Colosseum, back to the Piazza Venezia, the Corso, the twin churches at the Piazza del Popolo, and finally the bridge out to the Vatican. Crossing at the Ponte Regina Margherita might have been a bit out of the way, but he'd always preferred the area just across the Tiber, the wide avenues and trees that reminded him so much of Paris. As much as he loved Rome, there always seemed to be a kind of heaviness to it. Maybe it was in his own mind. Paris just seemed a little lighter.

His thoughts, however, were not of Paris tonight. *Perfect Light*—the more he walked, the more it gnawed at him. Augustine had referred to it as a collection of Jesus' sayings. By itself, Pearse knew that didn't set the prayer apart from any number of fourth-century tracts. He'd heard of the various collections that had floated around, most inauthentic, each trying to assert some sort of connection to the Messiah, a way to validate one strain of a burgeoning religion over another. That the four Gospels had eventually won out had done little to diminish the quest for the true words of Christ. What so many believers didn't realize—even now—and what Pearse himself all too often confronted in his own quest, was that the Gospels offered only a smattering of Jesus' words, each of the books steeped in interpretation, colored by the historical necessities that had faced their authors. Matthew, Mark, Luke, John, each essential to the task of shaping the church and its dogma, but each too far removed from the spoken Word not to fall prey to inconsistencies. Ever since his days in Chicago with John J., Pearse had believed that to read Christ's genuine teachings, to come face-to-face with their simplicity would clarify everything, remove all doubt, all uncertainty. A *Sola Scriptura* of his own. Faith at its most essential.

Something Petra had never fully understood.

Arriving at the Piazza del Risorgimento—rush-hour trams swallowing and spewing passengers by the dozens—he allowed himself a momentary flight of fancy. What if the prayer did connect to those words? What if the real Christ lay hidden somewhere within it? Freed from the structure that had engulfed them over the centuries, those ideas could breathe new life into a faith growing ever more static, distant. Ignite a genuine passion based on the purity of the Word.

As he stepped from the curb, however, an equally powerful thought entered his mind, brought on more by the events of the last few hours than by anything else. . . . *It's clearly important to someone. Important enough to take a man's life.* He had done his best to dismiss the possibility twenty minutes ago; now, he found it far more difficult. Could a scroll like that be seen as a threat—a single voice, Christ's teachings made plain at last? How might that be received? he wondered. Not as an answer to the complacency, but as a shock to its very core. Here would be something to strip away the layers of exegesis that sat atop the parables, the Beatitudes, all the dogma that had grown out of the myriad attributions of meaning. Could such clarity actually appear dangerous, even the hint of it prompt someone within the church to suppress it—better to maintain the current structure than to upend it, no matter how true to Christ's own insights the source of that clarity might be?

The real paradox of faith: Truth versus Structure. Pearse had to believe that the church was beyond such fears.

And yet, a man was dead.

He cut across the road and sidestepped his way through traffic, one or two angry horns spiriting him on his way. Once on safer ground, he moved along the sidewalk, the Vatican wall—sixty feet of weathered brown-gray stone and turrets—lowering above him; twenty yards down, he turned into the Santa Anna gate, an equally imposing archway, *vigilanza*—dressed in the customary blue tunics and capes—manning the gate. A few cars were making their way out—never more than a glance from the guards for those leaving, far more care with those trying to get in. Even so, the man nodded Pearse through, a token look at the Vatican *passaporto* of a familiar priest.

He might have felt a bit cheated by the world beyond the gate, so little in the way of real grandeur, but he never did. The affectations were reserved for the more public areas—the museums, St. Peter's. Here, it was a collection of administrative buildings, post offices, loggia, the only truly regal sight the fifty-foot archway leading off to the library and beyond. Even that was in need of a good cleaning. But, unlike anywhere else in Rome—perhaps the world—Pearse felt a genuine sense of security within its walls, a safekeeping that ostentation could only mar. And with it, that sense of lightness seemingly unavailable to him in the rest of Rome.

It was why he'd accepted the offer of rooms on his arrival, why he'd petitioned for Vatican citizenship a year after that. Spiritual refuge. Genuine connection to the heart of the church. A taste of the certainty he so desperately craved.

Unfortunately, his choice had dramatically changed things with his family, talks with Jack and Andy less frequent, a sense that the priest was somehow now even more off-limits. His parents hadn't quite known how to take it either, the final realization that their son was truly the church's and not their own. He'd tried to convince them otherwise, but there really wasn't much hope of that. Nor of any of them understanding what had prompted the move—that maybe, just maybe after all this time, Petra wouldn't be able to follow him inside the Vatican walls.

Then again, maybe not.

Managing his way along the cobbled drive—still slick from the rain— he thought about picking up a few pieces of fruit, something sweet at the market, but he couldn't muster the appetite. He remembered some cheese in his rooms. It would have to suffice. Stepping through another, more commonplace archway, he hurried across a stone courtyard before arriving at the entrance to his building.

Three flights and a corridor later, he turned his key and stepped into the two rooms that had been his home for the past few years.

Sofa, chairs, desk-cum-table greeted him as he kicked his shoes across the floor, two small windows on the far wall, neither of which—as far as he knew—having ever seen the sun. But there was always hope. He kept a plant atop the waist-high bookshelf between them just on the off chance a ray or two might creep in.

It was his eighth plant in two years.

Only at night did the light venture in, harsh, from somewhere above, enough to cast shadowed bars across the room from the rusted fire escape. Tonight was no exception. The slanted black lines were instantly erased as he flicked on a standing lamp. At the same time, he pulled off his collar—always the most relaxing moment of the day—and, stretching his neck, moved across the linoleum floor to the books. He crouched down and pulled several volumes out, placing them in a pile on the table just behind him. *Perfect Light*. Time to see how much he had remembered.

He pulled a ball from his glove on the floor and moved to the table. Sitting, he began to toss it back and forth between his hands. Always the best way to concentrate.

The first book was one of the red-bound volumes of the *Corpus Scriptorum Ecclesiasticorum Latinorum*, which contained Augustine's anti-Manichaean works. Pearse recalled several references to the prayer appearing during Augustine's own struggle with his faith. Long before he had decided to "take it and read," the hero of *Confessions* had wondered just how high the "true ascent" might actually take him. Those were the questions Pearse now scanned for, that sense of possibility so clearly felt by the young Augustine.

Much of the writing, though, concentrated on the Manichaean "Kingdom of Darkness," a realm for which Augustine had shown a particular fascination: evil let loose, as arbitrary as it was overwhelming. For a moment, Pearse wondered if perhaps he'd seen it for himself firsthand, the descriptions all too reminiscent of his days in Bosnia. Maybe the Manichaeans deserved more credit than Augustine had given them.

Forty minutes later, he shut the last of the books, no further along than when he had started, every reference too vague, too uncertain in its own understanding of the prayer. For Augustine, "Perfect Light" had remained a mystery. And for a man with perhaps the keenest mind in the long history of the church, such an admission only strengthened the case for its power, the unfathomable as somehow closer to the divine.

Pearse laid the book on the floor—he'd made his way to the sofa after picking up a wedge of cheese between books—and now stretched out his legs. He began to toss the ball in the air, hoping that something would click. But there was no use fighting it. Within a few minutes, his eyes shut, the sofa infamous for its nap-inducing allure.

Δ

It was an hour later when the sound of ringing woke him. At first, he thought it was his alarm, convinced for a moment it was morning. When he realized he was on the sofa, he began to orient himself, slowly aware that it was the phone. Trying to focus, he squinted across the room, the light from above verging on the painful; he forced himself up and moved to the table. On the way, he turned off the lights so as to make things easier.

"Hello?" His voice was raspy.

"Ian." It was Cesare, the sound of traffic in the background. Pearse could barely hear him. "You have to find it, take it." A sudden intake of breath, coughing.

"Dante? Where are you? What's going on?"

"Somehow . . . they came. They knew." More coughing, the words short of breath. "They will change everything. Everything."

"Who will change—" The blood drained from his face. "Dante, where *are* you?"

"It's still safe. . . . I didn't tell them. . . . Still safe."

A moment later, the line went dead.

two

Pearse took the steps two at a time, his hand chafing against the banister, Cesare's words ringing in his ears: *Still safe.* Reaching the ground floor, he bolted out the door, nearly knocking over an ancient monk—a Jesuit, given his robes—the old man trying to make his way in. No time for apologies. Pearse sped off through the archway.

He had waited a good five minutes for Dante to call back, staring at the phone, convincing himself that it was nothing more than a wiring miscue. It had taken his full concentration not to let go entirely, his mind as yet unwilling to accept the obvious. *They will change everything.* They.

Once outside the Vatican walls, Pearse glanced longingly at the taxi rank just off of St. Peter's Square. Not a cab in sight. The emergence of a bus rolling to a stop at the center of Piazza Risorgimento—its route taking it out toward Labicano—was enough, however, to propel him into high gear, his legs slipping along the pavement as he darted in and out of the tourists still making their way toward the basilica.

The last of the passengers was on board when Pearse sprang through the rear door, half the crowd within staring disapprovingly as he steadied himself against a near pole. The door slid shut, people continuing to look at him as the bus pulled out, Pearse only now aware that he had left without his collar. Instinctively, he brought his hand to his neck, smiling as best he could at the staring few.

Twenty-five minutes later, the bus pulled up across from Trajan's Park; Pearse stepped to the curb. Trying to draw as little attention as possible, he hurried across the intersection before sidling his way along the raised median as cars barreled past him in both directions. Hopping the metal fence that separated the two sides, he slipped through a gap in the traffic and settled into a resolute pace along San Giovanni in Laterano, San Clemente quickly in his sights.

Inside, the empty nave stretched to the altar, cavernous without the afternoon's chairs, strangely cool in the dank light, illuminated only by one or two overhead lamps. The permanent pews stood beyond the choir, thick black wood on stone, a single figure bent in prayer, another by the candles, eyes closed, peering up. Stillness, save for the sound of Pearse's own footsteps as he moved across the open expanse toward the stairs he had climbed less than five hours ago; neither of the men seemed to notice him.

At the steps, he suddenly realized he had no light—understandable in all the excitement—but how could he expect to find his way through the tunnels without one? He was about to go back for an offering candle, when he noticed the lantern—his lantern—still on the second step. He took it as a good sign, picked it up, and started down.

Dante's map was a far cry from clarity. Several times, Pearse found himself at dead ends, forced to retrace his steps, only to realize that an almost imperceptible curve in the drawing had indicated a ninety-degree turn. So be it. At least he was alone, no sound but that of his own breath amid the backdrop of rushing water; there was something comforting in that. By the time he reached the catacombs, he had grown accustomed to the monk's notation, taking less than five minutes to locate the room, dig through the pile of rocks, and retrieve the metal cylinder. When he reemerged in the church some ten minutes later, he tried his best at nonchalance as he strode across the empty nave, tube in hand. Once again, he went unobserved.

Outside, his shirt clung mercilessly to his back. He wasn't sure if the perspiration was due to the humidity or to his sudden possession of the scroll; regardless, the rain had returned, more mist than drops—a lifeless air, thick with moisture. The road remained serene, even under the keen gaze of the Colosseum lights some three to four blocks beyond. The glow continued to rise as he neared a fruit stand; he stopped and began to examine the apples, knowing he needed more than just the few pieces of cheese at his apartment to survive. It was an odd sensation, the realization that appetite could so easily detour the mind.

As he handed two of the larger apples to the woman behind the cart, his appreciation for the last forty minutes also came into slow focus, the first time since Dante's call that he'd actually had a moment alone to consider what he was doing. The manic reflex that had brought him to San Clemente was losing its edge. He had the tube; the question remained: What now? Any speculation about Ruini, Dante, the abrupt end to the phone conversation—even the cryptic warning—was just that: speculation. The recovery of the scroll changed none of it. And the police, regardless of the presence of Vatican security, would be the first to point that out.

Which left him only one choice—the prayer itself. Dante had known the truth: Somewhere within the scroll lay a clue to piecing together the disparate strands.

Pearse pocketed the change, took the small paper bag with the apples, and checked his watch. Five to ten. Mania might have lost its sway, but urgency remained a constant; he decided to make the call. Probably not too late, he reasoned, for a typical Roman. After all, hadn't she been the one to admonish him: "Never sit down to dinner before nine-thirty; they'll spot you as a tourist for certain like that"?

With the sound of her snap in his ears, Pearse moved toward the public phones across from the Colosseum. The first apple was all but core by the time he picked up the receiver.

"Attendere, prego." The operator retrieved the number in less than a minute. Another thirty seconds, and a phone somewhere in the Trastevere began to ring.

"Pronto." The voice sounded fully awake.

"Buona sera," answered Pearse, continuing in Italian. "Professor Angeli?"

"Yes?"

"It's Ian Pearse, from the Vatican. We spoke about the Ambrose papers a few months ago."

"Ambrose?" A moment's hesitation, then: "Ah, *Father* Pearse." The voice at once sounded more animated. "Of course. More questions on the old Milanese? Another one of those puzzles you were so good at?"

"Actually, not this time. I hope I'm not calling too late."

A laugh on the other end. "Yes, now I remember. Father Pearse, the *American.* Weren't we supposed to have dinner . . . something about eating too late for you?" Another laugh.

"I've gotten better. At least eight-thirty now."

"Thank goodness. Although anything before—"

"Nine-thirty. Yes. I remember. I'll take it, then, that I'm not calling too late."

"Absolutely not," she answered. "Now, what is it that I can do for you?"

Pearse did his best to concoct a story both reasonable and vague—few details, with emphasis on the extraordinary find—hoping that the possibility of seeing the prayer would allow curiosity to supersede skepticism.

"And no one has had a chance to do any kind of authentication? I would be the first?" Her response told him he had succeeded.

"As far as I know, yes."

"I see." There was a pause on the line. "And how, again, did you say this friend of yours located it?" Without waiting for a response, she continued. "San Clemente is, of course, the ideal place to have found it, but still—"

"Dumb luck," interjected Pearse, hoping to sidetrack any sustained inquiry. "I suppose he knew it was the sort of thing I was interested in. As soon as I got my hands on it, I wanted to find out as much as I could immediately."

"No, no, quite understandable." He could hear the childlike eagerness in her voice, even as the line again fell silent. "'Perfect Light.'" A certain wistfulness had crept in. "You know, they thought they'd found it at Nag Hammadi in one of the Berlin codices. It was '46, '47. Somewhere in there. I think it was Klausner who made the first breakthrough in the early fifties."

"I haven't really had a chance to look at it. I'm not all that sure—"

"Do you think you could bring it by tonight?"

He had been hoping for just that response; still, it came as something of a surprise. "I . . . certainly, if you're sure it's not too late."

"Enough with the 'too late.'" Another short laugh. "Father, how often do you get the chance to play with a seventeen-hundred-year-old piece of parchment? I imagine you're as intrigued as I am."

"Of course."

"Excellent. Then let me give you the address."

Forty-five minutes later, he pressed buzzer number 2 at 145 Piazza Santa Cecilia, a four-story building overlooking the courtyard of a fifth-century church and its convent. The narrow square had room enough for a few cars. The only signs of life came from a hole-in-the-wall restaurant—cutlery on plates colliding with the sounds of conversation—just off to the left. He had never been to her home before, their previous meetings always having taken place at the Vatican Library or a nearby café. The setting, however, fit Angeli perfectly.

A barely audible voice, crackling from an intercom, broke through to add to the din.

"Second floor," the voice said.

"Hello, it's—"

Before he could finish, a muted buzzing began to emanate from the lock. Pearse was quick to push through the ten-foot oaken door, a single bulb flashing on as he stepped into a corridor in need of several coats of paint. At the end, on his left, a curve of stairs swept upward. The sound of a bolt releasing echoed above, a door being pulled back. Light on the second landing. Halfway up the steps, he saw a familiar face peering down at him, a broad smile hidden within two ample cheeks. The eyes lit up at the sight of him.

"Father Pearse," she said, stepping back into the apartment as he reached the top, one hand inviting him in, the other at her side, smoke trailing from a cigarette.

"Professor Angeli." He nodded and stepped inside.

Immediately, she latched the door behind him. "Welcome, welcome," she said with a smile, then moved past him through the foyer and into a sitting room; he followed.

Inside, a desk sat at the center of the room, stacks of books piled high from one end to the other, a small empty square in the middle, one lone ashtray manning the border. It was clear why the desk was so overburdened. Ceiling-high bookshelves covered every inch of wall, each shelf packed to the gills with everything from ancient tomes to recent mass-market paperbacks. A yellowed sheen crept across the room from the far end, two standing lamps shadowing the few open paths that criss-crossed through the books on the floor, hints of a faded Oriental rug peeking through from below. Most of the weblike channels spun out from the desk, all leading to one long shelf across the back wall. No doubt her current project.

"This is exactly what I imagined," he said, still near the doorway.

"I think I'll take that as a compliment," she replied, and pointed to a chair not too far from one of the paths. Pearse sat. "A bit of a mess. You'll have to forgive me. An article I've been writing for an English journal. You know how the English can be about deadlines."

No more than five feet tall, with a tangle of gray-black hair, Angeli was at least sixty—though one could never tell with Italian women—and no doubt a bit more *cicciotella* than she had been twenty years earlier. The weight had done little to discourage a rather beguiling air, an easy wiggle in her walk as she moved to the only other chair that remained free of books. It was also the one closest to a second ashtray. "And it's Cecilia, please," she said with a smile as she sat, taking a long drag on the cigarette. "Don't you remember, 'Cecilia on Santa Cecilia'?"

A smile. "How could I forget?" he answered. "And I'm Ian from the . . . Vatic-ian."

She laughed out loud. "Yes. Yes, you are. Never did quite rhyme, did it?" Another quick puff before laying the cigarette in the ashtray. "And now for the scroll." Her hand was already extended, no request, simply a sudden jab into the air, fingers outstretched, impatiently waiting. Without a thought, Pearse leaned over and placed the tube in her hand. She sat back and opened the top. "Good, you've kept it sealed." Waiting for her to pull the scroll out, he watched as she did something completely unexpected; she sniffed at the opening. Several times. "It has the right oil base," she said, nodding as she pulled her nose from the tube. "Was it found in a jar?" When he didn't answer, she clarified. "An amphora? You know, the sort they found at Qumran or Nag Hammadi?"

He shook his head. "All I know is that it was in the tube the first time I saw it."

She nodded, said nothing, then slid her hand into the opening and pulled out the scroll; the tube found the floor. With tremendous concentration, she began to examine the sheaths wrapped around the parchment. Two pieces of leather string—tied about a third of the way down—hung loose, the only barrier between her agile fingers and the text underneath, but she didn't seem interested in them at all, or in what lay beyond. Instead, she continued to slide her thumb along the leather skin. It was clear she knew exactly what she was looking for, even if Pearse had no idea what the strange ritual was meant to unearth.

"The texture," she said, as if aware of his puzzlement, "the moisture of the leather, it's . . . something you become very attuned to if you've spent time with scrolls like these. If it went directly from jar to tube, you'd still be able to feel a springiness in the sheath." Her eyes remained transfixed on the leather as she spoke. "Klausner was extraordinary with such things. Managed to place two of the Dead Sea Scrolls at Qumran within a hundred years of their actual dating just by the feel." She looked over at Pearse, her eyes wide with excitement. "Wonderful fingers." Then standing, she headed for the desk; he followed immediately behind. He watched as she set the scroll on the empty square, which, no doubt, had been made available since his phone call. It was remarkable how well she knew her field; the scroll fit perfectly.

Setting it down, she deftly untied the leather cover, then slowly began to roll back the parchment. It must have taken her twenty minutes to lay out a section of no more than eight inches square, but her meticulous care kept Pearse rapt. Every so often, a word or two would escape her lips, pursed in concentration; her eyes would light up at those moments, her fingers, though, ever serene, precise, never giving in to the excitement. When she was fully satisfied that she had placed the parchment just right, she produced what looked to be four velvet sacks filled with sand and placed them at the corners. Then, with the section of scroll laid as flat as caution would allow, she pulled a large glass dome—an odd metal knob at its far side—from one of the desk drawers and set it over the scroll. In one fluid movement, she turned the knob and watched as the dome clamped itself to the top of the desk with a sudden hiss of air.

"Clever device," she said. "Not a vacuum seal, but close enough. Let's me spend some time with the scroll without damaging it." She pulled the last cigarette from the pack on the desk, produced a lighter from her pocket, and lit up.

"Handy to have around," he answered, craning his neck so as to try to scan the topmost portion of the text. "Glad to see you've cut down." He smiled.

"My one indulgence, Father."

Still staring at the text, he said, "If you think I believe that—"

A loud cackle rose from behind the cigarette. "Really, Father, you'll make me blush."

"Somehow," he said, his own smile wider, "I doubt that."

Another burst of laughter. "What a shame you're a priest. . . ." Without finishing the thought, she took a long drag and said, "Do you read Syriac, Father?" He shook his head; she continued. "Well, that's what's staring up at you. It's rather surprising. I would have thought—"

"Latin or Greek," he cut in.

"Latin or Greek?" She looked genuinely puzzled.

"Well," he explained, now a little less confident, "the few Manichaean texts I've seen were written in either one or the other."

"Really? That's odd. I was about to say Chinese. The only Latin text we have is the *Rule for Auditores*, the one they found just outside Tebessa, in Algeria. As for Greek—well, that's only in the later tracts. I assume you're referring to a specific collection?" No time to answer as she turned back to the scroll, a pair of half glasses emerging from a pocket; she spoke somewhat offhandedly, eyes scanning the words. "Actually, the fullest texts we have come from a group of seventh- and eighth-century sects who managed to survive on the fringes of the

Chinese Empire." She glanced up at him. "Can you imagine that? China?" Just as quickly, she turned back to the scroll. "There are even references to a Manichaean community as far east as—"

"Fu-Kien?" he said, unable to mask a rather coy smile. "Thirteenth century?"

She stopped and looked up, her surprise once again all too obvious. "Very good."

"Well, I had to make up for the Latin bungle. Show you I'm more than just a pretty face."

"True." She waited, then added, "I'd forgotten I have to be on my toes with you."

"Hardly. That was my best shot. I'll be lucky if I can keep up."

Her smile told him he had hit the mark. "Oh, I know that's not true. As I remember, you're very, very good at all these ancient puzzles." She took another quick drag. Evidently, Angeli could be equally coy when she wanted; Pearse couldn't be sure, but he thought he might just have shared a moment's flirtation with her, willingly or not. Another reminder of why he'd always enjoyed working with Cecilia Angeli so much.

She turned back to the scroll, once again caught up in the text.

"So, as I was saying, you'd expect Chinese, and if not Chinese, then Pahlavi, Soghdian, or Middle Persian. But Syriac"—she stooped even lower over the dome so as to peer at the words, smoke streaming from her nose—"that makes this a very strange document. A very strange document indeed."

She pulled her glasses from her face and stood upright. "And one considerably older than any of its Chinese relatives." Turning to him, she asked, "Would you like some coffee? I think I'm going to make a pot." Without waiting, she began to wend her way through the piles of books, the glasses quickly back in her pocket, a trail of gray smoke settling on the room behind her.

Pearse smiled to himself. It wasn't the fact that he was thirty years her junior that was holding her back. Just the collar, which, as he now recalled, he wasn't even wearing. She had been nice not to mention it. Or maybe that was what was egging her on. Pearse started to laugh as he edged closer to the desk.

He stared down at the strange script through the glass. The thick curve of letters melded easily into one another, yet each was distinct, a line of indecipherable signs linked only by the common touch of a single scribe's hand. In and among the letters, tiny sticklike figures littered the parchment—little men carrying daggers, what looked to be a lion poised in attack. Likewise, wrinkles and tears peppered the almost hypnotic flow of words and illustrations, choice bits lost forever, left to the reasoned imagination of the modern reader. Pearse knew Angeli would have no trouble filling in the gaps, offering up her own vision of continuity with intricate explanations, as if perhaps she had been there, peering over the shoulder of the ancient scribe as he had inked the original. She had done as much with Ambrose; somehow he sensed she'd be more at home here, more comfortable with the renegades and heretics.

"I was thinking," she said as she reappeared at the doorway, "there might be a link to the Mandaeans, given the little pictures. Mani's father was a Mandaean. It's a natural connection. Did any of your research with Ambrose take you as far afield as them?" She was reclaiming the glasses from her pocket as she neared the desk.

"The Mandaeans?" Pearse replied. "Actually . . . no. I can't say that it did."

"You know Fu-Kien, but you don't know the Mandaeans?" She was clearly having a bit of fun. "Really?"

"Shocking as it sounds, I know."

Her smile grew. "Actually, they're more of a strictly Gnostic group. Individual responsibility, hidden knowledge—the 'gnosis'—that sort of thing. There's certainly a link, but they're much earlier than Mani and Manichaeanism."

Leaving the banter aside for the moment, he asked, "So, if they were earlier, that means they would have died out by the time 'Perfect Light' was written?"

"Oh, no," she answered. "Most of the silver and gold markets in Basra and Baghdad today are run by Mandaeans. In fact, I once spent a very wonderful afternoon with one of their *nasuraiyi*, a 'guardian' of the secret rites and knowledge." Her eyes stopped momentarily on a spot on the rug. "Fascinating man. Tried to explain the five realms of light. Absolutely incomprehensible." She looked up with a smile. "It's just that seeing the Syriac with illustrations—well, it's a very odd choice. Naturally it makes one think of the Mandaeans." She drew up next to him and again began to scrutinize the scroll.

"Naturally." He now remembered how essential such digressions were to her work—essential, if equally incomprehensible. It was best to let her mind range as it saw fit. "So you *don't* think it's linked to the Mandaeans?" he asked.

"Of course not." She looked up. "Why do you ask?"

Now Pearse smiled. "No reason."

She turned again to the parchment. It was time to get down to business. Within seconds, she was translating as she read: " 'It is from the perfect light, the true ascent that I am found in those who seek me. . . .' " She let the words trail off as she seemed to reread the section to herself. "That's some sort of preamble," she continued. "There's a section missing here, and then it goes on: 'It is I who am the riches of the light; it is I who am the memory of the fullness. And I traveled in the—'" She stopped and bent closer in to get a better look, her eyes now scanning the next few lines, lips always moving silently. Pearse noticed another large tear just below her finger on the glass. "That's odd. This bit comes right out of the 'Secret Book of John,' the 'Poem of Deliverance,' at least in these first few lines." She read on. "There's another section missing here, and then it runs, 'And I traveled in the darkness . . .' something about a prison, and then picks up again here with 'And the foundations of chaos moved.' "

She stood upright, her eyes still on the scroll. "That's the Book of John all right. A Syriac version of the Gnostic Greek, but definitely John." She turned to Pearse. "I'm sure I could find a better translation of it; wouldn't be much help, though, I don't think. My guess is that the writer used it to set the tone, establish a link—although why he connects 'Perfect Light' with John . . ." Her words once again trailed off as she leaned in over the glass. "That isn't clear at all."

"Right," said Pearse hesitantly. "Actually, the Manichaeans might not be the only ones traveling in darkness here."

"What?" She looked up, clearly having been listening with only half an ear.

He smiled. "I think I missed class that day."

"Oh . . . I would have thought with Ambrose, you would have—" She cut herself off. "Or maybe not." She smiled, the teacher trying to find the right words. "I suppose it's all rather . . . obscure, isn't it?"

"A little earlier than my period, that's all."

"Always a good excuse."

"Then I guess I'll stick with it."

"Fair enough"—a cigarette back in her fingers—"No reason you should be familiar with any of this." She looked up at him, the smile in her eyes growing to a twinkle. "Well, is it to be the introductory lecture, or just the highlights, Father?" Once again, she left him no time to answer. "I suspect just the highlights."

She stepped away from the glass, turned, and sat on the lip of the desk. "Let's see," she began, taking a long drag, gesticulating with the cigarette to emphasize each point. "Dating. . . . John is written sometime in the first or second century, so it's a contemporary of the canonical Gospels; it's a Gnostic tract and therefore a threat to what would become orthodox Catholicism; it recasts the Genesis myth with God as a mother-cum-father entity prior to the God of the Hebrew Bible. . . ." Another long draw on the cigarette, her eyes now searching the air, the delivery no less staccato. "It focuses on self-knowledge and condemns the institutionalization of faith; it's supposedly written by one of Jesus' original disciples—John, the son of Zebedee—and purports to record the words of Christ Himself; and it's done in the narrative style of what was called an 'apocryphal act of the apostles,' a sort of Christianized novel." One last puff before she turned to crush the butt into the ashtray, speaking as she drove the cigarette deeper into the ash. "The poem is simply one section of the book, an explanation of how one might be able to achieve deliverance by reclaiming uncontaminated, or perfect, light." She looked up. "So there you have a link to the Manichaean prayer. A tenuous one, but a link."

Still trying to piece everything together, he asked, "And all of that makes John and its poem a typical Gnostic tract?"

"On a very fundamental level," she replied, "yes. It's one that conveys a secret knowledge—directly from Christ—which the initiated elite access in order to achieve an enlightened existence. Gnosticism at its most basic."

Feeling a bit bolder, he added, "And once the four Gospels are canonized, it slips into obscurity, along with the rest of the Gnostic scriptures."

"Well, *shoved* might be a better choice of words. Remember, at the end of the second century, the followers of Jesus—in all their myriad sects—were fighting for their lives. They needed to put up a unified front, rather difficult, given the number of gospels and apostolic letters making the rounds. Which meant internal debates among them ultimately amounted to a matter of survival, rather than theology."

"Expedience over spirit." Pearse nodded. "Kind of takes the sheen off of things, doesn't it?"

"Reality has a way of doing that, yes," she said.

"Glad to see you're not sugarcoating it on my account."

"Wouldn't dream of it."

He smiled. "I could hide all the ashtrays."

Another little chuckle. "I have them in places you wouldn't begin to think of."

He started to respond, then thought better of it. "So they needed one interpretation to stand supreme against the common Roman enemy, is that it?"

"Yes . . . but not just an interpretation. The early Catholic church needed a structure that could bring the faithful together. Something to turn the 'followers of Jesus' into 'Christians.' The 'Jesus movement' into 'Christianity.' Gnosticism defied any kind of structure and therefore made its believers difficult to control. No control, no unified front. You see where I'm leading?"

"To the end of Gnosticism."

"Exactly. Anti-Gnostic writings became one of the standards of the new orthodoxy, most famously from the pen of the Bishop of Lyons, a man named Irenaeus. He wrote several books. . . ." She stopped for a moment, her eyes again searching the air. "What was the big one? *The Overthrow? The Destruction?* Something about 'false knowledge.'" She looked back at him. "Whatever it was. It condemned all Gnostic gospels as heresy, and in so doing, helped to root out any internal squabbling. You had a common front." She seemed to have expected a bigger response from him; he obliged with an exaggerated nod.

"Thank you. At the same time, though," she continued, "that standard asserted an image of Christ that may very well have been different from the figure of Jesus His earliest followers had known. A shift. We, of course, will never really know."

"A different image of Christ?" For the first time, Pearse responded not as student. "I'm not sure I understand that."

Angeli smiled. "I don't mean to make you uncomfortable, Father."

"Yes, you do." He smiled. "What shift?"

"Oh, I didn't say there was a shift. I said there *might* have been a shift. No one's absolutely certain how people understood Jesus in those first few centuries. Too many versions of the Word floating around. There's Paul, the Gospels, the Gnostics, any number of Jesus sects—"

"Right, right," he cut in. "But there has to be a way to distinguish Catholic orthodoxy from Gnosticism? One Christ from another?"

"Naturally. We're just not sure which one is the authentic Christ."

"I understand. But the differences—"

"Are there. Yes." Evidently, this part of the discussion required a fresh cigarette. She fished through her pocket and produced yet one more from a seemingly endless supply. "I say all of this purely as an academic, Father, sugarcoating or not. As a Catholic—"

"Don't worry, you're absolved."

Angeli returned the smile, then lit up before diving back in. "Well then, two basic distinctions separate an orthodox and a Gnostic image of Christ. First, orthodox Catholics view God as a completely separate entity. Primal Other. We can venerate Him, attempt to mirror His life and piety, but we can never achieve a synthesis with Him. The Gnostics, on the other hand, claim that self-knowledge—the highest form of attainment—is actually knowledge of God. So, self and Divine become identical at a certain point of self-awareness."

"That's sounds like a very Eastern view of spiritual growth," he said.

"On some level, it is."

"And the second point?"

"Also somewhat Eastern. And politically far more explosive. For orthodox Christians, the 'living Jesus' speaks of sin and repentance. At His core, Christ is Savior, hence the need for His death, our sins, and His Resurrection. And that Resurrection is a literal one, confirmed by Peter. Without that doctrine, without Peter standing there saying, 'I was the first, I can vouch for His return, He gave me the keys and told me to tend to the sheep, and so forth and so on,' there's no need to have a group of men—the leaders of the church—sustaining that confirmation. In other words, without the doctrine of bodily resurrection, there's no way to validate the apostolic succession of bishops. No way to lay claim to the papacy."

"That's a little troubling, isn't it?"

"You might say that. For Gnostics, on the other hand, Jesus speaks of illusion and enlightenment. They reject a literal Resurrection altogether. So Christ becomes guide. Once again, a dramatic shift in the relationship occurs when the disciple achieves enlightenment. Jesus is no longer spiritual master. Instead, the two become equals through their knowledge. Self and Divine are identical. Hence, there's no need for a resurrection or a papal authority, with its subsequent structure. Even the few Gnostic tracts that hint at a Resurrection have Jesus appearing to Mary Magdalene first, not Peter. Imagine what that would have done for the papal succession? Pretty powerful stuff."

"So Gnosticism humanizes Christ?"

"No." Angeli shook her head. "It elevates human self-awareness to a deified status, and places the responsibility to achieve that status on the individual's shoulders. Jesus remains elevated. It's just now, He might not be alone."

"So we all become God?" Pearse asked somewhat skeptically.

"No, I don't think that's right," she said, this time a bit more thought before answering. "We all attain the knowledge, but Christ remains Christ. It's just that our relationship with Him is . . . not so distant. I can't think of a better way to put it."

"It sounds like you're saying we don't need a church."

For the first time, she hesitated. "On a concrete level, I suppose . . . yes." She seemed unsure of her answer, needing to convince herself. "Yes, I think that would be right. On a spiritual level, though, it's far more complex."

"Self-awareness was the only guide a Gnostic needed." Pearse was getting caught up in the idea. "No structure. Nothing to get in the way. An individually impassioned link to Christ. Pretty nice setup."

"As I said, to a greater or lesser extent. But don't forget, they never abandoned their commitment to faith. Or to Christ as the Messiah."

"Right, right. But it was a pure, unfettered faith." His eyes began to drift to a distant point.

"Yes." She noticed his expression. "Father?" She waited until she had his attention. "I'm sure some of this offends you. I don't mean to—"

"Not to worry."

"You're sure?"

"When I start humming and covering my ears, you'll know I've had enough."

"Anyway, you can see why orthodox Christianity needed to suppress it. It was their need for control. . . ." She stopped herself; best to leave the thought unfinished with a priest in the room, no matter what he might have said to the contrary. After several moments, she stood and turned back to the scroll. "None of that, however, helps to answer the question: Why put the Gnostic John at the beginning of a *Manichaean* prayer? Mani might have started out as a type of Gnostic, but he didn't end there." She turned to Pearse. "There are significant differences."

"Maybe it had something to do with the oral tradition. Something the scribe's own congregation said before chanting the prayer?"

A dismissive snort of air accompanied a quick shake of her head.

"I'll take that as a no."

"Unless he went counter to everything we know about liturgical tran-scription," said Angeli, "of course not."

"I preferred the snort."

"I thought you might." Within seconds, she was back with the parch-ment, her lips once again moving silently. "Here, you see, it goes off onto something entirely new." Without warning, she suddenly stepped away from the desk and headed for one of the bookshelves. Pearse was left to watch as she began to scan row after row, her plump little finger mov-ing anxiously through the air, until, with a jab, she turned to him. "You're tall enough. It's the green one on the fourth shelf, two in from the end." Half a minute later, they had the book at the desk. She flipped through several pages, a little hum to accompany her wanderings; each time, she returned to the parchment with a short "No" before moving on. After six or seven such dismissals, the hum almost a constant, she closed the book and laid it distractedly on a pile behind her. "Odd," she said, as she made her way back to the shelf; another retrieval by Pearse, another few minutes rejecting theories, one more on the growing pile of discarded texts. The next time at the shelf, she decided to take six books at once, with Pearse left to stand silently by while she hummed through each of them, her expression never drifting beyond the slightly intrigued. He guessed she would have made an excellent poker player. Finally, after nearly ten minutes, her eyes shot up. The look on her face was one of genuine shock. Pearse moved closer.

"The coffee!" she blurted out, and scurried along the central path and out of the room before he could respond. Only then did he fully recall what it was like to work with Cecilia Angeli. Always best to give her a wide berth. In fact, he'd begun to think it might be equally smart to let her spend some time alone with the parchment. There was very little he could add to her investigation, except as a distraction.

A day or so would also give him the chance to bone up on his Gnostic and Manichaean literature. A chance to feel more comfortable with the scroll before following its lead, whatever that might entail. A different image of Christ. Something so tempting in that.

More than that, it would give him time to try to find out what had happened to Dante.

Before she had returned with the coffee, Pearse decided he would leave the scroll with her, tell her nothing of Ruini or Dante, nothing of the monk's warning, and ask her only to keep the scroll's discovery to herself. He knew she wasn't someone to weather a visit from Vatican security all that well. Best to keep her out of range.

He also knew it was an unnecessary request. Angeli was famous for keeping everything close to the chest until she had pieced together the details. Hers was a professional insecurity at its most charming, if extreme. She'd insisted he approach Ambrose that way; it would be no different here.

She reappeared at the door, a tray of coffee and biscotti in hand, an empty chair serving as surrogate table. She began to pour.

"Just a quick cup," he said, "and then I should probably let you get some sleep."

"Sleep?" She laughed. "You think I'm going to get any sleep tonight? Why do you think I made the coffee? No, Father, we both know that's not the way I work. You've brought me a new toy; I want to play with it."

"And we also know that I'd only be getting in the way."

She handed him a cup, then took one of the cookies. With a little smile, she said, "Yes, that's probably true." After a healthy bite, she added, "Your friend won't mind if I spend some time with it?"

"Absolutely not." Pearse took a sip of the piping espresso. "Of course, if you find anything more than just odd—"

"I'll get in touch with you at once. Of course." She had taken her cup and another biscotti back to the desk, a tiny space between dome and edge all that was left for both. "You, after all, were the one to bring it to me." Another bite of the cookie. "I suspect I'll have something in the next few days. As you know, I like to work . . . alone, so I take a bit longer."

"I'll try and remember the access codes from last time," he said with a smile.

"It wasn't that bad, was it?"

"The results are always worth it."

"You're such a nice priest. Still, it's a shame. . . ."

Half a cup of espresso later, they stood at the door, Angeli clearly eager to get back to her "toy." The good-byes were brief.

By quarter past twelve, he stood on the Ponte Garibaldi, a starry sky having all but swept away the mist and rain, a hint of cool air off the water a belated apology for the day. He let the breeze sift through his hair and clothes as he walked, the sound of the Tiber constant as his own pace. He stopped for a few moments at the apex of the bridge, lights from each bank streaming onto the edge of the water, never, though, infringing more than a few yards, a narrow strip of deep velvet at center. Pearse stared out at the abyss, caught up in its imagined emptiness.

Light and darkness, he thought. The simplicity in contrast somehow so comforting.

▲

The *vigilanza* at the gate seemed surprised by his late return. Priests— even those without collars—were usually in bed at this hour. Pearse didn't recognize a single face as the guards gave both him and his identification a thorough examination before letting him through. The unfamiliarity evidently mutual, they continued to watch him as he made his way to the archway.

The change in weather had somehow eluded the Vatican, a dusty drizzle pressing at him as he walked up to his entryway. With no Jesuit to evade this time around, he managed the door with ease, the light from the foyer slipping into dim haze as he mounted the steps; the third-floor corridor waited silently. Trying to mirror its stillness, he tiptoed toward his room, gingerly pulling the key from his pocket before easing it into the lock. Inside, he slowly pressed the door shut, then placed the key on a side table.

"Quarter to one," came a voice from somewhere behind him. Pearse spun round, his eyes as yet unaccustomed to the dark, the striped shadows streaming in from the windows as he tried to pinpoint the unseen speaker. "That's rather late, isn't it?" His first inclination was to reach back for the door handle, but a figure suddenly appeared at his right, a large hand spread wide across the center of the door. Pearse turned back into the room, his eyes now clearer, the outline of a figure seated by the far window, another at its side. From his chair, the man flicked on a nearby table lamp. "Why don't you have a seat, Father?"

One by one, Pearse stared at the men, all three in dark suits. "How did you get in here?" he asked.

Stefan Kleist, still seated, reached into his jacket pocket and pulled out a small wallet. He flipped it open to reveal an identification card. "Vatican security," he answered.

The man in the chair was smaller than the others, far less overpowering, yet clearly more menacing. Or perhaps it was the accent, thought Pearse. The precision of an Austrian German as he articulated English; he couldn't tell. "I wasn't aware that gave you permission to enter a priest's private apartments in the middle of the night."

"Only under certain circumstances, Father." Kleist seemed strangely deferential, far less snide than with his initial quip.

"And that usually entails waiting around for one of them to return?"

"Why don't you have a seat?"

Pearse remained by the door, aware that the room had changed subtly since he'd last seen it. The books were back on the shelves, no longer on the floor by the sofa, the plate of cheese altogether gone. The ball was back in his glove. Someone had decided to clean up—perhaps too well—after what had no doubt been a painstaking overhaul of the apartment. He glanced once more at the man nearest to him—at least six foot seven, eyes vacant, no need to threaten, his frame imposing enough. Pearse slowly moved to the sofa and sat. A vicarious sense of déjà vu swept over him.

"Where's the scroll, Father?" asked Kleist.

The man's candor momentarily caught him off guard. Not that he had any idea what they thought they would find in it; still, given Dante's experience, he had expected a bit more finesse. "Scroll?" he replied.

"Tonight's not the night to play games." Kleist's expression remained unchanged, his tone enough to convey his impatience. "You saw the monk at Ruini's funeral."

"How did you know—"

"Do you often go out without your collar?" Kleist continued, producing the thin strip of white material from the tabletop. "Or is that only when you're in a rush?" Pearse said nothing. "What were you in such a hurry to find?" He waited, then asked again. "The scroll, Father—where is it?"

Pearse kept his eyes locked on the small man, trying not to display any of the panic mounting in his chest. He became acutely aware of the silence, second after second slipping by, until he heard the sound of a distant voice break through. "Don't you mean statuette?" Pearse was still staring, amazed that the words had come from his own mouth. He watched as a hint of uncertainty crept across the Austrian's eyes.

"What?" asked Kleist.

"Dante said there was some question of provenance," Pearse continued, no less stunned at the ease with which he let the words slip out. "That the monastery's claim was prior to the Vatican's."

"What are you talking about?"

"The fertility god he found in the catacombs. The statuette." He seemed to be gaining momentum. "He said you'd be eager to get your hands on it, although I'm not sure he thought you'd go to these lengths. Isn't that what this is all about?"

Kleist said nothing for several seconds, his gaze fixed on Pearse. When he finally spoke, precision once again laced his words. "This is much simpler than you seem to understand, Father." He paused, then continued. "We both know the monk never mentioned a statuette. Or any questions of provenance. He told you about a scroll."

Again, Pearse said nothing, the Austrian evidently willing to wait.

After nearly a minute, however, his patience had grown thin. He began to nod. "All right," he said, getting to his feet and buttoning his jacket, "then let's go and see this statuette of yours."

"What?" blurted out Pearse, trying to maintain some semblance of calm. "Now?"

"Yes, now, Father," he replied, standing patiently in front of his chair. "If it's where you say it is, then we've made a terrible mistake, and you have our apologies." The delivery was devoid of any emotion. "If not, then we'll have to start all over again."

Nothing in the words approximated what Pearse saw in the eyes staring back at him. Eyes that made it abundantly clear why the smallest of the three was issuing the commands. And it had very little to do with the accent. Remember the monk; remember the terror in his voice. With only a glance, the man had said as much.

Pearse's tone was far less controlled when he spoke. "Look, I'm a priest—"

"A Vatican priest," Kleist reminded firmly, without raising his voice. "Which places you under our jurisdiction."

"I'm also an American—"

"In an independent nation-state that houses no embassies." He let the well-practiced words sink in. "Vatican City recognizes no claims by foreign states to infringe upon the sovereignty of His Holiness, the Pope. As representatives of that sovereignty, we are equally unrestricted in our handling of those who claim citizenship within its walls." He waited, then continued. "The statuette, Father."

A nervous courage surged to the fore. "And what if I refuse to show you where it is?"

"Why would you do that?" he asked, again with no trace of emotion. "As I said, we're interested in a scroll. You show us this statuette of yours, and we'll have nothing more to talk about."

Pearse suddenly realized how well the man from security had played him. He tried to maintain his edge. "Except your apology."

For some reason, Kleist allowed himself a grin. "Yes, Father. Except that."

"This can't wait?"

"No." The grin was gone. "It can't."

With a nod from Kleist, the man across the room opened the door and stepped outside, waiting in the hall for the others to emerge. At the same time, the second man moved behind the sofa, again no need to threaten, his size more than enough to prompt Pearse to his feet. Kleist took a step closer to his quarry, then motioned for Pearse to join the man in the corridor.

No choice. No options. Whatever strands of reasoned argument Pearse had clung to now began to swirl in his head at a feverish pace. *Vatican priest.* The attribution had never sounded so threatening. He felt an overwhelming wave of panic sweep through him as he started for the door.

The closer he got to the corridor, however, the more his panic seemed to surrender to a feeling of supreme isolation, a sense that he was somehow removed, floating above it all, monitoring the entire episode from some distant point—its effect numbing. Under its ever-deepening sway, Pearse began to experience a kind of detached lucidity, his mind suddenly uncluttered by the frantic search for escape of only moments ago. His legs simply moved.

At the door, he watched himself as he calmly stopped and turned back to his captor. "I'll need the map," he said, the voice clearly his own. "Dante drew one up so I could find it."

Kleist, growing impatient with the ongoing charade, seemed unaware of the almost mesmeric quality in Pearse's voice and body. "So you could find the statuette?" he asked, the first tinge of anger in his voice.

"No," answered Pearse. "The scroll."

For an instant, Kleist didn't know how to respond. He'd expected the priest to play it out, maintain the ruse until its futility prompted the all-too-familiar lapse into hysteria—more often than not, once inside the car. He'd seen that sort of captivity work wonders in the past. And yet, this priest had done neither. He had admitted the truth without the usual ranting. "A map of San Clemente?"

Pearse nodded, his eyes fixed on the far wall. "Yes."

"Where?"

Pearse pointed to the bookshelf.

A twinge of frustration creased Kleist's lips. "We didn't find any map in there." Pearse started toward the shelf, Kleist's powerful hand quick to rein him in. "I told you, we didn't find anything."

The pressure on his chest seemed to release Pearse from his stupor. His mind, however, was still focused, rising above the panic. He kept absolutely still, his eyes trained on the far wall. Something was telling him he needed to piece together the last thirty seconds. Something in his subconscious. *What aren't I seeing?* "It's in a compartment in the back panel," he said. "You wouldn't have found it."

Kleist kept his arm on Pearse's chest. Neither said a word. After several seconds, the smaller man slowly released him, motioning for Pearse to find the map. Doing as he was told, Pearse moved to the bookshelf, his eyes still fixed on the wall. As he stepped to the side of the shelf, reality and subconscious began to collide, image into image—a moment of perfect fusion. *Not the wall . . . the window . . . the fire escape. . . . I've been looking at the fire escape.* He knelt down, now between shelf and window, careful to keep his movements slow, even, as if he were searching for something. He could sense the panes of glass directly behind him, both slightly ajar, a hint of air through the gap at the center. Ten seconds into the phantom probe, he saw Kleist begin to step toward him.

On pure impulse, Pearse launched the shelf out into the room, the wooden case scraping along the floor before crashing to a stop at Kleist's feet. An instant later, he swung his hand up against the lamp, it, too, tossed from its perch, wire plucked from socket, all light extinguished in a blinding instant. Pearse heard the movement, felt the rush of bodies within the room, amazed to feel his own back thrusting against the window, the two panes parting behind him as he tumbled out and onto the fire escape. A harsh glare hammered from above, a wild hand reaching after him, but he was already on his feet, hands grasping at the rails, rust grinding against his palms as he found the steps and began to hurtle his way down. No thought to the men above, to the sound of emphatic pursuit, only the stairs, the final row taken in a single vault, his feet landing on the ground, hands to the gravel so as to break his fall. The clatter from behind grew louder as he struggled to his feet, the alley far narrower than he had imagined from his third-floor roost.

He began to run, the path cutting to his left no more than twenty feet from the stairs, at once pitch-black as he continued on, hands now sliding along smooth stone, eyes squinting for any hint of a distance. He had no idea where he was, no sense of the buildings, only the need to keep moving. He was sure the Austrian was behind him, a pair of grasping hands ready to clamp down on his shoulder at any moment, throw him to the ground.

Without warning, the alley suddenly opened to a small courtyard, a single lamp at the far corner its only source of light. Delivery vans stood in a row by what looked to be a loading dock, beyond them a small entrance arch. To his right, a wedge of shadow clung to the walls. Pearse darted under its mantle, his eyes fixed on the entryway no more than thirty yards from him. The place was deserted, lights glowing in one or two windows from the adjoining buildings, the vans a desolate collection of black-visored sentries asleep at their posts. As he neared the arch, the sound of footsteps began to echo in the courtyard. Pearse froze. He planted himself against the wall and vainly tried to stifle his breath.

The small man appeared, a powerful physique in clear evidence as he ran out into the courtyard, stride compact, arms pumping in fluid motion, his chest straining against the confines of his suit. He stopped and began to scan the open space, no indication that he was even mildly winded. For an instant, Pearse thought the man had spotted him, his eyes pausing on the area of shadow now shrouding the priest. But just as quickly, he moved on, locating the arch and bolting toward it at full stride. Pearse held his breath as the sound of footsteps raced past him, no sign that the Austrian had sensed the figure no more than fifteen feet from him. In a matter of seconds, Pearse stood alone.

He was unable to move, certain that at least one more of the security men would appear at any second to drag him away. But the courtyard remained empty.

They weren't coming.

For a brief moment, he thought about returning to his rooms—the alley, the fire escape—the last place they would look for him. But the Austrian's words flooded back: *A Vatican priest . . . under our jurisdiction.* Again, no choice. No options. He had to get out of the City, easy prey within its walls. *Prey?* Another piece of absurdity, this one, though, all too real.

He pulled himself from the wall and, still in shadow, moved to the archway, its squat arc amplifying the echo of his footsteps. Beyond it, he came to a second courtyard—this one larger, mercifully empty—a partial view of the museum's rooftops in the distance. Again, he tried to orient himself. The trouble was, the two exits out of the square led away from the Santa Anna Gate, which, as he now thought about it, might not be such a bad idea. If security meant to keep him within its "juris-diction," the guards would have been told to keep an eye out for a col-larless priest. Hold him inside. Gates designed to ward off the overly eager tourist now called on to restrain a priest.

More absurdity. He had to find another way out.

Ducking through the closer of the two exits, he emerged to a part of the Vatican where the alleys snake from courtyard to courtyard, cling-ing to the sides of St. Peter's and the Sistine Chapel. Somewhere beyond, an expanse of gardens waited—the Governor's Palace, the Church of Santa Marta, the fountain of the Virgin—until tonight sacro-sanct in his mind, now nothing more than a cage. It was an odd sensa-tion, losing touch with the one place in Rome he had always felt most secure, protected. A stiff price to pay for something he still knew so little about.

Seeking out shadows wherever he could, Pearse edged his way along the narrow lanes, choosing what he thought were the most arbitrary routes, hoping in so doing to avoid any further confrontation. He knew that the Austrian would have a small legion at his disposal. It wouldn't be long before illogic met its match in sheer numbers. Which meant he had to find his means of escape now.

At every turn, though, the outer walls seemed to find him, endless sheets of brick and stone disappearing into a slate sky. *No way through, no way over.* The thought battered at him as he slipped from one court-yard to the next, alleys spinning him deeper and deeper into the private world of the Vatican, until, with a sudden upsweep of air, he sped out into the grasp of trees, several lamps casting insignificant beams on a car-pet of cobblestone. Pausing to catch his breath, he realized he had arrived at the Governor's Palace gardens, the dome of St. Peter's hover-ing above him to his left.

The wide piazza lay deserted, the palace facade a series of icy black windows—four, five stories high—staring back at him. He kept to the grass, relieved to slip under the widening cluster of branches, ears cocked for any sound around him. Silence. *No way through, no way over.* A deaf-ening mantra.

At the edge of the trees, he stopped again, resting up against a trunk to survey the area. The shadows shifted from a swirl of leaves, his eyes drawn upward to the dome, the cross atop peering out on an unseen Tiber, the world of Rome beyond. Ironic sanctuary, he thought, for one trapped behind these walls. How many, he wondered, had ever viewed it as such—St. Peter's, its two great arms of colonnades stretching around the square, grasping its faithful to its chest? Its intention to embrace. But also to insulate.

More so than he had ever imagined before.

Just then he noticed an isolated area blanketed in dim light. Unsure, he inched his way out to the edge of the shadow. As he continued to stare, a building came into sight.

The railway station. *Of course.*

He had completely forgotten about the single line that ran through the Vatican, the tracks some twenty yards beyond the station. Tracing them with his eyes, he watched as the rails disappeared into a tunnel. *No way through, no way over.*

So what about under?

He had no idea where the tracks led, or even if they remained unguarded farther on; still, they were his best bet, given the alternatives.

Of all the places he might choose for escape, though, the tracks were clearly the most exposed. He'd be out in the open for fifteen, twenty seconds. Again, he checked the area around him. No one. Steeping his lungs with air, he bolted out.

It was maddening to be so vulnerable, darting out in full view from a thousand different angles, the glow from the lamps almost painful to his skin. All he could feel was the utter stillness around him, an almost airless funnel from trees to station. Reaching the platform, he leapt onto the wooden boards that lay at the center of the rails. Everything seemed brighter still, more static, his only choice to duck down, plant his back against the low wall. He all but expected to hear the echo of *vigilanza* footsteps bearing down on him.

Nothing.

Another breath, and he propelled himself toward the tunnel, the twenty yards a final naked sprint before he felt the cover of darkness wash over him.

It seemed to go on indefinitely, tracks with narrow platforms on either side disappearing deeper and deeper underground. Still, it was better than what he had just left. He hopped up onto the platform to his left and started in. Twice, he looked over his shoulder, each time the light dipping farther from sight. On the third try, it vanished altogether. Only then did he notice the blue fluorescent lights evenly spaced along the wall. Dim to the point of futility, they seemed to grow brighter as his eyes became more accustomed to the dark. All the while, he tried to picture his whereabouts above ground, unsure if he had yet moved beyond the Vatican walls.

His answer came far quicker than he expected. No more than five feet from it, he began to make out what looked to be an immense door rising from track to roof, sealing the tunnel behind. No wonder there had been no guard at the station: Who could possibly find their way through this? Drawing up to within half a foot of the thing, Pearse confirmed his first impressions. Solid steel, all the way up.

Hoping to find a smaller door within, he began to glide his hands across it. Nothing. Undaunted, he dropped to the tracks and did the same with the door as a whole. Again nothing. He hoisted himself up onto the second platform and began to probe in the dark, when his elbow suddenly knocked against something jutting from the wall. Within seconds, he had the object, a piece of iron—as best as he could tell—rectangular, perhaps two inches thick, ten inches across. A few inches above, he found another, then another, all at regular intervals.

Rungs of a ladder. A minor miracle.

Ten or eleven up, he suddenly became aware of a landing no more than three feet above him, wrought iron, much like a fire escape's balcony. Continuing to climb, he grabbed ahold of its side and swung his legs over.

The perch lay open except for a glassed-in booth, large enough for perhaps two men, no doubt the operations room for the immense door. Stepping toward it, Pearse pressed his face against the glass—at least three inches thick—and discovered a console at the far end, buttons glowing in an amber hue, enough to reflect an inside door handle halfway down the wall. But no outside handle. Instead, a large metal box protruded from the glass. Fixed to its side was a long rectangular bar extending out toward the steel door.

Pearse dropped to his knees and began to fiddle with the box. It was totally unmanageable, even with a keyhole at the center. The bar, however, seemed strangely familiar. He ran his fingers along it, its texture that of a license plate, thin metal with raised lettering across it. He began to trace the letters, piecing together the text, SICUREZZA the first word to make itself known.

Within a few minutes, he had the entire message: TO BE USED ONLY IN THE EVENT OF A TRACK FIRE. An emergency exit, the warning of an alarm bell should the bar be pushed to open the door.

He could hardly contain his smile; modern technology had come to the Vatican.

At first, it seemed odd that this small lever was all that stood between him and his freedom. As he thought about it, though, he realized it was odder still that anyone should need to go to such lengths to leave the Vatican. Security throughout the City was minimal, because its sole purpose was to keep people out, not in. Another reason why the station had been deserted.

Why should it be any different here?

The thought was only moderately reassuring. With an alarm blaring, he knew everything would accelerate; the men from security would find their way inside the tunnel within seconds, still more of them to the spot where the mysterious escape route would deposit him. Inside the walls? Beyond them? He didn't know. Questions flooded his mind as he stood, his grip tightening on the bar. One last glance along the tunnel.

He pushed through.

The sound was deafening, but no more intrusive than the eruption of light that poured down at him from every direction. He stood in the middle of the cabin, his eyes adjusting as he tried to locate a second door. *There.* Just to the right of the console. Again, no handle, only box and bar. Without hesitation, he pushed through, this time arriving in a brightly lit corridor, narrow walls painted white, the ceiling lined with pipes less than three inches from his head. Processed air permeated the place, antiseptic, leaving a metallic taste in his mouth as he sped off.

It was impossible to concentrate on anything except the movement of his legs, the relentless sound of the blaring behind him, deeper and deeper, until, with a sudden choked cough, the Klaxon stopped. Its abrupt cessation felt like a blow to his gut. Still he ran, straining for the sound of steps, voices, anything behind him, his ears incapable of such focus—only the echo of his own feet on the bare cement floor.

Half-expecting to see a figure careering toward him—trapping him among those who were by now within the tunnel—Pearse noticed the pipes take a sharp turn to the left some thirty yards in front of him. Slowing, he managed the corner, at once barreling through yet one more door, his feet suddenly taken out from under him, his body wild as he slipped off a cement ledge, only to come crashing down onto a narrow strip of grass.

Everything seemed to stop. He lay prone on his back, completely disoriented.

Stars.

He was gazing up at stars. Outside. Glancing back, he watched as the door slammed shut, from this side, a rusted metal postern—no handle, no lock—nestled within the Vatican wall, a few scrawls of graffiti decorating its weathered facade. Otherwise, it remained completely nondescript. He spun around and propped himself on an elbow. A wide road—his best guess the Viale Vaticano—stood no more than ten feet from him. The pain in his back notwithstanding, Pearse felt an overpowering sense of exuberance, a nervous laugh erupting in his throat. He turned once again to the wall and stood. St. Peter's loomed directly beyond it.

Under our jurisdiction.

For several moments, he simply stared.

Not anymore.

The sound of a siren somewhere off to his left told him he had no time for victory celebrations. They would be coming, this only a momentary reprieve. Slipping into a web of pedestrian lanes across the road, he came face-to-face with a far more unwelcome truth: The Vatican was no longer his, its refuge lost.

What victory in that?

▲

Pearse had stopped running twenty minutes earlier, the furtive looks over his shoulder perhaps ten minutes after that. Since then, he'd caught himself letting up only once or twice, allowing the easy rhythm of a resolute pace to take his mind off of the last few hours. Those moments had passed quickly, a muted anxiety resurfacing to keep him alert. He'd thought about a hotel—the late hour notwithstanding—but realized a credit card could be traced. That the idea had even entered his mind stunned him. Angeli, of course, was out of the question—at least for the time being. Best to keep her isolated.

He'd crossed the river at the Aosta Bridge, opting for the Via Giulia, the summer lamps billowing against the high walls as he moved past the shops. One or two couples walked arm in arm along the lane, too few, though, to put him at ease; somewhere in the back of his mind, he knew he needed to find a more populated area.

He headed up through the Campo dei Fiori, passing by a favorite restaurant on the northeast corner, dark for the night, a momentary taste of Gorgonzola on his tongue. He'd eaten there two, three nights ago, a few friends from the library, now strangely foreign, a connection severed by the last eight hours.

For forty minutes, he walked, careful to keep himself situated within large groups—Piazza Navona, the Trevi Fountain, up to the Spanish Steps—the crowds growing younger and younger along the improvised route. Packs of students littered the steps and fountain, some camped around a single guitar strummed in adolescent serenade, others happy to gaze out at the spectacle of Roman summer. Still more couples wandered, while a few well-soused tourists snapped flashed shots of the bell towers looming above, pictures destined for blackened obscurity.

The refuge he sought, however, remained distant. Instead, he felt his own detachment like a spyglass tracing his every move, caught in the lens, all else a blur. Whatever sanctuary he had conjured beyond the Vatican walls during his flight quickly dissolved into a heightened sense of isolation, magnified against the backdrop of late-night revelry. The city itself seemed to goad him, his every turn met with an increasing sense of loss, even disorientation, all that was familiar somehow taken from him.

Even in the Piazza Barberini—its sudden collision of streets alive with cabs and cars—he felt as if he'd never seen the place before, everything starker, colder to the eye.

He was about to move on when he suddenly realized why he had come this way. Of course there was another refuge for him in the city. Of course there was a place where he could make sense of the last twelve hours. *John J.'s.* Just north of the Giardini del Quirinale. The priest's apartment. He couldn't believe it had taken him this long to think of it. Granted, he hadn't been there more than three or four times in the last two years—Blaney was always jetting back and forth to the States—but long periods without contact had never altered their relationship. Given what Pearse had been through tonight, he knew a two A.M. knock at the door wouldn't raise so much as an eyebrow, no matter how much in need of a good clipping it might be.

With renewed purpose, he made his way back the few blocks to Via Avigonesi, number 31, indistinguishable from every other building along the narrow street, endless walls of chipped russet stone visible in the shadowed lamplight. Pearse scanned the front windows, hoping on the off chance to see a light somewhere on the fifth floor. No such luck. He stepped to the door and rang the bell.

On the sixth ring, he again stepped back into the empty street and saw a light come on up above. A moment later, the crackle from an ancient intercom filled the air.

"*Sì?*" barked a woman's voice. "*Sa che ore sono?*"

"Yes, it's late. . . . I'm sorry," Pearse answered in Italian, "but I need to see Father Blaney."

"At this hour? Who is this?"

"Father Pearse. Father Ian Pearse from the Vatican. I'm sure he'll understand."

"Father . . ."

Pearse waited.

"The American?" Her tone was far less strident.

"Yes."

"I see." Another pause. "Well, Father, I'm sure he would, but he's not here. He's away for another few days. Is there something I can do for you . . . at two in the morning?"

The possibility hadn't even crossed his mind. "Not here?"

"I'm sorry, no. Was he expecting you?"

Pearse needed a few moments to respond.

"No. No, he wasn't."

"Well, he does call in from time to time. Shall I give him a message?"

"No . . . no. That's okay."

"You're sure, Father?" She waited. "Would you . . . like to come up? You're quite sure everything is all right?"

Another long moment. "Good night."

"Father . . ."

The voice trailed off as Pearse stepped away from the doorway, his sense of isolation now even more intense. The prospect of seeing Blaney had allowed him to drop his guard. *Another few days.* Pearse didn't have that kind of time.

Not sure where he was meant to go, he began to walk—back to the piazza, to the cabs, the lights, up along the Via Barberini—the city again cold and unforgiving. Why he felt the need for forgiveness, though, he didn't know.

It was only as he reached the top of the Barberini hill that he understood. There, across from the wide avenue, and tucked in at the end of a tiny cobbled piazza, waited the church of San Bernardo. It had always been a favorite of his, in appearance like a half-pint Pantheon, modest dome atop stocky walls—the troll on the hill—far less prepossessing than its more famous neighbors. It might have lacked the regal facade of Santa Susanna, or the Bernini treasure of Santa Maria della Vittoria, but Bernardo always managed its own quiet dignity, an almost medieval piety in its inelegance. More than that, its simplicity reminded him that, amid all the confusion, one thing remained constant and his own. Nothing so intangible as faith—although he knew he could find strength in that—but the far more patterned expression of prayer. What had Blaney always said? Sanctuary in the mantra of repetition. Another kind of refuge.

Why forgiveness? Because he had taken no time for it today, no time for the Mass he had abandoned, no time to quiet his mind. He slipped across the road, down along the uneven cobblestones, and through the door into the vaulted church.

Inside, the light was spare, enough to cast angular shadows from the statues of saints who filled the raised niches along the circular wall. Hard plaster faces stared down at him, cheeks and hands chipped here and there, pleated robes too rigid at the edges, the caress of Bernini nowhere in evidence on the austere figures. Yet all he felt was their serenity. He dipped his hand into the holy water, crossed himself, and moved to the wooden benches that stood in front of the altar. Sitting, he let the strain of the last ten hours seep from his muscles, a sudden sense of exhaustion overwhelming him. On the verge of sleep, he allowed his head to slip back.

Caught in that honeyed mist between conscious and unconscious, he found himself drifting. For little more than an instant, Slitna, Prjac, the countless other towns he had long ago forgotten, all seemed to rise up in wild assault around him—sounds, smells, tastes, nothing distinct, all of it trapped in dissonant haze, yet so palpable, it forced him to bolt upright, its grasp almost too much.

His heart was racing, his mind lost to an endless array of sensations. One, however, stood out as he tried to reclaim focus. A quiet resolve, strangely familiar, an echo from his days with Petra. Even then, he had understood it as an imperfect reflection of hers, a naïve courage that had all too often bordered on the reckless. Still, it had kept him alive on more than one occasion. Now, as he stared at the grained wood of the pew in front of him, Pearse allowed it to wash over him, resonate within. A moment with her. There might have been more to it than that, but he let it pass.

It wasn't difficult to understand why it had come to the surface now; he only hoped he could sustain it.

Lips moving silently, he began to pray.

Δ

Cardinal von Neurath held the large velvet drape back, his gaze drawn to the lights of Rome as they spread out in front of him. Half past four, still so alive. How many times, he wondered, had he allowed himself to stand in robe and slippers, peering out, the chill from the hour and the lure of sleep both forgotten? Too many to recall. The endless twists and turns of streets disappeared into the labyrinth of the city, landmarks dotting the landscape to give his meditation some bearing—the ivory cream of the Colosseum, the garish white of Il Vittoriano, and always the silent dome, crisp against a blackened sky, beckoning him, calling him. Only him. Perhaps tonight.

The sound of a taxi broke through, fatigue and chill suddenly more intrusive. Still he stared. Rome. It was almost too much to pull himself away.

"Why don't you get some sleep." Blaney sat in an armchair at the far corner of the large bedroom, lamp at his side, legs extending to a cushioned footstool. "I can wake you if any news comes in."

Von Neurath continued to stare out. "No, this is fine." After a few moments, he turned. "If you want to get some—" The shake of the head across the room told him there was no reason to finish the thought. They had known each other for the better part of forty years, tied together by what had once been so clear a path. In fact, it had been Blaney who had administered von Neurath's Rite of Illumination all those years ago. All so clear.

Things change. The priest, so devoted to his Manichaean faith, had never wanted more, content to be a spiritual beacon. Keep the teachings of Mani pure. Keep the Word alive. Blaney had always believed that the Word itself was all they needed to bring about the one true and holy church.

Von Neurath had recognized the weakness early on. Faith and teaching could take one only so far. There had to be a practical side to Mani's vision. And the more that pragmatism had asserted itself, the more Blaney had kept his blinders on, an attitude that made him appear all the more pathetic in von Neurath's eyes.

A relationship built on mutual mistrust. It was why they would both wait up for the call.

Von Neurath moved back to the bed and sat. "Any confirmation from Arturo on the transfers?" he asked, more to pass the time than anything else.

"About an hour ago," answered Blaney. "Our Pentecostal, Baptist, and Methodist friends were all very appreciative."

"I don't care how much they appreciate it," replied von Neurath, scratching away at a small stain on the bedspread. "I want to know that they understand what it's for." He brushed a few crumbs away and looked over at Blaney. "I can't start consolidating the fold without grass-roots support."

"I'm sure they're getting the message out, Erich."

A quizzical look crossed von Neurath's face before he turned to the stain again. "'Message'? That's a rather precious way of putting it, don't you think?"

"Perhaps. It's what you would call the 'soft sell,' I think."

Von Neurath laughed to himself; it seemed to catch Blaney by surprise. "I didn't realize you were so good at it."

"Hardly."

"Oh, don't underestimate yourself, John."

"No, I'll leave that to you."

Von Neurath looked up from the stain. "Have I struck a nerve?"

Blaney said nothing.

Again, von Neurath waited. "You've really grown to dislike me, haven't you?"

"Not at all."

"Don't tell me that you're disappointed?"

"Disappointment implies expectation."

A smile. "Touché."

"We see things differently," said Blaney.

"Yes, we do. I know the message isn't enough. One has to be certain that they understand it."

"Well, then, I'm sure you have the people in place for that."

"*We*, John. *We* have the people in place." He began to scrape away again. "Painting the world in black and white isn't that easy with all those other colors out there. One pure church won't just suddenly appear because you hope it will. You have to lead them to it. And the only way to do that is—"

"To manipulate them?" said Blaney.

Von Neurath didn't bother to look up. "A little crude, but, yes, that sounds about right."

Blaney nodded to himself. "'And when the light descends, and the darkness recedes, who shall be worthy of the mystery that has been hidden since eternities?'"

"'He who can make the world whole,'" answered von Neurath. "Epistle of Seth."

"I don't recall all that much about 'manipulation' in the epistle."

Von Neurath now looked up. "And what would you propose? Unless we have a willing constituency among our Protestant friends, no amount of papal encyclicals will make anything whole again, infallibility or not. The olive branch goes only so far."

"If, in fact, you're the one holding it," reminded Blaney.

"I don't think that will be much of a problem." The cardinal turned back to the bedspread, the stain clearly getting the better of him. "Sometimes the Word isn't sufficient to motivate people to action."

"I'm not sure Mani would agree with you."

"Mani wasn't dealing with such a complicated world."

"Oh, yes, I forgot. Poor, naïve little Mani."

Again, von Neurath laughed. "Sarcasm doesn't really suit you, John. You're much better when self-effacing. I'd stick with that." Von Neurath stood, stepped to a small washbasin on a nearby table, and began to dip a washcloth in the water. Wringing it out, he returned to the bed and went back to work on the stain. "Nobody's quite sure who or what the agents of darkness are nowadays. Too many would-be demons to choose from. If I can simplify that—"

"If *we*, Erich. *We*."

Von Neurath waited before continuing. "If we can simplify that, all the better. One clear threat. One ultimate demon to send them back into the arms of the true church."

"Even if that demon doesn't exist?"

A wry smile crossed his lips. "The last I checked, Islamic fundamentalism was alive and well."

"Playing on people's irrational fears isn't what Mani had in mind."

"We've been through this. And it's a little late to be questioning the method."

"I'm not questioning it. I'm simply interpreting its emphasis."

"Nothing brings people together like ignorance, John." Von Neurath seemed satisfied with his work and tossed the cloth back onto the table.

Now Blaney waited before answering. "'And nothing but ignorance can make the light—'"

"'Wither and die.' Yes. I know the verse. *Shahpuhrakan*, three-five. You might also recall *Book of Giants*, chapter six: 'And through the darkness He will conceive a light so worthy that it will say—I am born of the darkness, and yet I am the light itself!' Ignorance bearing wisdom. Not much to interpret there. Whether these fundamentalists actually pose a threat or not—whether Mr. Bin Laden and his ilk have more in mind for us than just some senseless bombings—we both know we can use their presence to create a genuine unity. Fear of a common enemy is a powerful incentive. We simply have to make sure that that incentive is strong enough. From there, it's a small step to the true church. Then you'll see the power of the Word." He paused. "If that isn't light born of darkness, I don't know what is."

"It all depends on how you use that enemy."

"Yes. Yes, it does. I wasn't aware you were so interested in the more mundane workings of all of this." He waited for a response. "No, I didn't think so." He stood and returned to the window. "Keep the faith pure, John. That's what you've always been so good at. All to make the church whole again." He waited. "Sometimes I wonder what you think that really means."

"Light set free. Triumph over darkness. It's not all that complex, Erich. 'The vain garment of this flesh put off, safe and pure; the clean feet of my soul free to trample confidently upon it.'"

Again, von Neurath laughed to himself. "Abstractions are so easy, aren't they? Especially when you can hide behind them."

"And what does that mean?"

Again von Neurath waited. "We make the church whole, John, and it's *our* turn to build from the ashes. Our turn to set doctrine, tend a flock, not just quote from a psalmbook. We're not exactly a feel-good bunch, now are we?"

Blaney said nothing.

"Two, three hundred elect among us? The rest, told to obey for a life of perfect asceticism? That requires a good deal of control. Limitations. How many of them, do you think, will be that keen to let their 'souls trample on the world of the flesh'? We'll have to take a lot of things away from them so that they can see how the Light can be set free. The triumph over darkness demands a great deal of discipline, a healthy dose of . . . reeducation. Not everyone's going to understand what we're doing for them." Again, von Neurath waited. "So don't tell me you're uncomfortable with how we'll be dealing with our enemies, real or not. You know as well as I do that it pales in comparison to what we have in store for our own followers. That kind of ascetic ideal requires sacrifice. And we don't have the luxury to pick and choose which ones we make."

Neither said a word for nearly a minute. Blaney stared at the phone, willing it to ring. Von Neurath suddenly turned to him. "It's defense, isn't it?"

"What?" asked Blaney.

"Defense," he repeated. " 'Satisfied slave turns up in armor.' "

It took Blaney a few seconds to realize what he was saying. "Oh . . . Yes." He now recalled the cryptic he'd given him earlier in the day. The word game they'd been playing for years, like all good Manichaeans. The mysteries hidden within language. There might have been a great deal of mistrust and disrespect in their relationship, but at least they had the cryptics to keep them on common ground. "That didn't take long."

"*Satisfied, fed. Slave, esne.* Turn them upside down," said von Neurath, "and you get *defense, armor.* Clever." Perfunctory praise.

"I do what I can," said Blaney. The phone rang; he picked up. "Yes. . . . I see. When? . . . No, that won't be necessary. . . . All right. Keep me informed." He replaced the receiver.

"Well?" the cardinal asked.

Blaney looked up; it took him a moment to focus on von Neurath. "What? Oh. No, that wasn't about His Holiness. We have a bit of a problem. The priest at San Clemente has disappeared."

"I thought Kleist was taking care of that?"

"As you said, I'm not very good with the mundane, but obviously he hasn't."

"And the monk?"

"I can take care of that. The priest should be Herr Kleist's focus now."

"Agreed." Von Neurath waited before continuing. "Do we know he has the scroll?" Blaney remained silent. "Do we know if he even understands what it is?" Again, no answer. Von Neurath stared out into the lights. "Then we do have a problem."

▲

Pearse felt a tap on his shoulder, his first sensation a grinding stiffness in his neck. For several seconds, he had no idea where he was, his eyes as yet unwilling to open to more than slits. He lay on his side, legs drawn to his chest, hands wedged between cheek and the hard wooden surface below. Trying to sit up, he nearly toppled from his perch. He placed a hand on the bench in front of him to steady himself. As his eyes strained against sleep, he noticed the church had grown brighter, a hint of sun peeking through the opening at the apex of the dome. Streaks of light cascaded across the top third of the walls. The saints, however, remained in dusky gray.

"Scusi," said a voice to his left. *"Ma non si può dormire qui, giovane."*

Pearse turned to see a priest standing over his shoulder, a man easily in his late seventies, thick black-rimmed glasses covering most of his face. His eyes refracted to enormous proportions through the lenses, giant brown balls filling the weighted glass. Still, there was a pleasant-ness to the face, thin lips drawn up in an expression of concern and understanding. When he noticed Pearse's clothes, his eyes seemed to grow even larger behind the frames.

"Oh," he continued in Italian, "I didn't realize you were a priest." The revelation, however, granted only a momentary reprieve, the slow real-ization that a priest had been lying asleep in his church even more trou-bling. He didn't seem to know how to respond. "Were you . . . in prayer, Father?" An odd question, but the best he could do.

"I . . . Yes. I came in to pray," answered Pearse. "I didn't mean to . . ." For some reason, his hand rose to his neck.

Again, the old priest appeared to be at a loss, the gentle face etched with confusion. A priest asleep, with no collar. How could one explain that? "I have some extra ones," he nodded, eager to move beyond his misgivings, or at least to distance himself from them; he started toward a set of stairs at the far end of the altar.

Pearse looked around; the church was empty. "Do you know what time it is, Father?" he asked.

"Just after five," the old man answered without turning around. "When I always come in." A wavering hand appeared, pointing to the top of the steps. "It's just up there. The collar." Pearse stood and fol-lowed, his legs tight from the cramped position of a lengthy nap.

The office was austerity itself, two straight-backed wooden chairs, no cushions, each standing guard before an equally uninviting desk, another chair stationed behind, all of them under the watchful gaze of a crucifix holding firm against the decay of crumbling walls. The domed ceiling of the small enclosure rose to perhaps eight feet at its height, the room clearly an afterthought, as if the space had been grudgingly ceded by a miserly sanctuary. The old priest shuffled to the desk, opened one of its drawers, and pulled out a new collar. "I always seem to forget if I have enough. Whenever I pass by Gammarelli's, I think I should stop and get one." Pearse nodded, recalling the *sartoria ecclesiastica* just off the Piazza Minerva. "An old man." He smiled. "I must have twenty of them tucked away in here." Pearse stepped across, took the collar, and fitted it into his shirt.

"Thank you."

"You're not Italian," said the priest.

"No. American."

"You have no place to stay?" he asked, continuing before Pearse could answer. "We once had a father from Albuquerque," the pronunciation thoroughly mangled. "He said he had lost all of his baggage, his papers. He had no collar, either. We gave him a hot meal."

"Albuquerque. Really?" Pearse smoothed out the collar, at the same time rubbing the cramp from his neck. "Actually, I have rooms at the—" He cut himself short. "Not far from here." He smiled. "I come from Boston . . . a small parish." He had no idea what had provoked the impromptu confession, but it seemed to have the desired effect. The man listened intently. "I came in to pray early this morning. I must have been more tired than I realized."

"Of course." A sudden gleam filled the old man's eyes. "Would you like to take the Mass?" he asked, an eagerness in his voice, eyes wider still.

Pearse began to shake his head, then stopped. Why else had he come in? When else would he have the opportunity? Given the last twelve hours, he had no idea what to expect beyond the doors of the church. If last night had been any indication—save for a momentary flash of distant resolve—certainly nothing of the familiar. He needed to reclaim something of his own. Something to take away with him. "Yes." He nodded, moving toward the old man. "Yes, I'd like that very much."

"I thought you might." The priest reached into a second drawer and pulled out all the necessary accoutrements—linens, chalice, wine, wafers. He moved slowly but with great care, the tarnished silver and weathered pieces of linen reclaiming a lost splendor in his hands. Setting them on the desk, he then turned to the small closet by the door and removed an equally ancient alb, then a lace stole, the cincture hanging on a hook at the side. Pearse moved toward him and helped him into the vestments, a bit of smoothing necessary on the wrinkled fabric; together, they retrieved the items on the desk and headed back to the sanctuary, taking labored steps, Pearse more and more relaxed in the old man's presence. The priest said nothing as he draped the corporal across the altar table, Pearse waiting until he had cast it just so before carefully setting down the pieces he had brought himself, all in neat order. A look of genuine delight rose on the old man's face as he turned to pour a healthy swig of wine into the chalice, a few drops of water.

"I prefer the Latin," he said. "When I'm alone. Old habits. I hope that's all right with you."

Pearse nodded, ever more at ease. *Old habits.* A sense of place, belonging.

"Good." The old priest smiled. Then, with a long breath—a moment of quiet thought—he began to chant, eyes somehow smaller behind the frames, concentrated, his body swaying back and forth, hands holding on to the table for support. An image of perfect serenity.

Pearse let go, as well. And for a few minutes, he seemed to forget everything that had brought him to the refuge of San Bernardo. Everything that lay beyond its doors.

▲

The second-floor lights told him she was awake; the shadow scurrying past the window confirmed she was still at work on the scroll. Pearse pressed the bell and waited.

As much as he hated to admit it, there really had been no other choice. The scroll was all he had to go on. More than that, it was his only leverage; at some point, he knew they would track him down. Better to understand what it was they wanted before facing the inevitable.

Another quick lesson from Angeli.

A hesitant voice answered. "Hello?"

"It's Ian Pearse," he said. "I saw the light—" The buzzer cut him off; he pushed through and stepped into the hallway.

Upstairs, the apartment lay under a veil of smoke, the smell of cigarettes thick on her breath as he followed her in. No word of hello, not even the expected smile, only the glass dome peeking out from over the barricade of books as they made their way through. Nearing the desk, he noticed she had managed to get to the end of the scroll, the right-hand side now laden with rolled parchment. He also saw how tired she looked, the red of her cheeks having faded to gray, her hair matted in odd clumps, obvious signs of long hours spent in deep concentration. A few crumbs of biscotti were all that remained from the once-full plate.

Her voice was hoarse when she spoke. "This is a surprise." She seemed distracted. "Or perhaps not."

He wasn't sure how to respond.

Whatever strain he thought he had seen in her face now showed itself to be something far more unsettling. Concern. Perhaps even apprehension. She returned his gaze, intensity, not fatigue, staring back. "Why don't you have a seat, Father." A disconcerting echo from last night. He did as he was told, taking the nearer of the two chairs, watching as she gathered up the various pieces of paper that lay scattered around the dome. She glanced at each page, trying, it seemed, to divine some sort of order out of them. "I see you've recovered your collar," she said, not bothering to look up, eyes darting from one passage to the next. Pearse said nothing. No reason to bring her up-to-date on the night's events.

Reaching for her cup, she moved around the desk and sat on the front lip of the second chair. She took a sip; her expression told him the coffee had long since lost its edge.

"Why didn't you tell me what the scroll was?" she asked.

Her tone surprised him. "I . . . didn't know what it was. I still don't."

"It wasn't found in San Clemente, was it?" Her response was no less accusatory.

"I was told it was."

"Then you were misinformed." She continued to stare at him. When he didn't answer, she elaborated. "The prayer by itself, I could accept. Even that bizarre preamble from John. But not this," she said, raising the papers in her hands.

Pearse followed the swirl of pages, unsure what she wanted to hear. After everything he'd been through last night, a grilling from Angeli was the last thing he needed. More than that, the attitude wasn't like her at all. He found it hard to imagine that she could actually believe he had purposely misled her. What could he gain by that? If he had known what the scroll was, why would he have brought it to her in the first place? Why the charade?

When she finally spoke, her tone was far less severe.

"You really have no idea what it is, do you?"

"No, I really have no idea." He was doing his best not to allow the last few hours to color his tone.

"Well, I suppose that's a relief."

When it was clear she was happy to leave it at that, Pearse prodded. "Any chance you might tell me what it is?"

She looked over at him.

He picked up the ashtray nearest him and placed it on the arm of her chair. "Does that help?"

At last a smile. "Ah, the art of seduction."

"If I'd known it was that easy, I'd never have taken the cloth."

Another tired smile.

"So what's in the scroll?" he said.

"'The scroll,'" she repeated. Looking across at him, she said, "Something I've never seen before."

"That sounds promising."

"Perhaps." A long breath. She eased herself back into the chair, then began to speak: "Well . . . to start . . . it's not a continuous scroll, which is what one would have expected. It's a series of unsewn single sheets, rolled together. That, by itself, is strange, but not unheard of." Before he could ask, she clarified. "Fire, decay, those sorts of things did, at times, leave groups of arbitrary single sheets lying about, which would then have been put together in a codex or scroll simply for storage's sake."

"And that's what this is," he asked. "One of those collections?"

"No. Which is even more surprising. In this case, each independent sheet is linked to the others in a very purposeful way, something, as I said, I've never seen. It starts out with a full text of 'Perfect Light'— which, by itself, makes it unique—but then becomes a series of epistles. Letters."

An image of Saint Paul wandering through Asia Minor fixed in his mind. "Apostolic?"

"Not at all."

"So Augustine got it wrong? It's not a collection of Jesus' sayings?"

"Evidently."

He allowed himself only a moment's disappointment before asking, "So whom are they written to?"

"That's a very good question."

"Thank you."

A smile. "To the 'Brothers of the Light.'" She was almost flip in her response.

"Manichaeans?"

"Yes, Manichaeans."

Silence. She seemed to be retreating again.

"How many ashtrays am I going to need?" he asked.

She peered over at him. "I'm not sure you're going to want to hear this."

"Now who's teasing?" He waited. "So the epistles . . . can I assume they're all written by the same scribe?"

"You'd think so, wouldn't you? But they're not. They're actually fifteen separate letters—not in Syriac, but Greek—that span a period of almost four hundred years." She stopped, her eyes fixed on his.

"*Four* hundred years?" he said. "That doesn't sound right."

"No, it doesn't, does it? But given the references to various emperors, Popes, and patriarchs, you can pretty much date the letters from somewhere in the middle of the sixth century, up through the end of the tenth. Considering that western Manichaeanism was supposedly wiped out by the end of the *fifth*, those are rather remarkable dates." Again, she held his gaze. "Added to that, all of the letters are connected to the prayer—they all begin with their own transcription of it. Another odd distinction."

"So where are they from?"

"All over. As far west as Lyons, northern Germany, Rome, Milan, Constantinople, Acre. The known world at the time."

"That's . . . incredible. There's nothing like that in the canon."

"I think I just said that."

"So what do these letters say?"

Her eyebrows rose in anticipation. "Ah, now that's where it gets interesting."

"Good. For a minute there, I thought it was going to be as dull as last night."

"Oh, really?" It was clear she was beginning to loosen up. "Well, compared to this, last night was—what did you always call it?" Pearse had no idea what she was talking about. "Minor-level? Minor—"

"Minor-league." He smiled.

She nodded. "Yes. Minor-league. Last night, we were playing in the 'bonies.'"

"Boonies," he said, correcting her.

"Boonies. Whatever."

"So what makes these letters so interesting?"

Again, she drew forward to the edge of the chair. "Each one is an apparent description of the writer's personal 'heavenly ascent.'"

"His what?"

"His tour of the divine realm, his ascent, where he's made privy to esoteric knowledge. All very Manichaean. Except that each one of these is written as if from the pen of one of the five prophets. Now, that's very strange."

Happy as he was to see Angeli back in full swing, Pearse needed clarification. "Prophets? I'm not . . . Which prophets?"

"Adam, Seth, Enosh, Shem, and Enoch," she answered, as if citing nothing more obscure than her own name. "The Manichaean prophets." It was now time for the cigarettes to reappear. "You'll also find Noah, Buddha, Zoroaster, and, of course, Jesus slotted into the list, but it's primarily the other five. Each appearing in cycles, and each bringing us one step closer to redemption." She lit one up. "Mani himself is the last of them, the Paraclete, 'the seal' promised by Christ."

"Right," he said, just to slow her down. "Why don't you take a few puffs." She was beginning to fly off; he needed to tie her down to something more tangible. "Let's hold off on the prophets for a minute. What do the letters actually say?"

Looking over at him, she, too, realized she was getting ahead of herself. She nodded. "They begin with the basics. Foretelling the end of the world, when all evil will be burned in a final fire, light set free, full knowledge attained—that sort of thing."

Slowly, he said, "Okay. So that would be . . . typical apocalyptic warnings. The light of Christ rooting out evil. Right?"

"Oh, it's not the light of Christ. That isn't it at all. That wouldn't make it Manichaean."

"No, of course it wouldn't." So much for the tangible.

"They're an easy bunch to get muddled with."

"Remember, I'm easily muddled."

"I'll try to dumb it down."

"Very kind."

She crushed out the cigarette and settled back into the chair. Waiting until she'd found the right approach, she began: "All right. You have to remember that the battle between light and darkness isn't a metaphor for them. It's real, manifested in the very way they chanted their prayers, the way they performed their rituals, even in the way they chose their foods. Unlike your basic Christians, or even Gnostics, the Manichaeans believed that light and darkness were substances scattered within the material world. For instance, they actually thought that melons and cucumbers held a great deal of light, meats and wine the dark elements. Eat a melon, promote good. Eat a chicken, foment evil."

"And that was what Mani developed out of Gnosticism? Evil foods?"

"It's not as silly as it sounds. How much sillier is the idea of separating spirit and matter—spirit good, matter evil? The Greeks got a great deal of mileage out of that one. And it's not as if Mani didn't find the material world as abhorrent as the orthodox Christians did; it's just that he managed to make it an essential part of salvation."

"Right, right." Pearse slowly remembered his brief foray into the world of "Light and Darkness." "And that's why Augustine and the church were so uneasy."

"Exactly. More than that, because Mani believed human beings are fashioned by demonic forces—bent on keeping the light trapped for eternity—he also thought that men had to play an active role in their own salvation: find those things that help to free the light, avoid those that don't. Melons versus meat. Augustine had said the will was free only when choosing God. With Mani, you've got something that grants a sort of cosmic feeling of responsibility to the individual, because he might be a bearer of the light. Catholicism never gave its faithful that kind of autonomy."

"Thanks for reminding me."

"I told you you weren't going to like it."

"I might surprise you."

"Anyway, a prophet's 'heavenly ascent' was simply the highest form of that responsibility, all of it geared to bringing the gnosis back to his followers and thus freeing sufficient light so that the last of the prophets—Mani himself—could return and bring about the final purification of the world."

"And that's what the epistles are all about."

"No."

"No," Pearse repeated. "Great." He was doing his best not to get frustrated. "So these 'heavenly ascents'—"

"Are where the epistles *begin*. Yes. What you might call Manichaeanism at its most attractive."

"I see." He had no idea what she was talking about, but he decided to press on anyway. "But it's not where they end."

"No."

Again, he had to hold back his frustration. "So where *do* they end?"

"With the *not* so attractive." She shifted in her chair.

"Meaning?"

"Well . . ." Again, she hesitated. "You have to remember that Mani's followers thought that theirs was the one true and holy Christian church."

"As did every other renegade sect at the time," he countered. "What's so unattractive?"

"Yes, but the Manichaeans were after a kind of hyperasceticism. They professed to be purer than the other churches, their scriptures more comprehensive and unambiguous, their methods of describing the world through their knowledge more quasi-scientific—something very appealing at the time—and their preparation for the return of the Messiah more complete." She began to sift through a pile of books, picking out one as she spoke. "That preparation, though, demanded that there be only one church standing when the Messiah returned." She scanned the pages, talking offhandedly. "All others had to be rooted out, or at least subsumed within the Manichaean system. Evangelicalism taken to its extreme. Even the Romans thought of them as some sort of 'superior Christians,' more pious, more devout than the rest."

"So the Persian dualism had unity as its goal? That doesn't sound right."

She nodded. "It's known as 'the Manichaean paradox.' Light and darkness waging war, but only to a point. The ultimate aim: one pure church in a world beset by darkness." She found the page she had been looking for. "Here it is. This is the catchphrase they used to summarize the whole theology: 'of the two principles and the three moments.' The two principles are, of course, light and darkness. The three moments are the beginning, the middle, and the end."

"That's innovative."

She continued, ignoring the comment. "In the beginning, light and darkness are separate; in the middle, they're mingled—that's where we are now, in that middle moment; and at the end, they resolve themselves in an eternal triumph of life and light over death. It's really quite simple."

Pearse did his best to nod. "Simple. I'm still not sure what makes that so 'unattractive.' It's not all that different from what the Catholic church was trying to do at the same time. You called it 'a unified front.'"

"Yes," she said, retrieving the cigarette, "but the Manichaeans were also seen as zealots, far too willing to brand those incapable of attaining the gnosis—that is, the vast majority—as threats to salvation. Only gnosis granted freedom; those without it, they felt, had to be controlled, maybe even manipulated. A sort of tough love. It was their methods for achieving that control that were unattractive and thought of as somewhat . . . suspect."

"Melons were actually evil?" he said.

"Very funny. No. Certain early Christian writers suggested—albeit in completely unsubstantiated ways—that the Manichaeans had more in mind for the material world than simply its purification. Or at least that their methods weren't as noble as they preached. Most scholars today reject those claims as another clever way the Catholic church managed to turn a rival group into pariahs."

"Right, right. Not only were their teachings heretical but they were deceivers and manipulators, as well. That part, I know. The church was very good at that for a while."

"Precisely." Smoke streamed from the cigarette. "And, from time to time, dating back as far as the third and fourth centuries, there's been speculation that they were . . . infiltrators—for want of a better word."

"Infiltrators?" His eyebrows lifted as he smiled over at her. "That sounds pretty racy. Into what?"

"I'm not sure I'd use the word *racy*, but"—she took a long drag—"infiltrators into other churches, where they would rise to positions of power, and then take those congregations in very specific directions. A sort of cancer within the Catholic hierarchy. Bolsheviks of the fourth century, if you will. And all in the hope of creating their one, pure church. There is, of course, no proof for any of that."

"Of course." His smile grew. "It still sounds pretty racy . . . Bolsheviks, infiltrators. In a purely academic way, of course."

"Yes. Very . . . racy." For all her playing, Angeli clearly had her limits. Still, Pearse was enjoying pressing at them. "Anyway," she said, "most of us believe that the Catholic church eventually became too powerful and well entrenched, and no amount of covert manipulation could have changed that."

"You make the Manichaeans sound like some sort of secret society."

"Oh, they *were* that," she insisted. "There, I can show you plenty of proof." She smiled up at him. "Very racy proof. Any number of documents describe how they developed a network of cells—à la the French Resistance—within the Roman Empire both to spread their own interpretation of the Word and also to avoid detection. Most scholars claim that the sect wanted to avoid detection by the *Romans*. As I said, though, there have been those who've suggested that the Manichaeans might have wanted to avoid detection by other *Christians*, as well." Angeli creased her lips around the cigarette and inhaled deeply. "And given what your scroll contains, I'm now somewhat inclined to agree with them."

Pearse knew there was more to her admission than merely an academic's reassessment. His encounter with the Austrian had been proof enough of that. The question remained: What? "So fifteen letters, describing some kind of transcendent experience, will change the way we view the Manichaeans? I can't see how that would be earth-shattering for more than a handful of people."

"Then you would be wrong." Nothing hostile in her tone, simply a statement of fact. Without waiting for a response, she bent over and began to lay the pages on the carpet, one by one. Whenever she needed more room, she would push the encroaching pile of books as far as her short arms would allow, eventually forced to drop to her knees so as to gain added leverage. Every so often, a few books would topple; she continued, undeterred, until the area from desk to Pearse lay hidden under a blanket of yellow paper. "Remember, it was a prayer passed down *orally*," she said at last, still fiddling with the order of the sheets. "Somehow, I forgot that little piece of information for nearly an hour. Stupid, stupid, stupid."

Pearse gazed out over the sea of yellow, the scrawl only slightly less daunting than the wild arrows that ran from one sheet to the next, exclamation points circled in red ink, whole paragraphs written vertically in the margins, the letters almost too small to make out. He watched as she twisted her head once or twice so as to follow the meanderings of several of the linked pages, the red pen emerging from one of her pockets to solidify the routing. When she was fully satisfied, she pulled herself up to the chair and sat.

"So, what do you think they are?" There was almost a giddiness in her tone.

Pearse looked across the pages. After almost a minute, he shook his head and turned to her.

"Oh, come on. You were wonderful on this stuff. Remember those bits from Porphyrius Optatianus, the poet-courtier of Constantine? All that wordplay? You were the one who figured those out, not me." She nodded again at the pages. "So come on. What do you think they are? It's right there in front of you."

The gauntlet had been thrown. Pearse moved to the edge of his seat and again began to scan the yellow sheets. Another long minute.

"Transposition of lines?" he said. Fatigue, lack of practice—either way, he knew it was a weak attempt, but he had to go with something.

"Too obvious."

"Thank you." He looked again. "Reverse sequencing?"

"Before the twelfth century? Oh, come on. You're not even trying."

He couldn't help but smile. "I promise. I'm trying."

"Think Hebrew scripture."

"Okay. It's . . . actually a pillar of salt."

"Ha-ha. I'm telling you, you're going to hate yourself." When he shook his head again, she conceded, "Oh, all right. It's a series of *acrostics*." She looked out at her handiwork. "Such a common device in prayers, and *Hebrew* literature is full of them. Took me an age to get that that's what they were doing here, but I thought you'd . . . well, anyway. They're acrostics."

He saw it at once. Following each of the lines, he confirmed it for himself. "The first letters of each line placed together spell out something else."

"And these are ingenious. Those pages there," she continued, pointing to the sheets closest to Pearse, "are the fifteen transcriptions of the prayer. Notice anything strange about them?"

He inched out farther on his chair. This time, he saw it immediately. "The lengths of the lines are all different," he answered.

"Exactly. Given that they're all the same prayer, you'd expect them to be identical, or at least close enough, perhaps a few words altered here and there. But in each one of these, the lines begin and end at entirely different points, while the individual words remain identical. Why?" He could tell she was enjoying this.

"The oral tradition," he nodded.

"Exactly. I knew you'd get it. There wouldn't necessarily have *been* established designations of lines and stanzas, because they would have recited it as a continuous flow of words—with a few pauses here and there—but with nothing absolutely fixed. An obvious explanation for the discrepancies. But was it?"

"I'm guessing no," he answered, eyes still glued to the pages.

"I began to ask myself, Why, given that tradition, did they find it necessary on these occasions—most of them separated by thirty years or so—to write down the prayer along with the letters? Plus, you would have thought that a natural cadence for reciting the prayer would have emerged over time, giving it some sort of shape. There should at least be some similarities among the copies. And yet, there's none. Why? And why include the prayer with each of the prophetic letters?"

"And that's when you thought of the acrostics." He nodded, getting caught up in her excitement.

"Of course. It ties in perfectly with the very thing that lies at the heart of any type of Gnosticism, Manichaean or not—secret knowledge. The gnosis. That's why they all start with that bit from John. An alarm bell, if you will. 'Remember the gnosis,' it's saying. In this case, the knowledge is literally hidden within the text." Her enthusiasm continued to mount. "Why the different line lengths? Because each transcription has a specific message of its own, thus requiring different first letters in each of the lines."

"So what's the message?"

Her cigarette now found the ashtray. "Unfortunately, none of my first fiddlings came up with anything that made sense. More than that, I began to realize how oddly constructed the prayer itself is. One would expect a prayer called 'Perfect Light, True Ascent' to be uplifting, begin with the mundane and progress to the divine. In fact, it works in precisely the opposite way. Sublime at the start, commonplace at the end. That's when I turned to the letters." She pointed to the sheets closest to the desk. "They were also about 'heavenly ascents.' Why include them? And why keep them all together?"

Pearse stared at the pattern Angeli had created on the floor, following the arrows, trying to make sense of it all. He became aware of her growing impatience. "I'm all ears," he said.

"Oh, come on, you must see it this time," she said, the childlike eagerness once again in her voice. When he shook his head, a smile crossed her lips; she quickly leaned over and began to sweep her hand through the air just above the pages, three or four times—desk to him, desk to him—before nodding in encouragement.

"Pillar of salt?" he said with a smile.

With a burst of energy, she threw both her hands into the air. "*Up.* It goes *up.* True *ascent.* You have to read the transcriptions from bottom to top. That's where the acrostics are."

He looked at the sheets; it was staring right up at him. "Form following content." He nodded.

"Exactly. The message is in the ascent. It's really quite marvelous."

"Granted, but I still don't see what's—"

"So earth-shattering?" she cut in, nodding to herself as she focused on the pages near the desk. "Neither did I for nearly an hour. Each acrostic produced coherent sentences, but their overall meaning wasn't clear— nothing more than unconnected catchphrases. I can't tell you how frustrating that was."

"I've worked with you before, remember? No broken plates this time?"

"That was an accident." She waited. "And no. Just a few snapped pencils."

"Then it couldn't have been that long before you figured it out."

"You know," she said, "I'm beginning to like you less and less."

He laughed. "I'm sure you are. You found the answer in the epistles, didn't you?"

Her eyebrows rose. "You are a clever boy."

"Each one was ascribed to one of the five Old Testament prophets." He nodded, "Which, of course, was impossible."

"Exactly. Oh, I wish you'd been here a few hours ago. Would have saved me an immense amount of time."

"Not to mention pencils." He smiled. "So why did the writers choose those names?"

"Why indeed?" she nodded, another cigarette emerging to fuel the fire. "To give the letters an added force, a certain sanctity? Maybe, but the very fact that each one included the written prayer was more than enough to set it apart. There had to be something else, didn't there? It was then that I began to think that the entire scroll might be based around the idea of ascent, or at least of looking at things from bottom to top. More of the gnosis. It had worked with the acrostics, so why not with the prophets, who just happen to be the most sacred within the Manichaean system?" A long drag. "Maybe their names were meant to focus our attention not on the sacred, but on the profane."

"Another way of flipping everything on its head. That's very good."

"Yes. I thought so." She nodded, smoke pouring from her nose. "So that's what I did. And that's when the acrostics finally made sense. I noticed that anytime there was a reference to a metaphoric path taken as part of the 'heavenly ascent' in one of the epistles, there was a line from the acrostic that directly corresponded to it and, in a very real sense, brought it down to earth. For example, in that one there," she said, pointing to a page a few rows up from the desk, "the letter describes the moment when the writer, calling himself Enosh, 'followed the hand of the Paraclete into a garden of scented chestnut trees and found sustenance.' In the acrostic that precedes the letter, there's a sentence that reads, 'In Trypiti, chestnuts grow lush.' Now Trypiti, as you know, is a town on the northeasternmost peninsula of Greece." Pearse didn't know, but, naturally, he let it pass. "I also saw that the word *chestnut* appears nowhere else in the acrostic or the letter. So it went. With each new allusion in the letter, the acrostic provided a real-world connection. And the further along I read, the greater the detail—location, direction, even distances. Between eight and ten such references in each twosome throughout the entire scroll." She waited before continuing. "The prayer and epistles aren't about ethereal quests for knowledge; they're about one very specific quest. Here. In the world of the material." She seemed to be on the verge of giggling. "What makes the scroll so earth-shattering is that it turns out to be an ingeniously coded map."

▲

Doña Marcella placed the ring on the white linen tablecloth, then laid the napkin across her lap. Three silver-domed dishes stared up at her. She removed the first to find egg whites, fruit, and a perfect square of clear gelatin; the second, wheat toast; the third, that awful concoction her doctors insisted on, grainy gray lumps peppered with some sort of chalky crystal. Her fight against cholesterol. Better now than later, they'd said. Take a stand against those evil foods. If only they knew.

She placed the lid back on the third and started in on the eggs. Dry and bland. She scanned the table for salt. None. They were making this difficult.

The train ride had just over an hour before Barcelona, four private cars hurtling through the Spanish countryside. She preferred it to flying, something about the numbing suspension of an airplane. At least on the train, she could feel the movement. That she was forced to use commercial carriers, unlike her father and grandfather before her, never seemed to bother the contessa in the least. The railway men were courteous, efficient, and accommodating. What more could she ask? None of her family understood. Even her youngest niece—already at work on her first marriage—had encouraged her to "join them in the modern age." There was enough in Doña Marcella's life that screamed of the late twentieth century; she certainly wasn't going to give up her one link to a simpler time. Half past ten, Rome. Good night's sleep. Barcelona by morning. Quaint, but ideal.

An idiosyncrasy to keep everyone guessing. A lesson she had learned from her father. With no sons of his own, he had brought her into the Manichaean fold early on, something virtually unheard of within the brotherhood. At most, a handful of women had ever been made privy to the inner workings, but the count had known his daughter was more than capable. He had also known it would set her apart. The amount of money she had funneled out of Spain on Franco's death alone had indicated her special talents. So unexpected from a woman. Keep them guessing. Keep them on their toes.

It was the role her father had trained her for, the role he himself had played before her. A watchdog, of sorts, someone to maintain their focus, keep their sights on the prize. So fitting a role for a woman among men.

She had left the sitting room car much as he had designed it, cutting-edge furnishings for the mid-1960s, sleek, straight lines of Danish craftsmanship, sofa, chairs, a card table bolted to the floor. A few pictures hung in what little space had been left between the windows, snatches of her extended family, no children of her own, but enough nephews, nieces, and even a few grand-nieces—parties, hunts, someone windsurfing—to give it that neatly cluttered look. She liked to take her breakfast here rather than in the more elegant dining car. Brighter, less formal. The hint of her father.

It was also far less intimidating to those she brought along as her guests.

"You're sure you won't give me a small piece of your yolk?" she asked, a naughty glint in her eyes. "I won't tell if you won't." The man began to respond. "No, I won't put you in that position," she continued. "After all, you were nice enough to meet the train this early, and on such short notice." A forkful of fruit now hovered above her plate as she spoke. "I'm sure it must be something of an inconvenience for you."

"Not at all," he replied. In his late forties, and wearing a suit to rival her own tastes, Col. Nigel Harris looked the perfect product of Eton and Sandhurst, wide face and high forehead below a neatly combed crop of ash blond hair. It was clear he'd spent time in the field, his skin a leathery red; what was so often that blotchy pink with Englishmen was smooth yet rugged here. A scar just below his left eye was a reminder of his final foray during the NATO mop-up in Bosnia, the explosion of a land mine sending him off after twenty-five years of service. They'd told him the eye would go sometime in the next five years.

Complete blindness within ten. Not much time, then, to make a lasting impression.

"I don't think that's entirely true, Colonel, but you're very nice to say so." She brought the fruit to her mouth, chewing slowly, aware that he was showing no signs of impatience. Promising. "I'd imagine your schedule is now quite full, both in England and the United States."

"There's a bit of a demand, if that's what you mean."

One would have been hard-pressed to describe any of his individual features as handsome, and yet his bearing, along with a highly fit body—posture firm, though far from rigid—made him a very attractive man, as easy with power as without it. Except for the eyes, ironically enough. There, if one were to strip away the soldier's veneer, lay the subtle shadings of an unfettered ambition. Doña Marcella had seen the signs too often not to recognize them. It made him all the more desirable.

She let a practiced smile crease her lips. "You're not on *Nightline* now, Colonel. False modesty doesn't play so well here." Again, his reaction was what she had hoped for. A momentary grin, a single bob of the head. "I will tell you that I found your sudden departure from the Testament Council rather odd."

"How so?"

"A heretofore minor organization becomes the new image of Christian politics, with you at its helm. No doubt a few feathers were ruffled, but they must have realized you were the one responsible for their newfound legion of followers. That must have put you in a position of considerable influence."

"Or made me the poster boy for 'one more shameful abuse of the cult of personality.' The *Mirror* was never one to stint on its appraisals."

"Still"—she stabbed at a piece of fruit—"the Christian voice was being heard."

"Evidently not loud enough, given the results of the last parliamentary elections."

"Your membership was growing every day. Given time—"

"We would have been marginalized." He showed no hesitation in challenging her, a measured deference as he spoke. "I really had no interest in being a gadfly for the next forty years, Contessa. The army taught me the futility of that. The council has influence now, but it has no idea how to use it."

"Christian leadership doesn't have quite the same cachet as political leadership?" It was time to see how well she understood her guest.

"They're not mutually exclusive."

"I think Tony Blair might have something to say about that."

"Yes, and that's the problem." A dusting of sugar for his strawberries as he spoke. "He's a rather limited target, wouldn't you agree? The British Protestant doesn't have quite the same zeal as one finds elsewhere."

"As I said, I've noticed your widening scope, Colonel. You've become very popular in the States."

"For the moment, yes. They seem . . . intrigued. Or it might just be the accent." Another smile.

"Or the charm," she countered.

He waited. "As I see it, they appear to have a genuine yearning for something beyond the cold manipulations of partisan politics, beyond the arbitrary whims of market economies. It's beginning to show in the rest of Europe, as well. Unfortunately, we English are always just a few steps behind on these sorts of things. People want something more stable, perhaps, if I may say, eternal." He placed the spoon back in the bowl. "Faith has become rather attractive again, and the Americans seem to be leading the way. Difficult not to make them a focus."

"Then your choice to leave the council," she answered, "seems even more perplexing."

"Not at all," he said, adding a touch of cream. "The TC was always a bit too parochial. We fell into the same trap that snared the Christian Coalition in the States. We became a tool of the radical right. One can't expect the voice of a fringe element to be the lodestone for mainstream Christians. Never really a chance for political change there. No, my choice to leave the council was not the least bit perplexing."

"But you still believe there's a large constituency out there eager for your kind of leadership." She let the phrase sit for a moment before continuing. "That's why you're here."

"Yes."

"And you think I can help."

"Yes."

For several seconds, Doña Marcella peered at the face across from her. She then slowly speared another piece of fruit, brought the fork to her mouth, and stopped, the melon tantalizingly close to her lips. Again, she stared at her guest. "But I'm a Catholic, Colonel Harris."

He held her gaze for a moment, then turned to his strawberries. "So they tell me."

The contessa watched him as he ate—healthy mouthfuls, though never more than he could manage. A refined precision, tipping the bowl ever so slightly away from himself so as to spoon out the last of the cream. "Faith isn't a tool for political gain, Colonel. Neither are the structures that guide it. As I understand it, they serve nothing other than themselves. I'm not sure we agree on that."

For several seconds, he remained perfectly still. Then, very slowly, he slid the bowl to the side and placed his hands flat on the table. He seemed content to smooth out the cloth, eyes fixed on the receding waves of white linen as he formulated his response, no doubt a well-worn tactic. When he was ready, he looked up, an unexpected severity in his expression. "Complacency, Contessa, is what tore the church apart five hundred years ago. Nothing more. I imagine a thousand years of certainty will do that to a monolith. And what began as a much-needed period of reassessment became that tool against which you've just warned me. Matters of faith placed a distant second to political expedience; a debate about rituals and hierarchy became the seed of our own demise. With each step away from one another, we eroded the one thing that had permitted us to define the boundaries of an uncertain world—cohesion. And yet, remarkably, the Christian faith survived despite that upheaval. Or perhaps because of it. I'm really no scholar. More likely than not, though, it maintained itself because nothing much stood up to challenge it. We were the only game in town, as the Americans like to say." His gaze seemed to intensify. "We don't have that luxury anymore. There are far more dangerous threats to us now than our own self-recriminations."

She had expected more of the politician, less of the pedagogue. Another point in his favor. Fully aware he was testing the waters, she pushed further. "Such as?"

"Growing pains." Before she could ask, he explained. "Fifteen hundred years ago, more or less, Mr. Mohammed leapt from his rock. Fifteen hundred years after the birth of Jesus Christ, our Mr. Luther emerged to challenge the existing authority. Growing pains," he repeated. "This time, however, those coming of age aren't aiming their recriminations at themselves. This time, it's a godless world they're after, and our Luther has become an Islamic fundamentalist. The trouble is, this go-round, there's nothing strong enough to rein them in. And they've much deadlier toys than we ever did."

"So you're proposing a Tenth Crusade, Colonel?" she said somewhat sardonically.

"Holy war cuts both ways, Contessa."

For a moment, she wasn't certain just how seriously he was taking himself. "And you really believe they pose that kind of threat?"

"It's not what I believe that matters. The threat is simply a tool. We didn't go into Iraq because Saddam was killing innocent Kurds. We went in because we needed to protect Kuwaiti oil. Not likely that NATO would have garnered much public support for the latter. Saddam was the threat. Saddam was enough. You want to bring a disjointed Christian voice together, give them something to rally around."

"I see." The politician had emerged.

"And the best guide, I've always thought, is the cinema." He had expected her surprise. "Oh, yes. Twenty years ago, the villain came in the form of the onetime Nazi; ten years ago, he was the renegade Communist. Now, he's the Arab gone mad. If that's what the public is buying, why not sell it to them wholesale? Does it really matter how genuine the threat is?"

"So what separates us becomes far less important than what connects us?" When he didn't answer, she asked, "Is that what you're saying, Colonel?"

His expression softened. "I believe what I'm saying is that we would be foolish not to use everything at our disposal, given the situation. As long as we can strengthen our position, does it really matter how we manage it?"

Watching him, she still couldn't be sure if what he said had come from the heart of a zealot or from the mind of a practiced politician. Whatever the answer, she realized Stefan had been right. Col. Nigel Harris would be useful in the months to come.

The question was, Who would be helping whom?

"And, of course, you've already started managing it."

"Of course."

She waited. "Well," she said, bringing the napkin to her lips, then laying it on the table. "You've given me so much to think about." She stood, then Harris. "Please, sit down. Finish your breakfast. If you need anything else, just ring for it. I have some things I need to finish up before we arrive. I believe we'll have a car waiting for you in Barcelona."

"Very kind."

She nodded and stepped out from behind the table. At the door, she turned. "So nice to have met you."

"The pleasure was all mine."

Another nod; she stepped out into the corridor and immediately into the adjoining room.

Stefan Kleist was standing in front of a two-way mirror, watching the colonel, who was now buttering a piece of toast.

"Well?" she said, kicking off her heels and moving toward him.

"Hard to know how easily we'll be able to control him."

"My thoughts exactly."

"There's always one way."

"Jealous?" She pressed up against his back; even without her shoes, she was a good inch taller than Kleist. She reached around his waist and unzipped his fly. Both of them continued to gaze at Harris as she probed within, the familiar thickness soon in her hand, his arousal growing as she began to stroke him with her fingers. She turned Kleist toward her, all the while her eyes fixed on Harris, who had pulled a cell phone from his pocket and was now making a call.

"Can we monitor that?" she asked as Kleist pulled up her skirt, leaving only a garter belt, never any panties, for him to deal with.

"It's taken care of," he said as he leaned back against the glass and hoisted her onto his thighs. He reached for his belt, but she stopped him.

"The zipper will scrape," he said.

"I know," she answered, and pulled him inside of her.

His thick hands clutched at her thighs, driving her up and down, momentary twinges of air from him each time he got caught on the zipper. It only made her buck harder.

"Quiet," she whispered, her eyes staring at the scar on Harris's face, watching it move as he talked. She could imagine licking at it, running her tongue along its narrow groove. She came, an instant later the feel of Kleist releasing inside of her. He continued to shudder, always a final few waves before he began to breathe again.

She wondered if it would be that easy with Harris.

A

" 'Map'?" The word seemed to catch Pearse by surprise. "To where?"

"To *what* might be a better question," replied Angeli.

"Fine. But they obviously meant to hide it from everyone except a very select few. I can't imagine too many Manichaeans would have been able to transcribe the prayer correctly."

"Given the oral tradition, none. And even if they had, the transcriptions would have been meaningless without the letters. You needed all of the parts together, which, as it turns out," she explained, "divide quite neatly into three subsections."

"How appropriate."

"Yes." She smiled. "Anyway, each of the subsections contains five letters—one each from Adam, Seth, Enosh, Shem, and Enoch. The first set—the earliest chronologically—gives general geography. Whatever they were hiding, it moved around quite a bit during those first few centuries. They even had it in the Taurus Mountains and Armenia—wild and woolly places, to be sure—for several hundred years. By the end of the eighth century, however, it finds its permanent home at the tip of the Greek peninsula, on Mount Athos. I had always thought that the first Athos settlements didn't pop up until the tenth. Obviously, the Manichaeans were there far earlier.

"Athos then becomes the focus of the next five letters, highlighted by scads of detail about a once-vibrant Manichaean monastery called St. Phôtinus. According to the Athos directory on the Internet, Phôtinus became a Greek Orthodox monastery sometime in the eleventh century."

"So you think there's a link between these Manichaeans and the Greek church?"

"The Greeks?" It took her a moment to understand what he was saying. "Oh, I see what you mean. No. Nothing like that. The Greek monasteries appeared on Athos only toward the end of the tenth century, before the Eastern church split with Rome."

"And Phôtinus predates the other monasteries on the mountain?"

"Oh, yes. According to this, by a good five hundred years. Clever, these Manichaeans. They picked a very appropriate saint, wouldn't you say?" When Pearse didn't answer, she said, "Phôtinus? From *phôs* . . . the Greek word for 'light.' It all seems to work, doesn't it?"

Pearse's expression was enough to get her back on track. "Anyway, the Athos monastery must have been built around 380. According to the directory, the Phôtinus monks chose the spot because it was 'as close to heaven' as they thought they could get. The Manichaeans evidently infiltrated the place sometime during the eighth century. And given what the letters say, there were several such infiltrated monasteries scattered throughout Greece and Macedonia from the sixth century on."

"The unattractive side of Manichaeanism."

"Exactly."

"And the last cycle of letters?"

"That's the one they reserved for the 'what.'" She looked over at him. "Unfortunately, they're not as forthcoming—even in code—about the very thing they went to such lengths to protect. But there's enough there to suggest it was something rather extraordinary."

"In more than academic terms?" he asked.

The exuberance of the last ten minutes seemed to slip from her face, her earlier apprehension resurfacing. "If something that could under-mine the legitimacy of the Catholic church is more than just academic fancy, then yes." Again, she waited. "They claim to have something that could pave the way for their own true church to emerge. Something very real to them, of 'highest authority,' higher even than Mani himself."

"Something like what?"

"I don't know. The language is very vague. As far as I can tell, it's some-thing that predates Mani, even the Gospels. A parchment written in Greek. That's the most specific I can get. What's most unsettling, though, is that it's clear they had a substantial number of cells scattered throughout the empire with which to unleash its power."

"Even as late as the tenth century?"

"Yes. The 'mapping' of the last two letters charts the locations of large groups of very powerful officials within the Catholic hierarchy who were tied to the Manichaeans. Names even I recognize, and it's not my period."

"Nice excuse."

"All of it suggests," she said, ignoring the barb, "that they never aban-doned Phôtinus, and instead simply blended in, as was their wont. The same evidently held true throughout the rest of Europe. Whatever they had hidden away in Athos, they clearly had the resources to make the most of it. The question is, Why didn't they use it when their network was so well established?"

"Maybe they did, and found out it wasn't as powerful as they'd thought."

She shook her head. "No. The letters are explicit in their warning that those listed remain prepared for 'the great awakening,' whatever that's supposed to mean. There's no battle cry to action, no sense that the Messiah's return is imminent, even with the millennium approaching. More than that, had they invoked whatever they were hiding on Athos, there would have been mention of a Manichaean heresy, or at least something like it, at some point in the history of the church. As I said, the Manichaeans disappear in the West after the fifth century—no mention of them, save for some false attributions to the Cathars, Bogomils, and Albigensians."

"And you think they survived." Statement, not question. An image of the Austrian flashed into his mind.

"Who knows how long they tucked themselves away? It's clear from the letters that they were extremely well entrenched, and had been for centuries. Who's to say they weren't able to maintain the subterfuge indefinitely? For all we know, they may still be waiting. I'd say that's more than just a little earth-shattering." Only then did she notice the change in his expression. "And from the look on your face, I might think you agree with me." Staring into his eyes, however, she realized it was more than that. When she spoke again, her tone was far less inviting. "Why did you come back this morning?"

The question caught him by surprise. Not sure how to answer, he hesitated. "I wanted to find out what was in the scroll."

"Yes, but why so early?" It was the first time it had occurred to her to ask. "If you had no idea what it was . . . I told you I needed time, that I'd—" She stopped abruptly. For several seconds, she said nothing. "You've come in contact with them, haven't you?" When he didn't answer, she pushed further. "You *know* they've managed to survive. And *they* know you have the scroll." Again, he said nothing. "That's why you made up all that rubbish about San Clemente."

"It wasn't rubbish," he insisted. "The person who gave me the scroll said it had been found in the fourth-century church."

"Which we both know is impossible; it could never have been found there."

"I realize that now."

"Who?" she pressed. "Who gave you the scroll?"

Again, he waited before answering. "Someone I trust."

"You might want to reconsider that."

He was about to respond, when the sound of three chimes, followed by a swirl of martial music, interrupted. Momentarily disoriented, Pearse tried to locate its source.

Without any reaction, Angeli checked her watch, then reached behind a pile of books at the foot of the desk. With her back still to him, she said, "The early news. Must be six-thirty." A moment later, she returned with a portable clock radio in her hands, the blue neon digits confirm-

ing the hour. "I sometimes fall asleep in here. Never can find the button
to—"The first words out of the commentator's mouth stopped any further searching.

"*A month of disbelief and prayers comes to its somber conclusion. Good
morning, this is Paolo Tonini. Ezio Palazzini, the supreme Pontiff of the
Catholic church, ordained Pope Boniface the Tenth, has died at the age of
sixty-seven. The news of his sudden illness sent shock waves throughout the
Catholic community when it was announced twenty-six days ago. Sources
at the Vatican have confirmed that His Holiness passed away in his
sleep. . . .*"

In rote response, Pearse quietly crossed himself, offered a few words of
prayer. Angeli jumped up, placed the clock on her seat, and strode to the
far corner of the room. There, nestled among various pieces of furniture,
she located a small television set behind a music stand laden with clothes
and papers. Pulling the mess to the side, she took a handkerchief from
one of her pockets and, with three or four quick flicks of the wrist, dusted
the screen. She then began to examine the knobs on the console, lighting on the one farthest to the left. The black void came to life, showing
old footage of the Pope in St. Peter's, a voice detailing the accomplish-
ments of his six-year papacy.

"Turn that off, will you," she said, motioning back to Pearse, not once
taking her eyes from the set. He switched off the radio and joined her.
The Manichaeans would have to wait a bit longer.

"*. . . a scholar, many have argued, the likes of whom hasn't been seen in
the Vatican since the fifteenth-century Pope, Pius the Second. The question
now,*" intoned the voice, "*is naturally one of succession. Rumors have already
begun to circulate within the Vatican of two prominent candidates. The first,
a longtime confidant of the late Boniface, and an equally accomplished
scholar, is Giacomo Cardinal Peretti, Archbishop of Ravenna.*" A photo of
the Italian, taken during an audience with the Pope, filled the screen. "*At
fifty-two, Peretti is one of the younger members of the Sacred College, and is
considered by many its most outspoken liberal voice. The other*"—a second
picture now split the screen with Peretti's, revealing a crisp Alpine background somewhere in the Tyrol—"*is Erich Cardinal von Neurath, Archbishop Emeritus of Linz, and, at sixty-eight, a champion of the Vatican's
most recent attempts at reconciliation with European Protestants through his
work with the encyclicals on faith. Both have strong support in the conclave,
although Peretti . . .*"

The words seemed to trail off as Pearse stared at the images. Something familiar about them, something that had little to do with either of the candidates. He stepped closer to the screen, his eyes settling on a third figure, a man directly to the left of von Neurath. He stood behind the cardinal's shoulder, his face, though, obscured in shadow. Pearse bent over, trying to make it out, Angeli aware of his sudden interest.

As the picture came clearer, Pearse felt a tightening in his chest.

There, staring back at him, was the man from the Vatican. The Austrian who had chased him from his home. *Remember the monk.*

Unable to take his eyes from the screen, Pearse felt the blood slowly drain from his face.

three

Giacomo Cardinal Peretti sat silently across from the canopied bed, the slight figure of Boniface X lying peacefully under white linen, head propped gently atop a single silk pillow. The room—three hours ago empty save for the two of them—now swarmed with doctors, security, clerics, lawyers, each caught up in whispered conversations, a collection of nuns kneeling in prayer, oblivious to the hushed activity. Peretti had been the last to speak with him, the last to hold his hand, his friend of forty years offering a final word of warning before drifting off: "Watch yourself, Gigi. Von Neurath wants to sleep in this bed more than you know." A quiet smile, and then gone.

Peretti hadn't needed the reminder, the halls even now alive with talk, his private secretary having brought him updates on two separate occasions as to the already-vigorous "campaigning"—none of it permitted by canon law, all of it greedily devoured by the Vatican's inner circles. No more than three hours since Ezio's death, and the politicking was well under way. The thought sickened him.

He stared at the ashen face, the high forehead dusted with tufts of gray-white hair, lips with a tinge of blue that matched the veins in his ears. The once-lined face seemed somehow smoother, even the neck taut under a stifling collar. The perfect facade for a spiritless body. Insignificant amid the self-serving swirl of motion all around him.

Peretti knew he had limited time with his old friend. The Cardinal Camerlengo—representing one of the more macabre offices within the church—would be arriving within the hour to lock up the private apartments, break the papal seal, and start the preparations for the *novemdieles*, the nine days of mourning. He had already announced that the conclave would meet on the ninth day, much sooner than was usual,

but certainly within his authority to decide. Most thought it was because
the current Camerlengo, Antonio Cardinal Fabrizzi, was in his late seventies, eager to make his interregnum stewardship as short as possible.
Peretti had other ideas. Fabrizzi was one of von Neurath's longtime allies.

"I need all of you to leave," Peretti said quietly, loudly enough, though,
to bring a sudden silence to the room. One of the security men started
to answer, but Peretti raised his hand. "Just a few minutes. I'm sure he'll
still be here when you get back." He remained seated, eyes fixed on the
body, face devoid of expression.

The nuns were the first to go, crossing themselves as they stood, each
turning to Peretti with a gentle nod before heading for the door—
Carmelite sisters, ever mindful of a cardinal's wishes. A slow trickle of
lawyers and doctors soon followed, the two or three security men the
last to leave. Finally alone, Peretti stood and walked to the bed. Again,
he stared into the lifeless face, hoping for some reassurance. He half-
expected the eyes to open, a naughty smile to creep across the lips.
"Gone at last," Ezio would say, a wink, spindly legs springing to the floor.

Peretti knelt at his side, his head drooped in prayer.

"What were you so concerned with on Athos, Itzi?" He looked up and
gazed at the serene face. "And why did you go without telling me?"

▲

Angeli moved to the kitchen table, two cups of coffee in hand. She
passed one to Pearse, then sat, the tale of the Austrian having required
another pot.

"On the other hand," she said, doing her best to convince both him
and herself, "the men from security might simply have been that—men
from security. They might actually have been trying to recover something they thought could be a threat to the church. A bit more aggres-
sively than one would have expected, but still—"

"No." Pearse shook his head, staring into the coal black of his cup.
"Even if you dismiss Cesare and Ruini—and I'm not saying you can—
think about who would want the scroll." He placed the cup on the table
and looked at her. "There are two possibilities. One, someone who hears
about its discovery, tracks it down, and then does what you did—
decodes the map and uncovers the link to Athos. At that point, he'd realize the prayer is only a first step, not the ultimate prize. He'd also realize
that he doesn't need it anymore—he'd already have the information

necessary to get him to Athos, before anyone else, and retrieve whatever is there. So even if he were to lose the scroll, there'd be no reason for him to hunt it down."

"True," she conceded.

"Or two," he continued, "someone who hears about it, but who never gets his hands on it, and therefore never has a chance to decode it. No decoding, no map. No map, and the prayer—in his eyes—would fall into the category of intriguing pieces of parchment rumored to exist, but lost to the ages. At best, he might do a little academic poking around to see if it wasn't all a hoax.

"Neither possibility, however, would prompt the kind of zeal our Vatican friends have displayed. Unless"—he leaned in over the table— "they knew it was a map *before* they'd heard about the discovery, a map to something worth a great deal to them. The question is, given what you've told me, how would anyone, except a Manichaean, know that?"

"I see." She let the words sink in before responding further. "No, you're right. No one has ever thought of the 'Perfect Light' as a map. No one *could* have, given that there's never been a written copy of it before."

"So the only person who would go to such lengths for the scroll," he concluded, "is someone who would have known it's a map before the written version had ever been found."

"And that," she admitted, "limits the field considerably."

The silence that followed only brought home the enormity of what they were saying. After a few moments, she spoke. "It would mean that those men from the Vatican are a part of something that dates back over seventeen hundred years."

"It would also mean," he added, "that, considering they're still after the scroll, they have no idea where it leads. That's why they're so eager to get their hands on it." Again, silence. Pearse took a long sip of coffee. "I suppose that gives me something of a head start."

"What?" When he didn't answer, she said, "You can't be serious. If what you say is true about Ruini and this monk friend of yours, we have to take this—"

"To whom?" His conversation with Dante—had it really only been yesterday?—flooded back. "No one outside this room is likely to see a link between the confirmed heart attack of a priest and a fifteen-hundred-year-old acrostic, much less the *un*confirmed disappearance of a monk and the promise of something older than the Gospels somewhere in Greece. Even the church would be hard-pressed—" He stopped, the sudden recollection of the television image storming back. "If von Neurath is involved"—the thought far more unsettling aloud— "who's to say how deep this goes? Or how mysterious the Pope's illness really was?"

"You're making a very big jump there."

"Am I? If we both agree these men are tied to the Manichaeans, you know better than I do what they had in mind for the Catholic church all those centuries ago. I can only imagine how their 'hyperasceticism' has evolved, their need for 'one, pure church.' Not the most pleasant place to be if they succeed. Plus, they'd have to destroy the current church to do it." He waited. "Given what's happened to Ruini and Cesare, not to mention my little run-in with security, are you willing to take the chance I'm wrong?" Her silence was answer enough. "The only way to find out is to get to Athos first."

What she said next took him completely by surprise. "We could destroy it."

"What?"

"The scroll, my notes, everything. Let whatever is on Athos stay on Athos. I can hardly believe I'm saying it, but it seems the only way."

"To do what? Leave these men totally unaccountable? Athos is the only thing that might explain what they've been waiting to do all this time."

"And with no way to find it," she insisted, "they won't have that chance."

"Of course they have a way to find it. They have you and me."

It was an obvious point, but one Angeli clearly hadn't grasped until this moment.

She started to say something, then stopped. Instead, she looked at Pearse; she then picked up her cup and slowly began to drink.

After several seconds, he said, "I . . . didn't mean to say it that way."

"No, no," she replied evenly, cup still clasped in her hands. "You're right. Of course." It was clear she was doing her best to stifle a growing unease. "They found your monk, you, no reason to think they won't track me down, get the name of the monastery."

"They want the scroll. They know I have it. They'll want me." He could see his efforts to placate were having little effect. "But if I get to Athos first . . ."

"Yes? And then what?"

He tried a smile, a shake of the head. "I don't know," he admitted. "Maybe it'll force them out into the open."

"That doesn't answer my question." For nearly half a minute, she sat there, staring at the table. Finally, she placed the cup down, swept a few crumbs onto the floor, and stood. "I don't have much of a choice, do I?"

Again, Cesare's voice echoed in his head. "I'm sorry I involved you in this."

It took her a moment to respond. Finally, she began to nod to herself. "I involved myself in this a long time ago." She turned to him. "You don't dream of finding a scroll like yours for an entire career and then run away from it when it's right in your hands."

"This is more than just a scroll."

"They're all more than just scrolls, Ian. That's what I've been telling my students for thirty years. Wouldn't make much sense not to take my chance to prove it, now would it?"

He knew she was grasping at anything to stem the anxiety. Who was he to argue with the method?

"There's a phone call I need to make," she said as she moved to the door. "And I'll have to transcribe my notes so you can read them." She needed to focus on the hunt, not on its implications. A map. Nothing more. She stopped and turned to him. "And some new clothes. A Catholic priest on Athos . . . now that wouldn't make much sense, would it?"

An hour later, she handed him a large manila envelope filled with yellow pages. Two hours after that, she returned to the apartment with numerous packages under each arm. He had used the time to catch a quick nap, then to acquaint himself with the envelope's contents. Even given the little he had read, he was astounded at how simple it all became when focused through an expert's lens.

She had done well. Pants, shirts, backpack—all the necessities. It had been a long time since he'd forgone the customary clericals. While he was trying on a green pullover, she removed one of the last items from the bag. A wad of cash. He looked at her quizzically. Before he could respond, she took his hand and placed the money in it.

"Lire, drachma, even some American dollars. They seem to like those wherever you go."

"I can't take—"

"Yes, you can." She smiled. "You probably won't need all of it, but best to be safe." He tried to hand it back, but she stepped away. "And how, exactly, were you going to get to Greece and back? On a credit card?" She shook her head. "That can be traced. So, too, can withdrawals from a bank machine." She was showing a great deal more savvy than he was himself. How *had* he planned to get to Athos and back? He realized he had no choice but to pocket the money.

"The man in Salonika is a former student of mine, Dominic Andrakos," she continued, now folding the bag. "I've told him you're a colleague. I gave you the name Peter Seldon."

"What?" Pearse was genuinely surprised.

"Well, I had to make up something. I don't want to get Dominic involved in all of this. Peter's a winegrower I know in California. Excellent Chardonnay. It was the first thing that popped into my head."

Again, best to let her handle it in her own way. Come to think of it, the alias actually made sense. More than protecting Andrakos—admirable in itself—he knew his own name might draw attention on Athos. She really *was* better at this than he was.

"You're interested in Ambrose and his possible link to St. Phôtinus," she continued.

"There *is* no link."

"Yes, but Dominic doesn't know that." She deposited the folded bags in a drawer. "His interests have always been somewhat later—ninth century, Photius's split with Nicholas the First, that sort of thing. Makes him very well connected on Athos. He said he'd be delighted to arrange things. He's expecting you sometime tomorrow, late afternoon."

She had obviously managed to put their earlier conversation from her mind. His was a research junket. Perhaps even something of a game. A wad of cash. A new name. A former student. Access to Athos. That he would have to use his Vatican passport at the border—something else easily traced—hadn't penetrated her defenses. He would get to Greece. That was as much as she cared to discuss.

He slipped his priest's shirt, jacket, and collar into the backpack. From experience, he knew how persuasive they could be at the borders. Together with the Vatican seal on his identification papers, they'd be enough to impress an indifferent guard. The manila envelope was the next to go inside.

"You know," she said, busying herself with something at the counter, "what you find might be more than you expect."

Her sudden willingness to revisit the real issue surprised him. "I realize that. Whatever the Manichaeans have—"

"That's not what I meant," she said firmly, her back still to him. He stopped loading the pack and waited for her to explain. "What if it is older than the Gospels? What if it does alter the way we understand Christ's message, the church?" She turned to him. "I know you've always had trouble with the structure, but this goes a good deal beyond that. They think it could actually tear down the church. Regardless of how the Manichaeans would want to use it, as a Catholic, Ian, how much are you willing to find?"

For the first time in hours, Pearse recalled his first reaction to the scroll. Not apprehension. Not fear. Only wonder. The possibility of Christ untethered. The purity, the connection that he'd always craved. *Sola Scriptura.* How much more powerful could it be than that? And if no longer in the scroll, then in whatever awaited him on Athos. Disentangled from the Manichaeans, it posed none of the threat Angeli was investing it with. At least not to him.

Maybe that was why he was so eager to go after it, why he had so quickly taken the task as his own. For the Manichaean threat? For himself? In all the excitement, he hadn't really bothered to ask. Nor could he have. The two were now inexorably tied together. The questions would have to wait.

"I don't know," he replied.

"You might want to figure that one out." She stared at him for a moment longer, then opened her purse and pulled a baseball from it. She tossed it to him. Without thinking, he reached out and caught it. "I found it in the Rinascente," she said. "Amazing what they have there these days."

Tracing his fingers across the seams, he smiled. "You remembered."

"A priest tossing a little ball in a café so he can figure out an ancient picture grid? Yes, that's not something one forgets." Now she smiled. "Just make sure the monks don't catch you. They'd probably confiscate it."

Λ

The surreal quality of their last hours together remained with Pearse for much of the train trip to Brindisi, sleep an impossibility. She had insisted on taking him to lunch, along with giving him a brief summary of Athos's history, all in a vain effort to lend some normalcy to the situation. More than not, though, they had eaten in silence. There was enough conversation around to relieve them of the burden. As one might have expected, talk of the Pope had monopolized every table. More like touts than a grieving flock, the clientele of the café had been placing odds: Peretti at two to three, von Neurath at even. Other names had entered the mix, as well, Pearse amazed by the familiarity the lunchtime crowd displayed with the inner workings of the Sacred College. Silvestrini at four to one (too old); Mongeluzzi at six to one (too young); Iniguez, Daly, and Tatzric all at ten to one (too foreign). Enough of a distraction, though, for both of them.

The good-byes had been brief, awkward at best, both trying to downplay the events of the last day. He had made it to the station by 1:30.

The choice of train, then ferry, had been an easy one. Overland routes would have taken days, not to mention the precariousness of a jaunt through the former Yugoslavia. And, Vatican ID notwithstanding, Pearse knew that passport control at the Adriatic was far less strict than at any of the airports he might have tried. Not that he thought the Austrian could possibly be monitoring all of them—although at this point, he had no idea how extensive the network might be—but best to make it as difficult as possible to track him. The Brindisi ferries sailed for two destinations: Albania and Greece. Unless the men of Vatican security had a sixth sense, the port wouldn't warrant much consideration. No, the boats were his best bet. Lots of tourists to get lost among at this time of year.

The train pulled in at 6:46. By 8:00 P.M., he had reserved a cabin on a 10:30 ferry—L140,000 for overnight passage to Igoumenitsa, on the southwestern coast of Greece. He would worry about the next leg of the trip tomorrow.

For two hours, he sat in a small Greek-style café by the piers, several cups of coffee, something resembling a gyro, and Angeli's notes to pass the time. He was trying to commit the layout of St. Phôtinus to memory—descriptions of benchmarks she had gleaned from the scroll with remarkable detail. But his lack of sleep was beginning to tell. Every so often, he found his eyes drifting, scanning the area along the street leading to the wharf, looking for what, he didn't know. Easier to concentrate on the casual meanderings of tourists than on the minutiae of a hastily scrawled map.

Those making the trip began to show up at around nine o'clock.

They wandered in the distance, their movements muted, the café too close to the strip of shoreline to permit anything but the sound of lapping tide against the pier. Pearse found himself listening intently to it, slowly attuned to the Adriatic's gentle glide, its beat less emphatic than the one he had grown up with on the Cape, the waves landing without the fullness he had come to expect of the sea.

And if only for a moment, he let his mind slip back to that past, recalling the hours he had spent alone on the beach, the glare angling itself lower and lower onto the surf—vivid blue into pale lemon—and all he'd had to do was cradle himself at the water's edge, the unmetered swish erasing everything and everyone around him. Not as a visual cleansing, but as a timbred one, the surge after surge of sound to engulf him.

Maybe that was what he was hoping to find on Athos.

A horn sounded near the ticket office. He looked up and saw the crew beginning to let people on board. The present resumed focus. Along the pier, the tourists were in full buzz, a rival ferry about to head out. He turned to the backpack and slotted everything inside, then made his way to the men's room at the rear of the café—priest's shirt, jacket, and collar to replace the green jersey he had been wearing since Angeli's, a quick wash of the face to snap some life into his eyes.

Within ten minutes, he was walking up the gangplank of the *Laurana*—another reminder of those summers on the Cape, the ferry a larger cousin of the boats he'd taken out to the Vineyard—his outfit and papers eliciting the desired response from the official. A few meaningless questions, his signature and stamp on various forms, followed by the deferential nod reserved for members of the clergy. Nothing out of the ordinary.

Pearse found his cabin—the room no more than six feet across, a narrow iron-framed bed bolted to the far wall, a tiny steel sink wedged into the corner. No window.

Perfect insulation. More comforting than perhaps he cared to admit.

⚠

His eyes bolted open at 6:00 A.M. to an overwhelming sense of panic. It lasted less than a second, but it was long enough to get him upright, the taste of stale breath in his mouth. Sitting in the pitch-black of the room, he knew exactly where he was, no need to remind himself of the last day and half. His appreciation for his surroundings had less to do with the momentary shock than with the way he had slept—on the edge of consciousness, eyes opening from time to time, dreams melding with the reality of an airless room, 3:30 the last time he had checked his watch. He was grateful for the last few undisturbed hours.

He had dreamed of Dante, uneven images returning again and again, always the same, the monk leading him through St. Phôtinus—a monastery neither of them had ever seen—but always away from the prize, away from the parchment he knew to be inside.

"You're taking me the wrong way, Dante. She said it's to the left."

"You don't want to go to the left. Please, Ian, do as I ask."

"But it's right there. I know it's there."

"They're old friends. Trust me."

"But it's—"

"Trust me. They will change everything." The face suddenly Petra's. "How much are you willing to find, Ian? How much?"

It wasn't difficult to explain the dream, or why she had appeared. At one point, his eyes had opened to the blackened cabin, certain that she was there with him. Hardly the first time. Anxiety, evidently, owed nothing to linear time.

By 6:30, he was showered and shaved, on deck with those who had taken the cheapest way across—a single seat. Most were still asleep, signs of late-night drinking, and who knows what else, in evidence. Even with the odd amalgam of smells, a crisp breeze managed to cut its way through, salted wisps on his tongue. Finding an area by the rail, he peered out.

He had never seen the Adriatic in sunlight, its coloring far more vivid than he had expected, almost with a dimension to it. Even the sun seemed sharper here, a constant pulse streaking the curls of water in a saffron blue.

It was exactly as Petra had described it, those moments when she would threaten to steal him away to Dubrovnik, find a boat, and just drift. The two of them. "Now, that wouldn't be so bad, would it?" He would smile, tell her about the Cape. And she would laugh.

"Either one," she would say. "Either one."

The first hint of shore appeared in the distance. He stared out for a moment longer, then checked his watch. Another forty minutes before docking.

It had been eight hours since Brindisi, time enough for the name of a priest to appear on a computer manifest, no sixth sense needed to place him on the Laurana into Igoumenitsa. Still less trouble to catch a flight to Athens—or perhaps a private airfield somewhere nearer the port— so as to meet the ferry. Pearse realized he needed to be a little less conspicuous. He looked around and saw a group of three young men beginning to shake off the effects of the previous night, yawning and speaking Italian as they joked with one another. He noticed their clothing, similar enough to his own—nondescript pants, faded shirts. He pulled himself from the rail and started toward them.

By 7:30, he would make sure they were all fast friends.

▲

Nigel Harris's last-minute announcement of a press conference had caught the media completely by surprise. Most hadn't expected rumblings from that quarter for at least another six months—Tony Blair's promised timetable for elections. CNN had been the first to jump, offering the 7:00 A.M. slot, completely at a loss, though, as to what the colonel—*former* colonel, they had to remind themselves—was proposing to unveil. His rather public departure from the council, and his subsequent tours through Europe and the States, had made him a hot topic. Several op-ed pieces over the last few months in the *New York Times, Corriere della Sera,* and the *Frankfurter Allgemeine* hadn't hurt his notoriety, either. If he wanted the early-morning slot—Nigel over coffee and toast—they were more than happy to oblige. It suited him. After all, "the new dawn" seemed to be a mainstay of his rhetoric.

He'd thought about the BBC. Bit more respectable. Bit more homegrown. But the Beeb didn't have the international cachet CNN could offer. They'd replay the conference again and again throughout the day, beaming him out to every one of their stations. And, if nothing else, *international* was the word of the day.

The pundits had been on the air since nine o'clock the previous night, speculating. *Nightline* had devoted an entire segment to the upcoming announcement. And given the time difference, they were promising to stay on the air—2:00 A.M. Washington time—to give their own spin on things when he finally got through talking. One guest had mentioned the possibility of a post in Blair's government. Given the PM's recurring run-ins with the Archbishop of Canterbury, he needed all the help he could get. Someone else had suggested that a new U.S. cabinet post might be more to his liking. The term *spiritual adviser* had been tossed around with a certain degree of playful cynicism. Still one more had speculated on a reconciliation with the TC, a way to solidify the "new Christian voice for the millennium" through a revamped Testament Council. Whatever it was, most of the major networks throughout Europe and the States were putting time aside. Harris was news. And news meant ratings. His own PR people had told him he'd be busy for the next few days. Wasn't that the point?

With a go from the producer in the London studio, Harris stepped to the microphone at 7:04. He pulled two note cards from his jacket pocket and began to speak.

"Good morning. My name is Nigel Harris, and let me first extend my thanks to CNN for organizing all of this at such short notice, and to you for allowing me to join you during your no doubt busy mornings. I promise to be brief.

"As many of you know, I stepped down as executive director of the Testament Council over a year ago. I was convinced, at the time, that an organization of its kind could achieve only limited gains within a secularized society, and that faith and politics, difficult as it was for me to admit, would never find a common ground in creating our future. I saw the selfsame efforts, both here in Europe and in the United States, coming to naught, and felt, perhaps, that our time had passed. I realize now that I was wrong." He paused. "It has never been clearer to me than today that those goals can be achieved *only* by the mutual cooperation of both. Faith must infuse politics. Politics must guarantee the rights of its faithful."

Again he paused, aware that, somewhere in the council's London headquarters, the phones were ringing off the hook. "No, we had no idea he was coming back, either," they'd be saying. He would have loved to have been there to see the surprise on their faces during the next few minutes. "I have also come to realize that such cooperation cannot be limited in its scope. At the council, we set our boundaries too narrowly. Our agenda alienated, rather than embraced. When the desire to strengthen the family, restore commonsense values, and foster religious liberty becomes the tool of political one-upmanship, then the issues of greatest concern to a faithful constituency can only become lost in the fray. I know that was not the council's intention to begin with, but, sadly, that is where the TC stands today.

"Several months ago, I therefore decided that there was a need for a new kind of leadership, an international organization that could meet the expansive needs of a new millennium, the new dawn. With the hope of stemming the cultural crisis that continues to batter away at the very heart of our social fabric, I brought together a group of political, civic, and religious leaders—names that will be made public at the end of this broadcast—who share my concerns. In the hope of inspiring inclusion, we have dubbed ourselves the Faith Alliance. At this very moment, the alliance is putting the final touches to a proposal, which we will present to various government leaders around the world, on how best to build a morally girded bridge to the next millennium. We are fully aware that this is only the beginning of the dialogue, but it will mean nothing without your support. I am, therefore, here this morning to tell you that a copy of that proposal, along with the alliance's mission statement, will appear in newspapers around the world one week from today. With it, our telephone numbers, fax numbers, and E-mail addresses, so that we can be certain that your voices—the voices of decency, civility, and cohesion—will be heard.

"We are taking this step because we feel that, in a world connected by the flick of a computer key, we can hardly sit back and allow the values dearest to us, and to our children, to remain at risk. Ours has been called a godless society, a great wasteland, a society so self-indulgent that we've become easy prey for those who would take advantage of our materialistic pride and our spiritual negligence. A new kind of terrorism abounds, which takes the godless as its victims. It becomes imperative, therefore, that wherever we can inspire faith, we must act with vigilance. Wherever we can find common ground, we must cultivate it so as to protect ourselves. Religious and, indeed, moral commitment can no longer be seen as quaint relics in an enlightened world of reason, where technology has become our surrogate divinity. Our children's future is too important to allow us to become so distracted.

"Let me say that the Faith Alliance will not be concerned with such divisive issues as national health, balanced budgets, tax reforms, deficit reductions, European fiscal cohesion, or any other such issues, which, though important in specific arenas and to specific politicians, have only shifted our focus away from what truly matters. Our message extends beyond political borders and therefore has no partisan agenda.

"In the next few weeks, you will come to know what we in the alliance hope to achieve. *Our* hope is that you will choose to embrace it. After all, it would be meaningless without your support. All I ask is that you take a look at what we have to say. Consider it. I feel confident that you will agree we must all find a way to reinject a spiritual and ethical purpose into every facet of our lives. If not for ourselves, then for the future, for that brave new dawn. What else is there?

"I thank you for your time and your patience. Are there any questions?"

Twenty arms sprang up at once. Harris pointed to a familiar face in the second row. Margaret Brown, BBC News.

"Mr. Harris," she began, "I appreciate your desire to keep things vague, but could you elaborate on what exactly you mean by religious vigilance? Which religion are we talking about?"

"Vigilance in inspiring *faith*, Margaret. I believe that to be a staple in every religion. The point here isn't to find what separates us, but what connects us. When the proposal comes out, I believe it will become quite clear that the issues we are confronting transcend those kinds of boundaries."

"Yes," she continued, shouting above the next surge of hands and questions, "but wasn't that the same claim you made when you were with the council? Not a Christian agenda, not a conservative agenda. And yet it turned out that wasn't the case at all when it came to your lobbying efforts with Parliament. Is the Faith Alliance just another special-interest front?"

"I'm not sure what you mean by 'front,' Margaret, but I will say that my choice to look beyond the council had more to do with the focus of the message than with the message itself. Spiritual commitment isn't something that should be marginalized. Jim," he said, pointing to James Tompkins from the *Times*.

"Yes. Mr. Harris, you said the proposal will be in papers around the world. That can run into a tidy sum of money. Where, might we ask, is the funding coming from?"

"That kind of information will be made clear in the mission statement." It was obvious to everyone in the room that the question period was going to be just that. Questions, no answers. Still the hands went up.

A reporter from the *Independent* jumped in. "You mentioned the Faith Alliance will be an 'international organization.' Could you give us a little more detail on that?"

"Let me put it this way. If, say, the Bank of England here, or the Federal Reserve in the States, has to take Japanese, Russian, European—what have you—economies into consideration when they set policy, I believe a crisis of values must also extend beyond borders. The linkages . . . that's the word they like to use now"—a few titters—"aren't just with our financial interests. The global community must be just that—global. And while we need to be sensitive to the cultural differences among us, we must also be willing to find that common ground so as to allow for some kind of connection when we tap into a part of the world that isn't our own. My son, like most of our children, I would venture a guess, is an absolutely avid Internet guru. To be quite honest, I use him as mine more often than not." More titters. "The point is, when he starts chatting with a little chap in, say, France, or Australia, or who knows where, I want to know that they're speaking the same language. That they have that commonality. And that they find comfort in it. That, ultimately, is what we hope to achieve."

One or two more pointed questions, followed by another series of less-than-coherent riffs from Harris, and the press conference came to a close. He was well aware of what the reporters thought of him and his meandering responses. So be it. He wasn't trying to impress them. The soon-to-be-released list of names would be more than enough to keep them happy. His concern wasn't the people who ran the media; it was those who watched it. And for them, bells and whistles were just fine. How many of them could get beyond the verbiage anyway? Bells and whistles. Best to leave it at that.

▲

The harbor at Igoumenitsa comes up quickly from the open sea, a wide U of coastline dotted with houses, apartments, hotels, all nestled by the shore, shielded to the rear by the northernmost chain of the Pindus Mountains. The hills slope more gently at the rim of the town, easy rolls of grass and trees lilting their way to within half a mile of the water. Once a bustling port where an Alcibiades or a Nicias might have gathered his fleet to sail against Sparta, the town now contented itself as a tourist hub, the central jumping-off point for Corfu, a few beaches and resorts all that remained of any particular interest.

Even so, Pearse stood astounded by the beauty of the place. As did his newfound companions. All four looked on in silence as the ferry docked, the beach a powdered white that seemed more snow than sand. And what had dazzled on the open sea now found definable texture in the wood and stone of the piers and buildings, chiseled gray topped by the ceramic red of undulating tiled roofs, each one shimmering under the gaze of an early-morning sun. If he had ever conjured an idealized form of Greece, Pearse now knew Igoumenitsa to be that image. The expressions on the three faces to his left told him he wasn't alone.

Over a quick breakfast, he'd learned they were making the trek to see a friend play in a summer-league soccer match in Beroea just west of Salonika. Amiable enough. More than that, they'd mentioned something about a bus. He'd asked to tag along.

Pearse made certain they were in the middle of the crowd as they took to the gangplank. Still not sure what he was looking for, he let his eyes wander—as casually as he could—along the faces of those waiting by the dock.

They were, as far as he could tell, all part of the tourist trade: hawkers of various activities, trinkets, transportation to the nearby resorts, all managing some semblance of Italian, articulated in thick Greek accents. Passport control was a formality; no one seemed to care that the priest had opted for mufti. Onshore, he stayed close to his friends, adopting the easy gait of a longtime confidant, arm on a shoulder as he laughed and nodded to the tales of their journeyman goalie friend. Evidently, the travails of what amounted to minor-league European soccer made triple-A ball sound like high living. Pearse tried to respond as if he knew what he was talking about. A few quizzical looks from the Italians, followed by bursts of jovial laughter—the much-hoped-for slap on the back—made the onetime trio into the perfect quartet.

As far as he could tell, no one showed any interest in them. Once or twice, he glanced around, ostensibly to check something in his backpack, tie his shoe. Nothing. At the bus station, he again made a quick sweep of faces—half the ferry, it seemed, hoping to squeeze onto the one bus out of town. Still nothing. Maybe Vatican security wasn't as keen or as capable as he'd thought. He bought a ticket, climbed on board—Igoumenitsa (in rather atypical Greek fashion) showing the good sense to coordinate ferry arrivals and bus departures—and settled in. Within twenty minutes, his three friends were well on their way to catching up on the previous night's sleep.

The more than eight hours necessary to travel the less than two hundred miles were due, in large part, to the pit stops along the way. First World and Third commingled with relative ease. At each station—a loose definition, to be sure—the driver took a few minutes to stretch his legs, chat with some of the locals, an occasion for everyone to escape the sauna inside. Sometimes, he even played up to the crowd, offering brief historical tidbits on the landscape—tales of the Centaurs, Jason and his Argonauts—although never allowing more than a few questions before shuttling everyone back on board.

At each town, Pearse marveled at the wide vistas of feral land, from a distance so lush. Closer in, the green patches tore up through the rough soil, wild vegetation seizing upon whatever turf it could. It was as if the earth here were too old to offer more than token assistance to anything staking a claim. Browned from the sun, the grass and trees tilted at an endless sky, faint hints of a distant past appearing from time to time on the roadside, all treated with casual indifference. A country of ruins could decide which it chose to celebrate.

The soccer trio managed to sleep through it all; their absence, however, didn't free Pearse from the obligations of small talk. An Italian, clearly uncomfortable in the heat—white handkerchief ever present at neck and brow—took each of the layovers as a chance to bemoan his situation to whoever would listen. A missed ferry, a business opportunity lost. After the third stop, Pearse was the only one not trying to steer clear of him. The burden of a priest's sensitivity. Only when the man began to ask Pearse about himself did the priest become more standoffish.

"Just on holiday," he answered.

"Where to?" the man pressed.

"Wherever the spirit moves me."

After that, he found reasons either to stay inside or to make his way to the men's room during the stops, avoiding the minitours altogether. He felt strange reacting as he did, innocent questions treated with such suspicion, but he knew he had no choice. From now on, he would have to set aside his more charitable instincts. Even in something as simple as a friendly chat. He watched as the man finally began to engage his seatmate; there, too, the saturation point came quickly. If not for the handkerchief man getting off at the next stop, Pearse wondered how long the other man could have taken it.

Reminding himself why he was on the bus, Pearse returned to the notes, piecing together the bizarre customs Angeli had detailed, each one attesting to the eccentricities of the Manichaeans. Albeit vague, the descriptions were no less intriguing: dramatized versions of the "heavenly ascent"; ritual ceremonies of "illumination" to test the commitment of an initiate; secret rites of bathing and eating imbued with mystical properties. Amid all the bumps and jolts of the ride, only one came across with any distinction: an elaborate ritual of greeting that appeared at the beginning of each of the letters. Unlike the transcriptions of the prayer, these showed no variation. Five identical steps, which, although not physically possible to experience in a letter, were at least described with enough detail to provide a clear picture. By the time they stopped for lunch, Pearse found he could recite the "signs of reception" himself.

One more insight into the Brotherhood of the Light.

The choice to stop at Kalambáka, he discovered, had less to do with the town's extensive choice of eateries than with its small railway station. Five miles off the Salonika road, it was the only chance to catch a train east or south—Larissa and Athens, and everything in between—before the bus headed north. More than that, it was an hour's break from the stifling heat of the midday sun.

Actually, Kalambáka was quite charming, far larger than anything they had come across thus far, and with a central square that boasted several cafés and restaurants. All, no doubt, for the tourist trade.

Before choosing one, Pearse decided to see if there was a train to Salonika—via Larissa—that might be quicker than the bus. Finding his way to the station, he discovered that, yes, in terms of hours spent, the train would lop off over three from the trip. In terms of real time, however, the one to Larissa didn't leave for another six. Of course, had he been going to Athens, he could have left within the hour. Not all that surprising.

So as not to make the jaunt to the station a complete loss, he stopped by the news kiosk and picked up one of the local papers. Probably a good idea to bone up on his Greek.

It was while he was getting his change that he noticed the handkerchief man's seatmate standing by the information booth. Evidently, Pearse wasn't the only one looking for something a bit quicker than the bus. And yet, if only for a second, Pearse thought he had caught the man staring at him.

He told himself it was nothing—after all, they had been on the bus together. It was natural for someone to glance at a familiar face. Hadn't he just done the same thing? Still, there had been something there, something in the sudden turning away of the eyes. In a moment of pure paranoia, Pearse imagined the hushed conversation between the two men on the bus, the first assault having come up empty. Stifling the urge to bolt out of the station, he slipped the coins into his pocket and, as casually as he could, headed for the exit. Even so, it was all he could do not to glance over his shoulder as he pushed through the door.

Crossing the street, he managed a peripheral view of the station; the man was also making his way back to the stores and cafés, and always at a constant distance. The more Pearse thought about it, the more he realized that the precautions he had taken in Brindisi, and again in Igoumenitsa, had retained a kind of fanciful quality. Watching a few tourists. Finding a group to walk with. Easy responses to an unseen threat.

He couldn't help but wonder if that threat had just made itself known.

And yet, it didn't make any sense. If either of the men were with Vatican security, why would they have waited until now to approach him?

Unless, of course, they had never intended to make contact at all. It suddenly dawned on him that the Vatican needed only to track him. They had no idea where the "Perfect Light" was sending him; all they needed to do was put someone on the bus, then let the priest lead them to the parchment. The possibility that he might be switching to the train had simply forced their hand.

He felt his face flush as his mind continued to race. He stopped and gazed into the window of a shop; from the corner of his eye, he saw the man pausing to tie his shoe. It was all the confirmation he needed. With no alleyways or tunnels in the offing, he realized he had no chance of losing the man before getting back on the bus. He had to find another way.

With that in mind, he headed into the square. A large group from the bus was sitting at what was clearly the best café Kalambáka had to offer. Too many people, he thought. Instead, he walked past the fountain to a far less prepossessing establishment on the opposite end of the square. Even the waiter seemed surprised by his arrival. Undaunted, Pearse sat and began to glance through the menu. As he did, he noticed that the man had stationed himself directly across the square, his view unimpeded. Pearse signaled for the waiter, pointed to something on the page, then asked for a coffee. The waiter nodded and disappeared.

Two minutes later, he returned with the cup and placed it on the table. Pearse took a sip, then asked for the men's room. The waiter pointed toward the inside of the restaurant, whereupon Pearse stood and headed back. Once inside, he kept himself far enough in so as not to be seen from the outside, but with a perfect view of the man across the square. Five minutes passed before the waiter drew up to his side with a plate of something brown. Pearse handed him several bills and told him to place it on the table outside. The waiter did as he was told, then returned to the kitchen.

And Pearse waited.

It was nearly ten minutes before the man began to make his way toward the café. The look on his face showed concern. Pearse pulled himself farther into the shadows. For several minutes, he watched as the man seemed unwilling to break the plane of tables and chairs, doing his best at casual surveillance. Finally, he had no choice but to step through. He was almost at the table, when Pearse suddenly emerged. Before the man could respond, Pearse drew up to him.

"Hello," he said with sufficient surprise. "Weren't you on the bus from Igoumenitsa?"

With no other choice, the man returned the smile. "Yes. Yes, I was."

"The talkative Italian. He sat next to you."

A second nod. "Yes. That's right."

"Well, you must join me for lunch."

Only a moment's hesitation. "That's very kind of you."

For fifteen minutes, they chatted about absolutely nothing, Pearse careful to keep track of the time. Without any prodding, he explained he was on his way to Athens. The train in twenty-five minutes. Amazingly, so, too, was the man. What a coincidence. Perhaps they could travel together? Pearse thought it a splendid idea. They finished their meals, headed back to the station, and, after buying two one-way tickets, made their way to the track.

Much to his relief, Pearse discovered that the Greek trains were all of the old European style: side doors to the platform from each compartment. He made sure that he and his companion picked one toward the back of the train. With five minutes to spare, they were seated next to each other, the conversation more and more insipid with each passing second.

Waiting another two minutes, Pearse suddenly winced.

"Is something the matter?" asked the man.

Pearse took several breaths, then said, "Stomach." He smiled. "It acted up back at the restaurant. Not sure Greek cooking agrees with me."

The man nodded, a look of concern in his eyes.

"But I think I can wait until we're moving," he added.

The man's smile returned.

With a shrill whistle, the train began to move. Waiting as long as he dared, Pearse stood and, with his apologies, slid open the door to the corridor and headed for the back of the car, having made sure to pick one without a rest room. As he moved, he could sense the man staring after him; still he continued slowly. With a sufficient show of frustration at not having found a men's room, Pearse pushed through the connecting doors and into the next car. He shot a glance back, the tint of the glass obscuring the view. Even so, he could tell that the man had gotten to his feet. Not waiting to see what he might do, and feeling the growing tremor of acceleration, Pearse broke into a sprint along the corridor. Darting into the last of the compartments, he bent over, opened the door—the tail end of the platform now sailing by at an ever-increasing speed—tossed the backpack out, and jumped.

The impact was instantaneous, his body rolling along the cement four or five times before he came to a stop. The pain in his shoulder and side was intense. His face, however, came through unscathed, locked within the protection of his arms. Lying flat, he glanced back at the train. The final car was just now slipping past the platform, the door he had used for his escape open and empty. Seconds passed before a figure appeared, too distant to make out with any accuracy. Its body language, however, was more than enough: frantic disbelief as the train banked away, its speed having become too great a deterrent for a second leap.

Pearse had lost his would-be tracker. Somehow, the pain in his shoulder seemed far less severe.

An official came running up, spewing Greek too fast for Pearse to keep up. Something about the company not being responsible for injuries. Pearse got himself to his feet, nodded, and, with a little shrug, answered, "No toilet paper."

Five minutes later, he emerged from the station rest room, having taken care of whatever scrapes and tears he had inflicted on himself. Five minutes after that, he was safely back on board the bus.

The audacity of the last half hour hit him only as the bus began to pull out. Rather than a sense of elation, or even relief, he felt overwhelmingly light-headed.

He pulled down his window and let the wind slap at his face.

▲

Beroea came and went, quick good-byes for his three friends. Half an hour later, the bus was driving through the outskirts of Salonika, city streets growing all around them.

Though bolstered by the misdirection in Kalambáka, Pearse remained cautious. It had been several hours since then, more than enough time for his lunch companion to get in touch with someone else. Sending them to Salonika was just too obvious a choice.

With that in mind, Pearse attached himself to the first clump of passengers off of the bus, he at its rear, head tucked low into the shoulders of those around him. Even so, he had no idea what he would do should someone appear. He'd used up his one flash of brilliance in Kalambáka.

Clutching at the strap of his pack, he stepped through the platform gate and into the central hall.

Far grander than he'd expected, the station opened up under a vaulted dome of steel and glass, a series of tobacco shops, shoe-repair stalls, and newspaper kiosks all littered about, the tinny sound of overamplification echoing with each muffled announcement.

Head still bent, Pearse noticed a man—no more than twenty-five—making his way toward the recent arrivals. A man who seemed to be staring directly at him.

For the second time in the last few hours, Pearse felt the blood drain from his face. He edged his way deeper into the group.

Still the man came, heading straight for him. Pearse knew it was pointless to run. From the corner of his eye, he spotted a guard by one of the exits. He was on the verge of breaking toward him, when the young man did something Pearse never expected.

He waved, a hesitant smile on his face.

The movement stopped Pearse in his tracks.

"Professor Seldon?" The young man continued toward him. "Peter Seldon?"

It took Pearse a moment to remember.

"Yes. . . . Yes, that's me," he answered.

"Oh, good," the man said, pulling up to his side. "I was a little worried. Dominic Andrakos. Professor Angeli—"

"Of course. Yes. Hello." The two men exchanged a handshake.

"You were worried you wouldn't find your way to my place?" Andrakos asked.

Pearse realized the relief on his face must have been all too obvious. "Something like that."

"Understandable." Andrakos smiled. "Salonika can be a bit tricky. The professor described you over the phone. She said you were coming by ferry. As there's only one bus a day from the west, I took the chance. My car is just out front."

"Lead the way," Pearse added in Greek.

"Oh? You speak," he responded in kind. "The professor didn't mention that."

"Enough to get by. I'm much better with the classical."

"Then this will be good practice for you."

Ten minutes later, they were fighting the traffic on Odós Egnatia, one of Salonika's broader avenues, Andrakos spouting bits and pieces of historical insight as they drove. Mario Andretti as tour guide. Pearse kept a hand on the car's dashboard, nodding each time the younger man took a breath. Had it not been for the speed and the still-unsettling few moments at the station, he might actually have enjoyed the ride. As it was, he was simply glad to be getting closer to the mountain.

▲

The guard at the desk nodded to Kleist, no need for identification, not even a second glance at the package in his hands. Security had been punched up since the Pope's death, most buildings within the Vatican under continuous surveillance. As a senior officer, Kleist was becoming a familiar figure around the City. In fact, he'd been to the Domus Sanctae Marthae four times in the last two days. Not that surprising, given that the six-story hospice would soon be home to the hundred or so members of the conclave. The cardinals had been forced to stay in makeshift quarters at the Papal Palace for centuries; now, they enjoyed far more spacious living during their deliberations. John Paul II had seen to that. Boniface had found no reason to change things back.

Having surveyed the building several times now, Kleist wished the late Pope had. The whole thing was too spread out, too disjointed, much more difficult to control.

His concern, however, had little to do with the cardinals' safety. In fact, it was quite the opposite. Trying to bury upward of a hundred men under fifty tons of marble and stone would, he was discovering, require twice as many explosives as would the Papal Palace. Much greater chance of discovery. That the plastique would be in the building for less than an hour once the call came through made little difference. Impromptu spot checks by the bomb squad—dogs in tow—could be expected each night the conclave sat in session. And once they had chosen a new Pope, Kleist knew security would be taken to an even higher level. All of which meant that while the world celebrated the election, he would be racing around the hospice, twelve to fourteen minutes to plant the bombs between the dogs' departure and the cardinals' return.

Added to that, von Neurath had been adamant that certain fragments from the explosives remain sufficiently intact to allow for positive identification. They had gone to too much trouble acquiring the casings— ones that their Syrian dealer had assured them had come from the private cache of the Dar Hadjid, one of the more ruthless militant groups out of Iran—not to leave enough detritus for the source to be traced. The choice to target the third and fifth floors, therefore, had as much to do with room assignments as with engineering. Certain crucial cardinals on the fifth; best chance for surviving fragments on the third. As von Neurath had said, two birds with one stone: Allah's stamp on the atrocity, more room for their own in the Sacred College. He had displayed a genuine delight in detailing the strategy.

And yet, the actual horror of what they were planning troubled Kleist far less than the cardinal's explicit instructions that he discuss the preparations with no one but him. Usual protocol required Blaney, Ludovisi, and the contessa to be kept apprised of every detail. Von Neurath had explained that the lines of communication needed to be restricted at this point. Why was not his concern. Still, it seemed odd.

Reaching the fifth floor, he pulled a collection of brackets from the package, along with a section of blueprint, and moved down the corridor. The schematic was surprisingly clear. Inside several heating vents and ceiling ducts along the hall, he attached two sets of the metal supports, less than a minute for the epoxy to harden at each stop. It had been the same that afternoon on the third floor. One or two more trips, and everything would be in place.

Back on the ground floor, he nodded to the guard on his way out. "Everything looks fine." Kleist smiled.

"Wouldn't have expected anything else," answered the man.

Good to hear, thought Kleist as he stepped out into the night.

A

The university's junior faculty housing made Pearse's Vatican rooms seem lush by comparison. Andrakos insisted on a glass of something before they headed out; given the last day and a half, Pearse readily accepted. They toasted over a tiny wooden table in what passed for the kitchen, both men downing the liqueur in a single swig.

"Hooo." Pearse coughed several times, his eyes filling with tears. He'd had ouzo before. This was definitely not ouzo.

"*Yamass,*" said the young Greek. "You won't get this quality booze for a couple of days."

"That might be a blessing in disguise."

Andrakos smiled and tilted back his glass, refilling both before Pearse could say no. "They water down everything on the mountain."

"I can understand why." If he'd had any concerns about Andrakos's driving before, he couldn't wait to see him on the road after two of these.

Surprisingly, the alcohol changed very little. In fact, it seemed to heighten his skills. While Pearse replanted his hand firmly on the dashboard, Andrakos took the car in and out of alleys, crisscrossing and circumventing the afternoon traffic with extraordinary ease. Amid the whirlwind, he even managed to throw in a few more sights—a fleeting view of the Arch of Galerius, sixty feet of weathered stone and marble, its side piers lopped off, leaving only a gated torso, several bands of reliefs chiseled below, a glimpse into the city's Roman past.

"A little reminder of home for you," said Andrakos.

"Doesn't look like Boston," said Pearse.

"Ah," said Andrakos. "I meant your current home."

"You'd love Boston. Just remember to take the car."

Pearse was permitted only a few seconds to take it all in before they were zipping past mosques and minarets, a quick glance at Atatürk's birthplace, confirmation of Salonika's role as meeting place between East and West. An equal-opportunity guide, Andrakos enjoyed recalling his city's tug-of-war history, secure in the fact that whatever her conquerors had tried to impose, they had never escaped her singular imprint. Salonika was forever Greek, its relics—Roman, Turkish, Armenian—infused with the image of that Hellenic past.

It was only when he realized they were making their way deeper into town, rather than out to the mountain, that Pearse spoke up.

"Travel visas," Andrakos explained. "No documents, no monks."

Less than five minutes later, they pulled up in front of the Ministry of Macedonia and Thrace, which, as far as Pearse could see, was Agiou Dimitriou Street's answer to Rome's Palazzo Borghese, though on a far less opulent scale. The ash gray building stood back from the street, a pebble garden leading to the entrance steps, with arched columns beyond. Inside, the fantasy quickly faded, stark walls amid a bureaucrat's maze of offices, along with two bizarre modern sculptures standing sentry at the door. A far cry from the Berninis he had hoped for.

Andrakos hurried them through the main hall, hellos and nods to just about everyone they passed. The same held true on the second floor, first names for most, smiles and waves following him down the corridor. Clearly, Angeli had chosen her contact well.

He headed for the office at the far end, not bothering to knock before venturing in.

"*Yasu*, Stanto," he said, moving straight for the desk.

The man in the chair looked up, a slightly older version of Dominic, a brother's glare in his eye. "Don't you even bother to knock, Nikki? I could have had someone—"

"I told you I was coming. We need the papers."

It was then that the older Andrakos noticed Pearse at the door. "Oh, yes. Hello," he said in English. "Please come in."

Pearse stepped inside, at once taken by the view through the window—picturesque church, several bubble domes atop a ceramic roof, clear indication of Stanto's favored position at the ministry. A view like that took years to acquire.

Dominic was already busy with various piles on the desk.

"They're not in there." Trying his best to curb his annoyance, Stanto smiled at his guest, then pulled the pages from his brother's hands, continuing in a hushed Greek. "Look, Nikki, I can't keep making last-minute arrangements for you. This is a serious office, not your private travel agency. The boys on the mountain can get very upset."

"They love me out there," replied Dominic, a wink to Pearse as his brother pulled a second set of pages from his hands.

"They love God, Nikki. They tolerate you."

"*Barely* tolerate." Dominic laughed. "By the way, the professor speaks Greek."

The older Andrakos hesitated before turning to Pearse. "Oh. Of course," he said, extending his hand. "I'm sorry. Constantine Andrakos. I'm not usually this—"

"No need to apologize," said Pearse, shaking his hand. "Peter Seldon. I'm the one you should be taking to task. It's my fault that this has all been so last minute."

"You're nice to say so, Professor, but you don't know Dominic. It isn't the first time." He reached into a drawer and pulled out two rather impressive-looking envelopes. Pearse noticed they were both addressed to the Holy Community of Mount Athos, the great imperial crest—the double-headed eagle of Byzantium—at the top. "They delivered the *diamonitirio* fifteen minutes ago. The ink is probably still wet."

Dominic took the passports and, trying his best at a pose of servility, asked, "And the boat? Did you get the boat, Stanto?"

"Yes, I got the boat," he replied, as if to a child. "It'll be waiting for you at Ouranopolis. Brother Gennadios will meet you at Daphne. He said he's looking forward to seeing you."

"I told you they loved me."

"I think he meant the professor." He turned to Pearse. "Gennadios mentioned he once did some work on Ambrose."

"Really." Pearse smiled. "I . . . can't wait to talk with him."

Dominic was already at the door. "I'm sure you've got plenty of work to do. Wouldn't want to get in your way."

"No, you wouldn't want to do that," said the older Andrakos. "Just try and get there in one piece."

The eighty miles to Ouranopolis—the Gate of Heaven, little more than a village at the base of the Athos Peninsula—took just over two hours, remarkable, given the condition of the roads.

"I once did it in an hour and forty-five." Andrakos beamed as they parked on a street barely wide enough for the car doors to open. "A friend of mine claims an hour and a half, but he did it alone. Mine still stands." He pulled out a piece of paper, scribbled something on it, then placed it under the wiper. "It's for the fellow who lives here," he explained. "Just telling him when we'll be back, and to move the car if he needs to." Pearse noticed the keys still in the ignition. A different way of life in Ouranopolis.

They emerged onto another street, this one slightly wider, a few patches of cobblestone in need of repair. It wended its way down through the village, the small houses on either side like giant sandstone steps leading to the shore.

"The place seems empty," said Pearse.

"Most of the boats are still out on the water. But it'll be loud enough in about an hour. Once they get back and start drinking."

"More of the stuff we had at your place?"

Andrakos laughed. "That's rice water compared to this. I won't tell you how many times I've come out here and not quite made it out to the mountain."

"Different kind of research." Pearse smiled.

They neared an ancient tower hovering by the water. One or two windows pockmarked its upper reaches, stucco unevenly slathered along its face, scars of brick peeking through. It peered down, superior only in its height, the one sign of real civilization against the timeless backdrop.

"From what I've heard," said Pearse, "you'd probably need something a little stronger than ouzo if you had to take care of these monks. They tell me they're a pretty austere bunch."

"Austere? These boys take it so seriously, they don't allow anything female on the mountain at all. Anything. No sow, no cow, no hen. And all because a couple of them got a little friendly with some of the shepherds' daughters about a thousand years ago. . . . Probably why they call it the Garden of the Virgin."

Pearse laughed. "I'm not sure the Holy Mother would agree."

"Why? Even she wouldn't be allowed out there."

Arriving at the shore, they headed out along a narrow jetty, its wood and spikes groaning under the weight. A small cabin stood at the end of the pier, a single light inside. Andrakos stepped toward it. "I'll be back in a minute."

The door smacked shut, followed by the din of conversation. It quickly faded as Pearse moved to the edge of the landing. For the first time in days, he stood alone.

It would have been enough to close his eyes, trace the lapping of the waves, once again less frantic than those he had known on the Cape; or to breathe in, the taste of tangerines mixed with hewn grass on his tongue; or to shut them all out and simply gaze at a sun already dipping to the Aegean, clouds streaked a beet red against the thickening blue of a summer sky. Instead, he had them all, a barrage of pure radiance, somehow releasing him from all thought. His eyes fixed on a point perhaps a hundred yards out, a patch of perfect stillness. Weightless. And for a few moments, he was there, freed from everything around him, floating, adrift. He could feel the water rise about him, cup his head and arms, effortless.

"Now you know why the monks come." Andrakos was by his side, silently staring out. "And why the mountain is theirs."

Pearse continued to hold it in his grasp, unwilling to let go until Andrakos had moved off. He then turned, the image almost too perfect—a small fishing boat tied up some ten yards back, squat captain, tangled gray beard.

Greece was making good on all its promises.

Andrakos remained by the wheel, chatting with the captain for the length of the trip, leaving Pearse alone to take in the full measure of Athos from the sea. He stood at the prow, hands clasped to the rusted metal rail, an ever-increasing sense of insignificance as the mountain opened up in front of him.

What began as a rise of grass and trees soon gave way to the surge of ragged stone, slopes crumbling toward the sea, rock clusters strafing the ground, green-and-white embers shimmering against a dusking sky. And wherever the blanketing of oak and brush tried to assert its will, wide scarps of serrated wall rose up to thwart all but the most vigorous attempts. Even the scattered tufts of misted cloud that floated above offered little more than false hope against the unforgiving and relentless terrain.

The God of Athos was a vengeful God, testing his faithful, unwilling to grant them an easy piety.

And yet, the mountain's beauty was undeniable, not simply for its fierce grandeur but for the totality of the place, a finite depiction of the rift between sea and sky. Unpeopled, it held a kind of primal wonder.

Pearse stood breathless, awed by its majesty, more by its carnality, a living, breathing earth. The mountain was holy, less for the men who chose it as their refuge as for the touch of the divine in its every aspect. A sanctity conferred by the brutality of nature.

That truth gained even-greater clarity as the first of the monasteries emerged, perfect linear form rising from the rugged chaos of the mountain face. Neat rows of balconies and roofs hovered above the slopes, a bell tower with fattened Byzantine dome peeking out from the tidy angularity. The sun lay too low to permit any real detail, lights from within shimmering a constellation's outline of the tiny city above. The pattern ducked and turned at odd moments, projecting wild limbs from the main body. Too soon, though, it slipped from sight, another configuration appearing in the distance, the mountain's zodiac taking shape against the now-darkened sky. Some of the monasteries had dared to climb high, blurring the distinction between earth and stars; others had pitched low in tapered valleys, their shape like the flow of untamed water. Each a pocket of perfect order, a thousand years of strict devotion.

And one, he knew, the guardian of a parchment whose truth transcended even the splendor of the mountain itself. Staring up into the sky, Pearse understood—perhaps for the first time—what it was that had brought him here. And what it was to be so close.

As the boat bobbed along the shore, his gaze fixed on the tip of the mountain, its peak lost in a crown of cloud. Even at night, though, one could make it out, the glow from the single monastery at its base bathing the nimbus in a golden hue.

St. Phôtinus stood alone at the edge of the peninsula, the most sacred of sites reserved for the holiest of the monasteries.

The captain slowed the engine and let the boat drift toward the piers of Daphne, the village—halfway down the peninsula—as far as he could take them. From here, they would go by mule or truck, depending on the severity of Phôtinus's approach.

Grinding the engine into reverse, he angled the boat in between the others moored at the dock, the sound jarring against the quiet of the place. Pearse saw Andrakos slip the man a few bills before grabbing his pack and joining him on the pier.

The place lay deserted, a few muffled sounds from the town above, nothing to compete with the boat as it pulled away. Andrakos headed up the stairs, surprisingly silent, Pearse behind. When they reached the road, they found it empty, as well. Andrakos dropped his bag and sat; Pearse did the same. Still, not a word. Obviously, there were new rules on the mountain. The only sound was the clink of glasses from some unseen tavern, a few drinks before the last of the boats headed back to Ouranopolis.

They didn't have long to wait before the sight of two bouncing lights appeared off to the right, Andrakos quickly getting to his feet. As the truck pulled up, he swung the pack onto his shoulder and placed his hands at his back. The sham supplicant from his brother's office now transformed into the real thing. Pearse followed his lead, a pose of quiet respect as the monk stepped out to greet them.

"Who are you fooling, Dominic?" Brother Gennadios laughed as he approached, rapping the younger man on the arm as he drew up. He wore the classic black robe of Greek Orthodoxy, the bonnet on his head tilted at a somewhat daring angle. His forearms, now around Andrakos's back, were thick and muscular, a rug of hair extending as far as his knuckles. Pearse noticed the impish smile on the younger man's face as Andrakos looked up.

"I had *him* going," he answered, nodding to Pearse, the familiar twinkle back in his eyes.

Gennadios turned to Pearse, eyes wider still as he grabbed both of his shoulders and pulled him in close, a kiss on each cheek. His grip was exceedingly powerful, the two men roughly the same height, the monk a good hundred pounds heavier. The softness of his beard surprised Pearse.

"Professor Seldon. What a pleasure. I'm Gennadios. I apologize for the time you've had to spend with this one, but life is filled with tests, none more trying than young Andrakos here."

"He's not so bad if you've had a few drinks."

Gennadios erupted in laughter, then cupped Andrakos's neck in his hand. "Like an open book, Dominic. Like an open book." He turned again to Pearse. "You didn't let him drive, did you?"

Before Pearse could answer, the monk was shuttling them into the truck, packs tossed in the back, the front seat a patchwork quilt of vinyl and duct tape. Squeezed inside the cab, Pearse guessed that the white Ford had been around longer than Gennadios himself, the crunch from the gearbox confirmation as they set off.

The drive at night was far less compelling than the view from the water, intermittent shots of the mountain quickly obscured under a tangle of leaves and thickets. What few openings they came to offered only momentary bursts of stars. Without someone familiar at the wheel, Pearse realized, the road would have been impossible to traverse, hardly a light to warn of the sudden twists and turns, at one point the monk forced to take the truck down to a virtual stop so as to manage one of the hairpins. Even at ten miles an hour, the constant bouncing from the combination of rutted road and shockless wheels made communication all but impossible. It was something of a lifesaver. Gennadios was pouring forth with what seemed to be everything he knew about Ambrose. Pearse smiled and nodded, happily unable to catch more than a word or two here and there.

Fifteen minutes into the lecture, the monk pulled the truck over.

". . . which might have changed Augustine's entire outlook. Anyway," he said, shouldering his door open and tossing the keys onto the dashboard, "you should come out my side. We wouldn't want to lose you over the edge on your first night."

Pearse peered out at the sudden drop off to his right, then slid across and joined the other two at the front of the truck. Gennadios handed him a lantern.

"The rest, we do by foot."

The climb did little to help conversation, a rigorous pace through the interior of the mountain. The trees and brush sprang up far thicker here, paths just wide enough for a mule laden with supplies, gnarled undergrowth making for precarious footing. The lanterns were more to keep Gennadios in sight than to give any sense of the tip of the peninsula. Even with a breeze off the water, Pearse felt the sweat mount under his shirt, a balmy midsummer evening moistening the air. It felt good, something his body had been craving. If not for Gennadios wheezing his way up, Pearse would have pushed the pace, happy to lose himself in the physical exertion.

They climbed in dim silence for perhaps twenty minutes before emerging on an open bluff, a tiered expanse of rock, earth and sage beyond. Fifty feet to their right, the mountain seemed to come to an abrupt end, the drop-off some eight hundred feet, a full moon perched just beyond the edge of the cliff. Below, they could hear the roll of the surf. Above, a faint glimmer of light poked through.

It was St. Phôtinus staring down at them.

"It gets easier from here," intoned Gennadios, clearly winded. "Another twenty minutes or so."

He was spot-on, the monastery inching out over the last of the hillocks some fifteen minutes later. Smaller by a considerable degree than the rest of the "cities" on the mountain, Phôtinus still managed a rather imposing glare from its frontal assault. A stern line of cypresses stood guard along the outer wall, bits and pieces of which dated back as far as the fourth century. Most of the loose stone had been replaced by brick and mortar over time, Byzantine and Ottoman architecture colliding in a wild mélange of turrets and flying buttresses. On either side, the walls matched the rise of the mountain, uneven steps climbing high along the slope, disappearing into an overgrown wood perhaps two hundred yards above, the overall effect that of a headless turtle attempting to take flight.

But it was the sight directly in front of them that demanded attention. Two ironwork doors—vast shields arching to a stone gate thirty feet high—recalled a time when the monks of Athos had been forced to fight for their piety, pirates a constant menace, a long-abandoned gunwale still visible along the topmost part of the wall. Even Phôtinus's motto, etched crudely into the stonework above the doors, conveyed the dual message of refuge and resistance.

Take Peace Within These Walls and Gird Yourself to Dwell in an Armor of Loveliness and Light.

As the peninsula's first line of defense against attack from the sea—and forever caught up in the squabbles of distant emperors and sultans—Phôtinus had long ago learned to guard its privacy well. Even now, it was considered the most insular among a community renowned for its isolation.

And yet, the doors stood ajar, three or four lamps from the courtyard inside lighting the last few yards of their approach.

As they entered, Pearse was astounded by the silence, no monks coming out to demand their papers. Instead, they walked undisturbed to the fountain at the center—a simple pool with a strangely ornate spout. It was a monk in prayer, the water trickling from his eyes, as if tears. Pearse stared at it for several seconds. He couldn't help but wonder if the tears were meant for the one true and holy Christian church, a disturbing thought as he joined the other two. They were cupping great heaps of water, Gennadios on the fountain's ledge, handful after handful to his neck. The hike had gotten the better of him. Only then did Pearse realize how thirsty he was himself. It was several minutes before any of them spoke.

"Nice climb," Pearse finally said. "I suppose you must make the trek quite often," he added, dabbing his neck and shoulders.

The monk breathed heavily before answering. "Maybe twice in the last six months. It's not something I look forward to."

"You don't get out much, do you?"

"Get out much? I don't understand."

"Well, if you've left only twice—"

"Oh, I see what you mean," he said, the smile returning to his face. "Dominic obviously didn't explain. I'm not a Brother of Phôtinus. My home is the Great Lavra," he added, giving a quick flick of a finger somewhere off to the east, "the *second* oldest on the mountain, a mere babe compared to this one. We go back only as far as 963. But Phôtinus, well, it's been around since—what is it, Dominic, 384, 85? No one's quite sure." He returned to the water.

"Not my period," Andrakos answered.

"Always the best excuse," said Pearse, Angeli's smile appearing in front of him.

Andrakos started to respond, then stopped.

Gennadios laughed. "You've actually shut him up with that one. I must remember it."

Pearse waited for Andrakos's smile, then asked, "So it's all right for us to be here?"

"Well, I wouldn't have made that trip with you if I weren't sure," said Gennadios.

"All of the monasteries have a kind of open-door policy with one another," Andrakos explained. "If you and I had walked in here alone, we'd be in a lot of hot water right now. As long as we've got the bearded one with us, they know it's okay. I've actually never been to Phôtinus myself."

"Five, six hundred years ago," added the monk, "that wouldn't have been the case. Now, with fewer than two thousand of us scattered among the monasteries, we've let things loosen up a bit."

"Without this one here"—Dominic placed an overly enthusiastic hand on Gennadios—"I wouldn't have been able to see half the archives I've needed for my work."

"And *with* this one," the monk nodded, taking Andrakos's hand from his shoulder, "you've managed to get me in all sorts of trouble with half the abbots on the mountain. Brother Timotheos at Stavronikita still isn't talking to me."

"That's because he's taken a six-month vow of silence." Andrakos laughed.

"It's still no excuse."

Pearse laughed as well, the sound echoing throughout the empty courtyard. It seemed to prompt movement from one of the far build-ings, a strange aggregation of striped archways topped by a maroon attic with gabled roof. A small figure appeared from a side door, another black cassock gingerly making its way across. He seemed to glide across the flagstone.

"I see you made it without too much trouble," he said as he neared them, catching Gennadios in middip, the larger man spinning around and at once pulling the diminutive monk into his barrel chest, an embrace that would have gotten the better of a man twice his size. Still, the little monk held his own.

"You need a bath" were his first words as he disentangled himself from the bear hug. "And our fountain won't do." The two laughed.

"It's good to see you, too," said Gennadios as he stood to make the introductions. "Professor Seldon, Dominic Andrakos, this is Brother Nikotheos, librarian of St. Phôtinus, and a man with a finely tuned nose."

There was an almost feminine quality to his face, delicate olive-shaped eyes, soft white skin amid the wrinkles. Even his beard seemed to soften its texture. His hands, however, betrayed his years, browned and bony. Pearse guessed Nikotheos to be somewhere in his early seventies. "We don't usually allow guests to arrive after the second meal—in fact, we don't usually have guests at all—but Gennadios explained your work on Ambrose. I wasn't aware he'd ever made the trip."

"I guess that's what I'm here to find out." Pearse smiled.

"Yes." It was clear he'd expected a bit more by way of explanation. When none came, he nodded to the little group and said, "Well, let's get you to your rooms, perhaps a quick tour. It's late for us."

Pearse's was the last of the cells they came to, more of the flagstone, stark white walls, a small desk and iron bedstead below a single window. The glass panes were pulled open, the smell of minted olives in the air.

As he had done for Gennadios and Dominic, the monk retrieved two bowls from the shelf by the door, one filled with dried fruit and nuts, the other with rose-scented *loukoumi*, the Greek version of Turkish delight. He placed them on the desk.

"In case you get hungry during the night. We're up before the sun, first prayer at four." He turned to go, then stopped. "Oh, I meant to ask— are you Orthodox or heretic?"

It was a question Pearse had hoped to avoid. He knew that the few non–Greek Orthodox they permitted on the mountain were generally of the harmless tourist variety. Those who wished to see the manuscripts were put to far greater scrutiny. Too long a history of disappearing documents, miraculously reappearing in the British Library and the Vatican, had made the monks justifiably wary. Their distrust of Catholics verged on mania.

"I'm a Catholic," Pearse responded.

"Oh, I see." Nikotheos's expression remained unchanged. "How sad for you." Again, he moved to the door, then stopped. "I wouldn't make that public knowledge. Several of the brothers feel quite strongly about it, the abbot included." A smile. "But we'll make sure you get to see the manuscripts. I'd love to find out how Ambrose ties in with us here." And with that, he was out the door, pulling it shut behind him.

Pearse tossed his pack onto the bed and stepped to the window, a light mist having settled in the last few minutes. Such was the whim of mountain air. It hung on the upper reaches of the buildings, the moon lost behind it. Even so, he could see the monastery stretch out in front of him, the slope of the mountain giving his third-floor cell a near-panoramic view.

It was far bigger than he had imagined, wide pockets of open area extending up to unseen distances, all of them surrounded by a wide assortment of fifteen centuries of architectural evolution. Closer in to his right, the fountain continued its endless trickle of water, the patter

echoing in soulful meter; only the occasional brush of leaves and a flap-
ping of wings broke through the silence. As he continued to stare out,
he saw Nikotheos arrive in the courtyard, the monk moving slowly,
snuffing out lamps as he went. The area grew dark, save for one or two
paraffin lamps glowing in the windows above, late-evening prayers, last-
minute assurances.

For the most part, Pearse had little idea what lay out in the darkness.
Nikotheos's quick tour had been just that—quick. One or two of the
smaller chapels, refectory, library—all in swift succession, only the last
of them, he had discovered, behind locked doors.

"There was an incident at the Great Lavra a few years back," the monk
had explained. "Raiders in motorboats with guns. They stole quite a few
manuscripts, gold reliquaries, even a few icons. They were caught, thank
heavens, but the damage had been done, illuminations ripped out,
destroyed. We keep these doors bolted at night now. Not what I would
like, but what can you do?"

Pearse had been relieved to hear that the rest of the place remained
open. From Angeli's notes, he knew he'd have no need for the library
and its manuscripts.

Unfortunately, that was all he knew. Little of what he now saw resembled the map she had drawn. Much had changed in nine centuries, most
of the buildings fourteenth- and fifteenth-century additions, still others
from the golden age of the czars, when Russian Orthodoxy had taken
Athos under its protective wing. The one piece that tied the ancient
Phôtinus to its more modern progeny was the outer wall itself, a basic
triangle, the entrance doors a fixed landmark situated at the center of its
base. He had to hope Angeli's calculations were accurate enough to lead
him from the fountain courtyard to the "Vault of the Paraclete," a room
somewhere within one of the more ancient buildings still standing.

It was odd to think how close he was to whatever was hidden within
the Vault, how long the parchment had waited to be found.

If, of course, it was still there. And if Angeli had deciphered the scroll
correctly. Too many variables.

A breeze lifted off the water, more of the olive and mint, a gentle
reminder of the world he now inhabited. For some reason, the face of
the priest from San Bernardo filled his thoughts, the ancient shoulders
swaying back and forth, the whispered chant from his weathered lips.
Pearse imagined the old man would have liked it here.

He turned to the bed, and he noticed a monk's robe hanging on the door, evidently the preferred garb even for guests. Perfect, he thought. He would rest for an hour, then go. Better with everyone asleep.

After all, he had to be back by first prayer.

▲

*"O existent in very truth.
O being which beholds the aeons in very truth.
Unseen unto all but me.
Unseen unto all.
Éeema, Éeema, Ayo.
O self-originate that lacks nothing and is free,
I have come to know you and to mix with your immutability.
I have girded myself to dwell in your armor of loveliness and light.
And I have become luminous."*

The boy, no more than sixteen, rose from his knees, trying his best to mask the relief pounding in his chest. It was the last of the prayers he would have to recite on his own. The rest, he knew, he could do in his sleep, *had* been doing in his sleep for the last six months. Preparation on preparation.

Hair parted neatly to one side, he wiped away the few beads of perspiration that had collected on his brow and upper lip. Dressing this morning in his hotel room, he'd assumed the air in the grotto would be cooler, the four floors of solid rock beneath the Ninety-fourth Street armory enough to fend off the heat. No such luck. The thick initiate's robe wasn't helping matters, either.

It just went to show how little an Ohio boy knew about New York summers.

Six others waited with him on the *beama*, the raised platform at the grotto's center, each of their faces illuminated in a billowing light from torches placed along the walls. Several ancient tapestries hung down as well, not even a hint of air to ruffle their faded colors. If the elect were hoping to shroud the ceremony in a kind of medieval patina, they were more than succeeding. The young men stood entranced.

"You have been formed within the orbit of the light," chanted the trio of elect, who stood behind the group of initiates.

"So that in your company I might have life in the peace of the saints," they responded as one.

"And so we welcome you. For the light is within your bosom, an unreproachable light, the sign of the prophets within you."

"O Iesseus-Mazareus-Iessedekeus."

"O Mani Paraclete, prophet of all prophets."

"Eternally existent in very truth."

"Éeema, Éeema, Ayo."

The *princeps*—the highest of the elect—now passed behind each of them, the ritual laying on of hands, a silent prayer. He wore a white cotton shawl pulled up over his head, the rest draping to his knees, a distant cousin of the Jewish tallis in all but the missing Hebrew lettering at the collar. Even the way he manipulated the fringed corners bespoke a connection to an Aaronic past. When he had finished, he kissed each of them on the cheek, followed by the sign of the cross on their foreheads, the sign of the trihedron at their breasts. One by one, the boys stepped down from the *beama* and took their places among the thirty or so men seated in the chamber. The boy returned to his father's side.

No words of congratulations. No recognition of any kind.

When the last of them was seated, the *princeps* removed the shawl from his head and placed it around his shoulders, the face of John Joseph Blaney now revealed to the assemblage. "Let us recall the Primal Aeons," he said; the gathering rose. "The Deep," Blaney began.

"The perfect parent, prior source, and ancestor," they responded.

"Silence."

"The betrothed. Thought, loveliness."

"The Intellect."

"The only-begotten, the parent and source of the entirety."

"Truth."

"The betrothed."

"The Word."

"The parent and source of fullness."

"Life."

"The betrothed."

"The Human Being."

"The Human Being."

"The church."

"The betrothed."

"These are the Primal Aeons. Through them, we bind our wills to Your knowledge; through our knowledge, we are bound to Your will. In the Father of Greatness, who resides in the realm of Light. In the Power of the cosmos, who brings our salvation. In the Wisdom of the ages, who returns us to the wholeness of our church."

"In the Father, the Power and the Wisdom."

Blaney stepped back to a small podium at center. "And let us recall the 'Perfect Light, the True Ascent.'"

As one, the voices began:

> *"It is from the perfect light, the true ascent that I am found in those who seek me.*
> *Acquainted with me, you come to yourselves, wrapped in the light to rise to the aeons.*
> *For I will illumine in your illumination;*
> *I will ascend in your ascension;*
> *I will unite in your union.*
> *It is I who am the riches of the light;*
> *It is I who am the memory of the fullness. . . ."*

The boy continued to chant, his mind wandering as the words flowed freely. For as long as he could remember, he had committed the prayers to memory, the rituals that had prepared him for today, his father as guide. Always in strict isolation, so different from the shallowness of Sunday, when he would watch his father play the role of minister, stand behind his pulpit and preach words that seemed so far from the truth.

As his mind drifted, so, too, did his gaze, faces all around him, many of which he recognized from neighboring towns—Davenport, Kenton, Elmsford—none of which he had ever associated with the private world he and his father had shared.

Until today.

The journey north to the elect. The day of illumination. Entrance into his cell.

Everything would change now. He had been told as much. How, he didn't know. Standing among his brothers, reciting the "Perfect Light," it didn't seem to matter.

Éeema, Éeema, Ayo.

Λ

The fruit was all but gone, the bowl of *loukoumi* licked clean. He'd been hungrier than he'd realized, the confection far better than he'd expected.

Waiting for the last of the paraffin lamps to flicker out, Pearse donned the robe and stepped out into the open-air corridor, a tree-lined atrium three stories below. The sleeves hung a bit too long, though an ideal spot, he discovered, to conceal the notes he had with him. Not that he was anticipating anything, but best to have the pages out of sight should someone appear. Looking to minimize that chance, he kept his lantern dark as he moved past the other cells, the monks either asleep or oblivious to his late-night wanderings.

With one hand flat against the wall, he inched his way back to the stairs, the moon having broken through, making all but the last few steps relatively painless. Once outside the dormitory walls, he found a darkened nook and fired up the lantern, careful to keep it low at his knees. No bonnet, no beard, but at least with the lantern shining out—and not up—he could see where he was going without casting any light on his upper body.

As quickly as he could, he began to retrace his steps through the various alleys and courtyards, one or two cats leaping out at inopportune moments to accelerate an already-lively heartbeat. But no monks. Even so, he found himself moving ever more stealthily, reduced to tiptoes for the last twenty yards or so, the area by the fountain far more exposed than he'd remembered.

Reaching the protective shadow of the great doors, he paused to reorient himself.

The collection of buildings he had seen earlier now appeared to meld into one another, a kind of flattened crescent, the moon offering just enough of a gloss to bring them into focus. Likewise, the water splashed in an ivory white, its lapping reflection trapped within the fountain walls, the area just beyond its reach somehow darker by contrast than the rest of the courtyard. Drawn in by the tranquillity of the scene, he began to feel far more attuned to the design of the monastery. Granted, he had only a small portion of it in front of him, but the discrepancies between Angeli's map and the actual layout seemed to melt away, the spacing far less compact, readable, a growing sense that perhaps he might be able to locate the signposts specified in the scroll. Or maybe it was just faith. Or the fact that the mist had lifted. Either way, he retrieved the pages from his sleeve, glanced at the first few, and set off.

It was remarkable how much she had teased from the text, or rather, how much the Manichaeans had been able to hide within their prayer. Half the notes on Phôtinus detailed landmarks chosen for what was, no doubt, their staying power: bends in the outer wall, ancient pieces of stonework planted deep in the earth, rises and falls in terrain that no amount of building or digging could disrupt. Those things that they knew would endure.

And, of course, as Angeli had promised, the distances between them.

Following the line of the wall to his left, he counted off the prescribed thirty-five paces to an arched hollow directly across from a small olive orchard, just as the notes described. Truth to tell, it had been thirty-one, but given the likelihood that he was a good deal taller than his tenth-century counterpart, Pearse quickly reasoned away the disparity. With that in mind, he shortened his gait, and arrived at the next landmark with extraordinary precision—"time placed in stone"—the first of two sundials situated at opposite ends of a garden at the orchard's center. Both sprouted an assortment of paths, only one of them leading up a short incline. It was the one he was meant to take, out beyond the orchard fence, past a natural spring, to the edge of the monastery's outer wall.

It was there that he met his first setback. For several minutes, he couldn't find a series of steps described as "notches in the great partition." His hands traced the wall face as Pearse became more and more concerned that he was somehow overlooking something. Struggling with a thick matting of overgrown saplings, he finally unearthed the first step, then the second, the rest of them so cleverly imbedded in the wall that had he not known what he was looking for, he would have missed them entirely. Even as he climbed, he needed his hands to feel out each one in front of him, lantern light insufficient to the task. Halfway up, he slowly realized that if not for the steps, he would never have been able to find his way past a group of buildings—thirteenth- or fourteenth-century, by his estimation—situated along the wall. How the Manichaeans had known to avoid what must have been open land back in the tenth century was anybody's guess. He continued to climb.

A gust of wind swept up as he reached the top of the wall, his hand quick to the stone face to steady himself. Momentarily staggered, he found it impossible not to stare out at the horizon, an explosion of stars so vast that he was forced to drop to one knee lest he lose himself over the edge. The Aegean swelled some three hundred feet below, its rhythm in strict counterpoint to the endless array of glitter quivering above. He tried to regain his feet, but his body refused, once again beguiled by the perfect synchrony of light and darkness. For all his doubts—his fears of a Manichaean ascetic—Pearse had, at least, come to appreciate its singular truth, palpable at a moment like this.

As close to heaven as they could get.

The echo of Angeli's voice roused him from his meditation. He forced his eyes back to Phôtinus and spotted the second set of steps just on the other side of the buildings. His body low, he traversed the top of the wall, then made his way down.

A courtyard opened up at the base of the steps. Scampering across it, he came to a bridge no more than ten feet across, a tiny rill below— more rocks than water—its trickle heard, not seen. He checked the notes; there was no bridge mentioned. Evidently, this was a "recent" addition. Instructed to follow the water upstream, he placed his hand on the bridge's stanchion and leapt down the five or so feet before making his way along the sod and mud, careful to keep his lamp high. The footing grew more and more tricky, slick rock causing him to keep one hand almost in the water so as to maintain his balance. Forty yards along, he pulled himself back up the bank.

What had appeared as a collision of trees and stonework from his cell window now opened up as the onetime heart of the monastery, the buildings retreating further and further into the past. And yet, the deeper in he moved, the more he sensed a loneliness from those he passed, too many of them abandoned, remnants from a time when Phôtinus had boasted five hundred monks within its walls. Now it held barely eighty, the rate of apostasy increasing with each year, the malady of "teddy-boyismos," as Nikotheos had called it—the lure of Salonika—having grown to epidemic proportions. The old monks were dying off, the novices fleeing, leaving the buildings to stand empty and alone.

Pearse felt only token sympathy. The fewer monks around, the less likely he might run into one.

All such concerns quickly faded when, at the top of a steep rise, he came face-to-face with a double row of columns, the facade for a cloister peeking out through the gaps.

This time round, he needed no cats to set his heart racing.

"Twin rows of eight will guard the Vault."

Somewhere within those walls waited the parchment.

Staring up at the building as a whole, he quickly understood why the Manichaeans had chosen it for their hiding place. He reckoned it stood almost at the center point of the three outer walls. More than that, it had been designed in such a way that, as far as he could tell, access to it was possible only from the route he had taken. The back and side walls seemed to grow out of the mountain, a half-chiseled sculpture tearing itself from the rock. Only the front colonnade was fully realized, the "twin rows" revealing an archway at the center. Pearse removed the last few sheets from his sleeve and started in.

Four portico walkways flanked a narrow quadrangle to form the interior, a courtyard of dusted earth and wild grass at its center. Unlike anything he had seen up to this point, the cloister clung to a late Roman past, a building that might very well have predated even the Manichaean presence at Phôtinus. Bringing his lantern to eye level— and relying on a suddenly lustrous moon—he followed the line of archways that extended to his left. The stone had softened over the centuries, but the rigid lines of each column could still be seen even in the half-light, the pedestals beneath linked in a continuous low wall. The arcade itself had not faired so well, the flagstones chipped and cracked, clumps of vegetation pushing their way through, odd mounds of dirt scattered throughout, the mark of animal scavenging. Every so often, a window or door would appear along the walled side of the arcade, the rooms within showing equal disrepair, some, though, with hints of long-faded mosaics—a partial crucifix here, the hand of the Virgin there—all shining back at him in the lantern light. From the varying sizes and shapes of the cells, it was clear that the place had once housed a virtually independent community within Phôtinus, far more than just the simple cloister it purported to be.

Further confirmation awaited him at the third corner of the quad-rangle—access to a subterranean level, highly unusual for a cloister of its age. Nestled within a miniature rotunda, he found a set of circular steps leading down. Eighteen of them. The notes were, once again, right on the mark.

Trouble was, it was the last of the detailed entries. The final two "clues" were far more cryptic, abstract phrases, with no directions of any kind. Even on the bus, they had struck him as out of place. "Those who enter may see the light," followed by the equally vague "The one unmoved takes wing." He had recognized the first as a biblical passage, somewhere in Luke his best guess, but pinpointing the source had done little to explain its meaning. The second had baffled him altogether. He had hoped that by now something would have appeared to clarify at least one of them; otherwise, why make the map so specific, only to leave the most crucial bits indecipherable? He was faced with two possibilities: Either the Manichaeans had thought the phrases obvious enough on their own or they had decided to throw in one last bit of "hidden knowledge" to keep things interesting. A touch of the gnosis at the bitter end. Had he been a betting man, Pearse would have opted for the latter, which meant that if he was going to find the parchment, he had to start thinking like a Manichaean.

Reaching the bottom of the steps, he could make out little more than ten feet in either direction, the lantern light only sharpening the vacancy beyond. It was enough, though, to see that the lower level was a virtual carbon copy of the cloister above, save, of course, for the central courtyard, which here had become a mass of solid stone. A pair of corridors branched out from the corner stairwell, the first legs of the quadrangle disappearing into a dusted emptiness. Gone were the sounds of the night that had accompanied him thus far, the absolute quiet matched only by the unrelenting darkness.

Lamp at arm's length, he started down the corridor to his left, his focus on the side walls, uneven rock chiseled from the mountain. From time to time, a rusted torch holder would appear, centuries beyond use, bits of stray iron hanging precariously from eroded pins. As to the cells, they came at regular intervals, six to eight paces between each, tiny hovels drawn of all air, dirt floors beneath. Surprisingly, several of them retained the faint aroma of burned leaves—why, he couldn't explain—instant memories of long-ago bonfires quickly erased by the immediacy of the place. More difficult was determining what most of the rooms had been used for—storage, prayer, perhaps even ritual—bits of mosaics once again scattered throughout. He spent several minutes studying the tiles, hoping to find something that would invite him to "enter" and "see the light," but there was nothing. Only a neat pattern of cells to bring him back to the stairwell, no farther along than when he had set off.

Undaunted, he retraced his steps. When he reached the stairs for a second time, he planted himself against the rock and closed his eyes. The need for a little guidance. Where would they have hidden it? The silence brought him back to the notes. *It's a game for them,* he thought as he stared down at the pages. *So how would they hide the "knowledge"?* For want of anything better to do, he counted out the Syriac letters. Thirty-five. No luck there; the cells had stopped at twenty-two. Evidently, the Manichaeans hadn't placed much stock in numerology. *Look at the words. It has to be in the words.* He continued to stare at the phrase. "Those who enter may see the light." *The light.* He knew it was no metaphor for them, no spiritual allusion, but something tangible, real. Up to this point, he'd assumed "the light" had referred to the parchment. That was real. Enter and find it. Clearly, that wasn't the case. *So what down here contains the light?* He began to wonder if he'd somehow missed a tray of melons along the way.

Frustration began to set in. He tilted his head back against the wall, eyes lost to the void in front of him. For nearly a minute, he stood there, thoughts of the notes slowly supplanted by an uneasy appreciation for the space around him—cold, slick walls, lifeless cells, all part of an ancient cavern left to its own decay, desolate in its entirety. What he had seen only moments before as a piece to the puzzle now took on a far more unsettling reality, one separated from any other living soul by a maze of alleys and walls and streams. Urged on by the profound isolation of the place, those images began to fly through his head in a dizzying array, so overwhelming that he began to lose all hope of retracing his steps. The pounding in his chest accelerated. Instinct snapped his head to the right, the lamp with it, a need to know that the other corridor remained empty. All that stared back was a swirl of dusty air clinging to the lantern light. Beyond it, pure darkness, childhood fears crowding in, lungs tightening, an overpowering desire for light, *real* light, to relieve him of his self-conjured frenzy.

Fighting it, he suddenly experienced a moment of perfect clarity.

"Those who enter may see the light." *The light.*

In that instant, he knew exactly what the phrase meant. The guidance he had sought. It didn't refer to the parchment; it referred to light itself. *Actual* light, to erase the darkness and dispel the fears. Light in its most tangible form, even for a Manichaean.

All he needed to do was find its source.

His heart slowed, the air once again breathable, the glint of possibility holding his panic at bay. Thinking back on the last fifteen minutes, he knew the source wasn't in any of the cells; he'd searched them too well to have missed something that obvious.

Or had he? It suddenly struck him that perhaps the light he was looking for needed complete darkness to make itself known. Any sort of shading would only undermine a Manichaean design, light and darkness understood as polar absolutes. The lantern he had brought with him had marred that purity.

In an act of Manichaean faith, he opened the glass and blew out the flame.

It took him several minutes to accustom his eyes. Oddly enough, he began to feel a kind of comfort within the pitch-black, his body somehow less delimited, unobtrusive, more a part of the rock than an affront to it. No longer defined by the ring of light cast from his lamp, he could almost fade into the darkness, safe in its embrace—a growing respect for the Manichaeans' subtle affinity for the two realms.

When the first hint of light did appear, he thought his eyes were playing tricks on him, not for the light itself, but for its location. Thin lines of white slowly formed along the ceilings of both corridors, threadlike streaks at perfect intervals, as if a hundred spiders had decided to weave one strand each of silk. Impossible to make out above the garish yellow of the lantern, they now glimmered pristine against a blackened backdrop. He moved out toward the first, brushing his fingers along the ceiling, the strip of light matching the topography of his hand. Cupping his fingers toward the side wall, he expected to catch the light in his palm. Instead, the beam disappeared. Only then did he see the light shining on his knuckles. Amazed, he turned toward the solid rock courtyard. The light was coming from in there.

At once, he began to trace his fingers along the topmost edge of the courtyard stone, only to find a pattern of tiny holes hidden within. Each time he covered one, another strand of web disappeared, reborn with the removal of his finger. He'd paid no attention to the giant hunk of rock situated at the center of the four corridors; now, he ignored all else. He lit the lantern and began to examine the fissured stone. Drawing up to within a few inches of the first hole, he discovered something far more provocative.

Etched into the wall was a disjointed collection of Greek letters, most of which lay hidden under a healthy layer of dust. Sweeping the grit away, he saw they combined to form a block of writing; on closer inspection, a verse from the Bible. Ephesians. The armor of God. Like the steps he had discovered in the monastery's outer wall, the letters here had been carved with such ingenuity that they virtually blended into the contours of the rock. His adrenaline started to rise. A few feet down, another verse. This one Old Testament. So it went, around all four sides, no sign, however, of the simple invitation from Luke.

When he realized how stupid he had been, he nearly smacked himself on the head. Of course the verse from Luke wouldn't simply be waiting for him. It, too, would be hidden in the text. Taking his lead from the "Perfect Light," he scanned each of the verses again, this time searching for an acrostic. At the far end of the second wall, he came upon the letters hidden within a passage from Revelation, the irony not lost on him. Once more, he read the inscription from bottom to top:

ινα οιεισπορευομενοι το φως βλεπωσιν.
"Those who enter may see the light."

He pulled back and surveyed the area around the verse. The rock face resembled a tiny mountain range, the cracks in the wall like rivers and streamlets crisscrossing its terrain. Lifting the lantern in a wide arc, he tried to locate some hint of a door in the fissures, but to no avail. *No way through, no way over.* A none-too-distant echo. With little else to go on, he ran his fingers along the lettering, unsure of what exactly it was he hoped to find. He took particular care with the word *light*, pressing against each of its letters as if one of them might miraculously propel him through the solid wall.

He wasn't far off when, pushing at the last, he felt something give way, the miniature ς burrowing deeper into the rock. A moment later, he heard the sound of releasing, an entire section of wall moving perhaps an inch backward, guided by some unseen hinge. Stepping back, he watched as a seemingly unconnected series of cracks—oddly etched beams—joined together to create the outline of a door. A remarkable piece of engineering. Muscling his shoulder into the rock, he pushed his way through.

The sudden spray of light from within—a milky white radiance far purer than anything he had expected—forced him to wince. It seemed to emanate from the walls, an undulating mass of flawlessly smooth stone. Directly in front of him, six steps led down to the floor, which reflected an equal luster, no less luminous than the arched ceiling above, the overall effect that of a cube of light dug deep into the rock. He made his way down, sliding his fingers along a nearby ridge of wall—cold, wet, tacky to the touch. It gave the impression of something primeval, as if it had been culled from the very soul of the mountain. Even when he noticed the real source of light—a group of torches placed at the far end of the sanctum—he continued to marvel at the stone's effect. That the flames implied a recent visit from someone other than himself didn't deter him. Instead, he concentrated on the torches, too dim to be producing the kind of light enveloping the space. Somehow, the walls, the floor, the ceiling were absorbing the torchlight and throwing it back with an added vibrancy.

Even from behind the six tapestries that hung along the four walls.

Putting the geological mystery to the side for the moment, Pearse drew up to the tapestry nearest him. Considerably faded—early medieval, his best guess—it appeared to depict the Ascension of Christ: a lamb asleep in the lower right-hand corner, angels flanking Him on both sides, more of the heavenly host above. Christ blessed them all as He rose, clouds parting before Him, His face and torso far rounder than one might have expected. More curious, He wore the robes of an Old Testament mystic, a book covered with astrological symbols clutched in His right hand.

At first, Pearse attributed the idiosyncrasies to a Byzantine style, but the longer he stared, the more he realized how much of the scene felt incongruous, the usual cast of characters somehow miscast—the Virgin Mother nowhere in sight, the apostles conspicuously absent. Even the way the light radiated from Christ seemed skewed.

It slowly dawned on him why. This was no Ascension, but a Heavenly Ascent. No Christ, but a Manichaean prophet. Enoch, as Pearse now recalled his Apocrypha. Who else would be holding the *Book of Celestial Physics*? He glanced around the chamber. Each of the tapestries wove a similar story of a Seth or an Enosh, the figures virtually indistinguishable from one another. Only one of them stood out—the largest, hung along the back wall, depicting a man twice the size of the rest. Miniature versions of the other prophets stood within his open palms, their tiny auras subsumed within his own brilliance.

Mani, the Paraclete, larger than life.

From his vaunted perch, the Great Prophet stared down on the chamber, gnosis issuing from his every pore in a stream of letters and symbols woven into the cloth, the focus of his attention a raised platform at the center of the room. His gaze seemed to indicate its special importance. Pearse followed Mani's cue and moved toward it.

A series of wooden sculptures, each no more than two feet tall, surrounded the four sides of the pulpit—Byzantine figures carved in narrow ridges, maroon and aqua pigments peeling from their faces and hands. They looked like typical Eastern icons, eyes peering up at the tapestries, each of the little men in a classic pose of humble piety. And yet, there were subtle differences among them—a hand gesture, the tilt of a head—enough to draw Pearse closer. As he moved from one to the next, he realized how much they varied, each one with its own specific identifying mark: an olive branch clasped to the breast, a garland rung about a shaven head, a tiny book held in the right hand. *A book?* At once, he turned back to the tapestries, instantly aware of the connection. Each of the sculptures represented one of the figures on the walls. Like Saint Jerome with his lion, or Saint Catherine with her wheel, the Manichaean prophets defined themselves by their own artistic props.

But whereas six of them hung from above, the grouping around the platform numbered seven. Pearse quickly matched statues with tapestries, the odd one out all too obvious when he finally came to it. Its short hair and lack of a beard had confused him at first. Only when he looked more closely did he see the tiny indentations at the center of each palm. Jesus as prophet. Jesus as one more in a long line leading to Mani. Why He had been denied His Heavenly Ascent remained a mystery. Perhaps to confirm Mani's elevated position. Pearse had no answer. What he did have, though, was far more exhilarating.

Compared to the others in the chamber, Jesus remained earthbound, static. *Unmoved.*

Pearse needed only to help him "take wing."

He placed the lantern on the platform and knelt by the figure. Its robes draped to the ground, a hint of sandal peeking out, enough to reveal a rusted nail driven through the arch. At first, Pearse thought it was merely decorative, a symbol of Christ's final agonies; bending closer in, he realized it was actually bolting the statue to the stone below. He glanced at the other figures; each was managing with a single brace attached to the platform behind. Jesus alone required a separate means of mooring.

Pearse dropped to his chest and began to examine the few inches between the back of the figure and the pulpit. This time, he could find no release mechanism. Pulling himself to his knees, he placed his hands around the statue's waist and gently tried to lift it. The wood groaned from the mild exertion, the stone below shifting ever so slightly. A hint of movement. More than that, he watched as a powder puff of dust rose from behind the robes as he released, caught in an unseen stream of light. He inched over to the side and lifted again, this time his eyes fixed on the stone. *There.* A thin shadow along the back edge seemed to deepen as he pulled, another crack of light. The stone was rising. More dust as he let go. He tried it several times, but the bolt refused to give way, no more than half an inch before it locked the stone in place. He needed something to wedge into the gap, something to force the stone up from below.

He surveyed the chamber. Nothing but tapestries and statues stared back. He glanced over at the torches, each one firmly affixed to the wall by a web of ironwork, thick bands of metal impossible to dislodge.

So what about a rusted one?

Jumping to his feet, he grabbed the lantern and ran to the steps. Two minutes later, he was using the lamp's base to hammer against an eroded pin hanging from one of the corridor walls. A long metal strip dangled at its side, both closer and closer to release with each strike. The sound jarred, its echo a dull thud within the wildly shadowed space, lantern light flying in every direction. With a sudden clang, both pieces fell to the floor. Pearse snatched them up. A minute later, he was maneuvering the long strip into the half-inch opening.

Again he tried to lift. And again the stone refused. He pressed his full weight onto the improvised lever—his arm and chest muscles straining at the effort—bringing the gap to nearly an inch before his body started to shake. With one last surge, he drove down onto the iron wedge, hoping to snap the stone from its bolt, but his knees began to slide out from under him, twisting him to the side. The lever shifted as well, forcing the stone away from him rather than up. To his complete amazement, both continued to move, the stone scraping a few inches across its neighbor before his arms finally gave out.

The bolt, he discovered, had been designed not to keep the statue in place but to act as its pivot. Reaching his fingers into the gap formed by the rotation, he shoved the stone farther, the sound of grinding slate on slate reverberating throughout the chamber. When he had opened up a wide-enough breach, he picked up the lantern and stared into the hollow.

A pit some two feet deep opened up below the statue, more of the luminous stone forming its walls. At its center sat a square metal box perhaps ten inches high, twice that in both length and width. He reached down and pulled it up. It was lighter than he expected. He set it atop the platform and stood, marveling at its simplicity.

A plain box, untouched for nearly a thousand years, more remarkable for what he knew to be inside.

It was almost too much to think of opening it, a kind of ecstatic wonder at the prospect. To this point, he'd been playing a game, prodded by a Manichaean dare, distracted by its ingenuity. Now, all the ciphers, the meanings within meanings, fell away. He stood alone, a single iron latch between himself and an unimagined reality. He didn't think of Angeli's warning, nor of his own desire for clarity. He felt only insignificance, the mountain before him again, a divinity he could revere but never fathom. Paralysis born of faith. He sat, light-headed, the shimmering whiteness of the chamber draining him still further.

He had no idea how long he had been sitting, staring, when a flicker of torchlight snapped him back into focus. He reached for the box, an instant of resolve enough to bring his hand to the latch. More a device to keep the agents of decay at arm's length than to provide additional security, it easily gave way under a bit of pressure. Evidently, anyone who had gotten this far could be trusted with the contents. He lifted the lid, a strange odor wafting out, somehow familiar, though he couldn't quite place it.

More unsettling, though, was what he saw. A small dome of glass rested on a swath of velvet, between them what looked to be a leather-bound codex, no bigger than the size of his hand. A waxlike substance coated the crease where glass met velvet—a sealant of some sort—further protection against the elements. Next to it lay a pile of gold coins, their presence equally jarring. But it was the dome itself that troubled him most, the glass far too pure to have come from the hand of a tenth-century artisan, its craftsmanship that of the fifteenth or sixteenth century. All sense of wonder quickly faded; he dislodged the glass from the strip and picked up the codex. Flipping it over several times, he realized it, too, belonged to a different age. In fact, it was no codex at all, but a prebound book, the style of binding mid-Renaissance, the texture of the paper—when he finally opened it—confirmation of the dating.

The final slap was the language. Latin. Angeli had promised Greek. Where was the parchment they had gone to such lengths to protect? *Where?* And what had someone left in its place? His frustration and disappointment began to boil to the surface.

"I don't suspect you'll find much on Ambrose down here."

The sound of the voice bolted Pearse to his feet, all traces of anger quickly lost to the momentary shock. He spun toward the door.

There, peering down at him from the steps, stood Brother Nikotheos, a small revolver in his hand.

⚠

The monk waited. He set his lantern on the top step and slowly made his way toward the platform.

"A monk with a gun," he said. "That doesn't look right, does it?" Pearse remained stock-still as Nikotheos spoke. "Then again, neither does your being down here. I can explain the first. The second . . ." He let the phrase trail off as he drew closer. "How did you find your way into this place?"

Pearse watched as Nikotheos caught sight of the box, then the pit, his sudden surprise all too obvious. A moment of confusion. And yet, he had shown none of it while moving through the chamber, no hesitation with the tapestries or statues. Only with the hidden cache. Which meant he had been here before. Felt comfortable here. And that could mean only one thing.

Once again, Pearse would have to think like a Manichaean.

Stifling the pounding in his chest, he tried to recall the words from the prophetic letters, the "signs of reception." He knew they were his only recourse. Placing the book on the pulpit and, eyes ever on the monk's, he slowly began to speak in Greek: "In the salutation of peace, I extend myself to you. In the radiance of light, I call you brother." He held out his right hand, palm turned to the ground.

For what seemed an eternity, Nikotheos said nothing. He looked down at the outstretched hand, then at Pearse, a slight narrowing of his eyes. In that moment, Pearse thought he had miscalculated entirely, the man in front of him no part of the Manichaeans. He half-expected him to press the gun closer; instead, he watched as the monk slowly let it drop to his side. A moment later, he was extending his hand, placing it on top of Pearse's. When he finally spoke, his words were barely a whisper: "For the light is within your bosom, an unreproachable light, the sign of the prophets within you."

Heard aloud, the phrase momentarily stunned Pearse, a thousand-year-old legacy come to life. Quickly recovering, he replied, "O Iesseus-Mazareus-Iessedekeus."

"O Mani Paraclete, prophet of all prophets."

"Eternally existent in very truth."

"Éeema, Éeema, Ayo."

The two men stared at each other, Pearse now unsure how to render the words he had read into action. He had no cause to worry, as the monk immediately released his hand and stepped toward him. Kissing Pearse on both cheeks, Nikotheos made the sign of the cross on his forehead—two fingers and thumb, in strict Orthodox fashion—followed by the tracing of what looked to be a triangle over his heart. *That's what that meant*, Pearse thought to himself. It had been the one part in the letters he hadn't understood. Pearse repeated the gestures, then both men embraced.

As Nikotheos pulled away, he said, "Be received into our community."

Pearse nodded once, eager to keep his responses to a minimum. A ritual of greeting was one thing; an entire canon of belief was another. The monk appeared to be thinking the same thing, his expression that of a man not yet fully convinced.

"It's been a long time since I've spoken those words," he began, the gun—albeit at his side—in plain view. "You're the first from an outside cell to come to the mountain in many years."

"Yes," answered Pearse

"And the first unannounced."

Again he nodded. Clearly, it would take more than a few memorized lines to quell the lingering doubts. However much he wanted to guard against anything that might expose him, Pearse knew he had to engage the monk, gain his trust. More than that, he recognized the opportunity that now presented itself. Here was a modern-day Manichaean, a man with insights into a world of which Pearse had only begun to scrape the surface. He had to make the most of it.

"None of them was allowed inside this chamber, though," Nikotheos added, the suspicion growing in his eyes. "None of them even knew of it. And yet, here you are. Without anyone to show you the way."

A telling admission, thought Pearse. The Manichaeans on the mountain kept their Vault hidden, even from their own, despite the fact that they had no idea what it held. Nikotheos's reaction to the pit had said as much.

"It's what I was sent to find," Pearse answered. "The Vault of the Paraclete." He expected the added detail to put the monk's mind at ease.

Instead, Nikotheos's eyes went wide. It was several moments before he responded. "How did you know that?" he asked, his tone far more pointed than only moments before.

"Know what?"

"The name. How did you know the name?"

The response puzzled Pearse. "I don't understand."

"The Vault of the Paraclete. Only those of us of Phôtinus know that name. It's been ours to protect for a thousand years. Yet, somehow you know it." Nikotheos tightened his grip on the revolver. "You find the Vault. You know its name. And you come from the outside. How is that possible?"

Pearse stood motionless. He slowly realized what he had unearthed— the final line of defense between parchment and pursuer. None but the monks knew of the chamber's name; and they knew nothing of what they protected. The ideal security system, one set up in such a way that should anyone ever have come across a reference to Athos or Phôtinus in his search for the parchment, his reward upon reaching the mountain would have been blank stares from the monks. "Parchment? We know of no parchment." Were that person to have mentioned the Vault, he would no doubt have met a far more unpleasant fate. Even now, Pearse couldn't be sure just how reluctant Nikotheos was to use the revolver. He imagined that the one thing holding the monk back was the fact that his captor was inside the Vault and not asking to be shown to it.

Pearse had little choice but to up the stakes. "Then there must be another source."

Again the monk's eyes narrowed, the suggestion even more perplexing. "Another— That's impossible. No one else knows of it. No one else *could* have known of it. Not even the *summus princeps*."

Not yet willing to dive into whatever the *"summus princeps"* might be, Pearse knew he needed to make the most of the monk's confusion. As casually as he could, he asked, "Do you know why you keep these torches lit all the time?"

The question had the desired effect. "Why we . . . What are you asking me? What other source?"

"Do you know why?" Pearse repeated.

Again, the monk hesitated. "We keep the name hidden, the torches lit."

"And yet you've never asked why?"

"Why?" His frustration mounted. "There was no reason to ask. We protect the eternal flame for Mani. What other source?"

Pearse let his eyes wander to the walls and tapestries. "It was so I could find this place," he said, his tone now almost inviting. He turned and looked directly at Nikotheos. "You've kept the torches lit so that the 'Perfect Light' could lead me here."

"What?" His reply was barely audible. "The 'Perfect Light'?"

"The other source." Pearse paused. He had to see how much the monk knew of the scroll. "Do you understand now?"

Nikotheos stared back, confusion slowly giving way to a moment of profound realization. "The scroll?" he asked in whispered disbelief. "You have the *scroll*?" The significance of what he had said only now struck him. "And it brought you here." His eyes grew wider still. "The 'Hagia

Hodoporia' is here." Pearse watched as the monk's gaze tracked the discovery from pit to box to glass to leather-bound book. His puzzlement returned. "That . . . can't be. The 'Hodoporia,' it's supposed to be—"

"Much older," Pearse cut in. "Yes. I know."

Hagia Hodoporia, he thought. *Holy Journey*. The treasure hidden away for almost a millennium. In two words, Nikotheos had confirmed not only his familiarity with the hidden knowledge of the "Perfect Light"—something evidently not restricted to the Roman Manichaeans alone—but also his complete trust in Pearse; who other than someone of the highest order could know of such things? The former explained away all the "impossibilities"; the latter gave Pearse the freedom to delve deeper.

"So you have it?" the monk prodded. "The written text of the 'Perfect Light'?" A moment later, he was looking around the Vault in childlike wonder, as if he'd forgotten Pearse entirely. "The 'Hodoporia' was here all along. And we never knew it."

"Yes," said Pearse.

The monk's eyes caught on the tapestry of Mani, a giddiness now in his voice. "You know, you grow up hearing the stories, all about how the scroll was hidden away from our enemies. Hidden so well that it became lost even to us. Or stolen. Or destroyed. The myth of the 'Perfect Light.' Mani's will, I suppose." He turned back to Pearse. "And you believe one day a man will find it, unearth its mysteries, and discover the path to the 'Hagia Hodoporia.' The stuff of adolescent fantasies." His smile broadened. "And yet, here you are. That one man." A genuine admiration animated his face. "Tell me, when did you find it? The scroll, I mean."

Pearse waited. "A few weeks ago. We needed time to decipher it."

"Naturally." The monk suddenly realized he was still holding the gun. He quickly placed it in the pocket of his robes. "You understand the precaution." He now sat back on the edge of the pulpit. "Had we been told, we could have helped—"

"It was best this way."

"Of course." He nodded, a newfound deference in his tone, even in the way he held himself. Pearse realized that if nothing else, a Manichaean knew his place in the hierarchy. Nikotheos truly believed that the man who had discovered the lost scroll—and who now had access to the "Hodoporia"—had come from the very highest echelons of the church; he thus warranted a considerable respect. Pearse had no intention of convincing him otherwise. Somewhere in the back of his mind, he recalled

John J.'s simple words of advice to a newly ordained priest, a young man uncomfortable with the pressures of the confessional: *Plant the seeds, Ian. Give them the room to unburden themselves. And listen.* Strange how appropriate they seemed in so incongruous a setting.

"The *summus princeps* made the decision," said Pearse, testing the waters.

"Of course." The monk nodded. "He's always been fascinated with the 'Hodoporia.'"

He, thought Pearse. A who, not a what. An invitation for more probing. "You can understand why he wanted to handle everything as discreetly as possible. Especially," he added, not sure what he hoped to hear in response, "given the events of the last few days."

"The cardinal has always been a cautious man," answered the monk.

Pearse tried to mask the astonishment in his eyes. *The cardinal.* Had Nikotheos just confirmed von Neurath's involvement? Pearse had no choice but to press further. "Nothing," he continued, "not even the 'Hodoporia,' can be allowed to get in the way of the election."

"I understand." Again the monk nodded. "Imagine it. With the 'Hodoporia,' he'll be able to use Rome as no one ever has. It will expedite everything."

Again, Pearse had to stifle his reaction. *Use Rome.* What else could Nikotheos mean but von Neurath on the papal throne? And expedite what? A Manichaean in the Vatican . . . the catalyst for the "one true and holy Christian church"?

Before Pearse could respond, the monk's eyes flashed with a sudden insight. "Or is it the other way around?" This time, he waited for Pearse; when no answer came, he continued. "The cells were alerted *because* he anticipated the recovery of the 'Hodoporia'? Which would mean"—he let the thought sit for a moment—"that the vacancy in Rome wasn't simply good fortune?"

The cells . . . alerted. Pearse knew he had to tread carefully; even so, the implications of what Nikotheos was saying demanded greater clarification. "The 'Hodoporia' and the great awakening go hand in hand," said Pearse. "The cells must be ready to act."

"'The church will be one and His name one,'" intoned the monk, as if reciting a well-practiced verse of prayer. Before Pearse could dig deeper, the monk added, "But this isn't the 'Hodoporia,' is it?"

No matter how eager he might have been to learn more about the cells, Pearse knew he had no choice but to follow Nikotheos's lead. The monk probably knew little of what was to happen beyond his own cell. A handful of monks on a strip of mountain weren't going to play too large a role in the "great awakening." Even so, Pearse couldn't help but regret the lost opportunity. "Not from what I've seen," he answered. "No."

"Then what is it?"

It was a question he hadn't had time to ask himself. "Another piece in the puzzle?" he mused.

Nikotheos nodded. "Still, I'm sure he'll be eager to hear about it."

"Yes."

For the first time, the monk seemed to relax, the night's excitement obviously having taken its toll. Stepping away from the pulpit, he said, "You can call after first prayer if you like."

"Call?" This time, Pearse's surprise got the better of him.

"It's not all paraffin lamps and outdoor plumbing these days," he countered, now beginning to make his way to the door.

Pearse did his best at a smile. "Of course." To his great relief, Nikotheos had misunderstood his reaction.

"We have a telephone, a fax machine." He pointed up at the steps. "Even something in the door. We installed it after the Great Lavra incident." He stopped and looked back over his shoulder. "You were the first to set it off. It was how I knew you were here."

Pearse nodded. As much as he wanted to hear the voice on the other end of the line, he knew contact with Rome was out of the question. It might confirm von Neurath's role, but it meant serving himself up. Without the 'Hodoporia,' he still had no leverage, nothing to force their hand. "I need some time to study this," he said, picking up the book and easing it into his pocket. "Before I make that call."

"Of course." Nikotheos had reached the top step.

Pearse bent over and slid the stone back into place. Jesus was once more in line with the other prophets. The monk, meanwhile, gazed out at the Vault, a newfound appreciation etched across his face. "The 'Hagia Hodoporia,'" he mused. "Who'd have thought it?" Pearse retrieved the glass, the velvet, and the box, then joined him at the top of the stairs. He, too, took one last glance.

Not surprisingly, his gaze came to rest on the larger-than-life figure of Mani. No doubt due to his own exhaustion, Pearse thought he saw a momentary glint of concern cross the Great Prophet's eyes.

Maybe he had more leverage than he realized.

▲

Giacomo Cardinal Peretti pored through the diaries, every thought—personal and papal—inscribed within their pages. Boniface had kept meticulous journals, all locked away in the bureau by his bed, unknown to all but his closest allies. That Peretti had removed the only key from around his lifeless neck, then borrowed the last three volumes—June through August—had gone unnoticed by the security men. It would be days before any of them would think to go through the late Pope's personal effects.

Now, sitting alone in his own rooms—his accustomed bedtime long past—Peretti sifted through the minutiae with tremendous care. Little in the first volume had drawn his special attention: a draft version of an encyclical on faith, lengthy diatribes on the continuing abuses in Kosovo, growing concerns about von Neurath's ambition. At the end of the second, however, each entry began to include several lines on something far beyond the daily tasks of office, sentences replaced by bullet points. Peretti read:

July 9: Istanbul discovery still too speculative. Documentation sparse. Islamic text? (Ruini convinced early Gnostic.) Language source uncertain. Some form of Coptic, Aramaic? R concerned by Kleist arrival. (K → von N??)

July 13: Source Syriac. Ruini not familiar with language. Second part Greek (letters??). Old Testament references → Apocrypha? Imagery unusual. Prophetic journeys (Seth as prophet??). Syriac text given to Professor Alihodja (Dept. of Coptic studies). R working with letters.

July 19: Partial translation → Secret Book of John. (Seth, Enoch not part of Gnostic tradition → misattribution??) 3rd or 4th c. Letters through 10th (????).

July 22: Gnostic text only as introduction. Ruini insists "Perfect Light" (???) (fifteen versions, variations). Alihodja unfamiliar with "PL" (all the better). R looking for textual indicators → language still problematic.

July 26: Ruini has text. Alihodja unreachable (???). Thinks has link with Athos (Orthodox???). "Vault of the Paraclete" (???). Return Rome tomorrow.

July 30: If Athos, Ruini speculating something 1st c. (time frame, scope). → If so, why Kleist → von N interested? Ruini no answers yet. Sudden news of Alihodja heart attack. (foul play???) R convinced.

August 5: Sebastiano dead, as well. Only myself to blame. No sign of text. What is on Athos?? And where??

The last entry ended with a prayer for Ruini, a personal recrimination for not having seen the obvious dangers, and one last question:

Von N → "Perfect Light" → Athos: Is what connects them worth killing for?

Peretti closed the book. His friend's death two days later was answer enough.

A Manichaean prayer and Athos. What was von Neurath up to?

▲

He had waited ten minutes in his cell, time enough to be sure that Nikotheos wasn't still lurking about. Keeping the robe and bonnet on, Pearse had then made his way back to the great doors, along the open bluff, through the wooded trails, before coming to the ancient Ford. Three in the morning. Another hour to matins. Enough time to get him off the mountain.

What had taken Gennadios fifteen minutes took Pearse forty, the road to Daphne no less treacherous on the return trip. With the first hints of dawn—a gray matted backdrop as yet unwilling to cede the day to the sun—so, too, came the first boats out of the harbor. Dressed in monk's habit, Pearse had little trouble securing a ride to Ouranopolis, the backpack accepted with a curious look from his still-groggy captain. A gift from a recent visitor, Pearse explained. God's will that he put it to use. The man shrugged, then pulled the boat out into the Aegean. Oranges, not God's will, were his concern this morning.

Ten minutes into the ride, the drone of the engine gave way to the echo of the *simandron*—the long wooden beams used for calling the monks to prayer—each with its own particular timbre, deep, resonant tones of muted whale song bouncing off the scarps of the mountain. Last night, their music might have drawn him in, heightened his sense of reverence; now, they only reminded him of the hunt.

Another ten minutes and the din began to fade as the first sign of sun peeked through from above the tower at Ouranopolis, the hamlet already alive, boats busy with early-morning cargo for the mountain. A lone monk easily slipped through the swirl of movement, the narrow street where Andrakos had left the car still hidden under predawn shadow. Pearse quickly removed the robe and bonnet, tossed them onto the backseat, and fired up the engine. Within minutes, he was back on the highway.

The question was, To where? Igoumenitsa, Athens, and Salonika were no longer possibilities; the news from Phôtinus would no doubt send the Vatican men to all three, and far quicker than Pearse would be able to get to any of them. More than that, he knew Nikotheos would waste little time in alerting the Greek police to the disappearance of one of the monastery's most valuable manuscripts. Not to mention the issue of Andrakos's stolen car. Given the time limitations, and the nature of the various border options, Pearse decided on Bulgaria, his best bet Kulata— according to the map in the glove compartment—an hour and ten minutes if the roads were kind. He had to hope Nikotheos had waited until *after* matins before checking on his guest.

As Athos slipped farther and farther into the distance, the Holy Mother seemed more than content to remain by his side, her watchful gaze keeping the roads all but empty, no trace of police during the seventy-five-minute hurtle through the Greek countryside. She was equally kind at the border, a shift in guards—men impatient to get home—a priest's collar and Vatican papers once again sufficient to grease the wheels. Ten minutes from the small outpost, he pulled the car over and exhaled, trying his best to focus on what to do next.

It was only then that he realized he had no idea where he was meant to go. Everything since San Clemente had propelled him along without much time to think, one task to the next, a small leather-bound book having replaced the scroll. Aside from that, though, he had to admit he was no further along than when he had left Rome. Granted, there was the confirmation from Nikotheos as to von Neurath's role, the hint of something to be "expedited," "cells" in the waiting—hardly enough, though, to bring the diverse pieces together.

Settling on what he did have, he reached for the backpack and pulled out the leather-bound book.

The first page revealed the now-familiar Manichaean greeting, this time in Latin. Though six centuries removed from the last of the "Perfect Light" letters—the date, "April 28, 1521," scribbled at the top—the "signs of reception" remained identical in form and meaning. New to the layout, however, was a small triangle—one half of it darkened, the other half empty—occupying the top right-hand corner of the page. As with the odor from the box, it momentarily registered with Pearse. But he was too caught up in the text below to give it much thought.

There, in a stylized Latin, read the tale of one Ignacio de Ribadeneyra:

For those who have happened upon this book in an act of plunder and sacrilege, let me assure you that you will find nothing in these pages to rouse your interests. Take the gold pieces I have left you as ransom. Leave the book unharmed as your first act of contrition.

For those, however, who have come to this through the "Perfect Light," do not let anger win the better part of your soul. Rather, accept from me, Ignacio de Ribadeneyra, a poor brother of the monastery of Sanctus Paulus, the deepest apology at your disappointment. You have only to recall the ravages of the day, the great schism wrought by an heretical priest, and you will understand the choice I have made to conceal the "Hagia Hodoporia" far from the walls of Phôtinus. If I am ajudged to have acted with recklessness or with fear, know that my decision was dictated by the strictest faith and guided by the hand of Mani.

My journey to the "Hodoporia" began in the second year of the reign of Giuliano della Rovere, known to Christendom as Julius II. My place within the world at that time was to the north of the great city of Valladolid, a gathering of monks of the Hieronymite order, ever vigilant in our work for the Savior. To those who ventured into our abbey, we were healers of the sick, devoted to the word of Rome, and constant in our Catholic faith. To ourselves, we were minions of the Great Prophet, men who awaited the signs of the great awakening.

It was in the winter of 1504 that I reached my sixteenth year. Having completed nine arduous seasons of study in the ways of the Living Gospel, *I was told that I should make the great journey, that my future was to be found in the search for the lost scroll. None from my poor monastery had ever been so chosen. Why such an honor fell to me, I do not know. Nor have I found an answer in these past twenty years. Quick of mind and eager of spirit, I know that it was the will of Mani alone that ensured my success, nothing else.*

With much anticipation, I set off from Palencia for the palace of Cardinal Vobonte, a man of considerable power at the court of the French king, and a brother devoted to the restoration of the scroll. I toiled for many months under his tutelage, schooled in the history of the scroll, and made privy to the wonders of the "Hodoporia." My mentor was a man of unending compassion, purity of heart, although his devotion to the scroll did at times overwhelm me, so fervent was his commitment. It was not long, however, before I began to share his great zeal, once again Mani's will that I should excel, my training quickly absorbed. With the last snow of the season freshly packed on the ground, I set out from Paris.

Would that I had carried my devotion as far as its gates. Would that I had been resolute. How might the world be changed now. But it was not to be. I was a boy of sixteen, unaware that I should not see France, nor my beloved Spain, for nearly twenty years. Perhaps, as I write now, ever again. It is, I know, just punishment for the life I have led.

Such is the price of weakness.

The first years of my journey came and went with a speed I cannot now fathom, lost in a haze of indulgence, for which I remain in constant struggle to atone. First to Lyons, then Milan, Bremen, all the while convinced that I was seeking out long-lost traces of the letters from the scroll; instead, I was steeping myself in the depravity of the age. For seventeen years, I let the world of darkness seduce me, not in wines and meats, nor in things of the flesh, but in a different kind of self-delusion, my soul profligate in its duty to the light. Like Augustine before me, I was too young or too prideful for the demands of such a journey; my faith was strong, but my head swam with questions, my place and purpose in the world undetermined. Was the scroll, its meaning, to be my own redemption? So much clouded my mind, a wave of indecision that forced me into a world I was perhaps too simple to understand. My love of God, my faith in Mani, though ever present, did not hold me to the task I had been set. A test of will? I cannot say. If so, I was tested, and I failed.

How often I wished that I had but copied a few lines from the Living Gospel, *taken with me the words of Mani to temper my own will. Then, perhaps, I might have curbed my distraction. (Or is that merely my pride speaking once again?) But to carry such things was too dangerous, the deception of the good Catholic never to be placed at risk. It was a role I learned to play all too well, my own corruption no exception within the world of the debauched popish church.*

And so unto this wanton life befell the ravages of the times of which I have spoken, and which, even now, consume the better part of the Christian world. When that heretic priest arose, I should have taken it as a sign to shake myself from my torpor, to seize the chance and redeem myself in the eyes of Mani. But I did not. Instead, I took this Luther to be a Brother of the Light, his contempt for Rome proof of his convictions. I convinced myself that he had found the "Hodoporia," for what else could so shake the gates of the ecclesia impura? *Surely his words at Wittenberg had been a prelude to the great awakening. Surely it was all evidence of the Great Hand of Mani. Once again, I was self-deceived. This Luther was no brother, his message one of division, not unity.*

How rife the world was for such upheaval. How perfect the time for the "Hodoporia" to assert its will. How miserable my own existence.

At last awakened from my slumber, I only compounded my iniquity. Like Jonah to Tarshish, I ran further from my duty, now to the East and the city of the Turks. Can I say that I knew I would find the scroll within its walls? I must confess, I cannot. I ran to Constantinople to bury myself in a world unknown. Yet even in my own depravity, Mani guided my steps. Even in my humanity, He allowed me to find the seeds of my salvation.

The story of my redemption is one of Mani's power. . . .

Pearse flipped through the next few pages—Ribadeneyra's own version of *Confessions*—his salvation, in keeping with Augustine's, at the age of thirty-three while sitting in a garden in Istanbul. But whereas Augustine had succumbed to the flesh—"give me chastity, and give me constancy, but do not give it me yet"—Ribadeneyra had fought a far less tangible enemy: his own self-doubt.

Pearse wondered if such uncertainty ran like a common thread through all those who sought the scroll. His own affinity for the Hieronymite monk grew with each page.

And yet, he couldn't help but ask just how seriously he was meant to take it all. The phrase "Take it and read" gave way to the equally inspiring, though now familiar, "Those who enter may see the light." Clearly, Ribadeneyra had chosen the phrase after having seen the scroll and deciphering its message. Still, it made for compelling narrative. Even more absorbing were the tales of midnight jaunts to abandoned churches, secret messages delivered by Orthodox priests, a vision of Mani himself appearing to set the wayward brother on his proper course—all of it ultimately leading the monk to "enter" an eleventh-century church, the scroll hidden within one of its long-forgotten crypts. Soon thereafter, the decoding of the text, the connection to Phôtinus, the Vault of the Paraclete. Piety rewarded. Certainty reclaimed.

Pearse could only hope for such results.

On unearthing the "Hodoporia," however, and on reading its contents, Ribadeneyra had made the momentous decision that the brothers of Mani, and the world in general, were not yet ready to confront its power. His certainty had evidently brought with it a residual serving of pride.

How much of the Pure Tongue flies through these pages. How simple the words, their source undeniable. Yet their power demands too much of us, their truth too great a threat. Are such thoughts a blasphemy? Perhaps. But a blasphemy we cannot confront in this age. Too much now conspires against the "Hodoporia" to unleash its power. Too much would be lost in the frantic swirl of heresies that abound. And if not lost, then abused in aid of this Luther, thus sealing the fate of Mani's return. No. The "Hodoporia" must appear when all is at peace, when the papal church once again grows well pleased with itself and is not armed against its enemies. (How I regret the chance I let pass. How long I shall live with the shame.) Then shall the "Hodoporia" assert its power, and thus make a place for the fullness of the light.

It was here that Ribadeneyra offered his truest indication of faith. Or perhaps the only rationale for his own inaction:

But it is for Mani alone to decide when that time shall come. He alone shall know when the "Hodoporia" shall be revealed.

Now certain he was acting in the best interests of all Manichaeans, Ribadeneyra had returned to Istanbul, reinterred the scroll (for the one "worthy enough to accept the task"), and concocted another bit of gnosis, so that, "centuries from now," another might discover it—Ruini, as it turned out—and "unmask the path to the Holy Truth." Mani would keep the scroll well hidden; Ribadeneyra would handle the "Hodoporia."

Pearse turned to the next page for the first installment of the monk's "hidden knowledge."

There is a town on the Drina. . . .

The Drina River. Bosnia. Pearse's eyes shot to the top of the page. The small triangle.

And he remembered.

▲

Half an hour from the Bulgarian border, he'd crossed into Macedonia, now three hours ago, each passing mile a nod to the Holy Mother's continuing generosity. Or perhaps to the ancient animosities between the Greeks and their neighbors to the north. Whichever it was, he was counting on that lack of communication to delay any alerts out of Athos. Still, he couldn't expect to sustain his run of good luck at the border posts. Ill feelings notwithstanding, there'd been too much time since his hasty departure from the mountain. The collar would soon lose its charm.

Unless, of course, the border he intended to cross lay in shambles. With one eye on the map, the other on the road, he knew he had only one choice: Kosovo. Over a year ago, the refugees had been pouring out, thousands of them crammed into camps littered along the Albanian and Macedonian borders. But there had been too many of them, thousands more shipped off to Turkey, Armenia, Greece—wherever friends or relatives had been willing to house them. Now, those same refugees wanted back in. Trouble was, there was no place to put them, entire villages buried under rubble. More than that, the Serbs weren't exactly encouraging them to reclaim their homes; mines were once again springing up all over the place. Still, the refugees came. And with them, a rebirth of the camps. Not that the rest of the world was taking much notice. That was last year's news. The horror of the camps, however, remained the same.

Callous as it might sound, Pearse knew that a priest on a relief mission could easily get lost in one of them. Or at least be deemed lunatic enough to be let through without too many questions. He was banking on the latter. More to the point, Kosovo would be the easiest place to disappear once Nikotheos's call went through to Rome. Mention of the "Hodoporia" would no doubt kick the Austrian and his cronies into high gear. Even if they should find the car—which he planned to abandon a few miles from the border—the chances of locating him within the mayhem were slim at best. Somehow, he would find his way to the Drina.

Where along the river, however, was another question entirely. The latest Manichaean word game had nothing to do with acrostics as far as he could tell; this time, the gnosis lay hidden in what Ribadeneyra had described as "language alchemically transformed." His explanation had done little to clarify:

Everything has not only one virtue but many, just as a flower has more than one color, and each color has in itself the most diverse hues; and yet they constitute a unity, one thing.

Still mulling over the sixteenth-century instructions, Pearse pulled into the "last petrol in Macedonia." He'd expected to see some signs of life this close to Kosovo; instead, the road had become empty, the last half hour driven in complete isolation.

And yet, the solitude shouldn't have come as such a surprise. During his first pit stop some eighty miles back—what had passed for a gas station, shack and seedy little pump—he'd been told that, this time, the UN was trying to keep the refugee camps to a minimum—Senokos and Cegrane to the south of the capital, Blace to the north. Those not involved had no desire to get too close.

The mayhem was at Blace—twelve kilometers on, according to the sign at the rest stop. On foot, Pearse knew, he could be there in a few hours.

The rest stop had clearly been designed for the onetime bus tours destined for the St. Nikita monastery, its minimalist cafeteria—glass as its walls—nestled into an opening in the trees. The pump here was pristine compared to the first he had seen, the name of the gas something unpronounceable, accents and consonants in the vast majority. Pearse pulled around to the back, grabbed the pack, and headed for the building. He left the keys in the ignition. If someone wanted the car, they were more than welcome to it. Let the men from the Vatican chase after an opportunistic refugee.

Inside, the place was equally bare, save for a man and woman at one of the far tables, both under a cloud of cigarette smoke. At the first sign of Pearse, the man jumped to his feet.

"Dobro utro." He beamed as he made his way across. A few more incomprehensible words, then a hand indicating the tables.

Pearse shook his head, and smiled, the international sign for "I have no idea what you're saying."

No less genially, the man continued. "How am I helping with you?" A nod. "You make to understand?"

Pearse returned the nod and said, "Telephone?" Immediately, he saw the disappointment in the man's face. "And food," he added, the man's expression at once brighter. Pearse then pulled out a few of the American bills. The man's face again beamed.

"Telephone. Food. Excellent."

Two minutes later, Pearse was doing his best with the operator. Eight minutes after that, he was being pulled away from a plate of something utterly unrecognizable, though surprisingly tasty, his call having gone through.

Professor Angeli's voice was a welcome relief. It took him no time to bring her up to speed on Phôtinus and the little bound book.

"Yes, but where are you?" she asked.

Pearse hesitated. "Probably best if you don't know that."

A pause on the other end of the line. "I see." When he didn't answer, she admitted, "I suppose you're right." He could sense her unease, the reality of his situation—and her own reacquaintance with it—a bit too much. "All right. . . . You say it's from a Spanish monk. Coded language. What did he call it?"

"'Language alchemically transformed,'" answered Pearse.

"No, no. The other phrase. The one from Pliny."

"Oh." Pearse turned to the page, quickly skimming through several passages. "'*Quaestio lusoria*,'" he read.

"Yes. '*Quaestio lusoria*,'" she repeated. Clearly, his warning had unnerved her more than he realized; her tone remained distant. More than that, it wasn't like her to need any kind of reminder when it came to the world of esoterica. "I might have a book on that. Hold on for a second." Pearse listened to the sound of her receding footsteps, followed by almost a minute of silence. When she picked up again, she seemed no less edgy. "Carlo Pescatore," she said. "*The Art of Renaissance Wordplay*. I knew I had it somewhere." He could hear her scanning the pages, the usual hum conspicuously absent. "Yes. Here it is," she began. "According to Signore Pescatore, a *quaestio lusoria* was a kind of puzzle. . . ." Another flip of a page. "Primarily the domain of poets. Steeped in classical references." She stopped, the first hint of the old Angeli creeping though when she continued. "Now that's interesting. He says it could be considered the great-grandfather of the modern cryptic." A few more flipped pages before she said, "You've always been very good at these. Like that Greek poem with Ambrose, remember?"

"Sure."

"Well, it's similar to that," she explained. "Except with this, it's more about anagrams and word reconfigurations, not just transpositions. That sort of thing."

"Sounds like fun."

"Good. Because, in some form or another, I believe that's what Señor Ribadeneyra has given you. It ties in perfectly with the Manichaeans. Meaning hidden within language." Again a pause. "How many entries are there?"

Pearse counted out the lines of text. "About twenty-five."

"I see." Again, a pause. "Might be a bit tricky in Latin. If you want, you could . . . read them to me over the phone. I'm not so bad with these things myself."

Pearse hadn't heard the request; he was already trying his hand at the first entry. It took him a moment to adjust his thinking. As he read, he began to see what she was talking about. On its own, the phrase made no sense whatsoever. Reading it as a cryptic—a bit of repunctuation here and there—he saw at once what Ribadeneyra was after. *He wants an anagram of a word that means "He that walks in battle,"* Pearse thought. He continued to stare. "He that walks in battle." Something so familiar to it, hours and hours of Catholic school and seminary Greek and Latin swimming in his head. His "gift" as he'd so often been told. He closed his eyes. "He that walks in battle." A moment later, he had the answer. Gradivus. From the *Aeneid*—the epithet of Mars. He quickly jotted down the letters on his palm. He read the rest of the clue. "Who turns the seventh to a fifth." *The seventh.* He let his eyes drift. *A musical seventh? The seventh Commandment?* He stared back at the word. *Or is it easier than that?* His eye stopped on the *u. The seventh letter?* "Turns . . . to a fifth." *The fifth letter of the alphabet?* With nothing else to go on, he replaced the *u* with an *e.* An anagram of Gradives. He then wrote the letters in a circle, the surest way to work out an anagram. Ten seconds later, he had the answer.

Visegrad.

"There is a town on the Drina. . . ."

At the same moment, Angeli broke through on the line. "Father?" Again, a pause. "Hello? Why don't you read me the first one?"

He was about to answer, then stopped. To this point, he'd attributed her hesitation to a concern for him. Now, something in her voice told him otherwise. "Is something wrong, Professor?"

"No." Her response seemed devoid of any emotion. "Nothing." Before he could answer, Angeli screamed into the phone. "Destroy the book! Destroy it! They—"

A momentary clattering on the other end, followed by silence, then the sound of another voice on the line. "Listen carefully, Father." It was a man, the accent familiar. The Austrian. "Find the 'Hodoporia.' Bring it to us. Do you understand?"

The line disengaged.

Λ

Pearse walked to Blace in a daze, the couple from the rest stop having insisted he take something strong to drink before setting out. Language aside, they had seen enough in his expression to know what he needed.

Rakija, homegrown brandy. Though far more lethal than the stuff Andrakos had served him, it went down easily, the color returning to his face with the second shot.

Now, alone on the road, he continued to see the image of Angeli in front of him. Screams, then silence. The men of the Vatican had been there all along, heard everything. He couldn't remember if he had told them about the Drina, Kosovo, the car. Had he mentioned Visegrad? All of it flew through his mind, the shock and the brandy making accurate recall impossible.

And yet, what did it matter? There was no need to track him now. No need to find out where Ribadeneyra's book would lead him. He was a priest. He wouldn't let her die. He would give them what they wanted. No matter what the consequences.

A reasonable argument four days ago. Now, he didn't know. Delivering the "Hodoporia" would assure both his and Angeli's deaths. That much, he did know. A surprisingly cold bit of analysis from a man of faith. Perhaps he was learning the ways of the Manichaeans too well. But to abandon her—and to convince himself that their methods were dictating his own callousness—was that really his only choice?

With no answers, he found himself on the ridge of a hill, below him the first signs of the madness sprawling out from Kosovo. A group of outsized tents appeared along the border, impromptu barricades circling large tracts of what, until recently, had been open land. Just beyond them, the rim of another mountain rose up thick with trees. He had been told that the police had cleared the camp weeks ago, a resettlement agreement with the Serbs all but signed. Naturally, it had fallen through, and Blace—a village of perhaps a hundred homes—was once again teeming with refugees.

From his vantage point, he saw the array of initials painted on the roofs of the tents—UN, NATO, IMC, ICRC, ACT, UNICEF, and a host of others he didn't recognize—all cataloging the impotence of a world unable to deal with the most recent Balkan flare-up. Seven hundred years of emperors, sultans, presidents, and kings hadn't managed to bring resolution. Why these thought they could, he didn't know. From the looks of it, most of those posted to Blace were simply trying to hold whatever they could in check.

The closer in he walked, the more unbearable the smell became. The first of the tents was still a good half mile off and already the stench of urine hung in the air. It was difficult to delineate the smells as he approached the first barricade: soiled clothes, unwashed flesh, an animal-like odor—wet fur doused in something sickly sweet—impossible to avoid. Not even a hand to the nose could keep it at bay, the air so thick with filth that it seemed to attach itself to every fiber of clothing, skin, hair. And yet, Pearse had little trouble ignoring it, the sights beyond the fence enough to overload his senses. Even from this distance, he could make out the faces, the thick frames of kerchiefed women, children—too big to be carried—clutched in weary arms. Some wandered about; others crouched in small groups, none talking, all with a stare of resigned helplessness, disbelief having long ago abandoned them. Bosnian, Kosovar—it made little difference. A new locale. Nothing else to distinguish them save the passage of eight years.

Pearse hadn't expected the place to jar him as it did, the "Hodoporia," Angeli, and all he had learned on Athos momentarily erased from his thoughts. Even he had let himself believe that the worst had ended a year ago. Not from what he saw now. No doubt it was the reason he failed to notice the soldier driving up from his left, the man outfitted in field camouflage, the Jeep with the UN insignia on its hood. The man pulled to a stop and stepped out.

"*Oproste te, Tatko. Mozam li da go vidam identifikacija?*"

Pearse turned, needing a moment to refocus his attention. Unsure what he had just heard, he shook his head.

In a slow, deliberate English—the accent pure Brit—the soldier repeated, "Your identification, Father."

"You're English," Pearse answered, pulling out the worn Vatican passport and handing it to the man.

"Yes," he replied, scrutinizing the papers. "And you're not Italian." After a few moments, he handed back the passport, a taut smile on his lips. "An American Vatican priest. Rather interesting. And what exactly are you doing here, Father?"

Pearse tried to return the smile. He needed something that sounded convincing. "I was supposed to join a relief group in Skopje, but my plane was delayed. They told me to come here. I managed to get a lift to St. Nikita."

"A relief group?" The soldier's smile widened. "We've plenty of those, Father. I'm afraid you'll have to be a bit more specific."

With only a momentary pause, he answered, "The International Catholic Migration Committee." It was the first thing he could think of, a dim recollection from a recent edition of *L'Osservatore Romano* that the ICMC was somewhere in Macedonia tending to the refugees. Pearse had to hope the Holy Mother was still by his side.

The soldier sized up the priest. "You're traveling rather light for a man on a relief mission."

"My bags are with the group," he answered, once again allowing the words to spill out on their own. "My itinerary, my contacts. All I've got is my Vatican passport."

"I see." A voice over a radio suddenly broke through, the soldier quick to respond. As he talked, he moved out of earshot, his eyes, though, never straying from Pearse. After several minutes, he returned.

"May I ask what you have in the pack, Father?"

Pearse shrugged. "A change of clothing. A few books."

The soldier reached out his hand. "May I? Security. I'm sure you understand."

Pearse nodded and handed the man the pack. He watched as the soldier tossed through it. He nearly flinched when the man pulled out the Ribadeneyra. He began to flip through its pages.

"It's . . . Orthodox prayers," Pearse said. "I thought, perhaps, being in this region—"

"Certainly, Father. I just have to check for anything concealed."

Pearse nodded again. The soldier moved on to his Bible. Again, a quick flip through. He then placed it inside, rezipped the pack, and handed it back to Pearse.

"Terribly sorry about that, Father, but we've had a bit of a problem with . . . people trying to get inside."

"I can understand that."

"Yes." The soldier smiled. "The ICMC. Nice chaps." Again, he waited, then said, "Well, we can't settle it out here. Hop in. We'll see if we can't find someone inside to straighten this out."

Grazie, Madonna.

Fifteen minutes later, Pearse sat inside a Red Cross tent, awaiting the attention of a harried young woman behind a makeshift desk. It became readily apparent that a lost priest didn't rate as a priority amid the constant flurry of activity. Pearse was more than happy to be viewed as an inconvenience, something to be shuffled along without too many questions.

As he waited, his gaze settled on a mother and her two sons sitting on the ground, boys of about ten and twelve, the younger held close to her chest, the other long and lanky, his chin resting on two propped fists, a worn leather satchel in his lap. The mother had somehow retained her impressive bulk, her boys not so fortunate, the older with a face well beyond his years. He was at that age when the nose grew too full, the ears too wide, a man's features on a boy's face. Awkward for most, it seemed sadly fitting here. The boy caught sight of Pearse, stared for a moment at his collar, then at his boots. He then looked directly at him.

"*Koje ste religije?*" asked the boy.

Pearse was surprised to hear Serbo-Croatian. "I'm a Catholic," he answered in kind.

The boy nodded, then pointed to the boots. "Those are good for walking."

Pearse looked at his boots, then at the boy. "Yes. You don't come from Kosovo, do you?"

"Yeah, Kosovo. Medveda. In the north."

"Your Serbo-Croatian is very good."

A hint of a smile. "It's a good language to speak now."

Pearse recalled the few encounters he'd had with Albanians eight years ago. All of them had spoken a second language. Often Serbo-Croatian. Sometimes German. Never English. "Are you a Catholic?" he asked.

"No. Muslim."

"Then why did you want to know my religion?"

The boy straightened up. "When the Protestant priests came to our village to tell us about Jesus, they had lots of money, drove nice cars. The Catholic ones were poor, told us that that was the way they were supposed to be." Again he looked at the boots.

Pearse understood. He glanced at the boy's feet, roughly the same size as his own, his shoes with little life left in them. Pearse reached down, untied his laces, and tossed the boots across. "How about a trade?"

Again, the hint of a smile.

The shoes were a remarkably good fit, the patches of ventilation something he would get used to. "Do you know how long you're going to be here?" Pearse asked.

The boy shrugged as he rubbed at a scratch along the toe of his new boots. "We can't go back to Medveda—at least that's what they say. Wherever they send us, they want the whole family together. My grandmother and sisters were sent somewhere in Turkey. They're not sure if they've come through here or not. And I don't know where my father and older brother are." He looked up. "Are you here to save people?"

The question, laced with as much cynicism as a twelve-year-old could muster, stunned Pearse. He stared at the boy.

For the first time since leaving Rome, he had no choice but to confront his own hypocrisy, a priest using his clericals as a means of deception. The boy, of course, had meant something entirely different. His was a disdain for the words meant to soothe a people trapped in a reality with no place for such gestures. Either way, the remark had the desired effect, Pearse forced to reevaluate his own intentions. People were dying here; worlds were being torn apart. Here. Where a priest should be. Yet the Manichaeans were forcing him to ignore that, disregard the one aspect of his calling he'd never questioned.

"I don't know," he finally answered.

From his expression, the boy hadn't expected that response from a priest. It took him a moment to answer. "Thanks for the boots, Father," he said, then nodded toward the desk. Pearse turned, to see the woman calling him over.

He turned back to thank the boy, but the boots had already reclaimed his attention. More buffing. Something far more useful than a priest.

Pearse stood and made his way across.

At the desk, he realized the woman was still in the midst of countless other tasks. She pointed for him to take a seat. Another few minutes, and she finally turned to him. "You've been very kind to wait so patiently, Father." Her English was tinged with a French accent, her tone genuinely apologetic. "Somehow, we've misplaced you, is that it?"

"Actually, I've misplaced myself," he said. "I'm supposed to be with the ICMC."

"Ah." She turned to a pile of papers on the desk, then brought up a new screen on her laptop. As she sorted through it all, Pearse looked back at the boy. He had nestled himself into his mother's side, eyes shut. Pearse watched, hoping to see even a hint of innocence slip across the face. None.

"You've missed them by three days," she said as Pearse turned back. She held a small folder in her hand, several stapled sheets within, her eyes fixed on the screen. "I'm afraid I can't tell you where they might be with any accuracy right now." She turned to him. "Is there someone we should contact, Father?"

"Then where would I be the most useful?"

"Excuse me?"

"Kosovo, Albania? Where would I be able to help?"

Her expression told him she wasn't prepared to deal with an overly eager priest. "Help? Father . . . it's not really a question of where—"

"I'm sure one more pair of experienced hands, not to mention a priest's presence, would be welcome somewhere," he said, his tone firm, though not aggressive. "I was in Bosnia during the war. I know the region, the language, the people. There must be someplace where they could use me."

The woman continued to look at him. Two of her coworkers suddenly descended, each one spewing rapid-fire French, the woman drawn into the exchange, her frustration more and more apparent as the debate went on. When they finally moved off, she turned back to him, her focus elsewhere. "You want to go someplace you can help," she said offhandedly. "Right." She placed her hands on the desk. "Look, Father, it's not our usual policy—"

"I don't imagine too much that's 'usual policy' is going on these days. I don't think I'm a threat to anyone."

"Of course not, Father. That's not the point."

"And I *was* supposed to be with the ICMC." He was actually beginning to believe it himself. "Doesn't that mean anything?"

"It's just that we can't take responsibility—"

"I'm not asking you to. I'll be responsible for myself. I'm just asking where you think I could do the most good." He could see she was beginning to teeter. "Or," he added, "I could continue to pester you for the next few days or weeks or months, until you give in and let a priest do his job."

"I see." A resigned smile inched across her lips. "Months."

"Months."

Her eyes narrowed; she began to sift through a pile of folders on her desk. "It's only because I'm a Catholic, Father." A moment later, she held up a single sheet in her hands. "There's a transport of medical equipment going out to Kukes in an hour. They're short one person." He couldn't be sure if her willingness to accommodate him had as much to do with his pleas as it did with the harangue from her fellow workers; he didn't really care. Again, she looked up at him. "You're sure you're comfortable with this, Father? Kukes is—"

"Far tamer than Omarska ever was." The mention of the former Serbian camp stopped her short, a newfound respect in her eyes. "I was there in '92. I think I'll be able to handle Kukes."

She pulled out another file, asked him to sign at several places, then handed him a laminated card. "The truck will be at the west gate in an hour." Before he could thank her, her two friends were back, more of the bluster. Pearse turned to go, the woman's voice quick to stop him.

"Father," she said, now standing, leaning into him as she spoke. "I was wondering . . . I . . . haven't taken confession since I got here. . . ."

Pearse smiled, aware of how long it had been since he had given it. "Of course. I'll be outside."

He would do what he could in Kukes. Spend a day. Token assistance. But the recollection of Angeli's voice told him it would be all he could afford.

Two hours later, he sat across from a Red Cross official in the back of a truck, a young Indian doctor at his side. No one bothered to talk. The ruts in the road were seeing to that.

Somehow, they even managed to dampen the sound of the exploding mine.

▲

"When?"

Blaney stared at the paintings on the wall across from his desk. He hardly noticed them, his focus so completely trained on the voice on the other end of the phone line.

"Yesterday. Around noon."

"And I'm only finding this out now?"

"They thought they'd be able to pick him up again before—"

"Before I found out that they'd lost him?"

Silence on the other end.

"We believe he made his way to Athos and—"

"Of course he made his way to Athos," said Blaney. "Even the cardinal knows that. The calls have been coming in since five this morning. And you're sure he wasn't hurt at the station in Kalambáka?"

"Yes. . . . I was told he got up at once. No injuries. But, as I said—"

"I know. No one was close enough to him at that point to be sure." Blaney took a deep breath. He couldn't let anger get in his way. "All right. We'll assume he's heading west. My guess is he'll try for Bosnia, maybe Albania. He obviously knows the region. And he knows he can get lost in there. We just have to hope he makes a mistake."

"Yes, Father."

"And I want you to get in touch with me the moment you make contact. No one else, this time. And no delays. Are we clear on this?"

"Yes, Father."

"Good." Blaney waited. "Then go in peace, my son." He hung up the phone and turned to the woman standing by the door. "You say he sounded well, Gianetta?"

"Yes, Father."

"But you didn't see him?"

"No, not really, Father. Only from the window as he walked off."

"And he didn't say why he wanted to see me? He didn't mention a . . . something he wanted to show me?"

"No, Father."

"All right," he said. "Thank you, Gianetta. You may go."

She nodded, then left the room, closing the door behind her.

Again, Blaney stared at the pictures. *No injuries.* At least there was some good news in that.

▲

Pearse had been lucky, a few bruised ribs, some lacerations, a twisted shoulder. The worst of it was the concussion. At least four or five days before the doctors at Kukes would let him go.

The Red Cross man and the young Indian had also escaped relatively unscathed. The driver, however, hadn't fared so well. He lay next to Pearse, a battery of tubes hooked up to his arms, little sign of life save for the slight rising and falling of his chest. The heat inside the tent wasn't helping.

It had been a day and half since the accident, Pearse only now able to focus his thoughts and prayers on the man for more than a few minutes at a time. Still, it was an improvement. It was also enough to get him out of his own cot; he stood. With his head pounding, he walked to the flap of the tent and stepped outside.

What he saw made Blace look like a resort. Pearse could almost taste the stench with each intake of air, thousands upon thousands of bodies more animal than human everywhere he looked. During the war in Bosnia, he'd visited two or three such camps, nothing to compare with the sprawl he now encountered. Hundreds of small tents dotted the mud-filled pastures, patches of gravel here and there where ICRC engineers had tried to stem the drainage problems. The toilets stood in a row along a steep slope, gravity their best hope against blockage. Everywhere, webs of rope line stretched from tent to tent, clothes hanging from them, an open-air tenement at eye level. Pearse knew the drill. Nothing to wash with, save the rainwater.

The town itself—bombed beyond recognition even a year after the official cease-fire—blended into the morass of canvas landscaping, the few remaining buildings given over to medical facilities. Even so, he was told that the spillover into the camp was beginning to take its toll, especially with the hot weather. Humidity meant flies; flies meant the threat of epidemic. A section of the camp had been isolated for several weeks, though never quarantined, family members insisting they be kept together. There was little any of the relief organizations could do to dissuade them.

An hour walking. It was all he could handle his first time out.

As much as knew he needed to get moving—Angeli's voice never far from him—he also knew the doctors were right. He needed to take the time to recover. What they probably didn't realize, however, was how much more they had given him.

For three more days, as his head cleared, he did what he could, "Baba Pearsic" allowed again to act the priest. Women, children, old men—the latter in the familiar flat hats, wool jackets, and countless layers of clothing—all seemed strangely comforted by him, those who knew they wouldn't survive the camp eager to talk with him. Not about God or faith, but simply to talk. There were plenty of village *hohxas* wandering about, holy men to handle the more elaborate Muslim rites.

At night, he managed what little sleep he could, trying to ignore the occasional screams within the camp, depravity, like a virus, having spread even to the hunted. It only sharpened his memories. No one ever talked of rape, he remembered. Not because it was a sin, or because it might be too painful for the women involved, but because husbands and fathers thought of its victims as abominations, forever unclean, no matter what the circumstances or who the perpetrator. Proof that barbarism played no favorites.

It wasn't all that difficult for the "Hodoporia" to slip to the back of his mind.

On the fifth morning, he was in the medical tent, the driver still stretched out on a bare mattress. Pearse had been with him through the latest surgery and half the night. When the most recent dose of morphine began to kick in, Pearse stood and started for the next mattress.

A voice from behind broke in: "I told you you could give absolution."

The words in English stopped Pearse in his tracks. Not sure if he had heard correctly, he turned. The face he saw nearly knocked him to the floor.

"Salko?" Mendravic was already sidestepping his way through the mattresses, the same immense figure he had known a lifetime ago, his embrace as suffocating as the last one they had shared.

"It's good to see you, too, Ian," Mendravic whispered in his ear. He then stepped back, the familiar grin etched across his face. "Father, I mean."

It took Pearse several seconds to recover. "Salko. What are you—"

"The priest's outfit suits you."

Still dazed, he asked again, "What are you doing here?"

"That's all you have to say?" He laughed.

"No, I'm . . ." Pearse could only shake his head. Without warning, he pulled Mendravic in and embraced him again. "It's so good to see you."

"You, too. You, too."

When Pearse finally let go, he was no less confused. "I still don't understand—"

"Fighting the Serbs. I've been smuggling people in from Priština for the last few months. Mainly through Montenegro."

"So why here?" It seemed to be all he was capable of saying.

"Because two days ago, I heard about a 'Baba Pearsic' in Kukes—an American who'd been in Bosnia. Slitna, to be exact. Most of the Catholic priests are either in the north or in Macedonia. I thought I'd come and see for myself. And here you are. So, how's the head?"

"That's unbelievable."

"You've stayed in one place for a few days. Not so unbelievable. Again, how's the head?"

"About ninety percent."

"So, better than it was before." He laughed.

Pearse was about to answer, when movement from one of the beds broke through.

"You do what you need to do here," Mendravic said. "I'll be outside."

Twenty minutes later, Pearse joined him. They began to walk.

"You make a good priest."

"You make a good rebel."

Again, Mendravic laughed. "Don't flatter me. I'm not with the KLA, but I understand what they're doing. It was the same with us. Except here, Dayton only made Milošević stronger. Until your friends in the West understand that, there's really no choice but to fight these people."

"So you never went back to Zagreb?"

"Of course I went back. It never felt right. It wasn't mine anymore."

"And Slitna? You knew the people there."

Mendravic took hold of his arm and stopped. "Slitna?" Pearse began to list names; again, Mendravic cut him off. "You don't know?"

"Know what?"

"Petra didn't tell you?" Before Pearse could respond, Mendravic continued. "The entire village was destroyed. Wiped out. The day after you left. You were very lucky."

" 'The entire . . .' " The news hit Pearse as if it had happened yesterday. "Why?"

The loss seemed no less immediate for Mendravic. He shook his head. "They never really needed reasons."

"But you and Petra—"

"We were also very lucky. Off getting something—I don't remember what. Whatever we were so desperate to find in those days. When we came back, it was as if the place had never existed. Except for the rubble. And the bodies."

"I . . . didn't know."

"Yes. Well . . . I was sure Petra would have told you—" He stopped abruptly, only now aware of the look in Pearse's eyes. "When was the last time you spoke with her?"

"Petra? A month, maybe two after I left. Why? Is she all right?"

"Oh, she's fine. She's outside of Sarajevo now. Teaching again." He started to walk. "She has a son."

Pearse smiled to himself. "So she got married. Good for her."

"No. She never married."

Pearse's reaction was immediate. "My God. Was she—"

Again, Mendravic cut him off. "No. Nothing like that. You didn't have to worry about that with Petra."

Pearse nodded.

"The boy turned seven just this May," Mendravic added, his gaze now straight ahead.

"Really?"

"Really."

It took another moment for Pearse to understand what Mendravic was saying. Seven years.

Pearse stopped. A son.

The Croat continued on, Pearse unable to follow.

Filius

four

Nigel Harris sat in the breakfast nook of his penthouse suite atop London's Claridges Hotel, fifteen newspapers piled on a small table in front of him. Nestled in among them stood a cup of weak tea, a plate with two hard-boiled eggs, no yolks, and a bowl of piping hot oatmeal—the same breakfast he'd had every morning for the past twelve years, save, of course, for his recent meeting in Spain. Not that he didn't enjoy fruits and jams and countless other savories, but the bland diet was all his stomach could abide. His eyes weren't the only casualties of a military career.

The brief meal with the contessa was still having its residual effects. So be it. He'd hardly been in a position to refuse, the contessa famous for her strict adherence to the rules of hospitality. How and what he had eaten had been as important as what he had said. He'd known that going in. More than that, he truly believed she would have taken a weak stomach for a weak character, and he couldn't have her thinking that. Thus far, the results of their meeting had more than made up for the few days of discomfort.

Bringing the cup to his lips, he took a sip of the tea, the first always eliciting a momentary twinge in the hollow of his gut. Something to do with acids, the doctors had explained. The sickly sweet taste of bile constricted in his throat, a compression of liquid and air, nauseous tightening gripping at the base of his tongue. He swallowed several times, the saliva only adding to the swell of gastric insurgence. He waited, then took a bite of the first egg. He had trained himself to visualize its path, the malleable white adapting to the contours of his esophagus, down through the center of his chest, every toxin absorbed within its spongy skin. The burning began to dissipate. He ate the second egg. Routine. It had gotten to the point where he almost wasn't aware of it. Almost.

He pulled the last of the papers from the table and flipped to the end of the A section, the op-ed pieces, with no hint of yesterday's events. Instead, they offered the usual *New York Times* fare: a Hoover Institution expert on U.S. policy in Kosovo; Safire on Clinton (one more chance to paint Nixon in a softer hue); the mayor on tax restructuring. No doubt tomorrow, things would be different. For now, though, he'd have to settle for the editorials. He'd already made it through fifteen of the world's leading papers, a mixed bag of responses to the Faith Alliance's mission statement. He'd saved the *Times* for last. Best to build up his stamina.

The title of the first piece said it all: "Savonarola in a Suit."

He sat back and read:

Yesterday, Nigel Harris, former executive director of the Testament Council, began his latest campaign to assert himself as moral beacon of the West. His most recent attempt comes in the form of the loosely defined Faith Alliance, a group that boasts a following from as far afield as Hollywood and academe, Wall Street and the church. A broad base, to be sure. With a set of Twelve Guiding Principles (the number only fitting), the new apostles of ethical pro-bity have decided the time is ripe to confront those elements within society that threaten the basic tenets of decency. Their answer: a cross-cultural, multifaith incentive "devoid of political ambition."

While on an abstract level we applaud Mr. Harris and his colleagues for their concerns, we find enough in the alliance's mission statement to raise seri-ous questions. Although never pinpointing the focus of the campaign, Mr. Harris does hint at where we might expect to find his alliance making its pres-ence known: rap music, the Internet, single-sex marriages, prayer in the schools, etc. It seems somewhat disingenuous to dive into these hotly debated issues while claiming to have no political agenda.

More troubling, though, is the ambiguous definition he gives for an "alliance of faith," one in which "religious differences fade in favor of a wider spiritual commitment." That Mr. Harris champions tolerance is commendable, espe-cially given the history of his former associates at the Testament Council, who shied away from such inclusiveness. That he chooses to characterize that coher-ence, however, as a response to "a threat from those who understand holy war as a form of diplomacy" paints a far more divisive picture. Islam as straw man hardly seems the best way to foster decency.

For the fifteenth-century Savonarola, the scourge . . .

Harris glanced at the final paragraph, the historical tie-in something of a stretch, though amusing, a stern reminder of the fate the Florentine preacher had met at the hands of his own followers. Given the response from the majority of papers, however, Harris had little reason to heed the warning. Overwhelming approval. Confirmation of the fifty thousand E-mails that had arrived just in the last two hours.

Not bad for quarter to eight in the morning.

▲

Pearse sat on a slab of rock, the mountainside strewn with countless such mounds, the camp some two hundred yards below. To the east, an artificial lake—courtesy of the Fierza hydropower station—spread out like a wide pancake, serenely smooth within a curve of mountains, the water long ago contaminated, unfit for drinking or bathing, according to the latest Red Cross bulletin. It didn't seem to matter. The refugees continued to put it to use, dysentery, diarrhea, and fungus acceptable trade-offs when pitted against their own squalor. He could just make out a small group of women huddled by the shore, too far, though, to see what they were doing. Still, from this distance, it looked quite tranquil, his perch a temporary refuge from the chaos below.

Mendravic sat at his side, silently waiting. They'd been here for over an hour, sitting, staring. Finally, Pearse spoke.

"She should have told me."

Mendravic said nothing.

"Does he know about me?"

Mendravic started to answer, then stopped. "An hour ago, I would have said yes. Now . . ." He let the thought trail off. "I thought she'd told you. I haven't seen them in months."

Pearse nodded and continued to stare out. His eyes fixed on a clump of burned grass, a spray of blackened roots, only the tips still green. He had no idea what had caused its singular presence. Nothing other than to stare blankly into the charred wound.

At some point—not quite remembering when—he'd reached up and pulled the collar from his shirt. Seeing it in his hand now, he turned to Mendravic.

"Still think it suits me?"

Mendravic waited, then answered. "What are you really doing here, Ian?"

"That's a very good question."

"That's not what I meant."

"I know." Whatever Mendravic had meant, Pearse had been asking himself the same question for the last hour, his only answer one that seemed to define the past eight years of his life.

Running.

Not that he'd known about Petra and the boy, not that he could have known. But whatever he thought he'd find in the church hadn't really been there. Not for a long time now. Granted, he'd never lost his faith in the Word, in its power—he did have that—but it didn't make much sense to be a servant of the church when the church itself was causing all the misgivings. He couldn't help but wonder: Except for a collar and an address at the Vatican, how different had he really turned out from his dad? Priest or not, he'd made a habit of keeping everything at a distance. He'd abandoned Bosnia and Petra to become a priest. He'd abandoned Boston to become a scholar. He'd abandoned Cecilia Angeli . . . What reason this time? Kukes was simply one more noble distraction in an all-too-predictable pattern. And one that rang equally hollow.

His devastation at hearing of his son had nothing to do with the profligacy of a priest, the corruption of canon law, the depravity of mortal sin. It had to do with a boy, a woman, and a man. And the realization of a life lived in flight.

"You're not here because you came to help the refugees," said Mendravic, as if having read his mind.

Pearse slowly turned to him. "Why do you say that?"

"Because you don't really belong here, do you? The ICMC had no record of you. And the Vatican thought you were in Rome. It looks as if you simply appeared out of nowhere."

"You contacted Rome?"

"I had to make sure I had the right priest, didn't I? I wasn't going to trek halfway across Kosovo for the wrong one."

It took Pearse several moments to answer. Somehow, the mention of Rome brought him out of himself. He looked at Mendravic. "I have to get to Visegrad."

The sudden shift caught Mendravic off guard. "What?"

"And then you have to take me to Petra."

Before Mendravic could answer, Pearse was on his feet. "You're right. I didn't come here for the refugees. And I let myself forget that."

Without waiting, he started down the mountain.

▲

Via Condotti on a summer afternoon is, more often than not, a swirl of wall-to-wall people. The spill of tourists from the Spanish Steps combined with the surge of shoppers on the Corso take it to critical mass at around 4:00 P.M., not the moment to be fighting one's way toward a building nestled at its midpoint. Poor timing, to be sure, for Arturo Ludovisi, whose plane from Frankfurt had been delayed just long enough so that he now had the pleasure of experiencing Via Condotti at its most lunatic. Still, given the ledgers he had taken with him, he knew it was best to deposit them back in the safe as quickly as possible.

Pressing his way through the crowd, he arrived at the stoop of number 201, a building remarkable for its ordinariness, four floors of gray-black brick squeezed in between two elegant boutiques, men's apparel draped over faceless mannequins. The shops' interiors mirrored that austerity, stark walls, hardly any clothing in sight. Ludovisi had never understood the point.

As he fished through his pocket for the key, he carefully glanced around to make sure that no one was taking any special interest in him. Satisfied, he turned the handle and stepped inside.

The smell of damp wool wafted up to greet him as he shut the door. He turned on the overhead light, the dilapidation of the place brought into clear focus. Beyond the tiny foyer, a narrow staircase labored up to the second floor, a pronounced sag matched by an equally crumbly banister. Matted brown carpet, worn and stained, stretched taut along each step, enough of a cushioning, though, to mute the creaks and squeals from the wood below. Along the walls, strips of blue-and-white wallpaper—flowers and vases, as far as he could tell—vainly tried to brighten the hall. Years of cigarette smoke had smeared the pattern with a yellowish brown film, relieving it of all such responsibility. All in all, a grotty little cave, four floors high.

And yet, if just for a moment, the place managed to transport Ludovisi to another seedy little hallway, another building now long torn down, the sounds of screeching violins and crackling trumpets filling the air. The tiny *conservatorio* in Ravenna of il Dottore Masaccio, the man's enormous foot pounding out the meter, thick fingers stabbing at the notes on the page, an ominous stare as the young Ludovisi tried again and again to master the dreaded triplet, always to no avail. He always seemed better in two-two time. Room after room of young virtuosi, all but a select few with the talent only to frustrate the great maestro.

Ludovisi hadn't picked up a clarinet in over forty years; 201 Via Condotti hadn't inspired him to reconsider.

No doubt because the old place conjured a far more powerful association than the strains of Mozart and Vivaldi. Strange as it seemed, 201 had once been the breeding ground for the most debilitating financial scandal in the history of the Vatican. The story's most poignant memento? The image of Roberto Calvi dangling at the end of a rope under London's Blackfriars Bridge—June of 1982—the end to a rather undistinguished career, an unwitting dupe brilliantly placed at the center of the entire mess by von Neurath. That the press, along with countless "conspiracy theorists," had managed to mangle the facts surrounding Calvi's death had only made the cardinal's scheme all the more ingenious. A tale so intriguing that none other than Mario Puzo had found a place for it in his *Godfather* trilogy. Freemasonry, Mafia money laundering, the death of John Paul I. All somehow linked together. It still made Ludovisi smile to think of it.

In all honesty, von Neurath had never meant to undermine the prestige of the Institute of Religious Works (the IOR)—known to the outside world as the Vatican Bank. At least not at the start. His target had been far less lofty: one Licio Gelli, an erstwhile rival for the position of *summus princeps*, the highest office within the Brotherhood.

Born in 1919, Gelli had chosen the political, rather than the religious, path within Manichaeanism, infiltrating the Blackshirt battalions in Spain in the 1930s, later the SS Hermann Göring Division during the war. In the 1950s, he'd established himself as a leading player in the Italian secret service, instrumental in operations Gladio and Stay Behind—the West's efforts to station anti-Communist guerillas behind the lines in the event of a Soviet offensive. But while seemingly ideal to spearhead the "great awakening," Gelli had become too visible. When, in 1960, he was passed over in favor of the much younger von Neurath, he'd decided his link to Manichaeanism had outlived its usefulness. Simple fascism would be more than acceptable.

With access to the most sensitive intelligence files in Europe— blackmail the surest way to fill his coffers—and with fifteen thousand operatives at his disposal, Gelli created Propaganda Due, a private shadow army with tentacles into every aspect of Italian life. At his trial in 1983, one prosecutor claimed that, by the late 1960s, P2 included "three members of the Cabinet, several former prime ministers, forty-three members of Parliament, fifty-four top civil servants, one hundred and eighty-three army, navy, and air force officers (including thirty generals and eight admirals), judges, leading bankers, the editor of the country's top newspaper (*Corriere della Sera*), university professors, and the heads of the three main intelligence services." Though limited in scope to Italian politics, P2 looked as though it might pose some serious problems, especially given Gelli's intimate knowledge of the Manichaean cell structure.

At first, von Neurath responded subtly. He would control Gelli, rather than destroy him. Realizing that Propaganda Due was the perfect distraction for anyone looking to expose a group like the Manichaeans—conspiracies all the rage, given the Kennedy shooting—the cardinal created the myth of the Lodge. Von Neurath let slip that P2 was actually the most recent successor in a long line of secret societies connected to the Knights Templar—Freemasonry, the Sovereign Military Order of Malta, the Carbonari. An organization not to be trifled with. Just for fun, he hinted that the Vatican had taken a hand in funding operations, all in the name of the great fight against the godless Left. (After all, the IOR had fostered some rather dubious affiliations over the years—Spider and ODESSA, the ratlines that had ferreted former Nazis out of Europe. Why not P2?) A few well-placed minions in the right offices were enough to substantiate the ruse. And while Gelli was certainly carrying on his own dirty war—albeit on a very rudimentary level—it was von Neurath who saw to it that P2 was linked to any number of terrorist activities throughout Europe and the Middle East, from arms sales to purchases of crude oil. A wonderful opportunity to test just how much influence a Manichaean could wield. In fact, for a period in the late 1970s, it was virtually impossible to unearth anything to do with "black ops" and not hear the name Propaganda Due. To those in the world of intelligence, Gelli's influence extended to South America (Juan Perón), and even to the United States (Alexander Haig and the Nixon administration). That P2 was actually involved with less than 10 percent of those activities mattered very little. Gelli—quickly dubbed "the Puppet Master"—was being held responsible for it all. Those looking for conspiracies had found their demon.

Von Neurath—perhaps naïvely (although Ludovisi would never have been the one to point it out to him)—assumed that eventually one of the myriad international crime-fighting organizations would step in and put an end to it all. Not so. In fact, Gelli's influence began to match the reputation von Neurath had concocted for him. Myth had turned to reality. The Vatican and Mafia were now two of P2's leading contributors. Evidently, subtlety wasn't doing the trick.

As much as von Neurath enjoyed having P2 as a diversion for any prying eyes, he realized Gelli had become a genuine threat. With the Lodge ever more active, he knew his old rival would need a place to launder the money he was receiving from his more unsavory connections, thereby protecting his association with the IOR. Enter Roberto Calvi and the Milan-based Banco Ambrosiano. Calvi had been in von Neurath's pocket since the mid-1960s, when the bank had gone through several lean years. Under the guise of private investment, the Manichaeans had been more than happy to bail him out. Those investors now called in the favor. Calvi became Gelli's middleman. Ambrosiano started funneling the dirty money. And the Vatican was kept clean.

Until von Neurath told Calvi to muck up the works.

The scandal surrounding Calvi, Gelli, the shortfall of nearly $1.3 billion at Banco Ambrosiano and its link to the laundering of reputed Mafia money through the IOR became front-page news in 1982 and set the ball rolling. Calvi's "suicide" forced the Vatican to establish an independent commission, introducing one of its junior members—a young investment analyst named Arturo Ludovisi—to the inner circles of Vatican finance. An added boon. The final results: a tremor through the very heart of the papacy, the imprisonment of Gelli—reported to have escaped Swiss jailers in 1986, his body delivered to von Neurath two days later—and the dismantling of Propaganda Due. For those seeking out secret organizations and the like, victory had been won. No reason to look elsewhere.

And all neatly orchestrated by von Neurath.

For the Manichaeans, the payoff proved even more beneficial. They easily incorporated the P2 cells into their own network—all of which came to believe they were still working for Gelli through his successor, one Arturo Ludovisi. They, of course, had been a bit surprised by the nervous little man the first time they had met him. Ludovisi's genius for numbers had more than won them over. After all, who would believe someone like that to be the head of P2? The cells had given him their full endorsement. As a result, the first seeds of Pentecostal, Baptist, and Methodist Manichaeanism had taken root in the States. And, to top it all off, Ludovisi was asked to stay on as senior analyst at the Vatican Bank—on special recommendation from the Cardinal Camerlengo—a position of considerable autonomy. Not bad for what had started out as nothing more than a bit of housecleaning.

In fact, it was Ludovisi's relationship with the old P2 cells that had made his recent trip so easy. Eighteen cities in nine days, another $30 million deposited with over six hundred cells. If the "great awakening" was on the horizon—as von Neurath had promised—the financials were more than in place. It was just a matter of making sure the ledgers he had taken with him remained consistent with the numbers on the Vatican database.

Hence the need for the quick trip to 201 Via Condotti.

Reaching the second floor, he headed for the back office, little more than a six-by-six square, room enough for a weathered desk and chair, the former bolted to the floor. An odd touch for anyone not in the know. A single window overlooked the alley below, little light, less air. Ludovisi liked it here. No one to bother him. No one to answer to. He turned on the table lamp, then pulled the cord for the overhead fan. Sitting, he retrieved a small card from his jacket pocket and began to glide his fingers along the underside of the desktop. Locating a narrow slot on the left-hand side, he slid the card in. A moment later, a key-pad—far more sophisticated than one would have expected—slid out from one of the drawers. He punched in a series of numbers, then watched as a panel opened at the center of the desk. Beneath it, a computer screen. Hence the need for the bolts.

As much as he recognized its technical wizardry, he'd never learned to trust the thing. Too great a chance that someone from the outside might hack his way into the files. It was why Ludovisi continued to use the written ledgers for the Manichaean accounts. One copy, safely stored. That the Vatican had switched over to the more modern system five years ago meant that he had no choice but to play with the gizmo from time to time.

He opened a file and began to type.

Twenty minutes later, the IOR database reflected the recent outlays—funds for relief projects, schools throughout Latin America, pro-democracy movements in the Far East. Nothing that could be traced with any real precision. That over half the $30 million had gone to finance the Faith Alliance was nowhere in evidence.

He pulled a second card from his pocket, and spent another few moments hunting for a slot. Finding it, he slid the card in—another keypad, another combination. This one released the door to a safe located within the two bottom right-hand drawers. Ludovisi placed the ledgers inside and closed the safe. Scanning the desk for anything he might have missed, he reached underneath and pulled out the two cards. The computer and keypads disappeared—the ancient desk restored. He then cracked the cards in half and tossed them out the window.

A minute later, he stepped out onto Via Condotti and began to make his way to the Corso. Almost at once, he felt someone grab his arm. Instinctively, he turned, a twinge of pain in his shoulder, as he saw a man directly at his right, the grip extraordinary.

"What . . . what are you doing?"

Another subtle twist of the arm. "Don't scream." They crossed the Corso, the rear door of a waiting limousine opening as they approached. The man helped Ludovisi inside, then closed the door behind him. The lock bolted shut.

Staring across at him sat Stefan Kleist.

▲

Pearse emerged through the canvas flap in a clean, if wrinkled, pair of pants and shirt, the priest's attire having been divvied up among his various tent mates. At first, they had hesitated. Priest's clothes. Not that any of them were Catholics, but, given their current situation, no one seemed all that eager to tempt the fates, no matter whose God was involved. Then again, an extra pair of pants and coat would certainly come in handy when the weather changed. It hadn't taken Pearse long to convince them that the clothes would be far more useful to them than to him, for more reasons than perhaps he cared to admit.

It had been forty minutes since Mendravic had gone off to rustle up whatever he could—water, food, and, more important, a ride west. Podgorica if possible. Not the most traveled route, but certainly the fastest. And with the sky promising imminent downpour, they both knew it was best to get going before everything turned to slop. That Mendravic had headed out without pressing Pearse for a more detailed explanation for the change in plans—the Croat more concerned that each of the men in the tent had enjoyed several swigs of the brandy he had brought—reminded the young priest just how comforting it was to have his friend looking out for him. Again.

Another nod from on high.

But it wasn't Mendravic's calming influence that confirmed a divine will at work. Nor his sudden appearance as ideal guide for the trip to come. Those would have made for too easy an affirmation of faith. It was the turmoil he brought—the news of Petra and the boy—the jarring intrusion of reality into Pearse's life. What confirmed the Divine here, as it had done on Athos, was a kind of brutality, there within nature, here within a single truth. One not to test faith, but to define its very essence: harsh, jolting, perhaps even gnawing, but ultimately human. A living faith in its fullest sense, a Teresian ecstasy born of genuine struggle, the human condition painted in raw, jagged lines. Gone was the notion of serenity nurtured in cloistered retreat. That brand of contentment could only dull clarity, cushion it under a haze of self-serving bliss. Faith required confrontation. Clarity demanded such vigor.

It was only now that Pearse was beginning to understand that.

"Baba Pearsic?" He looked down. A boy no more than ten was staring up at him, his eyes beginning to bulge from a lack of food and real shelter. Still, a hint of animation, a sparkle as he spoke. He seemed eager to talk with the priest. The change of clothing, however, was causing him some confusion. "Father?"

"It's me. What's wrong?"

"Some men. My grandfather told me. Men from the outside. They come to see you." Pearse had trouble keeping up with the Serbo-Croatian; he heard more than enough, though, to recognize the fear in the boy's voice.

"Did they say what they wanted?"

The boy continued to stare. He pointed in the direction of the western gate. "Some men. They come to see you." And with that, he sped off through the maze of tents and rope lines.

Men from the outside. It was an odd way to describe anyone. Pearse knew that a boy that age would have had no trouble identifying the uniforms of every relief worker in the camp, likewise those of the KLA, NATO, and the Albanian police. The vague designation "men from the outside" told him the boy's fears were warranted.

His first thought was the Austrian. It had been five days, ample time to grow impatient. Pearse had to believe that they still needed Angeli whether they'd pinpointed his location or not. Finding him—Mendravic's call to Rome, his search for a missing priest in a refugee camp, had seen to that—was only half the battle. They still needed something to keep him in line. He was praying that their hook remained Cecilia Angeli.

Then again, maybe the Greeks had gotten lucky? The discovery of Andrakos's car, the connection between Blace and Kukes?

Whoever they were, Pearse knew he needed to get a good look at them before they him. Sizing up his options, he quickly crossed the mud path and slipped into a tent three down from his own. At once, a line of familiar faces peered up at him, four women ranging in age from eleven to sixty, a boy of four, a man in his seventies.

Before any of them could ask, Pearse brought a finger to his lips. Silence. They had learned to appreciate its power early on in the war, hiding in basements, attics, waiting for the Serb patrols to loot and move on. A single gesture was all they required. Pearse nodded, then turned to peek through the crack in the flap.

Less than a minute later, he spotted them, conspicuous by their clothes, more so by their attitudes, four men who, from their expressions, had only recently entered a war zone, each trying his best not to show too great an aversion to the filth and disarray. Dressed in field khakis, windbreakers, and mountain boots—a muted yellow, tied halfway up the calf—they could easily have passed for members of a weekend climbing club, save, of course, for their physiques. Each stood at least six two, rigidly straight posture, broad shoulders, thick, powerful forearms. Everything about them screamed military. And yet, unlike their comrades in Rome, these men from the Vatican displayed none of the swagger Pearse had witnessed the first time around. Instead, they seemed far more . . . humane. It was the only way he could think to describe them. Even as they split up to take positions around his original tent, they indulged in none of the commandolike gesticulating he expected. One at the rear, one ten yards to the south, one ten yards to the north. Coordinated and precise.

With a nod, the fourth man entered the tent.

He reemerged a minute later with one of Pearse's former tent mates in tow: Achif Dema, the barber who had set up shop under a nearby tarp, the man who had accepted Pearse's jacket as a farewell gift. The obvious choice for consultation. Dema shook his head several times, pointing off in the direction of the medical tents, hands waving in a series of convoluted gestures, all accepted with an easy smile from the Vatican man. He knew exactly what the refugee was doing, or at least trying to do. A wild-goose chase for an inquisitive stranger. It might have done the trick had Mendravic not chosen that moment to return.

Dema, no actor to begin with, could hardly contain his reaction; at once, Mendravic became everyone's focus. Dressed as he was, he had no chance of passing for a fellow refugee, a fact not lost on the men. As one, they began to circle in—subtly, but again with a precision that bespoke a familiarity with such situations. Pearse was left to observe as the strange dance played itself out.

Luckily, Mendravic knew his way around the floor, as well. Pearse watched as his old friend moved along the path, his eyes aimed at the ground—seemingly oblivious—but with an intensity that indicated a plan of attack already in the making. As he drew to within earshot of Pearse's hiding place, he began to scratch his cheek. At the same time, and without breaking stride, he whispered under his breath:

"Wait for them to follow me. Meet at the north gate."

Pearse had no idea how Mendravic had known he was inside the tent. Nor did he have time to digest the information. Within seconds, Mendravic was springing to his left, a wild-bear version of the boy who had darted through the tents only minutes before. Instantly, the men from the Vatican raced after him.

Except for the one who stood by Dema. He remained perfectly still, only his head moving in a slow rotation, scanning the line of tents with great concentration.

His eyes came to rest on Pearse's. And he began to walk.

If faith required confrontation, Pearse knew he was about to enter a state of grace. The man quickened his pace. Pearse felt his heart accelerate, a sudden pounding in his throat. He had no choice but to go. Pulling the flap back, he bolted out—an instant of recognition from the Vatican man, Pearse ducking to his right through the web of rope lines.

The sound of pursuit was immediate. Forcing it from his mind, he began to weave his way through the tents, his head still groggy, his body crouched so as to avoid the lines, more so to gain as much shielding from the low canvas walls as he could. His eyes swept along the ground, never more than two, three feet in front of him, hunting for stakes, ruts, anything that might trip him up. Wherever the path grew wide enough, small gatherings of people appeared, obstacles to be run over and through. Their curses trailed after him, each a sonar's ping to trace his escape. A second wave always followed—the advent of his pursuer—the surest means of measuring the distance between them. The echoes were coming quicker and quicker.

Pearse did his best to keep himself moving northward in the hope of finding the gate. Several minutes in, he became acutely aware of a sudden shift in the air, a familiar sweetness, somehow lighter, the moment before deluge, when sky and earth darken under sooted clouds, a breathless hint of the coolness to come. He could almost taste the breeze as the sky began to open up, first gentle, then pail after pail of water, the sudden patter of clapping mud, Pearse drenched in seconds. The timpani of rain on canvas propelled him from tent to tent. All sound seemed to vanish, no sense for anything or anyone behind him, only his tiny bubble world shaped by the relentless barrage.

Underfoot, the ground grew slick with incredible speed, tiny inlets seeking out the low ground, rutted tracks from carts and trucks providing the network of conduits. Above, the clouds pressed farther down, a porous gray plummeting the afternoon into premature twilight. He had no idea how far he had ferreted his way into the confusion of tents, hardly willing to take his focus from the ground so as to gain his bearings. Instead, he continued to run, no chance at even a quick look back to see how close his assailant had drawn. The rope lines, once obstacles, now kept him upright, his hands sliding along the slick fiber in an attempt to maintain his balance, one narrow path to the next, improvised benches and chairs upended along the way as he raced by them.

Minute passed into minute—the gate nowhere in sight—his lungs and muscles starting to give out, his head beginning to pound, a burning in his throat, no amount of adrenaline able to stifle its hold. He tried to push himself on, but his chest began to constrict, his sides cramping. Shooting a glance over his shoulder, he fully expected to see the large man barreling toward him.

The path stood empty.

Amazed, Pearse slowed, then stopped. Slouched over, hands on his knees, he sucked in air, rain cascading through his hair, thick drops streaking down his face. He wiped them away. Again he turned, certain that the rain had somehow distorted his vision, the man only feet from him. Nothing. A flare of lightning illuminating the area, confirmation that he was alone. Not quite believing his luck, he stood upright, still breathing heavily, the pain subsiding, an uncontrollable grin spreading across his lips. He had lost him. With a sudden surge of confidence, he turned around, hoping to get a better sense of where he had brought himself.

His legs nearly buckled when, no more than thirty yards in front of him, he saw the man now propelling himself forward from rope line to rope line, knees brought high with each powerful thrust, the mud below no deterrent to the strangely mechanical leaping. Somehow, he had made his way around, anticipating Pearse's movements and positioning himself to cut him off. To the peal of thunder, Pearse swung around, too quick for his own footing, a hand to the ground as he began to tumble headfirst, trying to push himself forward, the boy's shoes no match for the sludge. He looked back for only an instant, a nightmare sensation, his own legs unable to move, his body in the grasp of the mud, his hands clawing to get himself to his feet. He lunged for the nearest line, hoisting himself up, the first hint of racing steps behind beginning to break through the rain's compulsive beat.

With the sound of the man's breath closing in, Pearse turned, catching sight of a pair of crystal blue eyes no more than fifteen feet from him. Their stare, however, exhibited none of the menace Pearse had conjured in his own mind. In fact, the man seemed to be slowing, his arms at his sides, a pose to pacify, not to intimidate. Strangely unnerving.

The image lasted less than a second.

From somewhere off to his right, a figure sprang out in a blur of movement, hands latching onto the man's chest, plunging him into the side of a nearby tent, spikes jerked from the ground, bodies trapped within the deflating canvas.

It was then that Pearse recognized Mendravic, now pulling the man upright and driving his knee into an unsuspecting groin. At once, the man doubled over, his head easy prey for a second assault. Mendravic swung his knee up, this time into the man's skull, the neck snapping back, the body instantly crumbling to the ground.

It had taken less than ten seconds. Pearse stared in astonishment.

Mendravic stooped down to check the man for papers. Finding none, he stepped toward Pearse and pulled him to his feet. "Don't worry," he said, yelling to him over the rain. "He'll be up and about in twenty minutes. He'll just have a very bad headache for a day or so. You know what that's like, don't you?"

Pearse was still unsure what had just happened. "Where did you come from?" he yelled back.

Mendravic led him to the spot from which he had just leapt, then pointed through the tangle of ropes. Remarkably, the north gate stood some forty yards from them, two cement block hovels on either side, checkpoint stations for those coming and going. An odd collection of trucks and vans sat parked around the open expanse, two Albanian guards in rain gear monitoring the area, their chosen perch the back of one of the larger trucks, shelter against the rain, rifles resting at their sides. Not exactly the most taxing duty in camp. Probably another two or three men inside the buildings. Pearse couldn't quite believe his luck at having gotten this close to the gate.

"I was here a minute, maybe two, before you," Mendravic yelled. "That's when I saw your head pop up, then the other one. Him," he said, pointing at the unconscious body. "At least I thought it was you." He started to make his way to the gate.

"And the other three?" Pearse asked, following.

"The rain helped." Mendravic seemed content to leave it at that. Pearse saw no reason to press for details.

As they moved into the opening, one of the Albanians jumped down from his perch. His smile made it clear that he and Mendravic had already done business. "He needs another two hundred dollars," Mendravic said under his breath. "I assumed you'd have it."

Pearse reached for the backpack, evidently too quickly for both soldiers. The one still in the truck reached for his rifle. The one moving toward them stopped, his smile gone. Mendravic raised his hands, a wide smile on his face; Pearse did the same. When they had drawn to within a few feet of the man, Mendravic began to speak in a cordial Albanian.

"My friend," he said, his hands now extended, "he's just getting the rest of your money. What did we say? One hundred American?"

"Two hundred," answered the man.

"Of course. Two hundred."

The guard's smile returned.

Pearse nodded slowly, as if to ask permission to open the backpack. The soldier motioned to his friend in the truck. The rifle returned to its resting place. Careful to bring out only the necessary bills, Pearse handed them to Mendravic who then handed them to the guard. After a quick count of the money, the man nodded again to his friend. He then waved for Pearse and Mendravic to follow him outside the gate.

A few hundred feet on, they arrived at the edge of a thickly wooded area. The guard pulled a flashlight from his jacket and let the thin beam cut across the rain-soaked bark of the trees. He found what he was looking for some fifty feet farther on, a virtually hidden path, but one with which the man was clearly familiar. It was nearly a quarter of a mile before they came to a small glade, a pair of run-down delivery vans—the small European kind, little more than a car with extended cab at the back, two cramped seats up front—standing side by side. Pearse guessed they had been "procured" from the streets of Pec or Prizren in the last two days, a cottage industry for the guards and any refugees willing to pay. Four hundred dollars seemed reasonable enough for an American priest and his Croatian friend. No doubt, the price varied considerably depending on the clientele. The guards had done well today.

"You've enough petrol to get you to Shkodër," the man said pointing to the van on the right. "There's a map inside. And some towels." He smiled. "Don't say you didn't get your money's worth." He started back, shouting over his shoulder as he walked. "And don't worry. The car won't have any trouble at the Yugoslav border."

Mendravic fired up the engine, doing his best to maneuver the van through the mud and roots, the rain pounding at the roof in a snare-drum frenzy. Pearse had squeezed the pack between them and was now making the most of the "towels"—ratty little handkerchiefs on a good day—to dry himself off and to clear the windshield, which had quickly fogged over. Mendravic pressed one of the tiny rags through his hair as he tried to jump-release the clutch so as to gain some added traction. It was several minutes before the bumps and jolts of the wooded floor gave way to something resembling a road.

Cranking his window open to combat the mist, Mendravic yelled to Pearse over the din. "So, who exactly are we running from?"

Not that difficult a question, thought Pearse, even if he was having trouble explaining the man's strangely nonaggressive attitude just prior to Mendravic's intervention. None of the swagger. None of the menace. Still . . . "How does Vatican security strike you?" He began to fiddle with the knobs on the dashboard in an attempt to get some air onto the windshield.

Mendravic glanced at him quickly. "What?"

"I'd need a phone to make sure," answered Pearse, the knobs quickly proving useless; he sat back and stared out at the empty horizon. "So unless we happen to pass a McDonald's somewhere out here, you'll have to settle for a best guess."

"I'm not much for fast food," said Mendravic, reaching into his jacket pocket and pulling out a tiny cellular phone. "Probably could have traded it for one of those NATO trucks back there. Maybe two." With one eye on the road, he flipped it open and pressed several buttons. "I piggyback onto the NATO satellite linkups from time to time." He handed it to Pearse. "Just enter the number."

Pearse knew he shouldn't have been surprised. Doing as he was told, he fished a piece of paper from his pocket. "By the way," he asked as he dialed, "how did you know I was in that tent?"

Mendravic laughed to himself. "Next time, keep your fingers *inside* the flap, not outside."

Angeli's machine picked up, her message brief. A trip to Paris. Research. She'd be back in a week. "It's Ian Pearse—"

The machine disengaged. "Do you have the 'Hodoporia'?"

Pearse didn't recognize the voice. "Let me speak with the professor."

"Do you have the 'Hodoporia'?" Pearse remained silent. It was several moments before the question came again.

"Have you found what they want?" Tired, clearly frightened, it was Angeli.

"Thank God," said Pearse. "Are you all right?"

"I've been better. They want to know if you have the parchment."

"I will. Soon. Have they—"

"*How* soon, Father?" The man was back on the line.

"Put her on the phone." This time, it was the other end that chose not to answer. "It'll take a lot longer if you keep sending people out after me."

There was a momentary pause. "Say again."

"The four men you sent to find me in Kukes," Pearse answered. "They didn't get what they came for."

Another pause, then the sound of muffled conversation in the background. Pearse thought he heard a second phone dialing. It was nearly a minute before the man answered. "Describe these men."

The tone on the line spoke volumes. The men in Rome were as much in the dark about his recent assailants as he was. They had sent no one.

No swagger. No menace. No Vatican.

The question remained: Where had they come from? And who had sent them?

"Describe them," came the repeated order.

Pearse waited. "Keep the professor safe." He then pulled the phone from his ear and flipped it shut. He handed it to Mendravic.

"So?" he asked.

Pearse let his head fall back, the pounding subsiding. "Not the best guess."

▲

It was after seven by the time the limousine deposited Ludovisi back on Via Condotti, his steps unsteady—to anyone nearby, a man clearly worse for the wine. The street had mellowed since his hasty departure, strings of multicolored Christmas lights hanging overhead to lend the place a kind of festival atmosphere. The sneers of boutiques had given way to the clownish smiles of gelato carts and rose stands, as always, the strains of an ill-tuned guitar echoing from somewhere on the Spanish Steps. Ludovisi noticed none of it, clumsily maneuvering himself through the crowd, the outer rim of the piazza fountain a welcome relief as he stumbled his way down to it and sat. Staring into the gurgling water, he tried to shake the haze from his head, unable to recall the last three hours with any precision.

As far as he could remember, the evening had begun in silence, Kleist stone-faced to his questions, their destination kept hidden behind windows tinted to the point of impenetrability, only the car's speed—too fast for the city streets—giving anything away. Somewhere on the outskirts of town. A villa perhaps. Kleist had finally offered him a drink— in the car, at the villa—he couldn't remember. Brandy, scotch, it made no difference now. The light-headedness had followed. He recalled something of an underground garage, a set of stairs, a rather grand library.

Once inside, they had thrown a barrage of papers at him, some to be signed, others simply to be held, each immediately retrieved by Kleist. Computer discs, as well. Endless questions about account numbers, funds deposited, all of it streaming by in an ever-growing fog.

By the time they had taken him back to the garage, he'd required a man on either side to help him down the stairs. The ride back to town had passed in a disjointed series of words and faces.

With a sudden spasm, he dropped his head between his knees and vomited. It only made his head ache all the more. A second wave followed, most passersby moving off as quickly as possible, one or two trying to offer some help, a collision of voices and hands swimming in slow motion in front of him. Ignoring them, he reached into his jacket pocket for a handkerchief to wipe his mouth; instead, he pulled out two cards, identical to the ones he had tossed from the window at 201. He stared down at them, unable to gain his focus. *I . . . destroyed these.* And yet here they were, whole. *What the hell is going on?* Nausea gave way to fear.

Without warning, the left side of his neck constricted, a sudden twinge in his arm. At the same moment, his head began to convulse, more of the vomit curling up through his throat, his body slumping to the cold stone below. Somewhere within the pain, he heard shouts, whistling. Nothing registered, his body no longer his to control.

By the time the ambulance arrived, Arturo Ludovisi had been dead for over six minutes, the cards still clutched in his hand.

▲

Shkodër came and went with a quick stop for gas, no letup in the rain, the car managing the border just as the guard had promised. The various passports and transit cards Mendravic had produced hadn't hurt their chances, either—Albanian migrant-worker ID required no pictures.

"So this book, the one in Visegrad, it will do what for them?" asked Mendravic, still trying to piece things together.

"Not really sure," answered Pearse, his attention on the final quintet of the Ribadeneyra entries. He'd been struggling with them for over an hour. "Whatever it's supposed to do for them, they're very eager to get their hands on it."

"And what you're doing there"—Mendravic nodded toward the small black book—"that's going to tell us where we go?"

Pearse hummed in response, not really having heard the question. He continued to stare at the words, bits and pieces he had scribbled on the page, countless little circles of crossed-out letters, words on top of words, side by side in odd configurations.

It hadn't taken him long to realize that Ribadeneyra's *"quaestio lusoria"* was far more complex than simply a series of arcane anagrams. His first stab at entry number two, during his second night at Kukes, had made that clear. There had been nothing to it that even remotely hinted at an anagram. The same held true for numbers three through five, each of them either too long or too short to make even the most subtle reconfigurations provide an answer. It was only when he had moved on to number six that he'd seen the pattern. Here, again, was an intricate yet solvable anagram. Seven through ten, impenetrable. Eleven, doable. Every fifth one. It had suddenly dawned on him what he was looking at. As with the "Perfect

Light" letters, the entries here held to the Manichaeans' predilection for divisions within divisions, and always in sets of five. In the scroll, it had been through the prophetic ascents; here, Ribadeneyra had managed it through the distinct types of wordplay. Five categories, five of each kind. The question remained: Aside from the anagrams, what sorts of manipulations would the other four categories require?

It had struck him that, perhaps, there was a simple way to find out. Stealing a few minutes on one of the camp's computers, he'd quietly scanned the Internet for anything on cryptogrammics. Not the most detailed or accurate source, but at least something to give the hunt direction. The result: long, drawn-out lists on the various forms of modern cryptic wordplay, far more than the five categories he was looking for. Procedures called "deletions," "reversals," "charades," and "containers" dominated, each with a quick explanation and an equally simplistic example. Tools for the elite crossword fanatic. The *quaestio lusoria* had clearly come a long way in four centuries. Pearse wondered how many of its modern enthusiasts understood its darker history.

Back in his tent, he had discovered that the two-line (as he had come to refer to those entries in the same category as number two) resembled a charade, albeit in a slightly less straightforward form. The modern version, according to the Internet, required the solver to break the answer into several words, each defined independently: syllables, as it were, of the final charade. For example, "sharpen the pen for truth" had produced the answer "honesty." The derivation:

hone (sharpen) + sty (pen) = honesty (truth)

A one-to-one relationship. Ribadeneyra had relied on more obscure references, some using only partial words, but all creating longer sequences between the clues and their combining forms, especially when the answer was a phrase rather than a single word. In all cases, though, they required a very creative understanding of a given definition.

To make things even more difficult, Ribadeneyra had rarely chosen to include the answer as part of the clue; he offered no phrases such as "for truth" to hint at the solution. One of his more vexing had read:

Ab initio, surgunt muti in herbam.

Loosely translated:

From the beginning, they rise without speaking into the grass.

Strange as it sounded, it made perfect sense, given the Manichaean influence. In fact, the real mark of Ribadeneyra's genius was his ability to construct entries that revolved around references to those things that could help set the light free: "rising," "fruits," "herbs."

The answer, Pearse discovered, was *"deversoriolum,"* the Latin word for "inn." The derivation had gone quite easily at the start:

> **DE** = from
> **VER** = the beginning (the Latin for the season spring, the beginning of all things)
> **OLUM** = into the vegetable (the accusative form of the word herb, *olus,* thus *olum*)

But what of *"sori,"* stuck in the middle? Here was where Ribadeneyra had shown his special gift (the kindest way Pearse could think to put it). After too many hours tossing the clue around in his head, Pearse had realized that the verb "to rise"—here *"surgere"*—could be replaced with the Latin *sororio* ("to swell," primarily as with milk in a mother's breast, another appropriate choice, given the metaphor of beginnings and birth). In conjunction with the second-to-last part of the clue, *"muti"* ("without speaking"), he saw he needed to remove the Latin word for "to speak" *("oro"),* so as to make the combining form, literally, "speechless." Removing *"oro"* from *"sororio"* (with a little tweak) left *"sori."* Hence:

De - ver - sori - olum

A lot of work for a three-letter answer.

So it had gone with the three- and four-lines, each a more opaque version of a modern cryptogram, naturally made more difficult by the interplay of Greek and Latin references. The three-line had worked primarily with deletions—single or double letters removed from one word to create another. The Internet example, "headless trident bears fruit," had given the answer "pear." The derivation:

$$\text{spear (trident)} - s \text{ (its ``head'')} = \text{pear (fruit)}$$

The most direct of all the categories.

The four-line, however, had proved the most difficult, combining elements from the other three to create the longest phrases. For example, to unearth just the single word *"pons"* (meaning "bridge") in one of the answers, he'd had to take the word *"pomus"* (meaning "fruit tree"), eliminate "the Greek Medusa" and replace it with the "the Roman Neptune." Here, "the Greek Medusa" had signified the letter *Mu*—the Greek for *M*, the first letter in Medusa; "the Roman Neptune" had implied the letter *n*. Replace *mu* in *"pomus"* with *n*, and you have *"pons"*—"bridge."

Granted, the gnosis here wasn't quite as deviously hidden as with the "Perfect Light"—no letters and cross-references to construct the map. Then again, the earlier Manichaeans had had five centuries to devise their puzzle. Ribadeneyra had taken a few months. An effort certainly worthy of their legacy.

Pearse quickly came to appreciate the beauty of the game, its precision. Everything was there from the start, no landmarks to be found, no mechanisms to be unhinged. A genuine alchemy, the gold trapped within the obscurity of a language waiting for release. A strange taste of the *Sola Scriptura*. Discovery in its purest form.

Pearse knew Angeli would have needed, at most, a few hours for the entire lot; he had taken the better part of four days. Even when helping with the refugees, he'd been aware that his subconscious was continuing to play with the clues, flashes of understanding bubbling to the surface at the strangest of moments, often a word or two in conversation enough to spark revelation. Though frustrating at times, the process nevertheless gave him a real sense of satisfaction, each of the entries offering up tiny moments of triumph. Given the mayhem of the last week, such fleeting brushes with resolution were deeply rewarding.

Still, he had yet to penetrate even one of the five-line entries, none of them coming close to anything he had seen on the computer. More than that, he had come to recognize that the last of the categories held the key to the entire puzzle. As with the acrostics, the rest remained meaningless—a mishmash of abstract phrases and words—without something to tie them together. With "Perfect Light," it had been the prophetic letters. Here, it was the five-line entries. Another map waiting to be discovered.

An image of Angeli came to mind, her plump little hand sweeping along the sheets of yellow paper, eyes staring up at him, so eager for him to see what she herself had already detected. The elation at her discovery. Her impatience with his thickheadedness.

He couldn't afford to keep her waiting too much longer.

At this rate, though, he had little to bolster his confidence. He had no idea as to what would help to unlock the last of the entries. He needed to clear his mind. More than that, his eyes needed a rest. The vibration from the van was hardly making the reading easy, his head still battling the last vestiges of the concussion.

He flicked off the flashlight, let the paper drop to his lap, and set his head back against the seat. After a few minutes—eyes gazing out at the blackened landscape—he said, "You're wrong, you know."

Not sure what Pearse was referring to, Mendravic remained silent.

"About your friends in the KLA," he clarified.

"Ah." Mendravic kept his eyes on the road. A return to the conversation they'd started over two hours ago.

"They're as much to blame for the refugees now as the Serbs were a year ago." Pearse continued to stare out.

"Five days in the region and you're an expert."

"They're a bunch of thugs, Irish Provisionals, Kosovo-style. Except maybe a little more brutal."

"I see." Mendravic nodded to himself. "I've always had trouble distinguishing Milošević from Tony Blair." Before Pearse could respond, he said, "A year after a peace accord, and the Serbs are still 'encouraging' people not to return home. I don't say I agree with everything the KLA does, but at least they're doing something."

"Like killing Serbs?"

"Yes. Like killing Serbs." He waited, then looked over at Pearse. "Not all that enlightened, I know. But there it is." Focusing again on the road, the hint of a grin now on his face, he added, "We're a sort of an eye-for-an-eye kind of people. Never really been that much room in this part of the world for turning the other cheek."

Pearse smiled to himself. "I wasn't aware the KLA set its policy based on scriptural debate."

"Just the overall strategy," Mendravic said. "Too many different kinds of scripture floating around these parts to map out the day-to-day game plan."

It was remarkable how easily they slipped into the familiar sparring, even after eight years. Pearse was about to let loose with his next jab, when he suddenly stopped.

Instead, he flicked on the flashlight and looked down at the pages on his lap. Something in what Mendravic had just said. Scriptural mapping.

"What?" prodded the Croat.

Lost in the pages, Pearse slowly realized that each of the five-line entries had a peculiar quality to it, something he would never have seen had he continued to attack each one as an individual cryptogram. Reading them as continuous phrases, he saw that each of them produced a kind of singsong cadence, almost a lilting meter, as if it was meant to be spoken aloud.

> *So do I stretch out my two hands toward You,*
> *All to be formed in the orbit of light.*
> *When I am sent to the contest with darkness,*
> *Knowing that You can assist me in sight.*
> *The fragrance of life is always within me.*

Like a piece of Scripture. Like the verse of a prayer.

He felt a swell of satisfaction, quickly doused by the realization that he had no idea what it meant. This was no verse he recognized. Pieces of Scripture or not, the five-line entries remained a mystery.

He was about to tell Mendravic, when he noticed a sign indicating a split in the road just ahead: east to Visegrad, west to Rogatica and Sarajevo. From there, another twenty minutes to the "town on the Drina."

When Mendravic opted for the Rogatica turnoff, Pearse shot up in his seat. He began to point in the other direction.

"What are you doing?" he asked.

"It's after ten," said Mendravic. "Visegrad's not exactly a tourist spot since the war. Much better chance of finding a hotel nearer the city."

Watching the Visegrad road disappear, Pearse knew Mendravic was right. After all, what could they accomplish tonight? He was too tired to make sense of the recent discovery. He needed sleep to clear his mind.

They drove for another half an hour, Mendravic intent on the roads, Pearse with his head in the book. Surprisingly, Mendravic was rather familiar with Rogatica and its surroundings. Mumbling street names to himself, he seemed to be in search of a specific hotel. After several miscues, they finally arrived at what looked like an apartment house, six stories of dull gray brick.

"This doesn't look like a hotel," said Pearse.

Maybe it was his preoccupation with the final set of entries, or the cumulative effects of the last week, but it wasn't until he saw Mendravic smiling back at him that Pearse realized where he had been taken.

"You're not very bright, are you?" asked Mendravic.

The Croat leaned forward in his seat and peered up at the building through the windshield. "Fifth floor. Second in from the right."

Pearse couldn't bring himself to lean forward.

"This was your second request, wasn't it?" Mendravic sat back, the grin once again in evidence. "Shall we see if the two of them have room for us tonight?"

Ⓐ

Doña Marcella pulled the half glasses from her face and placed the papers on the coffee table in front of her. She waited for Blaney to finish reading.

She hadn't been to his rooms off the Giardini del Quirinale in years, the priest, by the look of them, well taken care of by his Chicago archdiocese. Thick velvet drapes hung across the twelve-foot windows, the furniture distinctly Edwardian, a bulky mahogany roughness befitting the man seated across from her. Browns on browns, with a hint of maroon here and there. What few splashes of color he permitted came from a pair of large vases standing on either side of a rather dour sideboard.

"Am I actually supposed to believe this?" she asked when he finally looked up.

"I don't think you're the one they're trying to convince," Blaney answered.

"It's all tabloid." She reached for the paper nearest to her. "'Gelli's Ghost Returns,'" she read. "Complete nonsense." She tossed it back onto the table. "The morning papers won't be so quick to swallow all of this. Who's going to believe Arturo capable of such things?"

"He was found with the papers, the discs."

She waited before answering. "If what they say is true, this will make the whole Calvi business look like a minor inconvenience. This isn't going to be the usual mop-up. I'm going to need time, and I'm not sure I have it."

"That's not what worries me," said Blaney. "Weakening the bank only makes the church more vulnerable, raises the specter of corruption.

Which makes the job of the 'Hodoporia' all the easier. The question is, did he leave anything on those discs to link us with the bank?"

"That's exactly my point; the church isn't the issue." Frustration forced her up from her chair. "Tell me he wouldn't have been that stupid, John?" Blaney started to answer. She cut him off. "What does Erich say?"

He shook his head dismissively. "No idea. He's unreachable. The *novemdieles* concludes tomorrow morning. They've already started to convene the conclave."

"Not the best timing."

Blaney nodded. "Unless it's what he was planning all along."

It took her a moment to respond. "And what is that supposed to mean?" When he didn't answer, she pressed him. "You can't be serious? Why would Erich have had any part in this?"

"Let's just say I'm not so sure his faith in the 'Hodoporia' is what it once was." He let the words sit for a moment. "He's very fond of reminding me that it's a 'complicated world.' And a complicated world demands complicated answers." Again, he shook his head. "There's very little I'd put past Erich now. Despite all of Arturo's fidgeting, he was a remarkably fit man. Prided himself on it. He was also something of a hypochondriac. A man like that doesn't suddenly collapse in the Piazza di Spagna for no apparent reason."

"And you think Erich would have . . ." She couldn't finish the thought. "Why?"

Blaney sat back and let his eyes wander. For some reason, they stopped on a small crystal lamb nestled within a group of pictures—a gift from his very first parish. Something long forgotten. He stared at it, then turned to the contessa. "Because the thought of anyone else having something to do with this is even more unsettling."

⚠

She had sounded excited over the intercom, Mendravic announcing only himself, the real surprise left for upstairs. It had taken a good ten minutes for Pearse to get out of the car, the prospect of meeting his son somehow less daunting than seeing her again. He had no idea what to expect from the boy. With Petra, though, he knew what he wanted to hear, what had been running through his head since this afternoon. Nothing to assuage. No attempts to let him off the hook, tell him it had been for the best. He had outgrown that kind of coddling.

Inside, he quickly fell behind, nearly a full flight below by the time Mendravic reached the fifth floor. Moving slowly, Pearse heard the chirped "Salko" from above, an excited Petra at the top of the stairs, the sound of an embrace, an instant of laughter. He stopped, listened for a moment, then continued on. Rounding the final turn, he saw her arms clutched around Mendravic's enormous bulk, her face resting on his shoulder. Her eyes were closed, a moment to see her as she was, as he knew she would be.

And then her eyes opened. No change in expression. No hint of movement. Only the eyes peering down at him.

Somehow, Mendravic sensed it. Without a word, he pulled away and moved off down the corridor, the sound of a squealing hinge in the distance a few moments later.

The two of them continued to stare.

Whatever image Pearse had carried with him for the last eight years came to life as she looked down at him. If she had aged, it was only around the eyes, one or two creases. The battle with her hair continued to rage on, the familiar wisps draped along her cheek. She wore a simple shirt, skirt—something he had never seen before, never even imagined on her—ankle-length, bobbing atop her bare feet.

She leaned back against the railing. Silence.

"Hey," he said finally, regretting the choice before the word had even left his mouth.

"Hey," she answered.

"You look—"

She nodded to herself before he could finish the thought. "I look great, right?"

Again, he realized how stupid it must have sounded. He tried a smile. "Right."

She shook her head. "You still don't look like a priest."

"I guess some things never change."

"No, I guess they don't." She waited. "Amazing how long you imagine this, and it doesn't make it any easier, does it?" Again, she waited. "Why are you here, Ian?"

He wanted to move to her but couldn't. "It's a long story."

She continued to stare at him. "I never thought I'd see you again."

"I know." Another stab at the smile. "I wasn't sure you'd want to."

"Neither was I, for a while." She was about to say something else, then stopped.

Another awkward silence. Finally, he spoke: "Why didn't you tell me?"

"Oh, I see," she said. "Salko told you." A dismissive laugh. "Of course he told you. That's why you're here."

"It's not the only reason."

She'd become preoccupied with something on the step, her foot rubbing away at it. "I didn't know the last time we spoke."

"So why didn't you get in touch with me when you found out?"

Again, silence. When she turned to him, her expression was far from what he expected. Her own attempt at a smile. Not terribly convincing. "Right to the tough stuff," she said. "That isn't fair, is it?" He tried to answer. "Look, Salko's probably halfway through the fridge. Why don't you come inside?" Not waiting for him, she turned and headed down the hall.

The apartment was much as he'd expected it—living room, galley kitchen, narrow hall, rooms somewhere beyond. A low overstuffed couch took up much of the far wall, Mendravic now taking up much of it, already a plate of something in his lap. A small table perched under the near window, half of it reserved for a rather ancient television—an even older video game hooked up to its back—two chairs around the far end for mother and son. A bookshelf—slanting just a bit—stood by the entry to the hall, a wide assortment of knickknacks, pictures, and books atop its six shelves. Pearse recognized a few of the faces, Mendravic's the most prominent, one shot of him caught in midlaugh, the boy clutched in his arms, outside, winter hats.

"He was four in that picture," Petra said, noticing where Pearse's eyes had come to rest. "It's a park in Sarajevo. Veliki. I think you were there once. It still had some trees left. Near where we lived."

"Dusanov," chimed in Mendravic, his mouth busy with a piece of orange. "It was Dusanov, the other side of the river. Remember, he cut himself when he fell?"

Petra shook her head and moved toward the shelf. "That happened in Veliki." She picked up the plastic frame, slid the picture out, and flipped it over. A moment later, the smile on her face signaled her capitulation. "'November fifth, 1997,'" she read. "'Dusanov Park with Salko.'" She looked over at Mendravic. "How do you always do that?"

He shrugged as he finished off the wedge. "Must be that I love him more than you do." A smile peeked out from behind the rind.

"That must be it," she said. She was about to put it back in its frame. Instead, she handed it to Pearse.

He looked down into the child's face and realized he was staring into Petra's eyes, tinier versions to be sure, but the same deep charcoal, the same long black lashes above, that pinch at either end when lost in laughter. The cheekbones were hers as well, sharply contoured around the dollop of nose, lips already hinting at his mother's fullness. But where the individual features were hers, the shape of the face was not, most notably in the jaw, its curve more pronounced, its line more angular—a child's size of one Pearse knew all too well.

Five minuscule fingers squeezed at Mendravic's large nose, the howls of laughter from them both almost audible.

"He's beautiful," Pearse finally said.

"Yes, he is." She waited for him to hand back the picture. She looked at it for several seconds, then slotted it into the frame and placed it on the shelf. "He's asleep," she said. She looked at Pearse, the first hint of softness in her eyes. "You'll have to be quiet." Not waiting for an answer, she started down the hall, Pearse at once behind her.

With a finger to her lips, she quietly opened the door, the mustiness of a sleeping seven-year-old at once rising up to greet them. Waiting a moment for her eyes to adjust, she led the way through, a tangle of clothes and toys scattered along the path, a sliver of shadow cutting across the room through a slit in the curtains. When she reached the bed, she remained perfectly still for several seconds, Pearse at her side.

The boy lay curled up on his side, hands nestled under his chin, a thin blanket draped along his back, only his feet peeking out at the edge. Beneath the cover, a small shoulder rose and fell, the sound of gentle breath on pillow. Nothing else to break the silence. A few years older— the chin more pronounced, the lips having lived up to their promise— the face remained hers. Pearse couldn't help but marvel at him, the quiet wonder of this boy. He had a sudden need to reach out to him, hold him, equally desperate not to disrupt the moment's perfect serenity. Torn between the two impulses, he crouched down and brought his face to within a hair's breadth of the boy's cheek, the closeness almost unbearable. Shutting his eyes, he felt the warmth just beyond his grasp, and a sense of overwhelming loss.

Even then, he couldn't bring himself to hold his son, no matter how great the need. He hovered on the brink, eyes now open, his own breath growing shorter and shorter. When it became too much, he pulled himself back and turned to her. She had been looking at him all along. She continued to stare, her eyes unwilling to give into the tears.

Then, without a sound, she stepped closer into the bed, leaned past him and kissed her son. The child moved, his lips parting, a deep breath, as if he might say something; then, just as quickly, he was still. She waited, then nodded to Pearse and headed for the door.

When she had pulled it shut, she turned to him. She seemed unsure for a moment. "You could have held him," she finally said. "It would have been all right."

Pearse thought of answering, but couldn't. They stood there for a moment. The sound of a plate being dropped momentarily broke the silence. Instinctively, she turned toward the kitchen, then back to Pearse.

"Salko," she said.

She started down the hall; Pearse reached out and took her hand. He felt her entire body tense. Just as quickly, she relaxed and turned to him.

"Not yet," she said softly. She slowly pulled her hand away. For just a moment, she let it rest on his chest, then turned and headed for the living room. Pearse watched her go, then followed.

Mendravic was at the fridge.

"It's not going to be enough," he said, his head deep inside. "You hardly have a thing."

"It's not as if I was expecting you," she said as she sidled past him and opened several cabinets along the cupboard by the stove. From the one at the top, she produced crackers, a collection of boxes filled with foods Pearse had never heard of, and pasta.

Mendravic removed himself from the fridge and peered over at the scant offerings. Crinkling his face, he shook his head. "Crackers? This is Salko." When she continued to stare at him—no hint of mercy in her eyes—his expression at once became more benign. "The orange was good," he said sheepishly.

Ten minutes later, he had convinced her that they needed to go out. Ten-thirty. Not so late in this part of the world. The boy would be fine. Yes, he knew the right place. Yes, it was very close by. They'd be away half an hour. Forty-five minutes at the most. With tremendous reluctance, and a constant barrage of encouragement, she had knocked on her neighbor's door. Explanations of friends from out of town, nothing in the house. The woman had been more than accommodating.

"I know the place," she had said. "Go. It'll do you good. He'll be fine with me." A wink from Mendravic hadn't hurt, either.

True to his word, the café was no more than a five-minute drive from the apartment. A good deal more than crackers and pasta.

And, as with just about everything else, Mendravic seemed to be on familiar terms with everyone at the restaurant. The promised crowds, however, proved to be no more than a waiter and cashier, both eager to close up shop. Evidently, his recollection of late-night carousing wasn't terribly accurate. No matter. The two were more than happy to keep the kitchen open a little while longer. For an old friend.

"I'm in the mood for *burek*," Mendravic began, the waiter nodding his approval. "And some of the lemon-ginger *rakija*."

"'*Burek?*'" asked Pearse.

"Like Greek *spanokopita*." When Pearse continued to stare blankly, Mendravic explained: "Casserole. Spinach, cheese, light pastry. Delicious."

Pearse's expression showed far less enthusiasm. "Nothing heavier?" he said.

"One order of the *burek*, and one of the *maslenica*," Petra told the waiter. "And a bottle of *prokupac*."

"Masle what?" Again Pearse was at a loss.

"Trust me." She smiled. "Heavier. Much heavier."

Half an hour later, there was still plenty on the plate, even Mendravic too full to take a taste of the generous helping of stew. The wine and brandy were another matter.

"You're telling me one person usually eats this whole thing," said Pearse, having had a bit more to drink than he was used to, and unable to wrap his mind around the Bosnian capacity for consumption.

"Sure." Petra laughed. "Ivo has at least two of them each night for dinner."

Mendravic laughed as well, a few hums of approval as he now began to pick at the bits of feta that had broken free of the remaining heap of meat.

"Ivo?" Pearse couldn't recall an Ivo.

Before Petra could answer, Mendravic cut in: "Her son. Your son. Ivo. It's as close as you get to Ian in Croatian." He was hunting for the last of the mushrooms. Poking away with his fork, he added, "Two of them, easy." A lazy laugh as he pushed the plate away.

Ivo. Pearse realized he hadn't even bothered to ask. For some reason, he laughed as well. Only for a moment, but distinctly, a laugh.

"What's so funny?" asked Petra.

He shook his head, the laughter subsiding, a nervous energy competing with the effects of the brandy.

"Good a reason as any," Mendravic chimed in as he hoisted himself up. "Men's room," the declaration more to remind himself why he'd gotten up than to update his dinner companions. He picked one last mushroom from the plate, swallowed it, and headed back.

When Petra turned to him, she saw Pearse was staring at her.

"What?" she said.

"Hearing his name . . . it made me laugh."

"It's a good name," she said. "Good enough for you."

"That's not what I meant."

"I know."

"Yes, I know you know."

Petra refilled their glasses. She took a sip, then placed hers on the table.

After another awkward silence, Pearse spoke: "It's just when I first saw him, it made me . . . I can't explain it. To see him and know how much I hadn't seen, how much he was without my ever having . . ." The thought trailed off. "And then hearing his name. I don't know. It just . . . came out of nowhere." Without any thought, he picked up his fork and began to run it along the plate. "Does that make any sense?"

Petra continued to look at him. "He's your son. He has your name. Yes. That should make you happy."

Pearse nodded, his focus still on the plate. After several moments, he asked, "And you?"

"And me, what?"

"Does it make you happy?"

She waited before answering. "That's a silly question."

"Why?" he asked, turning back toward her.

" 'Why?' " Again she paused. "You saw him. It's a silly question."

Once again, an overwhelming sense of loss cut through him. "Then why didn't you tell me?"

"A priest with a son?" A smile, a shake of the head. "We both know you would have thrown that all away, done the right thing. And I wasn't going to do that to any of us. You asked me to understand." She held his gaze. "Don't you see, I finally did."

"Maybe better than I did."

She stopped, never for a moment thinking he would say that. "What do you mean?"

"I mean, it's never been as clear as I thought it would be. It's never made as much sense."

"As what?"

He continued to look at her.

"Don't . . . don't say that. Every day you didn't come back confirmed how right your choice was. That you belonged in another life. And every one of those days made me feel stronger about what I was doing. About the decision I made."

It was several seconds before he spoke.

"Does he know about me?" he asked.

"Of course."

"That I'm a priest."

Now she laughed. Her reaction caught him by surprise. "You don't tell a seven-year-old his father is a priest, Ian." She reached for her glass. "Don't worry. It's not that strange for a boy here not to have a father. Half his friends are the same way. Except theirs are dead. At least he knows you're alive."

"I guess that's something."

"Believe me, it is." She took a sip. "He knows you're an American. He knows you fought with Salko and me during the war." She stopped and placed the glass on the table. She then looked up at him. "And he knows you're a good man."

He stared at her for several seconds. "Thank you," he said.

"I'm not going to lie to my son."

"Except for that bit about the priest."

"Right. Except for that."

He waited. "Look, I'm sorry—"

"Don't do that, okay?"

Again he waited. "Okay." He took a sip, then said, "He must wonder why I haven't visited him."

"You're an American. That makes up for a lot of things to a boy here. You brought peace and chocolates and video games."

"That's not what I meant."

She was about to say something, but instead began to cradle the glass in her hands. Staring down into it, she said, "He has Salko, who's been wonderful. And he has an image of a father that makes him feel different from all the other kids. What more could he want?"

"So right now, I'm some generic American who's made of chocolate and designed in Japan."

"You're everything that's possible to him. Everything that's beyond here." She took another sip, her eyes again on the glass. "Most fathers dream of being that to their sons."

For the first time, Pearse realized he'd been missing something entirely. From his first moments with her tonight, he'd been focusing on Ivo. Everything they'd talked about had been the boy. Strange that in the car he'd been so concerned with how he would react to her. And yet it had all slipped from his mind the instant he'd seen her.

And now he'd needed her to remind him.

"So what about you?" he asked.

A nervous laughter erupted in her throat. Again, it caught him completely by surprise. "You really were never very good at this, were you?"

For some reason, he laughed, as well. "I guess not," he said.

"I'm telling you," said Mendravic, who chose that moment to reappear, "it's not that funny. Ivo, Ian. They're just names." It was clear from his expression that he knew exactly what they'd been talking about. Pearse couldn't be sure just which one of them Mendravic thought he was rescuing, or, more to the point, which of them he thought needed the rescuing.

Whichever it was, Mendravic was clearly eager to go, hovering by the chair, his eyes scanning the area by the door. He'd had his food. He needed a bed. Same old Salko. Pearse turned back to Petra, who was also peering up at Mendravic. "Well, we can't keep you waiting," she said, "now can we?"

She slid back her chair and was about to stand, when Mendravic said, "Wait here." His tone was direct, none of the charm of only seconds ago. Before she could answer, he was making his way to the door. She looked at Pearse.

His expression told her everything. "You didn't come just to see us, did you?"

She had been trained too well not to recognize an order. And she was too smart not to understand the implications.

Pearse stared blankly, then turned to watch Mendravic leave the restaurant.

Twenty seconds later, he returned. By his side stood Petra's next-door neighbor. In his arms, he held the boy, Ivo peering down from the height, his cheeks that puffy red from recent rousing. Even half-asleep, his eyes lit up at the sight of Petra. She was already to him by the time Mendravic spoke.

"We should move to the back," he said, releasing the boy into his mother's arms. With Mendravic, Ivo had fit perfectly; with Petra, he seemed to overwhelm her smaller frame. Still, she held him tightly to her shoulders, his head lost in her neck, legs dangling awkwardly below. The expression on her face betrayed none of the unwieldiness, her cheek pressed to his, whispering something into his tiny ear. Pearse watched as the two women headed back, the boy's eyes drifting into sleep, his hands lost in his mother's hair. At the same time, Mendravic stepped over to the waiter; they exchanged a few words, the man nodding. As Mendravic returned, Pearse saw the waiter move to the door and lock it.

"How did you—"

"I saw them across the street, through the window," Mendravic explained.

Now on his feet, Pearse realized the corner lamp illuminated much of the area outside. Not too difficult to pick up two figures on an empty street.

Once all four adults were settled into a booth—Ivo's head now on Petra's lap—Mendravic explained:

"She says a man came to the apartment."

"How he got into the building," the woman piped in, "I don't know, but there he was, five, maybe ten minutes after you left."

"At eleven o'clock at night?" asked Petra. She turned to Pearse, then Mendravic. "What haven't you told me?"

Mendravic shook his head once, then asked, "Did he say what he wanted?"

"You," the woman answered, nodding toward Petra.

Mendravic hesitated, then said, "Naturally. It's her apartment. Did he say why he wanted to see her?"

"No." The woman looked at Mendravic. "A police badge, or something like it. You learn to look at the eyes, not the badge. I'd seen that same stare plenty of times during the war. Men appearing in the middle of the night. I kept the chain on the whole time." She turned back to Petra. "I told him you didn't live there anymore, that it was my place. When he asked me where you lived now, I shrugged"—she demonstrated for the table—"said it wasn't my business. I waited by the window until I saw him leave. He got into a car with someone else. Ten minutes after that, I brought Ivo here."

"You walked here?" It was the first time Pearse had said anything.

"Don't worry," said the woman as she turned to Mendravic. "The basements of all the buildings on the block are connected. We went down, then came out on the street behind. They wouldn't have seen us." She turned and handed Petra a small bag she had been holding on her lap. "Some clothes for you and Ivo. I thought it might be a good idea." She then turned back to Mendravic, the smile almost coquettish. "I also fought in the war."

Mendravic nodded. "I can see that. Excellent work."

The woman seemed well pleased and sat back.

"What was the man wearing?" asked Pearse.

The woman's expression made it clear that she felt she had said all that was necessary. "Wearing?" She shrugged again. "I don't know. A jacket. Some pants. Oh . . . and some of those high boots. Tied outside the pants. The sort you take into the mountains." Again, she turned to Mendravic for approval. Again, he smiled with a nod.

"High boots," echoed Pearse, also peering over at Mendravic. He could see the gears working behind the Croat's eyes.

"All right," Mendravic said. "You need to stay with friends for the next few days." The woman's reaction told him she'd already taken the precaution. "And we have to get out of here now."

"We *all* have to get out of here now." Petra was staring directly at Mendravic.

Again, the gears cranked before he answered. "Right."

"We can't take them to—"

The woman cut Pearse off. "I don't want to know where you can't take them. I don't want to know where you *can* take them." She was clearly enjoying her return to Mendravic's world, the posturing far more compelling than any possible danger. She stood. "I'll wait to go back to the apartment for three days. You can contact me then." She turned to Petra, offered a smile, a kiss on both cheeks for Mendravic, and then headed for the front.

As he watched her go, Mendravic spoke under his breath, *"Vive la résistance."*

"Behave," chided Petra. "She saw more than you and I ever did during the war. And she knows exactly what she's doing. She's just a little lonely now. Without her, your friends in high boots would be standing here with us right now."

"We can't take them to Visegrad," said Pearse, picking up where he had left off.

"And we can't leave them here," answered Mendravic.

"Before we make any decisions," Petra said, "we all have to know exactly whom and what we're running away from."

"No, we don't." The tone in Mendravic's voice was one neither of them had heard in years. He stood, stepped around, and picked up Ivo before Petra could respond. The boy, who had fallen back to sleep, was now stirring, one eye lazily opening. Mendravic quickly whispered something to him, his massive hand rubbing gently along the boy's slender back. In a hushed voice, he continued. "We get in the car and we drive. And then we fill in the gaps."

He turned and headed toward the kitchen. Pearse and Petra had no choice but to follow.

▲

The coolness in the air surprised him, more than a hint of the coming autumn. He was glad he had brought a sweater, the walk to the church nearly a mile from the inn he had chosen on the edge of town. He'd had time enough to acclimate himself—two days since his flight into Heathrow—ample opportunity to monitor the comings and goings of Bibury's inhabitants, a typical Cotswold village, replete with teahouses, ancient Tudor shops, long barrow walks, and the usual infestation of summer renters up from the city. He'd opted for one of the more prominent villages, easier to go unnoticed, another tourist taking in the pleasant English summer. Even so, quarter to twelve, and only the central streets showed any signs of life. And what life there was kept itself to a minimum. The pubs and restaurants had closed over an hour ago—coming from the south of Spain, he'd never understood how the English could abide the early closings—leaving little else to do but head back home for the down quilts and goose-feather pillows.

A more and more inviting prospect the farther on he walked.

That there was hardly any light didn't seem to bother him in the least. The lamps were for town; out here, they would have been an intrusion.

He had walked the route perhaps fifteen times in the last day, committing to memory the exact number of paces required along each lane, the placement of each turn, the points when the road would rise and fall—but nothing visual. Too much conspired at night to make anything but the most precise measurements a reliable guide. The countryside could play tricks, tease with the appearance of a hedge, the outline of a house. He might as well have been blindfolded, for the attention he gave to his surroundings.

Concentrating on the numbers also allowed him to focus on the sound of his steps, barely audible even within the crisp stillness of the late evening. The last of the houses had come and gone some ten minutes back, his only indication a sudden quickening in the roll of the road, the undulation more and more aggressive during the last quarter mile of the walk.

As he reached the end of the count, he looked up and saw the small church in front of him, its outline cutting into the sky, its Norman lines lost to the blackness. He scanned the area to his right; the manse, a small cottage by day, was now little more than an amorphous hump on the horizon. He headed for the side of the church farthest from it, a window he had left unlatched during his visit that afternoon. Truth be told, he'd removed the latch entirely. No reason to leave anything to chance.

Hoisting himself up to the sill, he lifted the window, a momentary screech of metal on wood, nothing, though, to cause concern. He then pivoted himself through, slid down to the stone floor, and removed the pack from his back. Retrieving a laser-line flashlight from one of the compartments, he twisted its head and pointed the fine beam at the ground.

It would take him almost an hour to plant the explosives, most of the time devoted to positioning them so that enough of the fragments could be found and traced. That took some expertise. It was why he had been chosen.

Why others had been chosen.

Vienna. Ankara. Bilbao. Montana. Over a thousand names. Over a thousand churches.

One result.

Éeema, Éeema, Ayo.

▲

The humidity had returned, even in the short amount of time they had spent in the restaurant. Added to that, the alley outside smelled like three-day-old garbage, the neighborhood cats having made easy work of the cans and bags placed along the walls. One or two were still busy, unconcerned with the arrival of the odd quartet. A quick glance over, then back to the hunt.

As the four of them neared the alley's edge, Mendravic turned to Pearse. "Wait here," he said. "I'll bring the car around." He then handed him the boy and moved off down the street.

For just a moment, Ivo lifted his head, eyes half-asleep; just as quickly, he dropped his head down, nuzzling into the soft of Pearse's neck.

It had happened so quickly, Pearse had no time to react. The boy in his arms. The very thing he'd been unable to do himself back in the apartment now handed to him without a thought. Mendravic had had other things to worry about.

Strangely enough, Pearse couldn't recall what they were. Not with his son in his arms. For several minutes, he stood, eyes closed, arms wrapped around the sleeping boy, forcing himself not to hold him too tightly, the impulse almost too much. Mind a blank. The smell of sleep from his hair. The sound of breath on his neck. Here was the Teresian moment, felt, not thought, not even fully understood.

At some point, Pearse began to feel a hand on his arm. He turned to see Petra.

"You can let me have him," she said, her arms outstretched, waiting.

He was about to tell her that it would be easier for him to carry the boy, when he saw the expression on her face. She seemed torn, unsure whether to give in to a moment she had wanted for so long, or to take back what was hers—if, in fact, she could think of Ivo as hers alone anymore.

Pearse suddenly understood why he had been so afraid in the apartment. It was because of this moment. Having held him, and then to give him up. That was the loss.

With a simple nod, he reached up under Ivo's shoulder and carefully lifted him to his mother. Again, the boy's body draped awkwardly on hers, but it didn't seem to register with her at all.

Trying to focus on anything but the last few minutes, Pearse suddenly realized it was taking Mendravic a very long time to get the car they had left just outside the front of the restaurant. Motioning for Petra to stand back in the shadows, he slowly edged his face out into the light. He looked back over his shoulder. "Wait here."

An eerie quiet filled the street, heightened by the glow of two white lamps at either end. No signs of life as he slowly began to move out along the pavement, head low, his own shadow half a foot in front of him. The air seemed to grow more sterile with each step, a dryness in his throat. Nearing the corner, he heard his own voice begging him to turn back. Still he walked.

The sound of squealing wheels broke through, his first instinct to flatten himself against the wall. The car was coming from behind him, its lights on high beam, blinding him for an instant as it careened down the street. With a sudden choking of the engine, it stopped directly in front of the alley. Pearse pulled himself from the wall and began to run, the only image in his head that of Petra and the boy, his own horror at having abandoned them. With his hand up to guard against the glare, he saw the driver's door open, a man begin to emerge. Pearse propelled himself faster, lunging at the figure as he stood.

Mendravic caught him with a quick forearm, locking his throat in a viselike grip.

The two recognized each other instantly. Mendravic released, Pearse gasping for air as he steadied himself against the car.

"What the hell were you . . ." Mendravic had no time for questions as he moved to the back of the van, opened the trunk, and motioned for Petra to bring Ivo. Mother and son emerged from the alley, Mendravic taking the boy and placing him inside the van. Petra stepped up into the back cabin as well. Mendravic shut the door.

It was only then that Pearse saw the blood on his arm.

"Salko, what—"

"Get in the car," he barked, racing to the driver's side. Pearse leapt around to the other. He'd barely pulled the door shut before the car bolted out into the road.

Mendravic reached behind him and slid open a small glass partition to the back.

"Are you all right back there?" he asked.

"We'll be fine," Petra answered. "He's up, though." A small face suddenly appeared in the opening, eyes wide, a smile equally electric.

"Hello, Salko."

"Well, look who's up." Mendravic continued to glance at his side mirror, his attention more on what lay behind them than on the road ahead. "Hello, little man," he said. A hand now appeared and tugged at Mendravic's ear, evidently a game between them. Removing the tiny fingers, Mendravic said, "Can you do me a favor, Ivo? Can you sit back there with Mommy and not make a sound? Can you do that for me?"

"Can I come sit with you?"

"Can you sit with Mommy?"

It was then that Ivo noticed Pearse. "Hello," he said, his tone no less forthright.

"Hello." Pearse smiled.

"I really need you to sit with Mommy," said Mendravic, eyes still on the mirror. "Okay?"

The boy stared for another moment at the stranger, then back to Mendravic. Another quick squeeze, and then gone.

Mendravic slid the glass partition shut.

"He takes it all in stride, doesn't he?" said Pearse.

"What?" Mendravic was concentrating on the road.

"Nothing." Seeing the blood on Mendravic's arm, he asked, "What happened?"

"Obviously, our friend in the resistance wasn't as good as she thought she was."

"They found you?"

"No. I found them. At the car. Good news, it was only two of them this time. Bad news, I wasn't as effective."

"Meaning?"

"Meaning we could have company." He pulled the car around a corner, forcing Pearse up against the door.

"And your arm?"

"Is in pain."

Pearse said nothing, watching as Mendravic took the road heading up into the mountains. Evidently, Visegrad would have to wait.

After nearly twenty minutes of silence, Mendravic finally seemed to relax behind the wheel.

"We're not going to Visegrad," said Pearse.

"Not tonight we're not." Mendravic took the car to seventy. "And we're not taking Ivo anywhere near there."

Pearse nodded, suddenly angry with himself. It was something he shouldn't have needed to be told.

"Why did you leave them in the alley?" asked Mendravic.

The question felt like a slap to the face. "I . . . thought—"

"Next time, don't. If I tell you to stay someplace, stay there. Do you understand?"

Pearse didn't need to answer.

"I've got some friends," Mendravic continued. "We'll stay with them for a day or so until the boys with the boots move on."

Pearse nodded.

"Just like old times," said Mendravic, his attempt to lighten the mood ringing hollow.

Pearse looked back through the glass. Ivo was once again asleep in Petra's lap. Her eyes were shut, as well.

Just like old times. It was a nostalgia he could have done without.

five

"... **d**uring or after the election of the new Pontiff, unless explicit authorization is granted by the same Pontiff; and never to lend support or favor to any interference, opposition, or any other form of intervention, whereby secular authorities of whatever order and degree or any group of people or individuals might wish to intervene in the election of the Roman Pontiff."

The cardinal dean finished reading and began to make his way around the Sistine Chapel. One by one, the cardinal electors rose to acknowledge the oath.

Von Neurath sat with his hands comfortably in his lap. The hard back of the bench seemed to suit his posture, less so the velvet cushion underneath. On his right sat an Englishman; on the other, a South American. Neither had said a word in the last twenty minutes, better that way, since von Neurath couldn't remember if his Spanish colleague was Brazilian or Argentinian, Escobar de something, if memory served. Cardinal Daly, however, was another matter entirely, well known among the conclave as a *papabile*—a "good prospect"—according to the scuttlebutt that had been circulating over the last few days. Strange that they'd placed two of the prime candidates so close to each other. Or maybe it was simply geography, the Italians on one side of the chapel, the rest of the Catholic world on the other.

Usually brightened by the afternoon sun, the chapel lay under a glow of standing lamps, the gated windows above the Perugino frescoes draped behind thick cloth, a nod to both the solemnity and the secrecy of the conclave. Even in the half-light, the chapel lost none of its grandeur, the plaintive stares from above deepened by the shadows, thick, muscular tones—the pigment having been restored—once again fresh and alive.

Von Neurath stared at one or two of the faces above. He'd never been all that taken with the paintings, far too ornate for his tastes. He much preferred the line of a van Eyck, or a Breu the Elder, or a Lochner, or even a Fra Angelico, if pressed to name an Italian. Now there was the precision of faith. With Michelangelo, everything of value seemed to get lost—hulking, self-indulgent bodies twisting this way and that, no direction, no meaning. Perfect for the Italians, he thought, each of whom continued to gaze up, with self-satisfied grins, as if somehow they were reading a private message, the figures meant for them alone. Von Neurath brought his arms to his chest and waited.

Movement by the altar caught his eye. The Cardinal Camerlengo—his old friend Fabrizzi—began to set the chalice and paten in place, cue for the initiation of the first ballot. Von Neurath looked down at the paper in his hand, the printed Latin a simple reminder of what had brought them all together.

"Eligo in summum pontificem . . ."

"I elect as supreme Pontiff . . ."

And next to it, in his own hand, the words "Erich Cardinal von Neurath."

It was an odd sensation to see the name in front of him. The Italians might have their art, but he would have their throne. Looking up, he had to suppress a smile.

The dean approached him. Von Neurath stood.

"And I, Erich Cardinal von Neurath, do so promise, pledge, and swear." He placed his hand on the Gospels held out in front of him. "So help me God and these Holy Gospels which I touch with my hand."

Twenty minutes later, each of the 109 had sworn their troth. The voting began.

As the first of the cardinals moved toward the altar—always one by one—von Neurath scanned the faces across from him. How many of them were thinking of grandnieces and grandnephews? he wondered. Kleist had made over sixty tapes. He'd sent out fewer than twenty of them, but it was more than enough to encourage the crucial swing votes necessary to take him past the two-thirds majority for election.

The procession continued, at last his own turn. With a deep breath, he folded the paper in his hand, stood, and slowly walked toward the altar. Reaching the table, he turned back to the conclave, raised his ballot high for all to see, then placed it on the paten. He watched as the Cardinal Camerlengo lifted the gold plate and slid the ballot into the chalice. As simple as that.

Forty minutes passed before all the votes had been cast, time spent in silence. Some prayed, some stared longingly at the pictures. After all, it was the Divine Spirit who chose a Pope, not men. They could take the time to enjoy their surroundings—God's will, not theirs, managing this most pressing of matters.

Von Neurath thought of the "Hodoporia." He'd heard nothing from Kleist in over five days, the last message from Athos, confirmation that the priest had yet to get hold of the actual parchment. Some sort of book. One more step removed. Assurances that everything was close at hand.

Without the "Hodoporia," though, von Neurath knew the papacy would mean nothing, infallibility or not. Two hundred and fifty million Catholics at his disposal, and no way to convince them to follow a new path. No way to justify the shifts to come with a divine authority.

He had no choice but to trust Kleist, trust that he would deliver what he had promised.

"Peretti."

The sound of a voice brought his focus back to the altar. One of Fabrizzi's three assistants—the scrutineers—was reading out the first ballot. He then passed it to the next cardinal, who likewise read it aloud. So, too, the third, who then ran a needle and thread through the paper.

"Daly."

Von Neurath exchanged a moment's smile with the Englishman as his name was echoed twice more. No need to worry. Two votes. One hundred and seven to go.

Eighteen minutes later, von Neurath sat stunned. By his own count, he had fallen six short of the majority, Peretti having taken forty of the remaining forty-two.

Evidently, several of the swing votes had decided not to swing.

The cardinals sat silently as one of Fabrizzi's assistants gathered the twined ballots and notes and retreated to the small stove whose chimney had become so famous over time.

Black smoke.

Two more votes tomorrow morning, one tomorrow afternoon, if need be. For as long as it took.

The cardinals rose. Filing out, von Neurath noticed that Peretti was staring at him. The hint of a smile. He did his best to return it.

Kleist would have to make certain he wasn't put in so embarrassing a position again.

▲

Pearse had slept on and off for over twelve hours, his body finally giving out after more than a week of neglect. They had arrived in the village sometime after two, twenty miles west of Novi-Pazar, less than an hour from the Kosovar border, somewhere up in the hills. That they'd crossed back into Yugoslavia hadn't occurred to him until he'd seen the signs for Belgrade. No border post, no guards. Evidently, when he wanted to, Mendravic could avoid such inconveniences.

Pulling up along one more dirt road—a smattering of houses spread out along the surrounding hills—they'd stopped at the only hovel still showing some signs of life. Ivo had been quickly carted away to a bed while Mendravic had made the introductions.

Much as Pearse had expected, the men and women of the KLA proved to be none-too-distant cousins of the Irish Provisionals, less concerned with practical objectives than with the grand design. He'd talked with them for over an hour, stories of recent escapades, all dismissed with a fanatic's rationale. As it turned out, these were a new breed of KLA, taking their fight "beyond the borders," as they had explained. The rest of Serbia/Yugoslavia would learn to leave Kosovo alone.

By three, he'd had his fill, the brandy having taken its toll, as well. Hoisting himself up from the table, he'd found a bed and slept.

No dreams. Not even a hint of movement. Just sleep.

Now, at almost three in the afternoon, he emerged from his room to find Petra alone at the kitchen table, a mug of coffee in her hands.

Pearse found a cup and joined her.

"So, he finally appears," she said as he sat. "What time did you make it to bed?"

Small talk. He could manage that. "A little bit after you. Not much of a conversation. Where is everyone?"

"Gone by the time I got up." She took a sip, then glanced around the room. "This seems strangely familiar, eight years removed."

He nodded, memories of Slitna hard to ignore, especially during last night's diatribes. Pearse wondered if he and Petra had sounded as rabid, all those years ago. Probably, although he hoped not. They'd certainly never had rolls like the ones now beckoning to him from a dish at the center of the table. Better bread, greater mania, he thought. It seemed a logical enough connection.

He took a roll and tore off a piece, dunking the wedge in his coffee and quickly tossing it down.

"That, too," she added.

"Saves time on the digestion. You knew that." The second piece received a healthy slathering of butter. "Is Salko up?"

"Ivo wanted to go exploring. Mommy wouldn't do. He pulled him out of bed about an hour ago."

Pearse nodded, another sip of the coffee. "This doesn't faze him at all, does it?"

"Ivo? No. I'm sure it's like a game for him."

"That's quite a game."

"Not when you've played it before."

Pearse hesitated, then asked, "Ivo?"

"We were in a village like this for about three months in '97." Seeing his confusion, she explained, "When NATO pulled out? The trouble in Mostar?" Still nothing. "You do have newspapers in the United States, don't you?" she added.

Pearse grinned. "I think we have a couple. I suppose you have to remember to read them."

"I suppose you do. Although," she added more pointedly, "I'm sure we stopped being front-page news once Mr. Clinton got reelected."

No bitterness in what she said, just pragmatism. The same way she could talk about a seven-year-old being trundled from his bed in the middle of the night as part of some familiar game.

"He really takes to Salko, doesn't he?"

"Didn't you?"

Pearse nodded to himself, then rolled a piece of the buttered roll into a ball and popped it into his mouth. "Do they get to see a lot of each other?"

"About once a month. Maybe more, if something comes up."

"Something . . . like what?"

"I don't know. Little-boy things that a father would be—" She stopped herself. "Not really that often."

She was trying to be kind. Even if he'd known what to say, he knew he wouldn't have been able to find the words. He'd make her laugh, or put her in a position where she'd have to tell him to stop, just as he had last night. For some reason, he thought of the Ribadeneyra entries. The alchemy so manageable there. Here, impossible. Then again, better to leave unsaid what he couldn't say.

"It's good Ivo has him," he finally said.

"It's good they have each other," she echoed. "Salko probably needs the fix more than Ivo does."

Another ball of bread for him as she stared into her cup.

After a time, she said, "There are days, you know, when they disappear for hours. Just the two of them. Their 'little adventures.'" She was letting him in, if only for a moment. "It's funny. Ivo always comes back with this adorable look in his eyes, as if they've got some great secret. Something just the two of them know. The men." She smiled to herself. "I remember when Salko taught him how to whistle. The great event. And Ivo came running in, and he waited and waited while Salko told me where they'd been, the two of them passing each other little winks and nods. I pretended not to notice. And then, all of a sudden, he started to whistle. This sweet little chirpy thing through the giggles. And we all started laughing. He was so proud of himself." It was as if she were looking directly at them. "You should have seen his face when I whistled back. He couldn't believe it. He couldn't say a thing. Somehow, I knew the magic secret." She laughed. "That's when he told me I had a girl's whistle. It wasn't like Salko's or his." She stopped, eyes even more distant. "I wasn't Mom. I was just a girl."

Pearse took a sip of the coffee, then said. "Did Salko tell you why I'm here?"

She turned back to her cup. "Some of it." She reached for a piece of bread, something to keep her hands busy. "I don't think he's that clear on it himself."

"That makes two of us."

"Whoever it is, they're very thorough. They knew where to find me."

"Sorry about that."

She shot him a quick glance. A mock upbraiding. "They would have come whether you and Salko had shown up or not. Probably better that you did."

"You're being mighty nice this morning."

"Don't get too used to it."

Without thinking, he dipped the buttered piece into his coffee, the black liquid turning a pale brown. "That was clever."

"If you'd wanted milk, all you had to do was ask," she said.

"Yes, thank you very much." He stood and walked to the sink, then dumped out the cup. "It was pretty horrible anyway." Regardless, he poured himself a fresh cup.

"I guess . . . this must be a bit of a shock," she said.

"The bad coffee?" She let the comment pass. "I can't say it's what I expected when I left Rome, no."

"Right." She hesitated. "What did you mean yesterday? About it not making sense to you."

He was about to take a sip, but stopped. "I thought . . . you didn't want to talk about that."

"I guess I do."

He leaned back against the counter.

"Or . . ." She suddenly stood and moved to the counter, eyes fixed on the kettle. "Maybe not. Maybe now's not the best time." She picked up the kettle and, facing away from him, began to pour.

He tried to find something to say, but all he could come up with was, "Okay."

She placed the kettle down and stood there, staring, her hands on the counter.

"I don't even know why I asked," she said.

He turned to her, her face in profile. Once more, he reached out and took her hand. This time, she didn't pull away.

"Maybe . . . we should let this wait until after Visegrad," he said.

Her eyes still on the counter, she nodded slowly. "Maybe we should."

No movement. Then, slowly, she looked up at him, her hand still in his. She said nothing. A moment later, she let go and headed to the table, cup in hand.

"So," she asked as she sat, "what exactly are you looking for in Visegrad?"

It took him a moment to refocus. "Remember that parchment we found in the old church?"

"Of course I remember it."

"I think it's related to that."

Her eyes went wide. "That's . . . bizarre."

For the first time since he'd made the connection, Pearse realized he hadn't taken the time to admit how odd it really was. For the next twenty-five minutes, he did his best to explain what he himself was having trouble understanding.

"And you think they'll kill this friend of yours?" she asked.

Pearse shook his head. "I don't know."

He was about to explain further, when the sound of cars and vans broke through from outside. Both of them moved to the window, Pearse's initial assumption the boys from Kukes. When he recognized one of the men from last night's conversation, however, he relaxed. That is, until he saw the makeshift stretcher, a body in tow, being pulled from the back of one of the vans. The place was at once alive with running figures, a woman walking by the side of the stretcher, her hands clutching something below the laid-out man's shirt.

Petra was already out the door by the time Pearse could take it all in. He moved outside as well, two men pushing past him, no concern for their erstwhile guest.

"Some sort of raid that went wrong," Petra said, drawing up to him. "Two of them are injured. I told them you're a priest."

"But they're not Catholics."

"They don't seem to care. They're taking them in there."

Petra led him toward one of the houses, what passed for the village clinic. Not terribly sanitary, but certainly the cleanest room within a ten-mile radius. Inside, they'd already started on the man Pearse had seen through the window, the woman a doctor still at his side. The other lay on a second table, doing his best to hold back the screams, sudden bursts of air through his nose, a man who looked well into his forties but who was probably no more than twenty-five. Every few seconds, his back arched, the grimace on his face silencing whatever means of release he had found, the need for two others to hold him down. His leg was streaked red, a bandage drenched in blood around what remained of his right foot.

The other was at most nineteen, no screams, no movement, no need to hold him down. His eyes remained wide, a stare Pearse recalled all too well from another lifetime. This boy would be dead within minutes. Even so, the doctor was doing what she could. A small area of his shirt showed some blood, hardly enough, though, to prompt the distant stare. Only when he moved closer did Pearse realize that the front of the torso wasn't the issue. From beneath the gurney, a small pool of blood had begun to gather on the table. The boy lay flat because to move would mean to leave a part of himself on the canvas. The doctor called Pearse over. They needed help with the shirt. Pearse did as he was told. Kukes revisited.

In a sudden movement, the boy grabbed his arm and began to speak in a rapid-fire whisper. Pearse turned to the doctor, expecting her to bark at him to get out of the way—but she was too busy to notice. Without thinking, Pearse leaned over, trying to make out even one or two of the words as they raced by. The boy spoke with such intensity that Pearse found himself nodding, as if he actually understood what the boy meant him to hear. The whisper gave way to a strange sort of laugh, the grasp on his arm loosening, until the boy drifted back to silence.

Pearse stared at the face.

The clarity of that moment. The purity of its language, even unheard. Even as the gaze froze.

Pearse turned to the doctor. She, too, had watched the final moments; she reached over and shut the boy's eyes. Not a word to Pearse as she moved to the second table. With everyone preoccupied, Pearse silently gave the boy the last rites, whichever God he prayed to.

Forty-five minutes later, he stood outside with Petra, the shock slowly wearing off.

As if heaven-sent, Ivo and Mendravic chose to appear at that moment, making their way up the road, the tinier of the two skipping, his hands filled with rocks and sticks, and who knows what—treasures only a seven-year-old could find. "Here's to exploring," Pearse said as he and Petra moved out to them. Ivo began to run toward his mother as soon as he saw her.

"We came back about twenty minutes ago," said Mendravic as he drew up to Pearse.

"Did he see any of the—"

"No," Mendravic answered, continuing to walk, leaving Ivo with his mother. "I thought it a good idea to find another adventure."

Pearse nodded, continuing to walk. "One of them mentioned something about a raid gone wrong."

"They picked the wrong day to go," Mendravic replied.

Before he could explain, one of the KLA men had drawn up to them, now walking alongside. Youngish, mid-thirties, he'd been one of the more vocal around the table last night. Pearse couldn't quite recall his name.

"It was as if they were waiting for us, Salko," he began, ignoring Pearse altogether. "You wouldn't have believed it. Armored vehicles, road-blocks, the whole works. We had no choice but to run. I still have no idea how they knew we were coming."

"They didn't," answered Mendravic.

"I'm telling you—"

"You were an added bonus," he explained. "They weren't there for you." Before the man could ask, Mendravic said, "They were there because of what happened two hours before you left." Mendravic stopped. "Someone blew up a Catholic church around five this morning. I saw it on the news at that inn outside of Janca. The boy and I stopped for lunch. It was all over the television."

"Serbs?" asked the man.

"They have no idea," Mendravic answered. "No one killed. Just the building."

"So why the roadblocks?" asked the man, a growing frustration in his voice. "You'd think they'd be happy that the Catholics got it. Happier if it had been a mosque."

"I don't know what to tell you," Mendravic answered. "That's why they were there. You were lucky to get away."

"Because of some hysteria about a church, I lost a man?" Pearse could see the rage in his eyes, the utter disbelief. "They'll blame it on us, won't they? Catholic church. Muslim KLA. Probably did it themselves just for the excuse." The man began to shake his head, all the while staring at Mendravic, Pearse evidently still invisible. When the words wouldn't come, he finally looked at the priest, no hint of kindness in his eyes. For a moment, it seemed as if he might say something. Instead, he turned and headed back to the clinic.

"What weren't you telling him?" asked Pearse when the man had moved out of earshot.

"It's the stupidity that'll make him want to kill them even more now," Mendravic said, his eyes fixed on the retreating figure. When he realized Pearse had said something, he turned to him. "What?"

"There was something else you didn't tell him, wasn't there?"

Mendravic waited before answering. "When did you get to be so smart?"

"What didn't you tell him?"

His eyes narrowed for just a moment. "It wasn't only one church. There were three others. Two in Germany, another in Spain. Also this morning."

"And they think they're connected?"

"They? Yes, the TV people think that they're connected."

"Why?"

"I have no idea."

"Was there any news on the election?"

"Election?"

"The Pope."

"Oh. Black smoke. They'll do it all again tomorrow. What does that have to do with—"

"That's probably your answer." Stopping Mendravic short, Pearse added, "What better time to strike? The church preoccupied. No single authority. Catch them with their pants down."

"For what reason?"

"It might be more obvious than you think."

Again, Mendravic paused. "You think it has to do with your little book."

"So do you. That's why you didn't say anything to your KLA friend."

Another pause. "All right," he admitted. "Then what, exactly, is in that book that would explain all of this?"

It was now Pearse's turn to wait. "I wish I knew, Salko. I wish I knew."

▲

Kleist glanced over his shoulder one last time. Highly unlikely that anyone had followed him down here, but best to be sure. An endless assortment of pipes—all wrapped in plaster—ran along the low ceiling, the hum of a generator and furnace somewhere off in the distance. Otherwise, the basement of the Domus Sanctae Marthae lay in silence.

Above him, a hundred cardinals waited in their rooms, relaxing or praying, or doing whatever it is that cardinals do between conclave votes and dinner. Tonight, he had no intention of disturbing them.

Except for one.

Checking the building schematic for perhaps the fifth time in the last minute, he came to a small door located low on one of the walls, the hatch no more than two feet square. Fixed into its lower left-hand corner waited a simple lock, brand-new from the shine. Kleist pulled a ring of keys from his pocket, slipped one into the slot, and pulled back the door. Dropping to his knees, he angled his flashlight up and peered through.

No more than four feet across, the opening extended up beyond the reach of the light, equally distant to both his left and right. It was as if a four-foot wedge had been yanked from the center of the building, leaving this hollow tucked deep within. The light caught on a group of pipes perhaps twelve feet above him, open space above that, then another set of pipes twelve feet above that, so on and so on, the crude demarcation of the floors of the building. Kleist slid himself through and stood, pulling the door shut. He then flattened himself against the cement-block wall and again checked the schematic. The flashlight found what he was looking for off to his left—the iron rungs of a ladder built directly into the wall. Not an easy climb, but certainly manageable.

When he reached the "fourth floor," he stepped out from the ladder and onto the piping, using his hands along the walls to keep his balance. Flashlight in his mouth, he counted off four heating ducts before bringing out a razor knife from his pocket. At the fifth, he sliced an opening into the aluminum, then tossed both knife and flashlight into the vent and hoisted himself up.

Fifteen minutes later, he sliced a second hole for his exit. This one dropped him down into another narrow passage, Sheetrock having replaced cement. He aimed the light to his left and slowly traced it along the wall. About a third of the way back to him, the light flashed momentarily. It had caught on something. Quickly, he made his way to the spot. A hinge. Two feet below it, a second. He placed his flattened palm on the wall and pushed.

It gave way with surprising ease. Again on his knees, Kleist ducked his head under, then pulled the rest of himself through. He was met by a cushioning of wall-to-wall carpeting beneath him. To his left, a bed. He stood and shut the door.

"You're late."

Kleist turned to see Cardinal von Neurath seated in a chair across the room. It had been von Neurath who had discovered the approach to the room in the plans. Nothing easier than to install a door and arrange the room assignments.

"Yes, Eminence."

"Keep your voice down. These walls are paper-thin."

Kleist nodded and moved toward the cardinal. A chair waited for him; he sat.

"I want one of those children taken. And I want it on the news quickly." Von Neurath saw the momentary confusion on Kleist's face. "Doesn't matter which one. Any of them will send the message to the rest. I need those six votes, and I need them tomorrow."

"The news? How would that—"

"We're sequestered, Stefan. We're not sealed in a vacuum. We all managed to hear about this morning's events in Bilbao and Göttingen, and whatever that place is called near the Yugoslav border. You take the child, we'll hear about it." He let the words sink in. "Those weren't supposed to go off for another few days, were they?"

"No."

"What happened?"

"Miscommunication."

Von Neurath waited before answering. "Get word to Harris. He has a tendency to overreact. Tell him, nothing changes."

Kleist nodded.

"If for some reason the vote doesn't come through tomorrow, I want you to leak the Syrian link to the bank. And keep Arturo's name at the forefront." Even more pointedly, he added, "And remember, nothing about this to the contessa or Blaney. You don't have to understand why."

Another nod.

"Now, where's our priest?"

"Most recent contact was last night. He phoned."

"That was good of him." The irritation lasted less than a second. "Does he have the 'Hodoporia'?"

"He will in a few days."

"I see." Von Neurath saw the moment's hesitation in Kleist's eyes. "What?"

"At the refugee camp—he says four men were tracking him."

"What four men?"

"We don't know."

"You believe him."

"Yes."

"Do we know who they are?"

"No."

"Excellent." The word was laced with sarcasm. Another pause. "I want this cleared up by tomorrow. If he doesn't have the 'Hodoporia' by then, find him, take the book from him, and find it yourself. No more distractions. Do you understand?"

"Yes, Eminence."

"Good." Von Neurath stood. "Then unless you have something else . . ." Kleist shook his head. "They'll be coming around to call us for dinner soon. They're very keen that we all eat together in silence. Given the food, I can understand why."

Kleist wasn't sure if he was meant to smile or not. Instead, he simply nodded and stood.

"Oh, which reminds me," added von Neurath. "Send Mr. Harris my congratulations on his recent approval rating. Make it an egg. A hard-boiled egg. He'll understand." He nodded Kleist toward the tiny door.

Two minutes later, Kleist was crawling his way back through the heating duct, a constant trickle of sweat dropping from face to aluminum.

Hard-boiled egg. He wondered if he'd somehow missed something. Or maybe it was simply the cardinal's way of putting him in his place; it wouldn't have been the first time. Whatever he had meant, though, Kleist was sure of one thing.

The priest would be dead within the day.

At least now there was no confusion on that front.

▲

"Nige . . . you're sure we can't get you some dessert?"

Nigel Harris smiled to the man across the table from him. "I'm fine. Thank you." Three others sat across from him, as well. A lunch meeting engineered by Steve Grimaldi's office, very "developmental," high on the "no turnaround time," given Harris's current "breakthrough" status. The colonel was beginning to understand the advertising industry's lingo, although he couldn't be sure if it was the industry or Grimaldi himself, the latter more than happy to toss whatever happened to be running through his mind into the conversation. That notwithstanding, the rest of his staff seemed to understand his every word—everyone "on the same page"—especially when they took their little breaks to "detox" the details.

The lunch meeting had started at eleven. It was now nearly one.

While the plates were being cleared, Harris glanced out the window. He'd never gotten his LA geography down, not sure if he was actually in what they considered downtown. From the thirty-eighth floor, it certainly looked like a downtown, though with conspicuously few people on the streets. Maybe the trendy restaurants weren't in this neck of the woods, he mused. Or maybe in-house catering had just become too good across the board. From what he'd just had to suffer through—something "blackened" beyond hope—he was guessing the former.

"I think you're going to like what we've put together, Nige. It's very early—"

"Developmental." Harris nodded.

"Exactly. So we're not sure just exactly how we need to play with it. But we want to get them out there quick." Grimaldi nodded to one of his associates; she pressed a button at the center of the table and a large

TV screen lowered from the ceiling at the far end of the room. A second button, and the shades began to close. Harris turned to Grimaldi and raised his eyebrows as if duly impressed. The adman seemed to preen. The lights dimmed. "Your group's getting a lot of press right now, Nige, and we thought it might be nice to pick up on that newsy quality. An election kind of thing. Get people in your camp. This is one possibility. And don't be afraid to tell me exactly how it makes you feel."

Grimaldi pressed yet one more button, and the screen came to life, black at first, a counter running in white numbers along the bottom edge, the words "Nigel Harris Promo 1" next to it. When the counter reached ten seconds, the center of the screen filled with one of the quotes from a recent article on the alliance. The now-familiar voice from every movie preview produced in the last five years began to read the text in slow, sonorous tones.

"Its vision is for our future. . . . Its message is clear. . . . It's time we put our faith back into something we believe in. . . ."

A classroom of children filled the screen, eleven- and twelve-year-olds, a perfect hodgepodge of ethnic and racial backgrounds, all smiling faces, the word Tolerance written in large letters on the board, the children clearly in the midst of a discussion. The screen darkened, another quote. The voice returned.

"Our children need to understand what ties them together, not what separates them. And faith is that answer."

Next, an equally Stepfordesque scene appeared, people on a generic Main Street, again ample ethnic diversity, ideal families strolling along, stopping to chat with one another, three separate churches in the background—one seemingly a synagogue, the lines, though, too blurred to make it out with any detail. In some sort of high-tech special effect, the three buildings began to grow into one another, the happy little community watching the transformation. No quote this time. Just the voice.

"It's time to build an alliance of faith, where religious differences fade in favor of a wider spiritual commitment."

Images of Harris, several other notable members of the alliance, and an American flag peppered the screen, the final image that of a field somewhere in the Midwest.

"The Faith Alliance. It's our bridge to the next millennium."

The screen went black, the lights came up. Harris turned to Grimaldi, who was standing by the far window. Grimaldi was staring directly at him, a birthday-morning grin lining his face.

"I see," said Harris, trying to find the words. "I'm not exactly sure that's what we talked about. It was all rather . . . over-the-top."

The smile dipped momentarily. "Sure it was. But there's good over-the-top, and there's bad over-the-top. Which one do you mean, Nige?"

"The one that says that that advertisement won't be seen by anyone outside this office." Harris sensed a slight elevation in the tension of the room. "Exactly how I feel, Mr. Grimaldi? What I just saw was insipid, mawkish, and says nothing about the alliance."

"Don't underestimate insipid and mawkish," said Grimaldi, the first hint of something savvier beneath the veneer of the hip salesman. "They sell well."

"I'm sure they do, but I don't believe we're *selling* anything. We want to inspire. There's a considerable difference there. Might I ask what happened to the segments I filmed? I thought they made my position quite clear."

"Fair enough." Grimaldi nodded to one of his associates. "Let's call that a first stab." Again the lights dimmed. The second promo.

The image on the screen this time was far less polished, the angle of the camera slightly skewed. A young man, maybe in his mid-thirties, sat on a park bench, elbows on knees, chin propped on his hands. The camera shifted around him several times, close-up, then back, more odd angles, before it stopped on a medium shot. The man seemed to be looking at something in the distance, but the camera stayed on him. The voice-over began, this one without the husky pomp.

"Time was when I wasn't sure what to expect for his future."

A quick cut to a group of boys playing in the park, again choppy angles, long and short shots interspersed in rapid sequence.

"I thought about the usual stuff, high school, college. Get himself a job. And that one day he'd be out here, watching his boy, wondering the same things. The same endless cycle. And I had to ask myself, Is that all I can give him?"

The man stood and began to walk toward the boys. He stopped by a tree and watched as his son tore around with the ball, the other boys giving chase. The man smiled.

"Not by a long shot."

The man moved out from under the tree, his son catching sight of him, tossing the ball back into the melee before racing up to his father's side. As the man knelt down to straighten his son's jacket, the voice-over continued.

"If you've got some of those same questions, think about the Faith Alliance. I did. It's where we can make their future together."

The shot traced up to the sky, then back down, now the vista a wide beach, a far shot of Harris walking, pants rolled up to the ankles, his own two boys scampering in the tide just ahead of him. The camera moved in.

"I'm Nigel Harris, director of the Faith Alliance. If you're in need of something to put genuine meaning into your life, and the life of your family, consider joining us."

The camera followed Harris's glance to his boys.

"It's their future. Don't deny them a personal relationship with faith."

The camera pulled back as Harris darted over to his sons and began to splash water at them; they, in turn, splashed back.

Fade to black and the words *"The Faith Alliance. Our bridge to the next millennium."*

Fade-out.

The lights came up.

Grimaldi remained by the window. "I told you insipid and mawkish sell," he said as he moved back to his chair. "It's just how you package them."

Harris turned to him as he sat. It was only then that he realized how clever Grimaldi had been. The whole morning had been a prelude to this moment, the mindless jargon bandied about at lunch, the first promo. All designed to let this moment have its full effect. Harris now understood why Grimaldi had the reputation he did.

"Yes, I can see that," he answered.

"So this one's more to your liking, Colonel Harris?"

"Call me Nige." He smiled. "Yes. Yes, it is."

"Good. Then you're going to love this next one."

Δ

Everything had quieted down by dinner. They had taken the body to a small house at the end of the village, the home of the local *hohxa*. There, it would be bathed and cleaned, prepared for burial according to strict Muslim custom, Pearse's last rites washed away with the rest of the worldly taint on the boy's soul. They had managed to keep Ivo preoccupied during the somber processional to the *hohxa*'s house, the other children of the village not so fortunate, essential participants in the ancient ritual. Pearse hadn't asked; Mendravic wouldn't have been able to explain.

The leader of the failed raid continued to ignore Pearse throughout the meal, no doubt silently blaming him for the morning's debacle. Catholic priest. Catholic church. To him, they were one and the same. Skewed logic aside, he did manage to show a considerable warmth to Ivo and Petra, doing his best to keep the dinner conversation lively, the day's tragedy left for another time. Pearse kept quiet, happy to watch the interaction.

What quickly became clear was just how smart a little boy Ivo really was. Polite to the end, he showed no hesitation in making his points, less patience for anyone who treated him like a child. And always with something of Petra's swagger in the way he handled his confrontations. In fact, more often than not, it was Petra herself who was on the receiving end.

"That's not true, Mommy," he said. "Why should we care about the Serbs when they don't care about us?" There was always a hint of the parrot in what he said, little phrases that he'd heard from Salko or his mother—mangled just a bit—but always injected at just the right moment. It wasn't necessarily what he said, but how he said it that allowed his cleverness to shine through. Even when Petra was on the defensive, Pearse sensed her absolute pleasure in Ivo's little jabs.

"Well, maybe that's why we should worry about them even more," she answered.

Somewhere along the way, he'd busied himself with a wedge of bread, rolling pieces of it into tiny balls. Preoccupied or not, Ivo managed to keep up. "No, because Salko said that's what they want. And we'd be giving them what they want, and we can't do that."

"Like what?" she pressed, the rest of the table watching as the little boy kept his eyes fixed on his handiwork, every once in a while a bread ball popping into his mouth.

"Like letting them know we're afraid. And we aren't." Another piece into his mouth.

"Never let them know," chimed in the raid leader with a smile. "Even if you are, just a little."

Ivo looked at the man, hesitated, then nodded, a very earnest nod for a little boy. And just as quickly, he was back to the bread.

"Is he always like this?" the man asked, his smile wider still.

"No," answered Petra. "Sometimes he can get pretty serious."

The entire table erupted in laughter, Ivo continuing with his very intricate bread work. When he realized that everyone was looking at him, he suddenly became embarrassed. Sensing the moment, Petra drew him in close, kissing the top of his head as he buried himself deep in her side.

"It's just that they all think you're as wonderful as I do, Ivi. Must be terribly hard having everyone think you're so wonderful."

That only made it worse. Except that perhaps Ivo was enjoying the attention more than he was letting on. And Pearse seemed to enjoy that just as much. The little showman, he thought. Why not? He was, after all, Petra's boy.

Pearse wasn't that surprised, then, when, an hour later, Ivo appeared at the door to his room, no less bold than at the table.

"Hello."

Pearse looked up. He'd been alone on his bed with Ribadeneyra since dinner, the five-line entries no closer to unscrambling than when he'd started. He had managed to tease out some connection among the rest of the entries—even without the final piece to the puzzle—a pattern beginning to emerge, when the little voice broke through.

"Hello," he answered, laying the pages on his pillow. Ivo remained by the door, his courage taking him only so far. "You can come in, if you want. I won't bite."

With a little nod, he pushed open the door, sized up the room, and slowly wandered in, not quite tall enough to see over the top of the chest of drawers. When he was satisfied, he turned to Pearse, one hand lazily running along the edge of the bed.

"Do you come from America?"

Pearse smiled. He'd expected a thousand other questions, not the one, though, most obvious to a seven-year-old boy. "Yup."

"I knew it," he said, as if having uncovered some great mystery. "I asked Mommy. She said I should ask you."

Again, Petra was letting him in. He wasn't quite sure what he had done to merit it. "How'd you know?"

"The way you talk." He started to roam again, his fingers lighting on the backpack. "What's in here?"

"Nothing much."

"Can I open it?"

"Sure."

He watched as Ivo struggled with the zipper, a giddy anticipation of the unknown within. Or at least of something American. His disappointment on unearthing nothing more than a change of clothes and a few odds and ends was equally intense.

"Sorry," said Pearse. "No chocolate."

Ivo snapped his head up, the look now one of astonishment.

"Isn't that what you were looking for?" asked Pearse.

A coy smile crept across the boy's face. "How'd you know that?"

"Oh, I have my ways." Pearse smiled.

For a moment, it looked as if Ivo might not let it go at that. Then, just as quickly, he was on to his next topic. "Did you come from America last night?"

"Actually, I haven't been to America for a couple of years." Another flash of disappointment. "Have you ever been to America?"

The look now turned to one of utter disbelief, less to do with the possibility than with the fact that Pearse had even thought to ask. "No! I know only one person who's been to America. Except for you."

"Really?" Pearse knew where he was going, but couldn't hold himself back. "Who?"

"My father."

It was said with such confidence, such an affinity, as if he had just spoken with him before coming into the room. The connection so clear. Again, he had to thank Petra for that.

"And where does he live?" asked Pearse.

A look of confusion etched across the young face. "America. Like you."

Pearse nodded. Obviously, his geography had its limits. Not wanting to lose him entirely, Pearse reached under the papers and pulled out his baseball. "Here." He tossed it to him.

Ivo caught it, no hesitation.

"Nice catch," said Pearse.

"I'm pretty good." He examined the ball very closely. "What kind of ball is this?"

"It's a baseball," said Pearse.

Ivo's eyes lit up. "A baseball! From America?"

From Rome, but close enough. "I know you were hoping for chocolate, but—"

"No, no. This is great. Can I play with it?"

"You can keep it, if you want."

If possible, Ivo's eyes grew wider still. "You mean . . . it's mine?"

"Well, I might ask you to play catch with me sometime."

"You can play anytime you want."

"Thanks. Maybe sometime you could go to America with me and see a game."

It was almost too much for him. "America?" A hint of hesitation crept in. "And Mommy, too?"

"Of course. And don't forget Salko."

Before Pearse had finished, Ivo was running back to the door, shouting to his mother. Within a minute, he was back, pulling Petra by the arm. Once again, her expression was far from what Pearse expected: not strictly a glower, but as close as she dared with Ivo looking directly at her.

"And Salko, too," he bubbled.

"Yes, I heard you, sweetie," answered Petra as she stared at Pearse. "That's very nice of him."

Pearse smiled. "I just said—"

"Yes, I'm sure you did."

Pearse wasn't sure, but he suspected this was part of a family dynamic he'd never had occasion to experience until now. Something reserved for mommies and daddies. Even on the short end of things, it was awfully nice, more so to see Petra struggling with it as well.

Not sure what protocol demanded, he fell back on the slow nod.

"You have to go to sleep," she said to forestall any further discussion. At once, Ivo launched into the ancient bargaining ritual, all of it to no avail. As he mopingly made his way to the door, he turned to Pearse and, instead of a simple "Good night," shot a finger at him and winked. It was enough to provoke a moment's giggle before a quick dash out the door.

Laughing, Pearse asked, "What was that?"

"Mel Gibson did it in a movie. He thinks it's how all Americans say good night." She remained by the door.

"Isn't Mel Gibson Australian?"

At last a smile. "Don't tell him that."

A silence settled on the room. He thought she might go; instead, she moved toward him.

"So, have you figured out where this book of yours is in Visegrad?" she asked pointing to the papers.

"No clue."

"So you have no idea *where* it is, you don't really know *what* it is, and you have no clue *who* was chasing after us."

"Right. But aside from that, I'm really close."

She laughed and sat down next to him. "Maybe another set of eyes would help."

"Sure. How's your Latin?"

"Oh," again more playful, "not so good."

"Then maybe I'll have to stick with the pair I have."

"They've always been a pretty nice pair."

For several seconds, neither of them said a word.

"Was I just flirting with a priest?" she finally said.

"I don't know. Question is, Was the priest just flirting with you?"

She was about to answer, when Mendravic stepped into the doorway.

"Ian, have you— Oh, sorry."

"Don't be sorry," they answered in unison.

A bit perplexed, Mendravic answered, "All right . . . I won't be. But if you two—"

"We don't," they said again as one.

"Okay," he replied, still not sure what he had just walked in on, though happy enough to let it go. "Did you tell him?" he asked Petra.

"Oh, no," she said. "I was just about to—"

"Ian, have you seen any of the papers?" Mendravic asked.

"Sure," he said. "I have them right here. What's this all about?"

"No, the newspapers, the ones they drove up from Novi-Pazar."

"I didn't know they had any. No. Why?"

"And the last time you saw a paper was . . ."

"I don't know, five, six days ago. Why?"

"Petra pointed it out to me. Maybe you should take a look."

Two minutes later, the three of them stood at the kitchen table, eight to ten major European papers waiting on top. The KLA might have been provincial in their worldview, but at least they were more sophisticated when it came to the news they read. Evidently, they wanted to see what kind of an impact they were having outside their own little universe.

"I hadn't seen one in almost a week, either, until Petra showed me these," Mendravic said as he began to sift through them. "So I can't tell you how long these have been running." He pointed to the lower right-hand corner of the nearest paper, the *Frankfurter Allgemeine*. A small box was set off from the columns, the look of an advertisement, except, for some odd reason, the language inside was English. Before Pearse could read, Mendravic pulled over several other papers—French, Italian, Greek—noting the identical box in each, and always the same language: English. Pearse read:

> **Whatever was on Athos, you have friends, Father. In Rome.**
>
> **Day or night: 39 69884728**

Every paper the same. Pearse turned to Mendravic. His phone was at the ready; Pearse took it and dialed. Both men angled their ears to the receiver and listened.

It picked up on the second ring. *"Pronto."*

Pearse wasn't sure what to say. The line remained silent. He looked at Mendravic. Finally, in English, Pearse answered, "I saw your ad."

"Yes." The accent was Italian.

"And I'm calling."

"We've had many calls. I need a name."

A number in a newspaper. People with nothing better to do than to dial it. Pearse understood. Realizing why the man needed his name, however, was hardly a rationale for giving it to him.

"I'm not sure I'm comfortable doing that."

"Then we can't help you. We already know the name we're looking for."

True, he thought. Even so. "I'm still not comfortable."

"As I said, then we can't help you."

Pearse waited. Another glance at Mendravic. The Croat shrugged. "Phôtinus," Pearse said.

There was a pause on the line. "The monastery on Athos."

"The Vault of the Paraclete."

Another pause, this one far longer than the others. A decision was being made. "Father Pearse?"

He didn't know whether to feel relief or anxiety. He was about to answer, when Mendravic suddenly pulled the phone from his ear and hung up.

"What are you doing?" Pearse asked, stunned.

"Do you realize how stupid we both are? I can't believe I only thought of it now."

"Thought of what?"

"Think, Ian. What's the simplest way to find out exactly where you are?"

Pearse shook his head.

"A trace. They were keeping you on the line to pinpoint your location. Very easy to do, even with satellite hookups. I can't believe I was so stupid."

"But they sounded as if they were trying to help."

"I'm sure they did."

Pearse stood there, not knowing what to think. Of course Salko was right, but then who would these people be?

The image of the four men from Kukes instantly fixed in his mind. Especially the one who had come after him, the look in his eyes just before Salko had attacked. No threat. No menace.

But if they knew about Athos, why go after him? Why not go after the Manichaeans directly? It didn't make any sense.

"Do we need to get out of here?" he asked, unwilling, for the moment, to focus on anything but the immediate threat.

"I think we caught it in time," Mendravic answered. "But I don't know. We could go to Visegrad, if you want."

"And sit there?" Pearse said, his mood souring. "I still have no idea where the 'Hodoporia' is."

"The what?" asked Petra.

"The thing we're looking for. The parchment." The phone call had evidently taken more of a toll on him than he cared to admit. "I haven't . . . gotten it. I haven't broken the code. And I don't know if I can. Look, there's a woman in Rome—"

"All right," said Mendravic, trying to keep Pearse from sinking deeper into frustration. "We stay here tonight. We go tomorrow. Maybe . . . I don't know. I could take a look. You could show me how it works. . . ."

"Oh, that would be good," Petra piped in, also trying to lighten the mood. "I'm sure you'd be a lot of help."

"I'm just suggesting—"

"He's trying to move forward, Salko, not back."

"Your confidence is overwhelming. I'm sure you—"

"I've already been dismissed," she said. "I couldn't pass the Latin test."

"There's a test?" he answered.

Listening to the two of them was enough to snap Pearse out of his funk. "I get it. You've made your point."

"Good." Mendravic nodded.

"Look, I'll . . . figure it out. I have to figure it out."

"I don't think anyone was worried about that," she said.

Mendravic put his hand to Pearse's neck; he squeezed once. "My guess is, you get to Visegrad, and everything falls into place. Trust me. You're friend will be fine."

Pearse nodded. Why not? The alternative wasn't worth thinking about.

▲

The contessa had been right. The congregation seemed primed to hear him speak. Harris had spent the better part of the last hour listening to what many considered the preeminent Pentecostal preaching in the South. Archie Conroy and his Ministry of Peace. Five thousand strong had gathered in the largest amphitheater he had ever seen. Another 120,000 had tuned in for the early-morning services. That the contessa had set it all up on such short notice had astounded him. Thirty million on deposit was one thing. Having one of the most powerful ministries in the States at his beck and call was another. Conroy hadn't flinched. If the contessa was involved, Harris had carte blanche. He was learning not to underestimate her.

"Now, before I hand you over to the colonel, who has been so kind to join us here this morning"—Conroy's accent and demeanor reeked of southern hospitality, with a little medicine show thrown in just for fun—"I want him to know who is with him today, joining him in prayer." Conroy paused. "I think I would be right in saying it's a community of the faithful." Amens from the crowd. "Which embraces anyone of faith." He smiled and looked over at Harris. "Even an Anglican, Colonel. Even an Anglican." A wave of laughter from the audience. Harris could see Conroy wasn't quite ready to cede the stage.

"Because we *are* a community here, even though you may be sitting next to someone you don't know, whose own brand of faith is unknown to you. Look around you. Does he call himself a Baptist? Does she call herself a Methodist? Another a Pentecostal?" Again he turned to Harris. "I think it's a pretty safe bet you'll be the only Anglican here, Colonel." Harris nodded with a smile as the audience laughed. Conroy turned to his congregation. "But does any of it matter if we are a true community in faith? As Paul tells us in Romans, 'Then let us no more pass judgment on one another, but rather decide never to put a stumbling block or hindrance in the way of a brother.' Or elsewhere, when he tells us, 'With one voice glorify the God and Father of our Lord.' 'One voice.' For 'if the dough offered as first fruits is holy, so is the whole lump; and if the root is holy, so are the branches.' Look around you at those branches. 'One voice.' Can you say that with me?"

The entire congregation echoed, "'One voice.'"

"Again."

"'One voice,'" this time louder.

"Can you hear the power in that? Can you sense the power of that one indomitable spirit—unbroken, untarnished by personal desire, by personal lusts, by personal affectation. 'One voice.' Paul warns us in Philippians. He tells us that there are those who 'preach Christ from envy and rivalry.' 'Envy and rivalry,'" he repeated. "How? How can they preach it that way? Because they 'proclaim Christ out of partisanship.' 'Partisanship,'" each syllable given its due. "Those walls they build high, as if somehow they can keep the Word only for themselves, hold Christ within their churches? Can the Lord be so tethered? Can the Lord be kept for only one group, no matter what they call themselves? No. He alone flies free to all who would embrace Him. But to those who embrace 'partisanship,' He has only one answer: 'Affliction and imprisonment.' Choose to build those walls, choose to place those stumbling blocks between brothers, and you will not find Salvation in Him.

"It seems so obvious, doesn't it? One God, one salvation, one faith, one voice. How else would He hear us? Even when He afflicted us with the Tower of Babel—that voice scattered throughout, altered, and divided—His message was clear. Those differences don't matter. Language, culture, wealth"—he paused for emphasis—"denomination. Seek Him out, and you speak but one language. The language of God. The language of Christ.

"Now, I know there are plenty of preachers who think my views on inclusion only complicate things." He began to pace, nodding, eyes staring straight ahead. "'Leave things the way they are,' they say to me. 'Archie—Baptist with Baptist. Methodist with Methodist. We all have different needs,' they tell me. And maybe they're right. Who am I to argue with the status quo? Who am I to say we're stronger than that, that the only thing that matters is our faith in Christ? What other needs do we have? I don't know." He stopped and turned to face the audience again. "When the Pharisees told Jesus that His ways were too dangerous, His message of love and inclusion too bold, He continued on. I don't know if I have that strength. I can find it only through Him. But he never talked about different needs. He never talked about the status quo. He talked of love and salvation. He talked of 'one voice.'"

Archie turned again to Harris. "It's a kind of salvation itself, isn't it, Colonel?" For all his homespun rhetoric, Conroy knew exactly how to lead a crowd. He was making Harris an essential part of the message— . the dissolution of denominational differences, with its personification sitting up onstage with him. An English Anglican and a southern Pentecostal. What could be clearer? Harris was beginning to understand why the contessa had insisted on this venue.

"A kind of protection," Conroy continued, addressing the audience. "But protection from what? It's so hard to talk of inclusion when there are those whose very existence is bent on destroying that voice, whose sole aim is to maintain a 'noisy gong or a clanging cymbal'—as Paul tells us in Corinthians 1:13—rather than to embrace the singular Truth that is Him." He stopped. "And I'm not talking about my fellow preachers who say, 'Archie, give it a break.'" A few titters from the audience.

"We've been doing it to ourselves for centuries, haven't we? Allowing personal ends, political ends, commercial ends dictate the destruction of that 'one voice.' Within our own community of faithful." He paused. "And outside it." He waited for complete silence.

"How many of you think I'm talking about our friends in Rome?"

The response was minimal, the congregants having been too well prepped over the last few weeks of sermons not to know where he was going. "I'm sure I could find fault there. More so than with my fellow preachers. I could give you reasons for five centuries of animosities, bring in experts to explain why that conflict exists, justify the ongoing division. I'm sure the colonel here could tell you far more about that than I could.

"But I won't ask him, because I believe in 'one voice.' Because I believe that maybe, just maybe, we can begin to recognize what binds us and not what separates us. Maybe there's a chance that we can begin to see beyond our own history to our future. Maybe there's something in the air that gives us hope, a new beginning"—he again looked to Harris—"a brave new dawn. You'll forgive me, Colonel, but it is such a nice phrase." Harris laughed along with the audience.

"Things are happening here that give us that hope, organizations, like the colonel's, that are saying, 'Haven't we come to a point when we're sick and tired of using our faith to differentiate rather than to incorporate? Disharmonize rather than harmonize? Rend apart rather than heal within?' We must remember, 'if two make peace with each other in a single house, they will say to the mountain, "Move from here!" and it will move.' And there's never been a better time to make peace in our house." Another pause.

"Because there is something far more dangerous than our own bickering out there now that demands our attention. Those who want to talk about doctrines and rituals and five hundred years of contention might be too caught up in their own little worlds to recognize when something far more profound appears on the horizon. If we're to find salvation, we must remember that 'that day will not come, unless the rebellion comes first, and the man of lawlessness is revealed, the son of perdition.' Thessalonians 2:3. He who encourages that 'noisy gong,' that 'clanging cymbal' revealed. He who delights in our own disunion. He who so desperately needs to keep our house divided. For if we were to unite, he would have no hope of defeating us.

"He's an old foe in a new garb, still intent on his holy war. Who am I talking about?"

A murmur swept through the hall, all of those listening once again too well prepared not to understand whom Conroy meant.

"And he has the audacity to call us godless." He paused once more. "But I'm getting ahead of myself. I think it's time to let the colonel tell you all about that, and the wonderful work he and his Faith Alliance are planning." Conroy turned to him. "It gives me great pleasure to introduce to you, Colonel Nigel Harris."

The audience erupted as Harris stepped to the podium to shake Conroy's hand. The man had set him up masterfully. The audience was primed. Harris only hoped that the other ministries the contessa had scheduled would make his job as easy.

Éeema, Éeema, Ayo.

▲

Black smoke.

From his perch on a balcony above the Arco della Campane, Kleist watched as the mass of humanity let out a collective groan. The second vote of the morning. He could only imagine the cardinal's mood right now.

They had taken the girl last night in Berlin, centrally located enough so that the story had hit most of the European papers and television shows by midmorning. Maybe not early enough. Kleist had to hope that the news would find its way to the appropriate ears by the afternoon vote, for his own sake, if not for von Neurath's.

Even so, they'd already targeted a second child—in São Paulo, with enough traces left behind at the scene to point a finger at yet one more of the soon-to-be-infamous groups out of the Middle East. It would be sufficient to get the message across.

While he watched the horde pulse within St. Peter's Square, Kleist pulled what looked to be a calculator from his jacket pocket, the device no bigger than his palm. He flipped open its lid, revealing a small screen with three or four buttons below. Using the tip of his pen, he began to tap out various instructions, file after file appearing then disappearing before he reached deep enough into the system to find what he wanted. He pressed one of the buttons; the hum of a phone line began to emanate from the device. Within a few seconds, it was dialing, the sound of a fax connection moments later. With another quick tap, the information on the screen began its cyberspace journey to the editors of *Corriere della Sera* in Milan. Von Neurath's choice. Something about completing the circle. Kleist hadn't bothered to ask.

When the transmission was complete, he pulled up a second file, more information linked to the Syrian involvement with the Vatican Bank, various holes from the first file filled in, others made more ambiguous. This time, *La Repubblica* in Rome the destination. A third file for *La Stampa* in Turin. *Il Gazzetino* in Venice was the last to receive the anonymous tip. Together, the four papers would be able to piece together enough to make the story front-page news. And always with the name Arturo Ludovisi at its center.

Sacrificing one of their own for the sins of the many.

At least that was how von Neurath had explained it—the choice of words, thought Kleist, a clear indication that perhaps thirty years within the fold had affected the cardinal more than he realized.

No matter. By tonight, the entire world would be privy to the latest mind-bending catastrophe out of the Institute of Religious Works, a mere trickle of the deluge to come. But the bloodhounds would have to wait for at least a few more days. Time enough to place von Neurath on the papal throne.

And by that time, there'd be much bigger stories holding their attention.

Pen at the ready, Kleist stared at the delete command flashing up at him. For some reason, he was having trouble following von Neurath's instructions to erase the files. He stood alone on the balcony, the room behind him empty. Still, he felt the need to glance over his shoulder. No one. Kleist looked back at the tiny screen, his pen once again poised above.

With a gentle tap, he reengaged the phone line. Another connection, this one somewhere in Barcelona. A second tap.

All four files went at once.

Von Neurath had given him a direct order.

The contessa, however, had always given him far more.

And she would understand.

Λ

"No, no. That's more than enough." Mendravic placed what he thought was the last bag of food in the back of the van, the woman at his side insisting he take one more. "We'll be able to pick up what we need along the way," he tried to explain.

"Not if someone's looking for you," she answered, and pushed the bag into his arms.

The woman was somewhere in her late forties. She held her hands atop two full hips, broad shoulders below an equally wide, if almost square, head. Her face, though, was that of a much younger woman, lovely pale skin, with bright blue eyes that peered over at Mendravic. Pearse sensed there was something of a history between them. Funny that he'd never thought to ask about that part of Salko's life. Or any part of his life, come to think of it. An affinity built on circumstance.

"All right," said Mendravic, smiling, "but if I take it, I get to take you, as well." He bent over and placed the bag alongside the others in the van.

"You'd be so lucky. You barely fit inside the car yourself." She reached underneath and pinched the middle of his stomach. "You'd probably make me sit in the back with all the food."

"Would I do that?" Mendravic answered, still fiddling with the bags. "I'd have Ian drive. Then I'd show you what the back of this van is really good for."

A mighty wallop landed on his back, the woman looking over at Pearse, the paleness of her skin unable to hide the hint of a blush.

"He didn't mean that, Father," she said, the red growing on her face.

"Oh yes he did," said Mendravic, head still buried inside the van.

Another slap on the back.

She smiled. "Well, maybe he did." And with that, she turned, giving Mendravic a final swat before heading back to the house. "But not likely it's going to happen."

Mendravic emerged from the van just in time to see her step to the door. "Poor woman doesn't know what she's missing, Ian," he said, loudly enough for her to hear.

"Oh yes she does," she answered, not bothering to look back. A moment later, she was gone.

Mendravic laughed to himself, then turned to Pearse, handing him the keys. "Lady friend or not, you drive. I'm tired."

"I wanted to say good-bye to Petra and Ivo."

"Of course. So do I. You wouldn't be needing the back of the van, would you?"

"I can hit a lot harder than your friend can."

"Does Petra know that?"

Pearse started to answer, only to find he had nothing to say. "Do we know where she is?"

"I said quarter to. Give her another five minutes."

As if on cue, Petra emerged from the house, a pack on her shoulder. "Is he in the front?" she asked, tossing the pack into the back of the van.

"What are you doing?" asked Mendravic as he retrieved the pack and handed it to her.

"Getting ready to leave," she answered.

"I thought we discussed this."

"No, you told me what you wanted me to do. I've thought about it, and I've decided that we're going with you."

"I think that's a mistake," answered Mendravic.

"Yes, I know that's what you think. And I think we'd be worse off staying here if they did get a trace on the place." Again, she tried to toss the pack in; again, he stopped her.

"I told you this morning," Mendravic's tone more pointed, "they'd have been here by now."

"Maybe, maybe not. Getting out of here is the only way to be sure."

"She does have a point," Pearse piped in.

The look from Mendravic was enough to stifle any other helpful comments.

"If it were just you, I'd understand," Mendravic continued. "In fact, we'd be better off with you. But I've no interest in taking Ivo into God knows what. They might or might not show up here. Fine. But they'll definitely be in Visegrad. That doesn't seem like too difficult a choice to me."

"Then you stay here."

"You want me to . . ." His frustration was mounting. "Fine, then Ivo and I will stay here."

"Ivo comes with me."

Pearse had forgotten how the two of them approached "discussions."

"You're not making any sense here, Petra."

"No. You're just not understanding what I'm saying."

"I understand perfectly well what—"

"No, you don't."

"Look, if you're afraid of losing Ian again—" Mendravic stopped, realizing he'd overstepped the bounds. The ice in Petra's eyes was all the confirmation he needed. "Try and understand," he said, his tone less shrill. "My only concern here is Ivo."

Petra held his gaze, the venom no less intense. She tossed her pack past him and into the van, then started for the front. "I'll take him on my lap for the first part of the trip." She opened the door, the cold stare replaced by a look of confusion. She turned to Mendravic. "Where is he?"

It took a moment for the question to register. "What?"

"Ivo. Where is he?"

"I thought he was in the house with you."

An anxious look crossed her face. "I told you that he was coming out to help you with the car."

Mendravic continued to stare at her, his eyes replaying an earlier conversation between them. "I thought—"

"He never came out?" she broke in, now looking past Mendravic to Pearse.

Pearse shook his head. "He must still be in the house."

It was an obvious answer, but one that seemed to catch Petra completely by surprise. Without even so much as a nod, she raced back up the steps, shouting Ivo's name as she went.

Clearly addled, Mendravic turned to Pearse. "I could have sworn she said—"

"I'm sure he's just waiting for her."

Mendravic nodded slowly.

"He's not there," she said when she reappeared. "I told you that he was coming outside—"

"I'm sure you did." It was Pearse who spoke, trying to calm her. Strange, he thought, to have the roles reversed, Petra and Salko always so unflappable. Not that he didn't understand their reaction, but somehow he trusted little Ivo, sensed that he was all right, no reason for panic to cloud the response.

"He's probably just taken off on another adventure," Pearse continued, waiting for Petra to turn and look at him. When she did, he said, "I'm sure he's fine. We just have to find him." Before she could answer, he added, "I'll take the houses down this way, Salko can take the ones up that way, and you stay here in case he shows up."

Petra listened, then nodded.

Mendravic was already halfway to the first house, shouting out a resonant "Ivo" every few steps; Pearse turned and began to do the same.

The streets were all but deserted, everyone either enjoying lunch or an early nap. The few who were out hadn't seen the boy. Pearse was nearing the edge of the village, his faith in his own intuition dwindling, when he heard a voice from above.

"Little guy?" the voice said. Pearse looked up, to see a man sitting on his roof, various tools for repairing a leak scattered about. "Light brown hair, with a thousand questions?"

"That sounds like him," said Pearse.

The man nodded. "He had to know what each one of these pieces was for," he said, positioning a sheet of tin as he spoke. "Why I hadn't made the roof better the first time. Why I was the only one who had to fix his roof. Turned out that all he really wanted to talk about was Pavle." When Pearse continued to stare, the man said, "The boy who died yesterday."

Pearse nodded. Evidently, their distraction hadn't worked quite as well as they'd thought.

"You ask me, he was a little too curious. Things like that shouldn't . . . Anyway. I finally told him to go find the *hohxa* if he was so interested. He went in maybe fifteen minutes ago." The man nodded toward the holy man's house.

Pearse thanked him and made his way to the edge of the village.

It was clear why the little hut stood off by itself. Smaller than the rest, it seemed overburdened by its own dilapidation, a rutted heap of veined stonework lumbering against the hillside, the right-hand side with a pronounced hump. The two windows on either side of the door seemed equally downtrodden, staring groggily out from behind a haze of dirt and dried rain, no indication as to when they'd last been cleaned. But it was the roof that looked most out of place, unlike anything he'd seen in the village, a misshapen dome atop four clumsy walls. A distant reminder of the church of San Bernardo, pious inelegance reduced here to a rural oafishness.

And yet, it retained an undeniable spirituality, a stillness amid a world trampling it underfoot.

Pearse stepped up to the small porch.

The door stood ajar, a faint light coming from inside, the odor of incense wafting out to greet him; he pushed through, uttering a hesitant "Hello." The state of the windows made outside light an impossibility, a few candles here and there to bring the place to life—table, chairs, oaken chest lost to the shadows. Otherwise, the room slept in a kind of stasis, even the candlelight unwilling to flicker.

No response.

He moved farther in. He noticed a staircase along the left wall, uneven boards rammed into the stone, no railing, naked steps, barely wide enough for one. More light from above. He headed across the room and made his way up.

Reaching the second floor, he came upon the *hohxa* eating quietly in front of a flimsy wooden table, an equally ancient chair supporting what Pearse could only describe as one of the thinnest bodies he had ever seen. The man wore a brimless hat far back on his head, the panoply of colors having faded to a dull brown, a few threads of blue and red still visible at the crown. No less aged, a vest hung loose on his shoulders, a striped long-sleeved shirt—no collar—beneath. He kept his legs tucked neatly under the chair, his back and head stooped painfully over the bowl, a gnarled hand clutching at a wedge of bread that seemed more prop than meal. He squeezed at it repeatedly as he brought the spoon to his lips, always careful to scoop up the excess from his chin before plunging in for another helping. When the bowl was all but empty, he mopped the bread across the last few drops, then slowly began to gnaw at the soggy crust.

Only when Pearse had drawn to within a few feet of him did he look up.

"You've misplaced your boy," he said.

"Yes," Pearse answered, not exactly sure what protocol demanded.

"Nice little fellow," said the *hohxa*. "Clever. You don't seem too worried."

Pearse realized he wasn't. Again, no answer why. "I'm not."

"Good. Do you want some soup? I have plenty."

"Actually—"

"You want the boy."

Pearse nodded. There was something oddly serene to the little man and his bread, much like his house, both broken beyond repair, yet somehow comfortable in their easy deterioration.

With significant effort, he pulled himself up, his back only marginally straighter, a quick adjustment of the hat as he shuffled to the far end of the room.

"You're the priest, aren't you?"

"Yes. I'm the priest."

"Strange how it all comes together, isn't it?"

Pearse had no idea what the man meant; he nodded.

"It's important for children to see this. You could learn something." He slowly pulled back the edge of a curtain to reveal a tiny alcove, the smell of incense and camphor oil at once stronger. "This isn't something to protect them from."

Inside, Pavle's body lay on a bier, shrouded under three large white linen sheets. At his side sat Ivo, hands in his lap, baseball in hands, his back to the curtain.

"He wanted to know," said the holy man in a whisper. "And when they're curious, you have to tell them."

Pearse started in, but the *hohxa* held his arm.

"We sat together for a while. He wanted to stay. I told him to come out and eat when he was ready."

The *hohxa* released his arm; Pearse pulled the curtain farther to the side and stepped into the alcove as the man returned to the table. As quietly as he could, Pearse crouched by Ivo's side.

For perhaps half a minute, he said nothing. Ivo seemed content to sit, as well. "Pretty brave coming here by yourself," Pearse said at last.

Ivo nodded, his eyes still on the covered body.

He wasn't sure exactly what was holding the boy's fascination, beyond the obvious. He decided not to press it. Another few seconds, and Ivo finally turned to him. "It's different from last time."

Pearse nodded slowly.

"When you don't know someone," said Ivo, looking back at the body, "it's different."

Petra evidently hadn't told him everything about their stay in the country during the Mostar bombings. Again he waited.

"It doesn't make me as sad this time. Is that bad?"

"I don't think so," said Pearse. "It doesn't make me as sad, either."

Ivo turned to him. "You didn't know Radisav."

"You're right. I didn't. But I've known other people. When your Mommy and Salko and I fought in the war."

Ivo thought about it, then nodded. "I guess so. But you didn't know Radisav."

Pearse shook his head. "No, I didn't know him."

"It makes me sad when I think of him."

Very hesitantly, Pearse placed his hand on Ivo's shoulder. The two sat for several minutes. Finally, Ivo stood up. "It's just different," he said, clutching the ball in his left hand. With the other, he reached out to the shrouded body, placing his hand on it, a little boy's need to touch.

Pearse's natural instinct was to say a prayer. He quietly stood and crossed himself. Probably best, though, not to say a paternoster with a Muslim holy man nearby, especially given the events surrounding the young man's death. For some reason, the image of Ivo's outstretched hand reminded Pearse of the five-line couplets, the Ribadeneyra verse never too far from his thoughts, even at a moment like this. Somehow, the prayer seemed strangely appropriate.

With his eyes on Ivo, and not quite knowing why, Pearse began to speak the Latin, words for a young man he had known only in final whispers: "'So do I stretch out my two hands toward You, all to be formed in the orbit of light.'"

Ivo turned back and smiled. He took Pearse's hand, then looked again at the body.

Ivo began to sing the Latin: "'When I am sent to the contest with darkness, knowing that You can assist me in sight.'"

Pearse stopped. Ivo stopped as well, again the smile as he looked up at Pearse.

"I know that song," Ivo said. "Salko sings it with me. 'The fragrance of life is always within me, O living water, O child of light. . . .'"

Pearse stared down at the little face, his body suddenly numb. His mind frozen.

Éeema, Éeema, Ayo.

Spiritus

Pearse steadied himself, watching as Ivo sang. He heard nothing but a dull humming in his ears.

> *"So do I stretch out my two hands toward You,*
> *All to be formed in the orbit of light. . . ."*

Ivo turned to him; the boy was saying something. Pearse tried to hear, even as the walls seemed to constrict, the air heavier with each breath. Still, Ivo stared up at him.

> *"When I am sent to the contest with darkness*
> *Knowing that You can assist me in sight. . . ."*

Pearse felt his hand press against the wall, the chill of the stone offering an instant of release. The tiny voice broke through: ". . . if you know it?"

Pearse drove his nails into the stone, the pain forcing air into his lungs. The walls began to retreat, another chance to hear the boy.

"Why don't you sing if you know it?" Ivo repeated.

Pearse felt himself nod. The five-line entries. A child's first prayer. So obvious.

From somewhere within the haze, he found the words. "'The fragrance of life is always within me.'"

Ivo smiled and sang:

> *"O living water,*
> *O child of light.*
> *O name of glories*

In truth do I find You.
In search of a truth.
That tells of Your might!"

Pearse joined in: " 'Éeema, Éeema, Ayo.' "

Salko sings it with me. Pearse crouched down, forcing himself to concentrate. "Salko taught you that song?"

Ivo nodded.

The confirmation was somehow more devastating than the initial shock.

"I know another one." Ivo smiled. "Not as well. We sang it for Radisav. Salko says I have to learn it without a book. Do you want to hear it?"

There was nothing to do but nod.

Once more, the sweet soprano let forth: " 'It is from the perfect light, the true ascent that I am found. . . .' " He hesitated. " 'That I am found . . .' "

" 'In those who seek me,' " Pearse continued, his own familiarity with the prayer a momentary diversion from his staggering disbelief.

" 'In those who seek me,' " Ivo repeated, nodding. "Right. You know it, too."

Another nod.

" 'Acquainted with me, you come to yourselves,' " Ivo sang, " 'wrapped in the light to rise to the onions—' "

" 'Aeons,' " Pearse corrected, his head beginning to clear.

" 'Aeons,' " Ivo repeated. "That's about all I know. What are aeons?"

"Emanations of the unknowable," Pearse heard himself say, rote response from a mind not yet willing to confront what was standing in front of him. When he saw the look of confusion on Ivo's face, he tried a smile. "I'm not really sure myself. So Mommy and Salko taught you those songs?"

Another look of confusion. "Mommy?" A quick smile, eyes wide. "They're only for Salko and me. He says they're our special secret. Did he teach them to you, too?"

Pearse had no response. There was too much racing through his head to process it all: Salko appearing out of the blue, handling the men at Kukes—no menace, no Vatican—the church bombings, the telephone call, the trace.

Pearse tried not to condemn himself for what now seemed such obvious stupidity.

But Salko, a part of this . . . and for how long? A picture of Slitna fixed in his mind. How could he accept that? How could he accept that Ivo . . .

He might have collapsed from the weight of the last half minute if not for Ivo staring at him, waiting for an answer. Another instant of brutality, this time dispensed at the hands of an innocent, Ivo's gentle smile, his tiny hand clasped in Pearse's. Songs, not prayers. Words, not ideology.

"Yes," Pearse said. "Salko taught them to me, too."

He had an overpowering desire to cradle Ivo, hold him to his chest, hide him from a threat he couldn't possibly understand—its most tangible form wandering the village, looking for the boy.

Salko.

Crippling as the thought was, Pearse knew he needed to move. He needed to get them out of here.

He squeezed Ivo's hand, picked him up, and headed for the stairs.

Halfway down the steps, Pearse realized the *hohxa* hadn't been at the table. In fact, he hadn't been anywhere. The same held true downstairs. Pearse quickly moved across the room. Setting Ivo down, he slowly opened the front door and saw the empty road leading up to the village. Stepping back into the shadows, he knelt in front of the boy.

"So you never talked to Mommy about those songs?" he asked, peering into the little eyes.

Ivo's smile disappeared—a look of pure concentration. "No," he finally said. "Salko said I couldn't."

The boy's expression was more than enough to convince. Pearse nodded, a wink. "Then I'm sure you didn't."

Ivo's smile returned.

"So now the three of us have a secret," Pearse said as he picked Ivo up again. He moved to the door and slowly opened it.

Just as he was about to step outside, Ivo placed a hand on his cheek. "I'm glad you know the songs," he said.

Pearse stopped. For a moment, everything beyond them seemed to disappear. "Me, too." He then moved out through the door.

Less than ten feet up the main road, however, he suddenly realized he couldn't chance running into Salko with Ivo in tow. There'd be no way to keep them all from getting into the car and driving off—no way to separate themselves from Salko. And whatever else might have been running through his head, Pearse knew he had to view Salko as nothing more than an immediate threat. There would be time enough to try to understand the implications later on.

Making sure the road remained empty, he moved back to the side of the house and set Ivo down.

"How about a little adventure?" Pearse said.

Ivo's eyes lit up.

"And how about we make this one into a game?"

No less excited, Ivo asked, "What kind of game?"

"One where we surprise Salko."

"Salko!" The raw enthusiasm of a seven-year-old bubbled to the surface; Ivo's little hands pulled up to his mouth to stifle the near explosion of laughter. "That'd be great."

Again, Pearse winked. "Then that's what we'll do."

Pearse knew the game was more for himself than for the boy. Leading on a UN guard, the man from the bus, or even the Austrian had been one thing. Salko knew him better than that. And, given his old friend's apparent predilection for deception, Pearse also knew the Croat would sense something. Keeping his own focus on Ivo was Pearse's only hope.

He took the boy's hand and began to lead him down the hillside, behind the houses on the main road. Ivo skipped as he walked, every so often grabbing Pearse's side when he began to lose his footing. They made their way through tiny gardens, a few clotheslines, one or two low stone walls, until they came to the back of a house Pearse guessed to be within striking distance of the van. He peeked around the corner. Close enough. No more than twenty yards from them, Petra stood by the van's now-closed door, Salko at her side. The look on her face had grown to one of genuine panic.

He stepped back and crouched by Ivo. Any hint of anxiety quickly faded as he looked into the smiling eyes.

"Okay, here's what we're going to do," he whispered.

Again, Ivo's hands drew up to his mouth, the anticipation almost too much.

"I'm going to go to the car and talk to Salko and Mommy. I want you to watch me. If you lie on your tummy and crawl to the corner of the wall, I think you can see the car." Ivo dropped down and inched his way out. "Can you see the car from there?"

He looked back up at Pearse, giving him a big smile and a nod.

"Okay." Pearse pulled him back, then looked directly into his eyes. "But you have to wait here until I give you the signal to come out." He demonstrated with a big wave. "Only when you see me give the signal can you come out." He waited for Ivo to nod. "And then I want you to run as fast and as quietly as you can up to the car."

Again, Ivo nodded. "Boy, will Salko be surprised!"

"No sound. Otherwise, he'll know."

"No sound."

Pearse winked, waited for Ivo to take his position, then backtracked behind two of the houses—he couldn't chance them catching sight of Ivo, no matter how remote the possibility. Just before heading up to the main road, he glanced back; he could still see Ivo, prone on the ground, wirelike limbs outstretched, waiting. Pearse slipped around the side of the house and started up the road. As he passed the house where he had left Ivo, every instinct told him to check on the boy, but he knew he couldn't. Petra's voice was a welcome relief.

"Salko didn't find him, either," she said as she moved out to him. "He—"

"I found him," said Pearse, drawing up to the van. Before either of them could ask, he continued. "He's in the holy man's hut. For some reason, he wanted to see the boy who died yesterday."

It was clear from Petra's reaction that this wasn't the first time Ivo had shown such a morbid interest.

"The problem is," Pearse continued, "our friend from dinner last night wasn't that eager to let me in with the body still there. Something to do with Catholic priests and Muslim corpses. I wasn't going to argue with him. He said you should come and get him." He nodded to Salko.

Petra started to go; Pearse quickly grabbed her arm. "He said Salko. He was pretty adamant about it."

"Janos can get that way," said Mendravic with a nod. "I'm sorry if he—"

"Don't worry about it," said Pearse, aware that he was having trouble looking Mendravic in the eye. Instead, he looked at the ground and nodded.

Salko squeezed his neck. "I'll be back in five minutes."

He headed off down the road.

"You can let go of my arm now," said Petra.

Pearse turned to watch Mendravic move past the houses.

"I said you can let go of my arm."

When he was certain that Mendravic was out of earshot, Pearse released her, his eyes still on the retreating figure. "Get in the car," he said under his breath.

"What?"

He turned to her. "Get in the car," no kindness in his tone.

"Ian, what are you—"

"In thirty seconds, Ivo is going to come running out from behind that house. Get in the car."

Petra tried to look past him to the house; Pearse took hold of her arm again. "Did you hear what I said?" The intensity in his stare was enough to hold her. "*Get* in the car."

"What about Salko?"

"We're not taking Salko. If you want Ivo, get in the car." He paused. "You have to trust me."

Whatever she saw in his eyes was enough to send her to the door on the passenger's side. She opened it and sat.

Pearse turned back, to see Mendravic disappearing behind a curve in the road. He waited another five seconds, then turned and raised his hand high, waving it in a wide, sweeping motion. At once, the little figure of Ivo darted out from behind the house and began to race toward them, his tiny arms pumping away. Within seconds, he was in Pearse's arms; another few, and he was on his mother's lap. No time to explain. Pearse shut the door and moved around to the driver's side.

He had just opened the door, when he looked back and saw Mendravic racing up the road, remarkable speed for a man his size. Only then did Pearse see the stooped figure of the *hohxa* twenty yards behind him.

The old man had found Mendravic, a warning from the Brotherhood, too late to stop them.

Pearse pulled the keys from his pocket and leapt into the front seat. Within seconds, he was grinding the car into gear, the sudden burst of movement drowning out the shouts from behind. A winded Mendravic appeared in the rearview mirror, the figure more and more distant, clear enough, though, to see a tiny phone being brought to his ear.

Visegrad . . . They'll definitely be in Visegrad.

Salko's prediction now all but a certainty.

Λ

White smoke.

The throng in St. Peter's erupted, Kleist once more high above on his private perch. The spillover down the Via della Conciliazone reached almost to the river, over 100,000 bodies pressed against one another in anticipation of a single phrase: *"Habemus Papam!"* It would be several minutes before the dean of the College of Cardinals would step out to the balcony, time enough for the masses to build themselves into a good lather. Kleist had to hope it was von Neurath who was waiting in the wings.

Once again, he pulled the small device from his pocket and flipped open the screen. He pressed a button. Dial tone. Within half a ring, the line picked up.

"Have the dogs cleared?" Kleist asked.

"Eight minutes."

"I want the chessmen on the board until we have confirmation."

"Understood."

"Hold them until the king retreats. They move as a unit. The king stays on the board until the rest are back in the box."

"Understood."

Kleist paused. "Double the coverage on the Campane. No access to anyone, passes included."

"Understood."

He cut the line. He'd been the one to dub their quarry the "chessmen"—bishops, cardinals, it made little difference. Pawns this afternoon. Keeping them in the Palace until after the Pope's address was simply the best way to buy himself a little extra time. The men at the arch? A chance to dilute the crew inside the hospice still further.

The dean emerged. An almost eerie silence fell over the 100,000 bodies.

"We have a Pope!" A thunderous roar exploded, the dean holding his hands high in an attempt to quiet the crowd. Even the microphone had no chance, the introduction of the supreme Pontiff lost to the constant clamor: "His Holiness, Pope Lucius the Fourth."

Had anyone asked, von Neurath had actually considered the far more obscure Zephyrinus for several weeks. Not so much for anything Zephyrinus had done, but for his timing. Pope in 216. The year a child had been born near the city of Seleucia-Ctesiphon on the Tigris, the capital of Persia. His name, Mani. The Paraclete. The hope of the one true and holy church.

In the end, Lucius had won out. Harbinger of the light. Far more appropriate.

Kleist watched through binoculars as the former Erich Cardinal von Neurath—clad in the white soutane and skullcap, emblems of his office—stepped out onto the balcony, his arms already in the classic pose of pious authority. He swept the air in narrow circles as if he were somehow breathing in the scent of spirituality. The noise of the crowd managed to reach even greater decibels, waves of sound echoing throughout the colonnades, von Neurath already comfortable with his preening humility.

Kleist turned his attention to the arch. The two extra men had taken up their positions. Like all good Catholics, they were crossing themselves, waiting for their new Pope to begin the Apostolic Blessing.

Fourteen minutes, start to finish. That was what von Neurath had promised. After that, eight minutes for the cardinals to be led back to the Sanctae Marthae.

Kleist picked up the package and headed for the door. He was now on his own timetable. Four minutes to the hospice, twelve minutes to set the plastique, four minutes to return.

Which left him a two-minute grace period.

The Harbinger of the Light always liked to keep things as tight as possible.

▲

"Where's Salko?" Ivo said.

Once again, the seven-year-old was asking the most obvious question. And once again, Pearse was totally unprepared for it. Keeping his eyes on the road, he said, "Salko . . . is . . ."

"Staying in the village," Petra cut in, pulling Ivo closer to her chest.

"What about the surprise?" he asked.

"What surprise?" she said.

"The one we're going to play on him."

Pearse heard the disappointment in his voice. "Actually, he—"

Before Pearse had finished, Ivo's eyes lit up. "Oh!" he whispered. He turned to the glass partition and slid it back.

"Hello, Salko," he shouted, straining against his mother so as to peer into the back of the van. "I know you're back there." He waited. "You thought you were going to get me because I thought I was surprising you." He looked at Pearse, a big smile on his face. "You're pretty good at this." Before Pearse could answer, Ivo was back at the partition, howling away at the unseen Salko. "Helloooooo. I got you. You can come out now."

Petra brought him back to her lap. "Sweetie, Salko isn't there. I told you, he stayed in the village."

Ivo broke free again, his head deep into the opening. "Come on. I know you're here." When it slowly sank in, Ivo became very quiet. "Why? Why isn't he here?" He sat back on Petra's lap and looked across at Pearse. "You said we'd surprise him. You said he'd be here." Pearse could hear the first hint of genuine sadness in the little voice. "Why isn't he here?"

"He had to stay in the village to help his friends," said Petra, holding him closer.

"But why didn't he say good-bye?" The words were now choked.

"It all happened very quickly, sweetie," Petra said. "He didn't even say good-bye to me. I think he needed to help his friends right away."

"Why?"

Petra looked over at Pearse. "I don't know. Sometimes Salko has to help his friends, and sometimes he has to leave without telling us."

"But he didn't leave." He lifted a hand to stem the first tears. "We did."

"I know, sweet pea. I know." She cupped his head to hers. "But we'll see him soon."

"I didn't say good-bye." His words were now muffled in his mother's neck. "I didn't say good-bye."

She began to rock him.

Ten minutes of silence passed before Pearse spoke.

"I didn't have a choice," he said.

Petra waited before answering. "Is he asleep?" she whispered.

Pearse glanced over at the little boy. The morning had obviously taken its toll. Pearse kept his voice low, as well. "Close enough."

"Don't ever use my son as a threat again," she said.

The quiet severity of her tone stunned him. It took him a moment to respond. "What?"

"You said if I wanted to see him, I had to get in the car. Don't ever do that again."

Another few seconds to understand what she was saying. "No. I didn't mean—"

"Yes, you did." She let the words sink in before asking, "Now what's going on? Why did we leave Salko back there?"

"It's . . . complicated."

"Try me."

He waited. He had no idea how to make sense of the last twenty minutes; and as much as he wanted to trust Ivo, he had to make sure. "'Sic tibi manus meae intendeo,'" he said.

"What?"

"'Omnes fingi in gyro lucis.'"

"What are you saying? I told you, I'm no good with Latin. Stop it," she demanded, her anger mounting.

"You have no idea what I'm talking about, do you?"

"No, and now you're frightening me. Why did we leave Salko back there?"

He kept his eyes on the road. He was having trouble admitting it to himself. "Because he's involved with this."

"So are you," her tone no less pointed then before.

"That's not what I meant. He's after the parchment. That's why he showed up in Kukes."

"A part of it?" The confusion momentarily softened her tone. "You're telling me he's a . . ." She couldn't find the word.

"Manichaean," Pearse said. "Yes."

"That doesn't make any sense."

"Neither does Ivo being able to recite a seventeen-hundred-year-old prayer that very few people have ever even heard of. But he did."

"Ivo?" Confusion turned to shock.

"'So do I stretch out my two hands toward You, all to be formed in the orbit of light.' In the Latin, 'Sic tibi manus . . .' He told me Salko taught it to him. It's one of their secrets. He's obviously very good at keeping them."

Pearse knew exactly what she was feeling at that moment—disbelief, betrayal, an utter sense of helplessness. He knew because he was still feeling them himself.

"I can't . . ." She continued to stare. "Ivo doesn't . . . He barely knows any of the prayers at church."

Pearse pointed to his pack by her feet. "Open it."

"What?"

"Just open it."

She hesitated, then reached across the sleeping child and picked up the pack.

"The little book with the rope tie," he said. "It's about fifteen pages in."

She did as she was told. She flipped past Ribadeneyra's brief history until she found the entries.

"There," he said, quickly glancing over. "Try the fifth line, then the eleventh."

She read. "I can't believe Ivo knows this."

"Then ask him. Wake him up." Emerging from a series of back roads, they arrived at a deserted intersection, the first promise of paved surface. A sign for the main highway peeked out from behind a tuft of trees. Pearse headed west.

Petra stared at the page, then back at Pearse.

"Ask him," he repeated.

She continued to stare. When she realized he wasn't going to relent, she very gently placed a hand on Ivo's cheek, bending close into his ear.

"Ivi, sweetie," she whispered. "If you sleep now, you won't sleep tonight."

The boy breathed in heavily, a slight turning of his neck.

"Come on, sweetie. You have to get up."

Another long breath as two tired eyes blinked in Pearse's direction, a tiny hand to rub them as the boy straightened up.

"Are we going home?" The nap had done little to improve his mood.

Petra looked at Pearse. "I don't know, sweetie."

Pearse didn't have an answer, either.

Holding the book at her side, she did her best with the Latin: "'*Sic tibi manus meae intendeo . . .*'"

Ivo immediately sat up in her lap, quickly turning to his mother. His look of surprise was almost comical. Just as quickly, he turned to Pearse. "You told her," he said, disappointment now verging on anger.

"No, she's reading it."

Ivo flipped around, only now seeing the book in her hand. "Let me see."

"Be careful, sweetie. It's very old."

"I know, I know. Salko told me." Ivo waited for his mother to bring the book closer. He then looked back at Pearse. "That's not the book."

"Let him see the words," said Pearse.

Ivo turned. Petra pointed to the lines in the text.

"What are all the other words?" he asked.

"They're . . . other songs," Pearse answered. "They—" Cutting himself short, he quickly glanced over at Ivo. "What book did Salko tell you was old?" he asked.

"The book with the songs," Ivo answered.

"I thought you weren't allowed to write them down."

"That's only 'Perfect Light.' I have a whole book of the other ones."

A child's first prayer. Part of a prayer book. *Of course.* Eyes on the road again, he asked, "Does Salko have that book?"

Ivo shook his head. "No. He gave it to me. When I turned six. Everyone gets one when they turn six. You know that."

"Right." A Manichaean primer for initiates. What else could be more obvious? "And you still have the book?" Pearse asked.

Ivo nodded.

"What are you talking about?" asked Petra.

"Where's the book now?" Pearse said, ignoring her.

"At home," Ivo answered.

Pearse started nodding to himself.

"What?" asked Petra.

"It's how he made sure," he said to himself.

"What are you talking about?"

"Ribadeneyra picked that prayer to make sure that the person who figured out his puzzle was one of them. A Manichaean. Who else would know the child's prayer? Who else would—" He suddenly slammed on the breaks. All three lurched forward.

"What are you doing?" she screamed, one hand around Ivo, the other strong-arming the dashboard.

"There are lots of prayers in that book, aren't there, Ivo?"

The little boy didn't seemed bothered in the least by the sudden stop. "Prayers and pictures and puzzles." He turned to Petra. "Salko says when I learn enough of them, I can start doing the puzzles."

Now it was her turn simply to nod.

"It's something in that book," Pearse said. "Otherwise, why use the prayer? Something only a Manichaean would know to look for. Something to explain the other Ribadeneyra entries."

Forgetting Salko for the moment—and everything else that had happened in that last half hour—Pearse jammed the car into gear.

They'd be expecting them in Visegrad. Not Rogatica.

He checked his watch. With any luck, they'd be there by midafternoon.

▲

Peretti heard the explosion, then felt the tremor. His hand immediately went to the wall, one or two picture frames tipping over on themselves from atop his bureau, a painting on the wall losing its nail. A second explosion. Then a third.

Pushing himself to the window, he peered out, the source of the eruption rising in flame no more than a hundred yards from him.

The Domus Sanctae Marthae.

Holy Mother of God.

Through the smoke and fire, he tried to locate the upper floors, now little more than jagged cavities of glass and stone. *Inside the Vatican. Not possible.* He crossed himself, a prayer for those inside.

The words were barely out of his mouth when he suddenly realized how close he had come to being one of them himself. The decision to return to his apartments had been a last-minute one; even then, it had taken a mighty harangue to convince the guards to let him go. The order had been for all the cardinals—*all.*

He reached for the phone, only to be drawn to the sight of the first survivors stumbling from the building, their clothes torn, limbs and faces darkened by residue or blood—he couldn't tell which. There were more than five or six of them, each one falling to the ground, except for the last, who continued to wander aimlessly, lost in a concussed haze, strangely graceful amid the havoc. The others faded into the background as the pinballing man came into focus, unseen barriers sending him this way and that. It lasted less than four or five seconds; a guard arrived to gather him in, the man's legs still churning even as he was helped to the ground.

Arbitrary movements, thought Peretti, disconnected—at least from the vantage point of reasoned thought. For the man himself, though, the actions had had meaning, purpose—understood only by a mind lost to the shock.

Just as the mayhem itself had meaning. The question was, Whose mind had inspired it?

He picked up the phone.

The door behind him suddenly flew open. Two men raced in, guns drawn.

"It's all right," Peretti said, recognizing them. "I'm fine."

Both men holstered their guns. "We should take you to the *Gabbia,* Eminence, just in case."

The *Gabbia,* short for Gabbia per Uccelli—the birdcage—had been a bomb shelter during the war, six floors below the library, now transformed into the Vatican's safe house for just such occasions.

Peretti nodded. "I should make some calls first."

The nearer of the two men took the phone. "There are over a hundred lines downstairs, Eminence. We should go now."

Nodding, Peretti followed them out.

"You were lucky, Eminence," said the man now trailing him. "They think over a hundred of the cardinals were inside when the bombs went off. Whoever did this knew exactly when to set them off."

One more nod.

Who indeed.

▲

Pearse sat in the car, hands clasped in his lap. Ivo was doing the same in the passenger seat. Neither had said a word for the last ten minutes.

He had parked in an alley almost a quarter of a mile from the apartment—on Petra's instructions. Remarkable how quickly she had been able to take everything in stride, the freedom fighter once again in control. Or maybe it was simply a maternal instinct. No matter. She had been equally clear about who would be going for the book.

"You stay here." A kiss for Ivo as she'd opened the door.

Pearse had started to follow, Petra quick to stop him. "I was talking to you. You don't know the area. You don't know the apartment. And if they are here, they know exactly what you look like." Stepping outside, she'd turned to him, her voice with an intensity he hadn't heard in years: "And don't let Ivo out of your sight. Understand?"

The boy had obviously been through enough of these sorts of situations to know when to stay put.

A confirming nod from Pearse had sent her on her way.

That had been almost fifteen minutes ago.

Now, glancing over at his charge, Pearse couldn't be sure just exactly which of his transgressions was prompting the silence: the flight from Salko, the absence of Petra. Most likely, it was the forced disclosure of the book's location. Petra's tone had been sufficient to unlock Ivo's secret: a box hidden behind a loose slat in his closet. Salko had evidently helped him to make it.

"Do you think you might ever stop being mad at me?" Pearse finally asked.

Ivo crossed his hands at his chest.

"Can I take that as a maybe?"

The boy clenched his arms even tighter, a snort of air through his nose.

"Okay—a maybe, with a big hug and a very quiet sneeze. Am I getting close?"

Silence.

"Don't try to make me happy," Ivo finally said.

"Okay." Silence. "How about I try to make you orange?"

Ivo shot him a glance, his expression somewhere between anger and confusion. "Orange?"

"Well, you won't let me apologize and make you happy, so I thought I could make you orange."

Ivo's arms loosened. "How do you make someone orange?"

"I have no idea. But at least it won't be making you happy."

Ivo stared at him for a few seconds, then turned away. "That's silly. You don't make any sense."

"Then how about you let me say I'm sorry?"

Without looking at him, Ivo answered, "You shouldn't have made me tell. It was my secret with Salko. And you shouldn't have made us leave Salko. Salko wouldn't have made me tell Mommy."

"I know," said Pearse, watching as Ivo began to play with a rip in the door's vinyl.

"If it's so important," the boy said, "why didn't you give Mommy *your* copy of the book?"

Even angry, Ivo was still a very clever little boy. "Well . . . because your book is special. It's going to help us find another special book. And I know Salko wants us to find that other book."

"Then why didn't he tell you where my book was?"

Very clever.

"Because," said Pearse, retrieving the Ribadeneyra volume from the dashboard, "he didn't know I had this book."

Ivo slowly turned to him. Only slightly less ruffled, he said, "The one Mommy read from."

"Right," said Pearse. "Do you want to take a look at it?"

"I saw it already. When Mommy had it."

Pearse nodded slowly. "Okay. I was just wondering if you wanted to hold it. But if you don't . . ."

Ivo stared at the book, then glanced up at Pearse. "I guess I could." He took the book. "But don't think this is making me happy. You still shouldn't have made me tell."

"Fair enough."

For a seven-year-old, Ivo showed tremendous care with it, turning back the pages slowly and peering at the words with great concentration. If nothing else, Salko had taught him how to appreciate his past. His was a child's Latin, enough to pronounce everything correctly, even if he didn't understand most of what he was saying. He stopped at one point, eyes wide. He turned to Pearse, pointing to a word he recognized.

"Manichaeus," he said

"Yes, Mani." To hear Ivo say it with such reverence tore into him. "You know a lot about Mani, don't you?" he asked.

"I guess. I know the stories from my book."

"The stories about Mani."

Ivo nodded.

"Have you read all of them?"

Another nod. Ivo placed the Ribadeneyra on the dashboard and began to count out on his fingers: "'The Apostle of Light,' 'Shapur the King,' 'Sowing the Corn,' 'Kartir in Darkness,' 'Finding the Light.'"

Bible stories for the Brotherhood, thought Pearse. "Which is your favorite?" he asked.

"'Kartir in Darkness.'"

"Why's that?"

Ivo shrugged. "I don't know. Because he gets swallowed up by the darkness at the end."

"Kartir?"

Ivo nodded.

From what Pearse remembered, Kartir had been the rough equivalent of a Babylonian Pilate. He wondered how many thousands of other little boys had found Kartir's demise so compelling.

A troubling thought as the door opened and Petra slid in next to Ivo. He was already on her lap, back pressed into her chest, by the time she pulled it shut. A quick kiss, then back to the vinyl.

"Any problems?" Pearse asked.

"They had a car outside. I took the basement route. Don't worry, they didn't see me." She handed him the book. "And it wasn't just a box. It was like a little shrine." The anger in her voice was all too plain. "Statues, pictures. . . . I have no idea what they were for." She let her head fall back against the partition, her eyes staring out the window, totally unaware of the effect her tone was having on Ivo. "How could he have done that?"

With tears in his eyes, Ivo looked up at her. "I'm sorry, Mommy. Salko said it was okay."

She looked at him, at once squeezing her arms around him. "Oh, no, sweetie. I'm not angry with you. I'm not angry with you at all." She kissed the top of his head.

Ivo's tears slowed. "Are you angry with Salko?"

"Don't worry about Salko, sweet pea. That's nothing for you to think about."

"Don't be angry with Salko, Mommy."

"Okay." Another few kisses. "I won't." After a moment, she looked across at Pearse. "So, is it what you thought it was?"

He continued to stare at the two of them.

"What's in the book, Ian?" she pressed.

He held her gaze, then turned to the book. "Right. The book."

Its dimensions were that of a small laptop, though far thinner. Across the top—in Serbo-Croatian—ran the title, *Verses for Children*, nothing to hint at the Manichaean scriptures within. Opening it, Pearse realized the book had recently been rebound, the sheets inside far older than the cover. The title reappeared on the front page, this time in grander script, a sure sign of nineteenth-century publishing. Confirmation came at the bottom of the page, where the year 1866 was inked in thick lettering. Between title and year—in a single column—ran a list of perhaps eight handwritten names, each from a different pen. It was the last few that caught his attention: Alibeg Mendravic, Vlado Mendravic, Salko Mendravic, Ivo Corkan.

A Manichaean lineage brought to life in the scrawled signatures of four six-year-old boys.

Pearse didn't know whether to be more concerned with the deep-rooted familial devotion or with the book's obvious professional quality. This wasn't something that had been produced in a back room by a bunch of zealots, a hundred or so copies to be distributed by hand. This was something far more serious, clearly published on a much larger scale. And if that was the case with the Serbo-Croatian edition, who was to say how many primers had been produced in German or in English? A far more daunting prospect.

Obviously, the Manichaeans hadn't spent the last seventeen hundred years simply waiting for the return of their Paraclete.

"I wrote my name," said Ivo, his little finger reaching over to the page, tracing the lettering. "That's Salko, and Salko's dad, and his dad. It goes back a long way." He looked at Pearse. "You have one with your dad, right?"

Pearse felt that now-familiar ache, his own failure for having allowed Ivo to become a part of this. Or was it merely jealousy, Salko's bond with the boy made clear in the caress of a tiny hand?

"Right," he answered distractedly, flipping to the next page as quickly as he could.

The table of contents stared back, a list of stories and prayers, each with its first line printed just below the title. Not surprisingly, the only one he recognized was the Ribadeneyra prayer, appropriately titled, "The Awakening." The title *Treasure of Life* appeared next to it in parenthesis. He scanned the rest of the page. Each entry sported a parenthetical of its own, several of the titles appearing again and again: *Pragmateia, Shahpuhrakan, Book of Giants, Living Gospel,* and, most popular, *Kephalaia.* It didn't take long to realize that these were the sources for the various verses. Texts thought lost for centuries alive within the pages of a child's prayer book.

He flipped to "The Awakening."

As with the "Perfect Light" scroll, tiny sketches of men with daggers and lions on the prowl littered the text. He was about to ask Ivo what they meant, when his eyes stopped on a drawing halfway down the page. At first, he thought it was simply one more triangle—half black, half empty—the ever-present symbol in Manichaean literature. Looking closer, he realized it was far more. Words filled both sides:

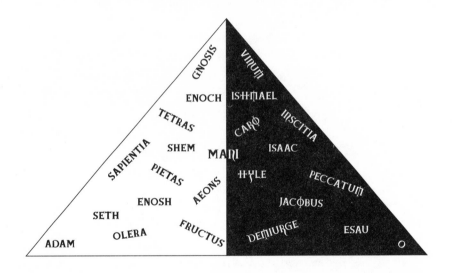

Those in the "light" represented the good—the prophets, fruit, wisdom, gnosis. Those in the "darkness," evil—brothers in conflict, meat, sin, nothingness. A child's guide to the two realms of the universe.

What Pearse saw, however, astounded him. Half of the words in the triangle coincided exactly with the phrases from the Ribadeneyra entries. It was only their location that puzzled him.

"Hand me my pack," he said to Petra, his eyes still glued to the page.

Ivo quickly leaned forward and picked up the pack; he wasn't quite strong enough to lift it, Petra lending a hand as he brought it to Pearse's lap. Staring a few moments longer at the page, Pearse then placed the open book on the dashboard and pulled the papers from inside the pack.

It took him less than five minutes to write out the answers he had deciphered from the one-line through the four-line entries, along with the unsolved five-line verse as Ribadeneyra had written it. He lettered the five separate sections A through E, each with its corresponding line entry. Staring down at the finished copy, he began to see where the Spaniard had been leading him all along.

1.	Visegrad	A-1
2.	Near the awakening	A-2
3.	Rises	A-3
4.	When light and darkness meet	A-4
5.	So do I stretch out my two hands toward You	A-5
6.	Esau	B-1
7.	Near the sin of Jacob	B-2
8.	Becoming	B-3
9.	Noble bridge	B-4
10.	All to be formed in the orbit of light	B-5
11.	Wisdom and piety	C-1
12.	Over the herbs	C-2
13.	Opens	C-3
14.	The Inn	C-4
15.	When I am sent to the contest with darkness	C-5
16.	Gnosis strikes wine	D-1
17.	Floating above	D-2
18.	Enoch	D-3
19.	The hills make ascent	D-4
20.	Knowing that You can assist me in sight	D-5
21.	Treasure	E-1
22.	Revealed	E-2
23.	The enlightener speaks	E-3
24.	To his disciples	E-4
25.	The fragrance of life is always within me	E-5

The first series was clear enough. "Visegrad, near the awakening, rises when light and darkness meet." The light and darkness were meeting in the triangle; the triangle was near "The Awakening" in the prayer book; and Visegrad was "rising" from it. Ergo: The triangle somehow represented Visegrad.

Now to the geography of the town. Pearse noticed that the first two or three lines of each set pinpointed different areas in the triangle.

"Esau near the sin of Jacob"—Esau, Peccatum, Jacobus: lower right.

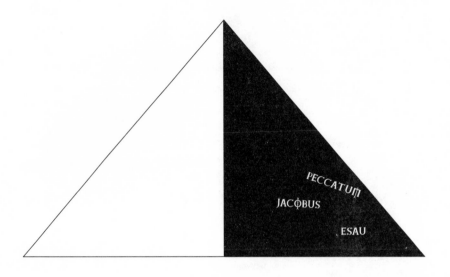

"Wisdom and piety over the herbs"—Sapientia, Pietas, Olera: middle and lower left.

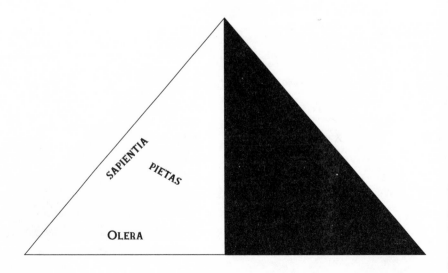

And finally, "Gnosis strikes wine floating above Enoch"—Gnosis, Vinum, Enoch: upper left and right.

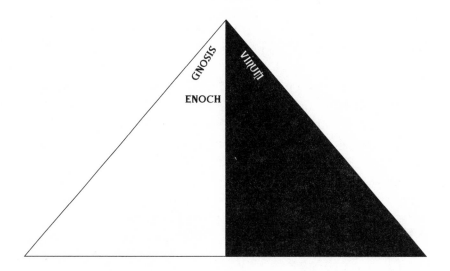

Three sides of the triangle.

The last line of each set held the ultimate key. Esau on the lower right became the "noble bridge." Wisdom on the middle left opened "the inn." And Gnosis up top defined "the hills." Three landmarks within Visegrad. Three points of a triangle.

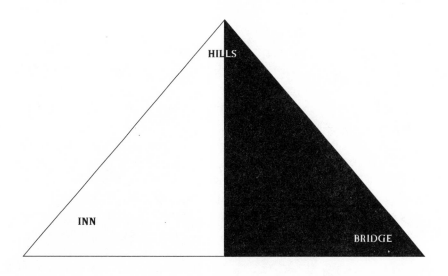

Even without reading the last set, Pearse knew exactly where the "Hodoporia" lay hidden on the map. Where else could it be but with Mani at its center? The treasure revealed in "the enlightener."

His disciple? The one to solve the mystery.

Like all good Manichaeans, Ribadeneyra had chosen his landmarks well. The bridge, though bombed in the recent war, remained roughly intact. The hills were the hills. The only question was, Where was the inn? Without that third point in the triangle, it would be impossible to locate the center.

"Where can I find an old map of Visegrad?" he asked, tracing the triangle from Ivo's book onto a separate sheet.

"How old?" Petra asked.

"Sixteenth, seventeenth century."

She watched him as he continued to draw. "Now where did I leave my sixteenth-, seventeenth-century map of Visegrad?"

Not bothering to look up, he said, "I'm serious."

"A four-hundred-year-old map? I have no idea. Maybe at the city hall. Why?"

"Because I need to know where something called 'the inn' would have been in 1521."

"At the entry to the old marketplace," she said matter-of-factly. "Where the road to Mejdan starts to climb."

"I said I'm serious."

"So am I."

Now, he looked up.

"I promise," she said.

"How do you know where—"

"Because anyone who grew up in this part of the world knows the story of the old inn. It's one of the first things you learn in school."

"In school?"

She turned to Ivo and began to sing: "'The boy from the hills, when he grew to a man—'"

"'Was known to the world as the Grand Mehmed Pasha,'" Ivo continued with a wide smile. "'He gave us the bridge near the mighty Stone Han, from Rade the Mason of the great Turkish Empire.'"

Pearse stared at both of them. "What are you talking about?"

Ivo giggled; Petra smiled. She sang again: "'So went the wood and the hay and stables, the inn tumbled down by the Grand Mehmed Pasha.'"

"'Say good-bye to the wood and the hay and the stables,'" sang Ivo. "'Make way for the Han of the Grand Mehmed Pasha.'"

"The Grand who?" Pearse asked.

"Mehmed Pasha of Sokolovici," she said in her best kindergarten-teacher voice. "He was one of Suleiman's viziers." When she saw no change in Pearse's expression, she said, "A local boy who made good. Around 1570, he decided he wanted to bring civilization to Bosnia, so he built the bridge, and, with it, the Stone Han—'the great caravanserai.' Hence the song."

"And what does that have to do with the inn?"

"The inn stood on the spot where they built the Stone Han," she explained.

Pearse began to nod slowly. "But first he tore down the wood and the hay—"

"'Tumbled down,'" said Ivo.

"Right. 'Tumbled down.' Sorry, Ivi." He waited for a nod. He then turned back to Petra. "And the old inn would have been there fifty years before this pasha decided to be so magnanimous?"

"Well, no one's really sure when the old inn was built," she said, "but the legend goes back to at least the early 1400s. That's why it was such a big deal when he 'tumbled it down.'"

"So anyone who came through Visegrad, say in 1521, would have known about the old inn?"

"Absolutely."

Pearse thought to himself for a moment. "Would you be able to pick out the spot where the old inn would have been on a current map of the city?"

"Sure."

He handed her the pages, the book, and the pack.

Half a minute later, they were on the road to Visegrad.

Λ

There was something distinctly non-Vatican about the rooms buried under the library, a coldness in gray steel to repel even a spiritual fire. Peretti had never been to the *Gabbia* before, the place an odd mixture of 1950s nuclear-provisioned and 1990s high-tech-obsessed. Doors several feet thick separated one room from the next, each fitted with an air-lock device, what he could only describe as an iron steering wheel wedged in at the center. They were archaic contrivances, however, when compared to the electronic gizmos that lined the walls, the once-spacious bunker now turned into very cramped quarters. Living areas had become computer rooms, open-atria communications centers.

A base from which to maintain the faith, even in the face of Cold War annihilation.

The only space that retained any link with the city above was the chapel, two stories high, squeezed in at the back of the complex: marble panels camouflaged the steel walls and floors; the flicker of chandeliers replaced the hum of fluorescent lights; paintings hung above the altar—Peretti recognized a Filippo Lippi—a gentle reminder of what they were here to protect; and, along the nave, twin rows of richly grained pews extended to the back wall.

All of them empty save for the nine shaken cardinals sitting alone in silent prayer.

Peretti glanced at the bent figures. They were, for the most part, *i vecchii*, "the old ones," cardinals beyond eighty, who no longer voted in the conclave but whose spiritual presence remained essential. It was their age that had saved them, too slow to get back to the Sanctae Marthae in time for the explosions. Little consolation in that. The oldest was Virgilio Cardinal Dezza, long ago Archbishop of Ferrara, a tiny rail of a man with a full head of white hair. Peretti had talked with him just this morning, nothing about the vote (of course), but about the beauty of the Sistine. Dezza had admitted he had always had a certain soft spot for the pagan sibyls on the ceiling—a thought that perhaps Michelangelo had painted them with a little more care, just to get a jab in at old Julius II. It had made him laugh; Peretti had laughed, as well.

Now, Dezza seemed a broken man.

Peretti dipped his fingers in the holy water, crossed himself, and knelt in the aisle. He then made his way to Dezza's side. The old man's eyes were closed. Peretti closed his as well and began to pray.

When he opened them, Dezza was looking up at him, a pained smile on his lips.

"Peretti." He placed a hand on his knee. "You weren't . . ." He couldn't bring himself to finish the thought. "Thanks be to God. It's a terrible thing. Terrible."

Peretti nodded.

"And the rest of it," the old man continued. "Is it a sign? Hail and fire, mixed with blood, falling to the earth. Is He coming?"

Dezza had reached that point in life where tragedy could be understood only as omen. Not unusual for men so long devoted to the church. "Terrorists, Eminence," Peretti said. He had known Dezza for too many years—first as bishop, then as cardinal—not to call him by anything but his title. "They were bound to find their way into the Vatican at some point."

The old man looked at him. "But it isn't just here, Giacomo. It isn't just the Vatican, is it?"

Peretti wasn't sure what to make of the expression—a genuine terror or a hint of senility—peering up at him. "The church is strong," he said. "There are others who will take their places."

Confusion crossed the old man's face. "Take their places?" he said. "Even if they're rebuilt, who will have the courage to step inside one?"

Peretti stared at him for several seconds. "What are you talking about, Eminence?"

"The churches, Giacomo. The churches."

"What churches?"

"The ones they destroyed," he said. "Hundreds of them."

Again, Peretti stared at the old man. "What are you talking about?"

"In the room with the screens," Dezza said. "It's all in the room with the screens. The church in flames. Hail and fire, mixed with blood. Hail and fire." His focus was back on the altar, his hands clasped in prayer. He closed his eyes, the conversation all but forgotten.

Peretti stood, a quick devotion, then back into the maze of corridors that made up the *Gabbia*. Three minutes later, he found his way into "the room with the screens." Thirty or so televisions filled the far wall, each one tuned to a different channel. The pictures were all too similar. Destruction on a massive scale. Stepping farther into the room, he saw von Neurath sitting on a sofa, a group of young priests in chairs around him, each one either jotting furiously on a pad or talking on the phone. It was clear who was dictating their every move. Every so often, von Neurath looked up to catch a report on one of the news programs. Otherwise, his energy remained focused on his entourage. It was during one of his quick glances up that he noticed Peretti in the corner.

He turned to him at once.

"Cardinal Peretti," he said. "They told me you were safe. Thank God you're alive."

Peretti remained by the door. "Yes, Holiness."

"A terrible tragedy, Giacomo. You and I were very lucky."

When he spoke, Peretti's words carried no emotion. "Then there must be a reason why He spared us, Holiness."

The two men continued to stare at each other. "Yes," von Neurath said finally. "There must." He turned to the screens. "And then this," he said. "It's all quite unbelievable."

"Yes, Holiness."

"I thought we had enough trouble with the bank," von Neurath added, passing a few notes to one of his lackeys. "But I see I was wrong."

"Trouble at the bank?" Peretti asked, his tone more confirmation than surprise.

"You haven't heard?" Von Neurath looked up, waiting for a response. When Peretti shook his head, he continued. "Not surprising. I found out myself less than an hour ago." He turned again to the notes. "It looks as if one of our analysts has placed the bank in a rather precarious position with a group of Syrian investors. It's Ambrosiano all over again, except this time there's talk of terrorist funding. I'm not really sure of the details."

"Remarkable timing, Holiness."

"Yes. Yes, it is. And they say all of this might be only the beginning."

"They, Holiness?"

Again von Neurath stopped and turned to Peretti. Pointing to the screens, he said, "They, my son. A thousand churches bombed, every continent, every denomination."

It was the last word that struck him. "Denomination?" Peretti asked.

"It's the Protestants as well, Giacomo. And the Greeks and the Russians." He began to scribble something on a pad. "It seems as if it's an all-out war on Christianity."

Peretti waited before responding. "Do they say from where, Holiness?"

"An old enemy," von Neurath replied, handing a sheet to the man seated across from him. "From the East. Given this new wave of fundamentalism, I suppose it was bound to happen at some point."

"I see." Peretti stared up at the screens. It was more than just destruction he saw. Groups had already begun to rally, outraged men and women waiting to unleash their venom, not a pastor or priest in sight to calm them. Blood lust left to run wild. He turned to von Neurath. "Then we must do what we can to ensure that our church remains strong, Holiness."

Again, von Neurath looked over at him. "Yes. We must."

An explosion on one of the screens drew the attention of everyone in the room. Peretti took it as his cue to leave.

He let himself stand in the corridor for a moment, the enormity of what he had just seen and heard quickly relegated to the back of his mind. *An all-out war on Christianity.* Orchestrated from within the Vatican? If so, it meant that the last place he should be was inside its walls. Peretti headed for the entrance.

A pair of guards stood silently by the door, a third at a desk, all three with guns at the ready. Peretti approached the man at the desk. The guard recognized him at once and stood.

"Is something wrong, Eminence?"

Peretti shook his head quickly. "No, but I need to leave the *Gabbia* for a few minutes."

"That's not possible, Eminence. It's still not safe."

"Then when will it be safe?"

The question seemed to fluster the man momentarily. "I . . . would imagine once the City has been secured, Eminence."

"And how long do we think that will take?"

Again, the guard had no answer.

Before he could respond, Peretti continued. "Because if it's later than tonight's first Mass, then we have a problem. His Holiness has asked me to retrieve a certain book from the library. For the Investiture of Office." Peretti was making it up as he went. Von Neurath had become Pope the moment he'd answered the cardinal dean's question, "Volo aut nolo?" with a resounding "Yes." That he'd have to wait a few days to have the woollen pallium bestowed on him made no difference whatsoever. Chances were, though, that a young Vatican guard knew none of that. "His Holiness must be ordained as quickly as possible, especially given the situation. It's a simple task, but we will need that book."

"Of course. I can send one of my men—"

"Will he know where to find the *Ritus Inaugurationis Feudalis Praedicationis?*" Not that there was an actual Investiture Proclamation lying around the library—not that such a proclamation even existed— but it sounded reasonable enough.

"Well . . . if someone tells him where it is."

"That wouldn't make any difference. It can't be handled by anyone but a cardinal. Am I now making myself clear?"

"No. I mean, yes, of course, Eminence." The man glanced at the two other guards. Both stared straight ahead. No help there. He looked back at Peretti. "You mean he isn't Pope yet?"

Peretti waited, then responded. "I can stand here and have this conversation with you for as long as you like. But at some point, you're going to have to open that door and let me get the *Ritus.*"

"But His Holiness—I mean His Eminence . . ." The guard leaned over the table; in a whisper, he said, "Cardinal von Neurath said that no one was to leave. He gave an express order."

Peretti leaned in, as well. "Well, until he's Pope, that order carries no more weight than my own, now does it?"

The guard needed a moment for that one. With a newfound resilience, he walked to the door, punched a few numbers into a keypad, and watched as the air lock released. "You," he said to the man nearest him. "Go with His Eminence. Gun cocked at all times. Understood?"

"Yes, sir."

The guard turned back to Peretti. "And if you could, Eminence, come back as quickly as possible."

"Of course," said Peretti. "I want to keep myself as safe as I can."

▲

The bookshop had all the tourist trappings: picture books on the bridge, postcards, even a few coffee mugs. Ivo had been particularly interested in a scale model of the bridge, the dust on the box saying more about the region's recent history than any number of news stories could have. The man at the cash register had virtually beamed at the sight of the three of them perusing the stacks, less enthusiastic when Petra had pulled a map from one of the shelves and moved them to the back of the store. No need to be by the windows. Not that she expected Salko's friends to be prowling the outskirts of town—less so a bookstore—but she'd done too much to make their arrival as inconspicuous as possible to jeopardize those efforts now.

They had stopped in Ustipraca—a town halfway between Rogatica and Visegrad—Petra friendly enough with the shopkeepers to rummage for something a little more provincial: long skirt and kerchief for her, coat, brimless cap, and a new pair of boots for him, along with a bundle of cloth put together to look like an infant in her arms. Three became four with a small blanket and a few pages of newspaper crumpled up inside. Most bizarre was her insistence that Ivo don a girl's long skirt and kerchief of his own. He'd giggled his way through it all, Pearse thinking it a bit much, until he'd looked at all of them in a mirror. By then, she'd applied some stipple from a child's makeup kit to his face, five days' growth of beard to add to the image of the nondescript Bosnian family. Pearse had had trouble recognizing them himself.

Now, gazing at a map of the town, and acutely aware of the few other customers in the shop, he was grateful for the camouflage.

"There," whispered Petra, pointing to a spot on the map. "The old inn would have been there."

Pearse pulled a sheet from his jacket and placed it above the map. Tracing the inn, bridge, and hills, he marked an X for Mani's location in the original triangle. He then peeled the page back.

"That can't be right," he said as he stared down at the area.

"That's where the inn—"

"It puts him in the middle of the river," he said, trying it again so as to make sure he hadn't miscalculated.

"Let me see," she said, taking the map.

Pulling the tracing away, Pearse pinpointed the three landmarks. "There, there, and there," he said. "Which puts Mani there," he added, his finger in the middle of the Drina.

"That can't be right."

"I just said that."

Her eyes still on the page, she asked, "Which are your three landmarks?"

Trying not to show his frustration, he said, "The bridge, the hills, and your inn, which obviously wasn't where you thought it was."

When she looked up, the expression on her face only served to annoy him further.

"What?" he said.

"I'll give you the inn and the hills, but you've got the wrong bridge."

"What?"

"1521, Ian. The great bridge wasn't built until fifty years later. Remember the song?"

Pearse didn't answer.

"It's the bridge over the Rzav River, not the Drina," she said. "That's the one your Manichaean was referring to." She placed her finger on the map. "The Rzav is the other river in town, which happens to be there."

Pearse brought the tracing up to the map. Angling it so as to accommodate the new landmark, he saw where Mani's X had come to rest. Nowhere near the Drina. Luckily, there was only one site of interest in the vicinity, the name all too obvious as Pearse thought about it.

"'Izvor za Spanski,'" he read. "Ribadeneyra was obviously more homesick than he let on." He turned to Petra. "What's a Spanish fountain doing in Visegrad?"

She looked more closely at the map. "It's in the *Cetvrt za Jevrejin*, the old Jewish Quarter."

Pearse began to nod. "Makes sense. A lot of Jews came east after the Spanish Expulsion. It's the right time frame. They must have built it as some sort of memorial."

Before he could ask, she said, "About fifteen minutes from here."

He carried Ivo, she the "baby," the streets relatively quiet for the late afternoon. The farther on they walked into town, however, the more the place began to fill, stores reopening after the protracted midday nap, more bodies on the streets to make Pearse feel a bit more comfortable.

It was when they reached the old marketplace that he recognized the first of the outsiders, men flaunting their conspicuousness—receivers with wires attached to their ears, handheld radios, not to mention the telltale dark suits of Vatican security. None of them seemed to notice the stares from the locals.

Pearse started to turn down a side street so as to avoid them, when he felt Petra slip her arm through his. She began to lead him directly toward one of the Vatican men.

Instinctively, he began to tug her back the other way. Almost at once, he stopped, aware that the movement would only draw more attention.

A numbing sensation began to course through his legs and torso as they drew closer to the man. In that instant, he knew only the betrayal: *I'm no good with Latin . . . You're frightening me.* He had shown her where the "Hodoporia" was. There was no need to keep up the pretense any longer, no need to lead him around by the nose. Of course she had known what Salko was teaching her son. Of course she had been a part of it all along. *How could I have been so stupid?*

They were within a few feet of the man, Pearse ready for the final Judas kiss, when Petra simply glanced at the man, then continued moving on. With his heart pounding, Pearse moved on, as well.

"It's only if you look like you're trying to avoid them that they'll notice you," she said when they were out of earshot. "They're not look-

ing for a family of four with a seven-year-old girl, remember? If we'd
gone down that side street, we'd be running for our lives right now."

The best Pearse could do was nod.

He was still breathing heavily when she led them up into an area of
town where the houses were packed in tighter together, narrow streets
making it difficult for the sun to break through.

"I though for a minute back there—"

"I know," she answered without looking at him. "Remember, you have
to trust me."

The moment in the village repaid in full.

They walked along the cobbled shadows for several minutes until she
turned down a short alley—no sign of the Vatican faithful this far off
the beaten path. Following the curve of the passageway, they came into
a small courtyard of dirt and grass.

"'Izvor za Spanski,'" she said.

Pearse stood there, staring at the small fountain at its center. All was
forgiven.

The square itself was perhaps thirty yards in either direction, the
buildings along the perimeter sagging under the weight of ancient stone
and wood. No more than four stories high, they looked to be resting
against one another, squeezing out what little support they could as they
peered out into the courtyard. Two trees stood at the opposite corners,
wide branches filled with leaves to blanket the square in even deeper
shadow. A group of children was playing soccer in front of one of the
more ancient houses, its decay helped along by the constant thumping
of the ball. None of them seemed to notice as the small family neared
the fountain.

Drawing to within ten feet of it, Pearse stopped again. He was hoping that, with the "Hodoporia" so close at hand, he might reclaim that
same sense of wonder he had known at Phôtinus; instead, all he felt was
a strange kind of ambivalence. Not that he was any less drawn to the
promise of clarity, but somehow it seemed tied to a part of himself that
sought release in isolation. And that no longer made any sense to him.

He placed Ivo on the ground, took his hand, and together they began
to circle the fountain. A second memory of Phôtinus fixed in his
mind—Gennadios scooping handful after handful of water to his
soaked neck—a thought that perhaps Ribadeneyra had chosen the
fountain not for its reminiscence of home but for its uncanny resem-
blance to the one on Athos. The only significant difference was that this

one hadn't seen water in quite some time: cracks lined the inner pool; once-green algae deposits had turned an inky black; and, at the top, where the Phôtinus spout had sported a monk in prayer, here the figure was a man looking back over his shoulder. Pearse noticed that, at one point, the water had streamed from the top of his head, a fitting stain now on his cheek, perhaps the last tears for a country he had been forced to leave behind.

Pearse couldn't help but wonder if he might be looking up at old Ribadeneyra himself.

Compelling as it was, there was nothing to indicate where a Manichaean might have chosen to hide his stash in the stone. And given its contents, Pearse couldn't imagine that the Spaniard had picked a spot anywhere near the water. He crouched down and began to examine the underside of the fountain. Ivo did the same.

"What are we looking for?" the boy asked, forced to bring his skirt up over his knees so as to avoid tripping over it.

"Not really sure," said Pearse.

Ivo nodded and continued to scrutinize the stones.

"It might be something you've seen in your book," Pearse said, busy with his own investigation.

Again, Ivo nodded, now on hands and knees, crawling in the opposite direction around the fountain.

"He's getting filthy," said Petra.

As one, Ivo and Pearse looked up at her, the expressions of annoyance identical.

"Wonderful," she said as she sat on the fountain's ledge. "Now I get it in stereo."

Crawling to within a few feet of her, Pearse located the date of the fountain's completion: 1521. Ribadeneyra had evidently been here for its construction, further confirmation that they were in the right place. He was just moving past her when Ivo popped his head up from the other side.

"I found it! I found it!" His reaction was enough to warrant a momentary break in the soccer match.

Pearse jumped up and moved around to him. "Great, great . . . but remember, we have to be quiet."

"But I found it," Ivo answered, no less excited.

Again, Pearse crouched down. Immediately, he understood why Ivo had called him over. Where the rest of the stones along the fountain's base were rectangular, Ivo had found one made up of two distinct triangular pieces. More than that, each triangle had a lighter and darker side, hardly visible from a distance, but there nonetheless.

Not only had Ribadeneyra been around for its construction, he'd obviously taken part in the stonework. Pearse glanced up at the figure again. They really were a very clever bunch.

"Excellent," he said, shooting a finger at Ivo and winking. Ivo's eyes lit up; he returned the gesture, then gave a little giggle as he looked over at his mother.

"See, I told you Americans do that."

"Yes, you did," she said, then looked at Pearse in mock appreciation.

Her reaction was lost on him as he was already busy with the stone. Placing his hand on it, he tried to move it. No chance. He pulled back and stared at the surrounding area. Ivo immediately placed his hand on the stone and pressed against it. He, too, shook his head and pulled back.

"What do you think?" said Pearse, still trying to locate something else on the stone face that might hint at a way through. No acrostics, no levers.

Ivo shrugged and again pressed at the stone. "It's pretty hard."

"Yup," Pearse said, his eyes wandering along the strips of mortar. "Pretty hard." He began to feel around the surrounding stones. Not so much as a crack. Remarkable craftsmanship, he thought, except that, as he now stared at it from ground level, Pearse saw that the fountain leaned a few inches to one side. Or if not leaned, then at least sat on an uneven foundation. The closer in he looked, however, the more it struck him that the stones had just settled over time. Which meant that whatever Ribadeneyra had left for the "disciple" to discover might simply have gotten buried as sections of the fountain had sunk deeper into the ground.

Taking that as his cue, Pearse began to run his fingers along the spot where stone met dirt, the soil coming away with a bit of effort. Within a minute, he'd created a little gully, enough to use a small rock for digging. Ivo, of course, had begun to help with a rock of his own. Meanwhile, Petra was keeping an eye on the passageway into the courtyard; she was also monitoring the soccer players, each of whom was becoming more and more interested in the group by the fountain.

"You have an audience," she said to Pearse under her breath.

He glanced over at the children, then turned back. "Hopefully, it'll be a short show."

A few more inches, and he began to make out tiny markings chiseled into the stone. Brushing aside the excess dirt—but with no angle to read it—he began to trace his fingers across the symbols. It took him nearly a minute to figure out what they were. Letters. Four of them. Greek—χῶμα, "earth."

Not terribly helpful, but at least it was a start. Another few inches, and a second word. This one, three letters. His old friend φῶς, "light."

Pearse realized that Ribadeneyra had returned to the original "Perfect Light" scroll for his final message. Once again, everything was flipped on its head. Earth above light, the mundane over the sacred. And, as with everything having to do with the Manichaeans, he was meant to take it literally. The earth was covering the light.

He continued to dig.

By now, the soccer quartet had moved closer, still keeping their distance, though with the ball wedged under an arm, the sure sign that their interests had shifted. The biggest of them, a girl of maybe twelve, tried to peer past Pearse to see what he was doing. "Did you lose something?" she asked.

Pearse looked over his shoulder, then at Petra. Before he could come up with an answer, she said, "My husband's a stonemason. He wants to see what kind of stones were used on the fountain."

The girl nodded and continued to stare. After another few minutes, she asked, "Is there something special about our fountain?"

"It's very old," said Pearse, repositioning himself so as to dig wider and deeper. "Strong stone."

Again the girl nodded. It seemed enough to satisfy her curiosity. The children returned to the wall, the digging once again accompanied by the thump-thumping of the ball.

"Did you hear that, Ivo?" Pearse said, pulling up another handful of loosened soil. "I'm Rade the Mason of the great Turkish Empire."

Ivo giggled, more eager to get his hands as mud-filled as possible than to remove the dirt. "'So went the wood and the hay and stables,'" he sang, "'the inn tumbled down by the Grand Mehmed Pasha.'"

"'Say good-bye to the wood and the hay and the stables,'" Pearse answered, "'when the inn tumbles down—'"

"Noooo." Ivo laughed. "You got it wrong." And then in a tone he could have borrowed only from his mother, he said dismissively, "You Americans."

Pearse stopped digging. He began to laugh as he looked up at Petra. "I wonder where he heard that?"

She couldn't help but smile. "I wonder." She reached over and planted a kiss on Ivo's head, a quick muddy paw up to discourage her.

"Mommy, we're digging. You can't interrupt our job. Me and Ian. It's very important."

"I know. Very important." Another kiss.

"Mommy!"

"Okay, okay. I'll let you get back to your job." She glanced at Pearse, then turned to the courtyard entryway.

How different from the last time he'd tried to unearth the "Hodoporia," thought Pearse. No children's songs or soccer balls. No Petra in the Vault of the Paraclete. The change in venue seemed somehow appropriate, less of Mani and more of the stonemason. Or carpenter. Either would have done.

The hole was nearly a foot deep when he uncovered what felt like an iron bar sticking out from the base of the fountain. He traced it to the wall. There, he discovered a small indentation in the stone, one that extended some four inches up, and which was exactly the same width as the bar. It was caked with mud. He chiseled into the dirt and found that the slot went deep enough into the stone for him to place his fingers fully inside of it. More than that, he found that the bar continued on through the slot, into a hollow in the belly of the fountain.

He had simply cleaned out the groove along which the bar could be moved.

His first inclination was to pull up. After all, what else would the slot be there for? Then again, these were the Manichaeans. Up meant down. Even so, he reached in and tried pulling up. It wouldn't budge. After the third attempt, he decided to continue digging below the bar. There, too, he found a groove, the continuation of the slot heading straight down. Reaching underneath the iron handle, he did his best to clear it out. With enough room to get his fingers around the handle, and with the now eight-inch groove unblocked, he turned to Ivo. "Okay, watch out," he said, repositioning himself so as to gain as much leverage as he could. Ivo moved to the side.

Going with his first instincts, Pearse put his full weight onto the bar and began to push down. It took several seconds of constant pressure to make it move, but when it did, he realized why the slot ran in both directions: the handle inched downward on an angle toward the wall. The other end of the bar—the one extending into the hollow—was moving up, filling in the upper groove like a counterweight. He had no idea how the mechanism worked, nor did he care as he saw the lower of the two triangular pieces begin to dislodge from its partner. It was forming a gap in the fountain's base.

"Look! Look!" said Ivo.

Pearse nodded and again pushed down with all his weight. Another quarter of an inch.

Ivo brought his hands to his face, his muddy little fingers shaking with anticipation. Petra did her best to keep them out of his mouth. Ivo at once latched onto her arms, eyes fixed on the stone, his feet hopping every time there was even a hint of movement. "Look, Mommy! Look!"

"I see it, sweetie." She tried to rub the mud from his hands with her own.

On the fourth try, the stone finally gave way, the bar rotating flat into the slot. Pearse pulled his arm up from the hole and sat, a little winded from the exertion. As he looked into Ivo's eyes, he felt a faint tremor of anticipation, a distant echo of what he had known in Phôtinus.

The "Hodoporia" was here.

He reached his hand into the gap and blindly groped his way through. There was an odd feel to the air, somehow heavier, yet with none of the dampness he expected. The few times his fingers rubbed against the stone, there, too, he was surprised by the texture, dry and cold, flawlessly smooth, no signs of decay. He attributed it to the strange mechanism, the bar and counterweight evidently having produced an almost perfectly insulated space. With his arm halfway down the opening, he hit on something metallic with rough iron edges, the feel of tiny bolts running under his fingertips. Another box.

Ambivalence or not, his heart kicked into high gear.

He reached his fingers around the side of the box and began to lift. He half-expected it to be tied down, one more trick to unravel before bringing it into the light. Instead, it came up easily. Angling it through the opening, he set it down at his side.

The box was identical to the one Ribadeneyra had used on Athos. Same size, same meaningless latch. Pearse looked up at Ivo and Petra.

"Well, here it is," he said. Channeling his nervous energy, he reached back into the hole and pulled up on the bar. The two stones came back together. He then began to push the dirt back in.

Ivo quickly knelt down, the same chocolate-hopeful expression spread across his face as he offered to help. "It's pretty old, isn't it?" he said.

"Pretty old," answered Pearse, tamping down the last of the soil. He brushed away as much of the dirt on his hands as he could, then picked up the box and sat on the lip of the fountain. Ivo stood and edged in close to his side, his eyes transfixed on the prize now in Pearse's lap.

The mud was still thick under his nails as Pearse struggled with the latch. It finally gave way, the same velvet and gold coins waiting inside. This time, though, the glass dome was considerably bigger. It had to be; a scroll, not a booklet, lay underneath. Like its "Perfect Light" counterpart, it was bound in leather, two tie-strings holding it together. He was about to separate the dome from the velvet, when he saw the state of his hands. He turned to Petra.

"I probably shouldn't touch it," he said. "You're going to have to open it up."

She hesitated.

"I could do it," piped in Ivo, ready to grab the dome.

Petra moved in quickly. "That's okay, sweetie." She reached over and placed the box on her lap. With a nod of encouragement from Pearse, she gently pulled the dome from its sealant. She looked at him.

"Go ahead," he said, a strange tingling now in his throat.

She placed her hand on the scroll and immediately pulled it away. "It's . . . oily."

The moisture of the leather . . . Pearse could only marvel at Ribadeneyra's ingenuity. He'd created enough of a vacuum both inside the fountain and the dome to keep the scroll in relatively good condition.

"That's a good thing," he said. "Try untying the straps. Gently."

She started to touch them, then stopped. "You're sure you don't want to do this yourself?"

He smiled. "Did I leave my sink next to your sixteenth-century map?"

"I just think—wouldn't it be smarter if you did this?"

As much as he now desperately wanted to hold it, he knew he couldn't take the risk of harming the scroll. "I think we should see what's inside."

Again she hesitated. "All right." She deftly inched the knot apart, then laid the strands at the side.

"Now peel back the binding. If you feel anything start to give, stop."

She did as she was told, rolling back the first inch of leather. A strip of vellum appeared, straw-colored, gritty even to look at. She turned to Pearse. He nodded; she rolled back a bit more.

The edge of a separate sheet of parchment, distinct from the scroll itself, suddenly appeared between leather and vellum.

"What do I do with that?" she asked.

For a brief moment, Pearse entertained the frightening thought that perhaps they'd uncovered the next clue on the wild-goose chase. Unwilling to indulge it for more than a few seconds, he said, "Just keep rolling it back."

Another few turns, and she had unrolled enough so that the separate sheet could be pulled out easily. With a little encouragement she did just that, holding it out in front of him so he could read it.

"It's from Ribadeneyra," he said as he read the Latin. "April 1521. 'Take the gold . . . leave the scroll' "—his eyes racing along—" 'let this be an act of contrition. . . .' " More nodding as he explained. "It's the same thing he did on Phôtinus. Except this time he finishes up the story." Paraphrasing as he went, Pearse read, "He got here in 1520. . . . He knew he wasn't well. . . . Mani found him this spot to die. . . . 'Praise be to Mani,' so forth and so on." He nodded for her to flip the sheet over. "That's interesting."

"What?"

"It says he helped design the fountain. He even laid some of the stonework. . . ." Reading several lines, Pearse said nothing, his eyebrows arching as he scanned the text. "Wow. That's why," he finally said.

"That's why what?" she asked.

"You really were very clever, weren't you?" he said to the sheet, disregarding her question. "A Manichaean through and through."

"What?" she asked again.

He looked over at her. "Ribadeneyra. He explains why we found those pieces of parchment eight years ago in Slitna." Before she could ask, he continued. "According to this, before he died, he sent a handful of men out with packets of pressed vellum, each filled with messages written in Eastern Syriac, not Latin. Something about the purity of the original tongue."

"Eastern what?"

"It's not important. The point is, the men were told to hide the pieces in churches throughout Europe. That's what we found. Each of the packets had a clue to where the 'Perfect Light' scroll was hidden. In other words, he basically had them replant the clues that he'd found himself during his twenty-year search. He'd already reburied the 'Perfect Light' scroll back in Istanbul before heading west, and he was banking on the fact that someone, at some point in time—depending on Mani's will—would piece the packets together and find his way to the 'Perfect Light.' "

"The scroll your monk friend gave you in Rome."

"Cesare. Exactly. His friend, a man named Ruini, actually found the 'Perfect Light' scroll in Istanbul. He then gave it to Cesare, who gave it to me. The 'Perfect Light' was what lead me to Phôtinus, where, instead of finding the real prize, I found Ribadeneyra's own little book—the one with all the cryptograms—which was simply meant to add one more step to the hunt for the ever-elusive 'Hagia Hodoporia.' "

"This," she said, holding up the recently unearthed scroll.

"Right. Before he died, Ribadeneyra hid the 'Hodoporia' inside this fountain, and then sent his last helper back to Phôtinus to hide the little book of cryptograms in the Vault of the Paraclete. End of story."

"Cautious man," she said.

"Or terribly devout. The two seem to go hand in hand with these people. At least when they're dealing with their 'Hodoporia.' "

She thought about it, then said, "Don't you think it's a little strange that you happened to be there when one of those packets was found outside of Slitna, and now you're here?"

Pearse looked up from the page. It took him a moment to respond. "We gave those pages to Salko, didn't we?"

She nodded.

Again, he waited. He turned to her. "I can't worry about that now. I need to find out what this thing is. There's a woman in Rome who's depending on that."

She placed the sheet back in the box, then looked at him. "Things have gotten a little more complicated, I think." She held his gaze, then looked past him to Ivo, whose head was resting up against Pearse's shoulder. "How are you doing, sweetie? You holding up okay?"

Ivo nodded quickly. He then looked at Pearse. "How are you doing, Ian?"

"Fine, Ivi. Fine."

Ivo pulled in even closer, and, in a whisper, said, "Can I have one of those gold coins?"

Pearse smiled. "Sure. Take as many as you want."

Petra reached into the box and handed him several of the coins. "Why don't you go play with them over there, sweetie. We still need to read some more of this."

Ivo skipped off, hands cupped around the coins. He picked a spot about twenty feet from them and sat down.

Petra continued to watch him. "Much more complicated."

Pearse watched the boy, as well. And he nodded.

Without warning the sound of an explosion rocked the courtyard, followed by a violent tremor. Ivo quickly got to his feet. At the same instant, the children playing soccer darted into the middle of the courtyard and lay flat on the ground. Within seconds, others were emerging from the buildings—the old and the young—the courtyard's center their focus, as well. Petra handed Pearse the box and ran toward Ivo, who had already run out into the open area and was now lying facedown with the rest. Pearse followed, all of them flat on the ground when the sound of sirens began to blare.

"That didn't sound like an artillery shot," he said.

"It wasn't," she answered.

"Then why are we all lying out in the open like this?"

She looked over at him. "Because some habits die hard, Ian."

He remembered his days in Slitna, the first rule of survival: get out of the buildings. He peered around at the old women and children, all of them facedown in the grass and dirt. Slowly, the heads began to rise. Each one listened intently for the sound of another blast. As the minutes passed and the sirens grew louder, they began to get to their feet. En masse, they headed for the passageway.

Pearse, Petra, and Ivo fell in behind, close enough to hear snippets of conversations, the word *crkva* the most frequent.

Pearse leaned into Petra as they walked. "What church are they talking about?"

"Your guess is as good as mine."

The maze of alleyways took them back toward the marketplace, more and more people on the streets as they neared the open area. Pearse felt the heat of the explosion before he saw it, that once-familiar tang of gasoline and sulfur. With the rest, he stopped at the edge of the marketplace, far enough out, though, to see a building rising in flames no more than a hundred yards from them.

The scene was mayhem, people lying in the street, two cars on their

sides, undercarriages on fire. Storefront glass lay scattered everywhere; a
few larger shards had landed with such force that they looked liked great
crystal teeth imbedded in the pavement. Nothing was more harrowing,
though, than the sight of the bloodied survivors screaming their way
down the street, one woman carrying a child who was clearly no longer
alive. Others had raced out to help them, some from an unseen ambulance corps, still more from the growing crowds, the area a haze of
zigzagging bodies.

Pearse pushed his way through, unaware that he was still toting the
iron box in his hands. He never felt the tug from Petra as he raced out
and headed for the first person he could reach.

She was a woman in her twenties, seated almost serenely on the
ground, staring mindlessly at her leg. Somehow, something metal had
twisted its way into her calf. Pearse pulled off his coat and draped it
around her shoulders; she didn't seem to notice he was there. He looked
up to see if there was anyone even remotely medical nearby, but there
were too many people to make out anything clearly.

"And the fish," she said, now looking up at him. "Before he runs out
of it."

Pearse looked down. There was hardly any focus in her eyes. He nodded. "You're going to be fine," he said.

He noticed an area across the way where they were beginning to bring
the wounded. He looked back at the woman. "I'm going to pick you up
now. Is that all right?"

The woman said nothing.

As carefully as he could, he placed one arm under her leg, the other
around her back, and began to lift. At once, she started screaming. Moving
as quickly as he could across the street, he arrived at the makeshift triage
area, a voice somewhere in front of him telling him where to put her.
Pearse set her down.

"That's great. Thank you. Now you need to clear this area," the man
said. "No more heroics today."

Pearse began to answer, but the man was gone.

It was then that he realized he had left the box in the middle of the
street. He spun around to try to find it, only to see Petra and Ivo standing with it. She no longer had the "baby"; Ivo had lost his kerchief. More
than that, his skirt remained up around his waist, his muddied pants in
full view. Pearse started toward them. He was barely out into the street
when he saw a man in a dark suit converging on them.

Pearse began to run. Ducking through the mayhem, he watched as Petra began to make her way into the crowds at the edge of the marketplace, the black box in hand. It was clear from her body language that she was fully aware of the man trailing after her. She and Ivo slipped into the mass of people, the man—speaking into a radio—ten yards behind them. Within seconds, he, too, was moving through the crowds. Pearse fell in behind all three.

At once, he realized Petra was trying to use the crowd to get herself around the perimeter of the marketplace. With Ivo in tow, though, she had no hope of losing the man; the spacing between them began to close. Pearse drew nearer as well, the man so intent on his prey that he never considered the possibility that he might have a tail of his own. Only once did Petra look back, Pearse certain that she had seen him. He wasn't sure if it would make a difference, but at least now she knew he was there. How long Ivo could keep up with her was another question entirely.

When she broke away and headed down a side street, Pearse guessed she was banking on his help.

Out in the open again, the gaps separating all of them widened, the man unwilling as yet to move in for the kill. It might have had something to do with his radio, thought Pearse. He watched as the man began to shake it rather than speak into it. The explosion had created a communications overload. Maybe it was interfering with the Vatican frequency? No backup. No reason to draw in too close. Whatever the cause, the man was holding back as he placed the radio in his pocket.

Pearse made sure to keep his distance as well, hugging to the sides of buildings, once or twice losing sight of Petra, who continued, with Ivo, to duck and weave through the alleys and streets. Everything was deserted, anyone who had ventured out by now at the marketplace, the sounds of it all receding farther and farther into the background. Pearse heard nothing but the near-silent patter of steps up ahead of him. He kept his focus on the man, not knowing if he should run at him or stay back. A fumbled attack would only leave Petra and Ivo more vulnerable. He had to trust that she knew what she was doing.

Entering a part of town he thought he recognized, Pearse saw her glance back again. It was clear she had meant for the man to see her looking at him. Pearse, as well. She immediately darted down another side street. Pearse watched as the man pulled a gun from his jacket and followed.

It was now or never. Still close to the buildings, he waited for the man to make the turn. He then sprinted out after him, careening around the corner.

In an instant, Pearse saw what Petra had contrived. She was standing twenty feet from the man, Ivo tucked in behind her, the box held out at arm's length. The man had stopped, the gun aimed at her.

But it was only for an instant. Before the man could react, Pearse came crashing into his back, the collision propelling them both to the ground. Still on top of him, Pearse drove his fist into the man's neck, rote responses from a part of his mind he hadn't tapped into for years. With his other hand, he grabbed the man's hair and pummeled his skull into the cobblestone, the second thrust enough to leave the body limp.

Trying to catch his breath, Pearse rolled off the man and stared up at the sky.

Only then did he hear the screams from Ivo. He immediately flipped over and saw Petra sitting up against one of the buildings, Ivo clutching at her, his face contorted in tears.

Pearse struggled to his feet. He raced toward them. Dropping down at her side, he saw her hands holding an area to the left side of her abdomen. They were stained red.

"It's okay, Ivi. It's okay. It's not so bad," she said breathing through the pain. She looked up at Pearse. "It went off when you jumped him."

Pearse hadn't even heard the gun discharge. All thought seemed to vanish. He pulled off his shirt and placed it over the wound. "We need to get you to—"

"I know."

"I need to find a car."

Petra nodded her head toward the next street. "It's down there."

Pearse looked up. That's why it all looked so familiar. That's why she had brought them back here. He jumped to his feet and started running. "Stay with Mommy, Ivo. I'll be right back."

He tore down the side street, the van no more than thirty yards from him. Two minutes later, he was lifting her from the pavement, laying her flat in the back of the van. Ivo climbed in by her side.

"So that's how you take out a catcher?" she said, the look of pain no less intense on her face.

"Something like that." He found a blanket and placed it under her head.

"Did he drop the ball?"

Pearse looked into her eyes, his hand brushing back the hair from her forehead. "Yeah. He dropped it."

She tried to smile. "The main road. Take a right. The hospital's about a half mile down."

Pearse shut the back door, picked up the box, and got in behind the wheel. He slid open the partition. "It's going to be okay. We'll be there in five minutes."

As he pulled the car around, he heard Ivo singing to her, his tiny voice echoing from the back.

▲

No one had bothered to ask about a bullet wound. The hospital had been too overrun to quibble about the details. They had been nice enough to find him a shirt.

It was two hours since they'd taken Petra—Pearse and Ivo left to sit with the rest of the shell-shocked, waiting for word. Ivo, cradled on his lap, had alternated between sleep and tears, his first half hour without her almost frantic. He had started by punching at Pearse, blaming him for everything, until his little body had given out. The first nap, followed by complete disorientation, more hysteria, a second breaking point, then a third. Finally, he had simply sat, eyes staring out blankly. Pearse had tried to talk to him, but it had made no difference.

One constant: the ball he clutched in his hand.

From conversations around him, Pearse had discovered that the explosion hadn't destroyed a church; it had blown up the Velika Dzamija, the Great Mosque. Unjust retribution, he had been told. Only when he'd moved to the television in the corner of the waiting area had he understood what they'd meant. The three churches yesterday had been just the beginning. News reports brought him up-to-date on the atrocities occurring across Europe and beyond. And, of course, the Vatican. The mosque had simply been one instance of Christian backlash—at least that was the way Bosnian television was interpreting it. They were expecting a good deal more. The Middle East was already up in arms about the accusations. The Vatican was calling for all Christians—all—to come together in peace. The battle lines were being drawn.

And all to bring about the one true and holy church. The thought sickened him.

A doctor approached. "You brought in the woman with the abdominal wound?" he asked.

Pearse stood, petrified by what he might hear next.

"She'll be fine," he said. "The bullet went straight through her side, no vital organs, but she obviously needs to stay with us for a day or so. You can see her now."

Pearse picked up Ivo and followed the doctor along a series of corridors before coming to a room with eight beds. Petra lay in the one nearest the window. The doctor nodded toward her, then headed out. Before Pearse could take a step, Ivo had dropped down and was racing to her side. He lay his head next to hers on the pillow.

She looked remarkably serene given what she had just been through.

"Hey, Ivi," she said, still well drugged. She brought her hand up and began to stroke his hair. "Mommy's going to be okay."

Pearse pulled a chair over and sat down. He didn't know what to say.

"I've had worse," she said, her smile weak, Ivo now clutching at her arm.

"I didn't think the gun—"

"Neither did I," she said. "Just unlucky." She stared over at him. "I guess you could tell me you're sorry." Again the smile.

"I guess I could."

Ivo started to cry.

"Mommy's okay, sweet pea. We're just going to have to be here for a few days. The doctor says you can sleep right next to me. They're going to bring in a cot, and blankets. How about that?"

Ivo kissed her cheek. "Okay."

She looked back at Pearse. She took his hand.

Gazing down at her, he realized how scared he had actually been. To lose her again.

"No cot for you," she said.

"I need to stay."

"No, you need to go." She waited. "I want my son back, Ian. No more little shrines. If what's in the box can do that, then you have to go and do that. Okay?"

Pearse looked into her eyes. "I need you to know—"

"I do. I know."

For several minutes, neither said a word.

"Ivi and I will be just fine here, won't we?"

Ivo pressed his head closer into her.

Again, Pearse said nothing. He leaned over and kissed her. Pulling back, he ran his fingers along her cheek.

Finally, he stood and looked over at Ivo, happily tucked into his mother's neck.

"I'll see you soon, little man."

Without moving, Ivo looked up at him.

"Keep an eye on Mommy for me, okay?"

Ivo smiled.

What more did he need than that?

seven

The last day and a half had been nothing short of a miracle, the first bombings—including the devastation at the Vatican—merely a prelude to the madness of the past nine hours. The wave of fear, mixed with outrage, was producing a kind of support Harris had never experienced in all his years connected with mass movements. Even the millennium nuts were getting involved. Religious commitment—whose death the pundits had been tolling for years—was having a genuine rebirth. Spontaneous rallies were springing up all over the place, doctrinal defensiveness evidently inspiring action. And what had begun with groups in the hundreds—petitioners in city squares, others outside state assemblies demanding greater "spiritual" security—had grown to ten times that number in a matter of hours.

And everywhere that blind hatred and moral indignation were commingling, the alliance was there.

Faith with firepower.

Those not so fortunate to share in the right system of belief were starting to feel the repercussions. Incidences of violence against Arab, Indian, even Chinese communities were occurring in every major city in Europe, as well as in the States. Kreutzberg, a section of Berlin, with the largest group of Turks outside of Turkey, had been the target of prolonged rioting. Stateside, several of the more outlandish radio personalities had taken to reminding their listeners not to forget who would benefit most from a clash between Christians and Muslims. Why not include an old favorite in the new brand of anti-Semitism?

In the meantime, Harris had been called by the PM to help devise a plan for calming the growing hysteria. Ten Downing Street was told it would have to wait. Harris needed to put the finishing touches to a Saturday-afternoon rally at Wembley Stadium. He'd been planning it for months—at the time, nothing more than an appearance to coincide with the alliance announcement. In fact, it had been Stefan Kleist who had suggested the date. The original sale of thirty thousand tickets had ballooned to over seventy in the last twelve hours. English television crews had been told to make space for the internationals, the Times Square Jumbotron in New York even promising to broadcast bits of the session.

Evidently, Savonarola would have his day after all.

▲

The three-hundred-mile drive from Visegrad to Zagreb was eerily quiet, everything, Pearse noticed, virtually deserted. It was as if all of Bosnia and Croatia were holing themselves up. And why not? Who knew better how to gear up for the kind of conflict now boiling to the surface than those who had been caught on its dividing line for centuries?

He'd called the hospital twice along the way. Both times, she'd been asleep. Ivo, as well. No reason to bother them. He'd call again.

Pulling off the highway at Zagreb, he made his way to the station. He'd realized an hour back he needed time with the scroll, time to find out what lay inside, and he wasn't going to get that in the van. It was why he was now opting for the train. More than that, he knew a train would meet far less rigorous security at the border than the van. Why take the risk? Five to midnight, and he was on board the last overnight to Italy, the scroll—wrapped in velvet—tucked deep inside his pack. The iron box, and everything else Ribadeneyra had placed inside it, remained with the van in the parking lot.

Except for the coins. Those he'd saved for Ivo.

Finding an isolated foursome and table at the end of one of the cars, Pearse settled in. He waited until the conductor had made his rounds, then turned to the scroll.

If he'd anticipated any awe or wonder as he undid the straps, he felt almost none. The scroll was no longer a piece of scripture existing in and of itself. It had a far more defined purpose, regardless of the imagined purity of its message. It was simply one more device to be used. And Pearse knew he was no different from the Manichaeans in that respect. They needed it to establish their church; he needed it to save Angeli and get back to Petra and Ivo. Who was to say which was more noble?

No vacuum dome at his disposal, he laid it out as best he could and began to read.

It took him nearly four and half hours to get through it, his only inter-ruption at the Slovenian border some twenty minutes into the trip. The officer had checked his papers, uninterested in the roll of papyrus carefully placed on the table. Given the events of the past day, it wasn't an American priest—even one out of black clericals—they were concerned with.

After that, he'd sat undisturbed, his astonishment growing with each verse he read. Device or not, the "Hodoporia" was far more than he expected, especially in its last few verses, his own familiarity with them at first unnerving. Almost disorienting. *Why would these be in here?* Until he realized what he was reading. He'd been so caught up in the Manichaeans that he'd let one of the most obvious choices slip from his mind.

Q.

My God.

Eight hundred and forty-five verses, and he'd only recognized it in the last half dozen or so.

The "Hagia Hodoporia" was Q, from the German word *Quelle*, mean-ing "source." *Die Quelle.* The answer to a pedant's dream.

Q.

Staring down at the ancient script, he couldn't quite believe that this was what he had been after all along. Incredible.

Up to this moment, Q had been nothing more than an hypothesis, a scholar's way to make sense of the central dilemma in Christian theol-ogy, the Synoptic Problem. In essence: if Matthew and Luke had used Mark as a common source (as they certainly had), what, then, of the par-allel passages in the two Gospels that bore no connection to Mark? In other words, how could either writer—without ever having seen the other's work—have come up with nearly identical elaborations in his own telling of the story? How? The only answer: another source beyond Mark. And one which, by definition, had to predate the Gospels.

A source contemporary with Christ, and thus unlike any of the four Gospels.

Q.

Reading through it, Pearse knew it was far more than just another exegetical tool. It stood as the last great mystery, even beyond that of the Dead Sea Scrolls.

A link to the Divine. Jesus' sayings, untouched, pure, written in His lifetime.

Clarity at his fingertips.

Though no expert, Pearse was familiar enough with the scholarship to recognize Q from several of its final verses: "The Coming of John the Baptist," "John's Preaching of Repentance," "John's Preaching of the Coming One," and "The Baptism of Jesus." Matthew 3:1–17, Luke 3:1–22, the first of the non-Markan elaborations. Later still, the "Inaugural Sermon," "Jesus on Blessings and Woes," "Retaliation," "Judging." More stories: "Jesus' Temptation," "The Healing of the Roman Centurion's Slave," "The Exorcism of the Mute." And, of course, the critical passage for any Q scholar—Luke 10:4–6, Matthew 10:10–13:

Carry no purse, no bag, no sandals; and salute no one on the road. Whatever house you enter, first say, "Peace be to this house!" And if a son of peace is there, your peace shall rest upon him; but if not, it shall return to you.

It was astounding enough to see the verses, one after another, stripped of their usual surroundings, now laid bare on a piece of parchment nearly two thousand years old. The true marvel, though, lay in the earlier passages—the vast majority of the scroll—those that appeared nowhere in the canonical Gospels, and which gave the words a meaning Pearse had never conceived, something to take it far beyond the narrow scope of scholarship.

It wasn't simply the new collection of Jesus' sayings, unseen until now, that made it so remarkable, but the structure itself, the form of the discourse, that placed the scroll in a context he couldn't quite believe. Or perhaps accept.

Q was half Gospel, half diary, one that traced twenty years in the life of a Cynic teacher named Menippus. Like Diogenes—the father of Cynicism, who had walked about with a lantern in broad daylight, looking for an honest man—Menippus was a wanderer, no purse, no bag, no sandals. His mission, to teach the Cynic ideal: flout convention, scoff at authority, disbelieve in civilization itself, and embrace a poverty that could grant freedom and thus a kind of royalty. To be king within a kingdom unknown by those still mired in the excesses of a material world.

A Cynic through and through.

How like another school of thought.

Driven by a force he couldn't explain, Menippus had set off on his "Hagia Hodoporia" from his home in Gadara—a Greek city east of the Jordan River, overlooking the Sea of Galilee—traveling to points as far west as Salonika, as far east as Jaipur, in India. Along the way, he had lived in Sepphoris, not far from Nazareth, then spent several years with the Nozrim ha-Brit, the Essene community at Qumran—those who had written the Dead Sea Scrolls, the Keepers of the Covenant. But not alone. Never alone:

I found Him when He was but a boy, but with such power, such thought. I knew why I had been brought to His side.

Menippus had wandered with a companion, at first the boy's teacher, then his student, ultimately his "Beloved Disciple." Menippus, the man forever unnamed in the Gospels, now revealed in the rolls of the "Hodoporia."

Q was nothing less than a history of the lost years of Jesus' life, his development from ages twelve to thirty, all transcribed by the pen of a Cynic teacher.

Pearse sat amazed.

To read the sayings in that context created an image of Jesus he had never seen before:

Blessed are those who have grown confident and have found faith for themselves!

Do not worry, from morning to evening and from evening to morning, about what you will wear. Consider the ragged cloak to be a lion's skin.

When you know yourselves, then you will be known, and will understand that you are children of the living Father. The task lies within you, the journey yours alone. Do not look to another to find a guide to yourself. He will not be there.

When you make male and female into a single one, so that the male will not be male and the female will not be female, then you will enter the kingdom.

And so with all instruction and teaching, men and women share equally in perfection. In me, there is neither male nor female.

Jesus was, in point of fact, a young Jewish radical firmly rooted in the teachings of a still-thriving school of Greek thought. His mission: to unleash a social experiment based on the rejection of traditional constraints in favor of the individual as part of a wider human family. The rituals associated with eating and drinking, the insistence on a voluntary poverty, the loving of one's enemies, even the choice of dress that Jesus insisted upon all came directly from the Cynic influence:

And how is it possible that a man who has nothing, who is naked, houseless, squalid, without a city, can pass a life in peace? See, God has sent you a man to show you that it is possible. Look at me. And what do I want? Am I not without sorrow? Am I not without fear? Am I not free?

Diogenes himself might have said it.

What was most clear from Q, however, was how strange the message had become in the hands of the writers of the Gospels and beyond. Not only had they inserted certain events—the Last Supper (and thus the Eucharist) was nowhere to be found in Q—but they had eliminated key sentiments that Pearse could only guess had run counter to the needs of the early church. The role of women as preachers (in keeping with the Cynic tradition), the constant emphasis on the individual's responsibility to maintain his or her own commitment, all disappeared once out of Q's hands.

Why no women? Why such import to the Last Supper and the Eucharist? No doubt to confirm the crucial role of the male apostles after Jesus' death.

And yet, the power structure of an elite corps of disciples had had no place in Q. Menippus had gone to great lengths to recount several sermons by Jesus—still in His twenties—that expressly denounced such hierarchy. His was a populist movement, meant for the people as a whole. Everything about it portrayed Jesus not as a harbinger of a mighty structure but as a railer against such monoliths:

And He said to them, "For what would you find through others that you cannot find in me alone? What walls exist that can house my power? And if they should try, I shall throw down this building, and no one will be able to build it."

For God does not have a house, a stone set up as a temple, dumb and toothless, a bane which brings many woes to men, but one which is not possible to see from earth, nor to measure with mortal eyes, since it was not fashioned by mortal hands.

It was all too clear that Jesus had sensed His own power, and that He had done everything He could to warn against its misappropriations and abuses. His was a brotherhood of believers, not a church of followers. The true authority came from God alone. The individual's personal and creative experiences of that faith—not the dictates of an institution— were the catalysts of that power:

> For those who name themselves bishop, and also deacon, as if they had received their authority from God, are, in truth, waterless canals.

Here it was, thought Pearse. Faith at its most personal, and thus most powerful. There was no denying the clear condemnation of his own calling. *"Waterless canals."* And yet, Q also offered the most perfect affirmation of his own brand of faith, one freed of a structure built around detached hierarchy.

The simplicity of Jesus' sayings had been lost, funneled through Mark, Matthew, Luke, John, Peter, and Paul to assure the connection with a Messianic past—the prophecies of Isaiah—and to establish the foundations for an infallible church. But had that been the message?

Not according to Q. Jesus as wisdom teacher, yes. Jesus as apocalyptic Savior, no.

Nothing was more clear on that point than the Beloved Disciple's retelling of his visit to Jesus' tomb three days after His death:

> And at that time, a great noise went up through Jerusalem, a wailing for the death of this Son of Man. And with it came word of a resurrection, His tomb laid empty, His being risen and returned. "But this will not be so," He had told me, "though some will come to say otherwise. It is but the folly of men to need such signs, their folly to place their faith in the body and not in the spirit."

In a single phrase, Menippus had brought down two thousand years of church authority: *"But this will not be so," He had told me, "though some will come to say otherwise."* Not from the distance of the canonical or Gnostic gospels, but from one who had spent his life with Jesus, and had been there at the bitter end, and beyond. No need to interpret. No need to explain. No need for a Luther to divine his priesthood of all believers from an ambiguous text. The message here was clear as day. And while Luther's ninety-five theses had been more than enough to shake the very core of Christendom, here was the Word of Christ, unambiguous and unassailable. Imagine how much more shattering it could be.

Angeli's words raced back to him: *without Peter standing there saying,*

"I was the first, I can vouch for His return . . ." *without the doctrine of bodily resurrection, there's no way to validate the apostolic succession of bishops. No way to lay claim to the papacy.*

Pull out the pin, and the entire structure falls.

At first, it seemed strange to Pearse that so monumental a shift could require so little ink. More so that Matthew and Luke had so easily glossed over it. But the more he read, the more it made perfect sense. Q wasn't the story of Jesus the Destined. That was for the Gospels. It was the story of a life built on faith and wandering, of a dream of revolution, inspired by ideas such as love and tolerance and spiritual equality. More than that, it wasn't advancing an image of Christ that no one had ever seen before—violent or self-serving, or whatever other character flaws iconoclasts had come up with over the centuries to debunk the mythology. It was Jesus at His most essential. The Messiah was still there, but it was a messianic message drawn from the pages of Cynicism, Indian mysticism, and Essene wisdom. Resurrections and the like only distracted from that message. The meaning was in the life, not in the death.

And for Pearse, it made Jesus all the more powerful, all the more holy. Pure divinity.

What Q made abundantly clear was that the revolution *was* the faith—the spirit, not the body—the rest of the structure merely trappings, more for the exploitation of men than for their salvation, something that Pearse himself had always believed. The shift from Q to the Gospels was a shift away from the individual to an overarching and alienating edifice. No wonder the Manichaeans had seen it as the answer to their problem. Here was something to undermine that structure.

And by the fifth century, the church *was* the faith. Topple one, topple the other. It had been no different for Ribadeneyra in the sixteenth. For over a thousand years, Q had truly held that power.

The question was, Could it pose that kind of threat today? Except for the passages on Resurrection, Q put forward an image of Jesus and faith that the modern church would have been only too happy to embrace. Q's commitment to individual rights and responsibility, and its view of women and their role in the church—anathema to a fifth- or sixteenth-century mind—were perfectly designed to resolve any number of contentious debates now ripping Catholicism apart. And all through the Word of Christ. Where was the hyperasceticism the Manichaeans had promised? Where was the gnosis they said they would be called upon to reveal? Everything in Q was plain as day. The irony, Pearse realized, was that their beloved tract, the scroll destined to bring about the ruin of the church, looked like it might actually be the device to save the church from itself.

That is, of course, if one could discount the passages on the Resurrection. Those were equally unambiguous. And given recent events, Pearse wasn't sure if the church could survive that kind of assault, real or not.

More than that, he understood why the Manichaeans had gone to such lengths to get their hands on it, especially now. Whatever madness they were planning to unleash would mean nothing without a way to justify the emergence of their unified church, something to show that the old one had been corrupted from the very start. The only response to a world gone mad? Remake the church. Embrace unity through a new notion of faith. No doubt most of the scroll would remain "hidden" or "lost." Keep only what was necessary. Use Jesus to secure Mani. The Resurrection sections would suffice.

How like the Manichaeans to distort the message in the name of gnosis.

The door to the car suddenly opened, the sound prompting Pearse up from the parchment for the first time in hours. He glanced back, to see another passport controller making his way down the aisle. The Italian border. He looked out the window, the sun already creeping out from behind a group of hills in the distance. He checked his watch: 6:15. He'd been so wrapped up in Q, he'd missed the sunrise entirely. He suddenly felt very thirsty.

"How soon to Trieste?" he asked as the man took his papers.

"About forty minutes." The man pulled what looked to be a tiny hole punch from a holster on his belt, ready to stamp Pearse's passport, then stopped. "The Vatican?"

Pearse wasn't sure how to respond.

"They just announced the body count, Father. Eight cardinals survived." He crossed himself. "Those people are animals." A quick squeeze of the imprint.

Pearse crossed himself, as well. "You have to learn to forgive," he said.

"I suppose, Father." He handed Pearse the papers and began to move on. "I suppose."

A

Trieste came as the man had promised, the station alive with early-morning travelers. Now, back in Italy, Pearse knew he could take the chance on a plane—no computer network checking his passport, no security on alert. Even if the Manichaeans did manage to get hold of a passenger manifest, he'd be in Rome an hour after takeoff, too short a period of time for them to do much about it.

Just in case, though, he'd decided to call in the cavalry. The puzzle was solved. It was time for someone else to put it to use and end this.

Stopping at the nearest news kiosk, he picked up a paper and looked for the private message, the phone number from his "friends in Rome . . . day or night." The fact that Salko had cut them off was reason enough to make the call.

He scanned the page. It was filled with stories on the travesties spreading like wildfire throughout Europe, an article on the Vatican Bank and the Syrian infiltration. What an appropriate word, he thought.

But no box.

He flipped through several other papers, the news seller becoming more and more irritated.

"Either buy one or move off," he said finally.

"Are there any from yesterday?" asked Pearse.

"Yesterday? Why would anyone want—"

"Do you have any papers from yesterday?" he insisted.

The man's irritation mounted. "I have today's papers. You want something else, try outside the station. Maybe Buchi's, two blocks down."

Five minutes later, Pearse stood inside the small tobacconist's, walls lined with papers from around the world. The most recent copy of *Helsingin Sanomat* out of Finland was two days old. He pulled it from the rack and immediately located the box in the lower right-hand corner of the page.

> **Whatever was on Athos, you have friends, Father. In Rome.**
>
> **Day or night: 39 69884728**

Pearse scribbled the number on his palm, bought a phone card, and headed out into the street. Within half a minute, he was inside a booth dialing.

A recorded voice came on the line: "We're sorry. The number you have reached is no longer in service. Please check the listing and try again. . . . We're sorry. . . ."

He slowly replaced the receiver.

Why would they have disconnected the line? The answer came to him as he stood there staring at the phone. His window of opportunity had been slim at best, too great a chance that the Manichaeans could trace the number, find whoever had been on the other end, and eliminate them. Once Salko had cut the line, the window had closed.

Flying back wasn't sounding all that clever now. Without his "friends in Rome," what exactly was he planning to do once there? Walk up to the Vatican and tell them that the Pope was a Manichaean, but not to worry—the scroll would solve everything? Or better yet, just hand the "Hodoporia" to von Neurath and explain to him that it might not be all that he'd hoped it would be? Nice try, but better luck next time. Now please tell everyone that Islam isn't our enemy so we can all go home.

For some reason, Pearse started to laugh. It was perfect. A Manichaean dream come true. Everything flipped on its head. Now that he had the "Hodoporia," he was powerless to use it. It only made him more vulnerable. Flight manifests notwithstanding, the Brotherhood would find him soon enough—here, or in Rome. And if he had the scroll with him, everything and everyone would become expendable. Which left him only one choice: confront them head-on. He picked up the phone and dialed Angeli's number.

It was the same message as before.

"It's Ian Pearse. I have the 'Hodoporia.'" He waited. "Hello. . . . Hello. . . ."

After fifteen seconds of silence, he placed the receiver back in its cradle. Again he stared at the phone. Then, slowly, he let his head fall back against the glass.

They wouldn't have. . . .

He suddenly stood upright. *Of course.* As much as he didn't want to involve anyone else in this, he really didn't have any other options. He picked up the phone and began to dial.

He just had to hope Blaney was back in Rome.

A

"Eight minutes, Mr. Harris."

A quick nod as he sipped at a glass of ice water, Wembley Stadium packed to the gills beyond the window of the luxury box. Harris waited for the man to leave, then turned and stared out at the crowd. The contessa, seated, kept her gaze on him.

"Your new army," she finally said.

The hint of a grin. "I don't think it's completely mine."

"Oh, I don't know. Still, that doesn't seem to be a concern of yours, does it?"

He looked over at her, momentarily at a loss. "I'm afraid I don't follow."

"Don't you?" She waited. "The churches. The Vatican. You put our money to quick use, didn't you, Colonel? And here I thought we were talking rhetoric, not mass hysteria. Evidently, I was meant to take the term *holy war* literally."

A slight squinting of his eyes. "That's not the way I work, Contessa." When she didn't answer, he continued. "I won't say it hasn't helped things enormously. Hysteria does have a way of rallying the troops. But I won't take credit for something I haven't done. I assumed that was your people."

Not convinced, she said, "And who exactly do you think my people are? Or did Mr. Kleist fail to bring you up to speed on that?"

Again, he waited before answering. "I'm now wondering if I should be asking you that same question." She said nothing. "I have connections, Contessa, but even I couldn't organize what's taken place over the last twelve hours in a matter of days. Something like that takes weeks, if not months, to plan. I can't say it fills me with confidence to hear that you're not quite clear on who orchestrated the attacks." Another pause. "Or perhaps you are, but aren't willing to admit it just yet?" He placed the glass on the bar. "Either way, I need to get down there." He moved to the door, then turned. "I suggest you make a few phone calls before all of this gets under way. Oh, and give my best to the cardinal. And my congratulations. Tell him I appreciate everything he's done." A single nod of the head, and Harris was gone.

She sat staring after him. She had come to rein him in, make sure he understood his role. What else had the bomb in Rome been but a message, a colonel's way of reminding them that he knew exactly who, and where, they were? The rest of the churches, she could almost understand, the first seeds of his holy war, misguided or not. Evidently, that wasn't the case at all.

More troubling was his none-too-subtle reference to Erich. Obviously, Harris hadn't appeared on Kleist's suggestion alone, as she had been led to believe.

The crowd roared. She stood and moved to the window. Harris was emerging from one of the runways, bodyguards in clear view. She watched as he made his way toward an enormous structure rising forty feet off the ground at the far end of the field. Two huge screens stood on either side of the raised oval, his entrance beamed out larger than life. A single cameraman led the pack, backing his way up the ramp so as to capture Harris up close. Music blared, grating yet inspirational. Harris waved to the throng. It was clear he'd picked up a good deal from his time in America. The whole thing had that National Convention feel to it. When he finally reached the podium at the center, his entourage fell back, only the cameraman down on one knee to continue the feed. For the contessa, there was something strangely familiar to the man, even from the back, the way he moved, the way his shoulders nestled into the camera. She picked up the binoculars and took a closer look.

Nearly half a minute of wild adulation passed before Harris spoke, the contessa continuing to scrutinize the cameraman.

Harris raised his hand: "My friends—"

He never had a chance to finish. Adulation turned to screams as four cracks erupted over the loudspeakers, the sight of the cameraman racing at Harris, gun in hand, blood everywhere. It was then that she saw it. The hair and skin color were darker, the facial hair, the contours of the face more acute, but it was him, his face screaming wildly, his eyes beyond madness.

Stefan.

An instant later, the bodyguards let loose, the barrage sending Kleist over the platform's edge. He fell, somehow in slow motion for her, his body arching gracefully until it crashed down onto the field below.

The contessa stared in disbelief. A single phrase fixed in her mind: *There's very little I'd put past Erich now.*

Maybe it was time for her to accept that, as well.

▲

"No, take a left there." Pearse leaned forward in the cab and pointed across the piazza.

"No, no, signore," said the cabbie. "Avigonesi is on the right."

"I know. Just take the left."

With a shrug, the man did as he was told.

Pearse had taken the cab from the airport, his flight and arrival uneventful as far as the Manichaeans were concerned. His sudden change of plans, though, had everything to do with the scroll. He wasn't going to chance holding on to it for too much longer. Should anything happen, it remained his only bargaining chip. Best to keep it safe. Plus, there was no reason to put Blaney at more risk than necessary.

"Here," said Pearse.

The driver pulled up along the cobbled piazza; Pearse got out. Three minutes later, he was making his way up the short flight of stairs to the office of the church of San Bernardo. He knocked on the door.

It was half a minute before he heard the sound of shuffling feet. The door opened, revealing the wizened priest, his eyes puffy from sleep, though no less enormous behind the thick glasses.

"Yes. Hello. Can I help you?"

"I was here last week." No sign from the old man that Pearse was registering. "The priest . . . who fell asleep on—"

"Ah, yes." A long, slow nod. "From Albuquerque." Before Pearse could correct him, he said, "No, no, from . . ." He thought for a moment. "No collar. Of course. Come in, come in."

Pearse stepped through. He waited until the priest had taken his seat behind the desk before pulling up one of the other chairs. He sat.

"Father, I need your help. . . ."

▲

Twenty minutes later, Pearse was at the front door of 31 Via Avigonesi. Gianetta answered and ushered him in, her hair, as ever, pulled back in a tight bun. At no more than five feet tall, and with a paper-thin figure beneath a dour black sweater and skirt, she needed a bit of effort to pull the thick oaken door closed behind him. She then led him across the foyer, stopping in front of what Pearse recalled as the door to the library. Equally imposing, it was situated at the foot of a narrow set of stairs leading up to the second floor. She knocked once.

A moment later, Pearse heard the familiar voice. "*Sì?*"

"*Padre Pearse, Padre.*" Not waiting for an answer, she smiled and headed back to the kitchen.

From behind the door, Blaney bellowed. "Ian. Come in. Come in."

Pearse opened the door and stepped inside. Blaney was seated by the empty fireplace, looking far older than when they'd last seen each other. Pearse guessed it was almost a year now.

"Hello, Ian. Hello. Please, come in."

The large study was exactly as he remembered it—a college reading room replete with thick-stuffed maroon leather chairs and sofas amid wall-to-wall bookshelves. Blaney stood as Pearse drew toward him. The two men embraced.

"It's good to see you, John J." They sat.

"You look tired, Ian."

Pearse smiled. "I'm fine, mom."

"Just concerned, that's all. But since you bring it up, how are they, mother and dad?"

"The same. I think they're out on the Cape. End of summer. You were at the house once."

"That's right. I remember a very cold midnight swim. Less refreshing than advertised."

"Family tradition."

"Yes," Blaney said. "So . . . you know I'm always delighted to see you, but your message . . . it didn't sound like this was going to be a social visit. What's wrong?"

"Actually, I'd love a glass of water."

"I'm sorry. Of course." Blaney pressed a button on the intercom next to him. "*Gianetta. Puoi portarmi dell' acqua e forse un po' di frutta? Grazie.*" He didn't wait for a response. "They insisted I get this thing a few months ago. They're very keen to make me feel as old as they can."

"You look fine," said Pearse.

"No, I don't, and neither do you." A look of playful concern crossed his eyes. "It's not Ambrose, again, is it? You're not in the midst of one of those binges without sleep? It's not healthy, Ian." Father as father. Pearse had gotten used to Blaney's paternal instincts a long time ago. "You need to take a vacation once in a while. Lie on a beach. That sort of thing."

"A few midnight swims?" Pearse was about to continue, when Gianetta appeared at the door.

"*Eccellente,*" said Blaney, indicating the table between the two men. "*Va bene di là. Grazie.*"

"*Sì, Padre.*" She moved across the room, placed the tray on the table, and quickly poured out two glasses. She then retreated to the door.

Waiting until they were alone, Pearse inched out on his seat, taking a glass as he spoke. "I've found Q."

Blaney was retrieving the other glass. He sat back and took a sip. "Q?"

" '*Quelle.*' The Synoptic Problem. I've found the scroll."

It took Blaney a moment to respond. "That's . . . remarkable. Where?"

"'How?' might be a better question. Or 'Why?'"

"You're sure it's Q?"

Pearse nodded as he drank.

"And it's a collection of Jesus' sayings?"

Pearse thought he heard the slightest hint of disappointment in Blaney's tone. "Yes. But in a context you won't believe. It's the lost years, John. Jesus from twelve to thirty."

"'Jesus from . . .' Remarkable," he repeated.

"And that's only the tip of the iceberg. It turns out that the 'Beloved Disciple' was actually a Cynic teacher who wandered with Him. There are nonparable conversations with Jesus, transcriptions of early sermons He gave, a recounting of the two years He spent in Jaipur with a group of Buddhist monks. The Eastern and Cynic influences are unmistakable."

"Cynic? You mean the teachings are . . ." Blaney had to think for a moment. "You're not telling me we're in danger of having to rethink the entire tradition, are you?"

"No. That's what's extraordinary. Q gives us the same Jesus, the same faith we've always known, except maybe with a little expansion here and there. It's the way we'll look at the *church* that's going to change."

"The church?" Blaney's enthusiasm seemed to return. "You think it might cause problems."

Pearse sat back. "I don't know. That's where it gets tricky. There are things in Q, things that could rock the foundations as we know them."

"So there *is* something dangerous."

"Yes, but it's not the real threat. That's not why I came to you." Again, he leaned forward. "Your connections at the Vatican are still—"

"Can I see it?" Blaney interrupted. He slowly placed his glass on the table.

"Q isn't the problem, John. Trust me. You might find this hard to believe, but there's a group of—"

"Still, I'd like to see it."

Pearse hesitated, momentarily uneasy with Blaney's insistence. "I don't have it with me," he said.

Now Blaney paused. "Why not?"

"It wouldn't have been safe. That's what I've been trying to tell you."

"Where is it, Ian?"

"You don't have to worry about the scroll, John."

"The 'Hagia Hodoporia.'" Blaney paused again. "Where is it, Ian?"

The two men stared at each other. For nearly half a minute, Pearse couldn't move. Then, slowly, he sat back in his chair.

"I was hoping you'd just bring it to me," said Blaney.

Pearse continued to stare.

"Not that you had too many other options, I imagine." He waited for a response. When none came, he reached again for his glass. "Q. That's a bit of a surprise. Although I suppose it does make sense." He took a sip.

Another long silence. Finally, Pearse spoke. "How long?" No anger, no accusation. "Slitna? Chicago?"

Blaney held the glass in his lap. "It's a bit more complicated than that."

"How long?" repeated Pearse. "I'd like to know when I stopped making decisions for myself."

"Don't get dramatic, Ian. You've always made your own decisions."

"All that talk about the 'purity of the Word,' 'faith untethered.' Only you weren't talking about my faith, were you?"

"Faith in the Word is faith in the Word. It ultimately amounts to the same thing. Now, where is it?"

"When?" Pearse asked again, still no sign of emotion.

"That doesn't really matter, does it?"

Pearse didn't answer. The two men sat in silence.

"All right," Blaney finally said. "About . . . a year and a half ago. When we found the last of the 'Perfect Light' packets. When I knew we were getting close."

"A year and a half? I met Salko over eight years ago."

"Yes, you did." Blaney nodded. "And it was completely unrelated to all of this. I wanted you to come out of that war alive. I asked Mendravic to look after you. As a friend. Nothing more. That we unearthed one of the packets while you were there . . . Mani's will, I suppose. You have to believe me."

Now Pearse waited. "So, you and von Neurath—"

"Erich? No. He has no idea who you are. That was the whole point."

"'The whole point?'"

"There are things going on here you don't understand."

It took Pearse a moment to respond. "So *you* were the one who sent the Austrian to the Vatican?"

"The Austrian?" Now Blaney needed a moment. "Ah," he finally said. "Herr Kleist." He shook his head. "No. Not at all. In fact, it was my men who made sure you got out of there that night. Why do you think I sent Mendravic to Kukes? I've been trying to protect you all along."

"Protect me?" The first hint of anger. "Did that make it necessary to involve the woman and the boy?"

"Von Neurath's men would have tracked them down," he answered, "used them as bait, or worse. They did it with your friend Angeli. That's why Mendravic picked them up. Yes. In order to protect them."

"So you knew about Angeli, and you just let her sit there."

"Interfering would have shown my hand. I had no choice."

"Protect me from what?" asked Pearse again. It slowly began to dawn on him. *"Von Neurath?"* He continued to stare at Blaney.

"Where is it, Ian?"

"Why?"

Blaney waited. "I need the scroll."

"And how did you know the 'Perfect Light' prayer would fall into my hands?"

This time, Blaney said nothing.

"How?"

"Don't put me in a difficult position, Ian. I need the 'Hodoporia.' "

"And you think I'm actually going to give it to you?"

"Yes. I think you will." Before Pearse could answer, Blaney pressed the intercom. *"Puoi portarli dentro adesso, Gianetta."* He released the button and looked at Pearse.

"Did I tell you to go to seminary even when you were having doubts? No. Did I tell you to continue with the classics after seminary? The ancient puzzles? No. You made your own choices. That was Mani's will, as well. I'm sure you can see that."

The two sat silently.

A knock at the door, and Gianetta stood waiting. Blaney turned and nodded to her. She stepped aside. A moment later, Ivo's little head appeared in the doorway.

For the second time in the last five minutes, Pearse slowly sat back, stunned.

With a little prodding, Ivo moved into the room, Mendravic directly behind him. Two guards remained by the door.

"The woman is upstairs," said Blaney.

Pearse stared at the little face. Ivo looked slightly confused; as ever, though, he was holding his own.

"Hi, Ian," he said.

Pearse tried to focus. "Hi, Ivi."

"I took a plane trip," said Ivo, his hand now locked in Mendravic's.

Pearse nodded. "That sounds great." He waited for the little nod. He then turned to Blaney. The words almost caught in his throat. "You knew all along, didn't you? Even before I went back to seminary?"

Blaney said nothing.

"You knew about them, and you said nothing." Pearse had never felt such a rush of violence. "A year and a half? This goes back a lot further than that."

"There are things going on here—"

"That I don't understand. Yes. You've said that."

"Did you want me to let von Neurath's men find them?"

"You turned my son into one of you." Pearse was having trouble stifling his anger. "What? You couldn't find someone else who knew how to play with the scrolls? Who knew how to decipher the cryptograms? Or was it just that you knew you could use the two of them to keep me in line? Just in case."

"Ian—"

"Let me see her," said Pearse.

Blaney remained silent.

"I need to see that she's okay."

"When I have the 'Hodoporia.'"

Pearse waited. "Still protecting me? Them?" He continued to stare at Blaney. He then stood. The guards inched farther into the room. Pearse ignored them. "You want your scroll, I'll need half an hour."

"I think we can send some of my men."

Pearse shook his head. "I don't need you 'protecting' the person who's got it. You want the 'Hodoporia,' you let me go." He glanced at Ivo, then back to Blaney. "You've made sure I'll be coming back."

Blaney thought for a moment. "All right. But you'll take my men along with you. Just to make sure you come back alone."

Rather than answering, Pearse stepped over to Ivo and crouched by his side.

He tried a smile. "Was the plane fun?"

"My ears hurt for a while."

"That happens to me, too. A little gum usually helps."

"Mommy doesn't let me chew gum."

"I guess I'll have to talk to Mommy about that, won't I?"

Ivo smiled. "Mommy said . . . she said it wasn't my fault what happened yesterday."

"And she was right, Ivi. None of that had anything to do with you. I promise."

He nodded. Then, in a whisper, he added, "She said it wasn't your fault, either."

Pearse reached out and gently pulled Ivo in close. At once, the little arms squeezed around his shoulders, the tiny cheek buried in his neck. The boy released. It took Pearse a moment longer to let go. He turned to Blaney.

"I'll bring it to you, but then the boy and the woman go with me. And you leave us alone. I don't care what you do with it."

"You know me better than that, Ian."

"No, I don't." He stared for a moment, then turned to Ivo. "I have to go for a little while, Ivi, but I'll be back soon. You take care of Mommy, okay?" Another nod. Pearse winked, then stood. He moved past Mendravic. He couldn't bring himself to look at the man.

Without acknowledging either guard, Pearse stepped through the doorway.

Two minutes later, all three were on the street, making their way to a Jaguar parked at the curb. The first man reached out to open the door, Pearse ducking his head to get in.

He was halfway there when he was suddenly pushed to the floor of the car. He tried to get up but was held immobile for perhaps fifteen seconds before being pulled back, the grip on his arm unbelievably strong. Outside the car, he saw the guards lying flat on the pavement, unconscious, two men in yellow boots standing over them. The sound of screeching wheels brought his focus to the road as a sedan drew up behind the Jag. Before he knew what was happening, Pearse found himself shuttled into its backseat, thick tinted glass all around him. The door slammed shut. The car pulled away.

Alone, Pearse sat stunned.

A

"That still doesn't explain why you're here," said von Neurath. "It's not the best timing."

Seated across from him, the contessa stared in silence. He was strangely less imposing tucked behind his desk, deep within his bunker.

He seemed much smaller by contrast, a man in need of protection. Hardly the image of a Manichaean Pope with the "Hodoporia" at his fingertips. Or maybe that was just what she wanted to see.

The stark quality of the *Gabbia*'s private room—a few chairs, a sofa, a bed up against the far wall—mirrored what she had just witnessed on her drive in from the airport. The height of the tourist season, and she'd seen no one at the Colosseum, no crowds in the Piazza Venezia or along the Corso, Rome all but deserted. Most jarring, though, had been the barricade barring entry to St. Peter's from every direction, a surreal backdrop to the detachment of regular army stationed on the Vatican wall. They had made the *vigilanza* at the gate seem more than a little redundant.

The Catholic church at its most desperate, she had thought. Where was the accompanying titillation she had always expected?

"Watching Harris die and seeing Stefan pull the trigger?" she answered. "You don't think that's sufficient reason to pay you a visit?"

It was now von Neurath who took a moment. "I wasn't aware you were there."

"Well, then it looks like we're all full of surprises, doesn't it?"

He poured himself a glass of water. "You should know, the response has been extraordinary. Even in the last hour. Amazing how five hundred years of contention can melt away when the Devil himself makes an appearance."

"I didn't realize your aspirations were so high."

He laughed. "You've got it backward, Contessa. I'm going to be their savior. The father of a new church that recognizes the need for a unified front against our common enemy. The message is already going out as we speak."

"Everything according to plan."

"Don't sound so derisive. You're hardly the innocent."

"We're not talking about me."

For several seconds, von Neurath didn't answer. "What are you really here about? I can't imagine the loss of a lover would matter that much to a woman of your . . . stature. Or is it the fact that it was two in one day? My condolences."

"Ever the gentleman, Erich. And no, it doesn't matter to me in the slightest."

"Then why come here? It only draws attention. As I said, not the best timing."

"It might not be the best timing for many things."

Silence. "Harris is already being touted as a martyr," he continued. "He's proving far more useful to us dead than alive. The ground swell is enormous. You made a very good choice there."

"Did I?" She let the question sit. "I think we both know I didn't have anything to do with that. At least not according to the late colonel. He wanted me to send on his congratulations, thank you for everything you've done." She waited. "Was he meant to be some sort of distraction? Keep me preoccupied while you ascended the throne?"

"You have such a vivid imagination. I've always liked that about you."

"Yes, I'm sure you have." She watched as he placed his glass on the desk, slowly spinning it in a pool that was forming below it. "Was the fact that you had Arturo killed also part of my imagination?" Von Neurath looked up. "The distraction obviously worked. Blaney was much quicker on that than I was."

He let go of the glass. "You two really have been spending entirely too much time together. John Joseph's always been best when concentrating on his prayers. I wouldn't put too much stock in anything else he has to say."

"Why Stefan?"

"I don't like betrayal."

"To whom?"

Von Neurath started to answer, then stopped. "Did you enjoy the files he sent you?" The contessa remained silent. "I gave him the opportunity to make amends. He took it." Again, she said nothing. "Blaney has the 'Hodoporia.' That's what this is all about, isn't it? Turns out the priest was an old friend of his. It took us a bit too long to figure that one out." He waited. "Surprises all around."

His response caught her off guard. Not a pleasant experience for a woman who had spent a lifetime making sure she knew exactly what was going on. It slowly dawned on her what he was talking about. "This has all been about jockeying for position, hasn't it?" Before von Neurath could answer, she said, "My apologies. I'm usually much smarter than that. Neither of you really cares what the 'Hodoporia' has to say, do you?"

"Actually, that's not true. To be fair to the good Father, I think he truly believes he's preserving the 'purity of the Word.'" He shook his head. "How many times have I heard that phrase? Rather endearing, don't you think, if you let yourself forget everything we're trying to accomplish."

She stood and took a glass of her own. "And what exactly is that, Erich?"

Again he laughed. "You're even beginning to sound like him."

"I can almost accept the bombings. I'm not quite the idealist John J. is," she said, pouring out the water. "But Arturo, Harris, Stefan . . . it's hard for me to believe that they were sacrificed just to create greater panic. You can see how their deaths might look to someone like me, can't you?"

"Rather threatening, I would imagine."

"Interesting choice of words."

"Yes."

"Said the spider to the fly." She took a sip, then looked around the room. "I like what you've done with the place. It has that cozy, insulated feel to it. One might even say . . . isolated."

"We don't have to do this, you know."

"You never answered my question." She looked back at him, placing her glass on the desk. "What is it, exactly, that we're trying to accomplish here?"

"Why, our one true and holy church. Isn't that right, Contessa?"

"Why does it sound so hollow when you say it, Erich?"

Von Neurath smiled. "More and more like John J. every minute."

"He was right. The 'Hodoporia' means nothing to you."

"That shows how little you understand."

"No, I don't think it does."

For the first time, his composure seemed to dip. "What do you want?"

"Obviously, something you gave up a long time ago. I just never saw it until now." She turned from him and reached up under her skirt. When she turned back, she was holding a revolver, barely the size of her palm.

Von Neurath didn't flinch. "I won't ask where you were keeping that toy."

"Security's rather tight for the Pope these days." She waited. "It is a Manichaean Pope, isn't it, Erich?"

"Don't make this mistake." He pressed a button on the side of the desk.

"Too many of them have already been made. I'm just here to clean up the mess."

"You know we'll never have an opportunity like this again."

"No, *you'll* never have an opportunity like this. The rest of us have always been very good at waiting for the right moment. It's making sure we get beyond the surprises along the way. The loss of focus." She paused. "And the sacrifices."

The door to the room opened. A guard entered, his gun out.

The contessa aimed and fired.

▲

"This way, Father." A man stood waiting at the open car door. Pearse had no choice but to step out. Forty-five minutes in darkened silence to arrive inside a garage, five identical cars in a row, the smell of gasoline and oil. He glanced through what few windows there were—trees, a drive disappearing into the hillside—as he was led to a door at the far wall, a second escort now behind him. Neither said a word.

When they reached the door, the first man turned and started patting Pearse down, arms and legs, a flat palm across his back and chest. He then produced a small box from his jacket pocket, flipped a switch, and ran it the length of Pearse's body. The box remained silent. He turned and opened the door. A staircase. They headed up.

Two minutes later, Pearse sat in a rather formal library, a fuller view of the countryside through two high oriel windows. Everywhere else, bookshelves and paintings climbed to the ceiling some two stories above, a narrow balcony extending along three of the four walls. Access to the books. Except for the somewhat modern desk situated between the two windows, the room might have passed for a Vatican gallery. The men waited by the door. Still, no word of explanation.

Pearse sat patiently. He was long past even a mild apprehension. It wasn't quite resignation. He knew that. But the mechanism to shock had shorted out sometime in the last hour. In its place, he'd found a numbing fatigue, a kind of heaviness he couldn't quite shake. But also a calm, a token gift from a psyche beyond the saturation point. It had been over thirty hours since he'd last slept, but he knew that wasn't it, either. He placed his hands in his lap, his head against the soft cushion of the chair, and stared out at the trees. And waited.

When the door finally opened, he didn't bother to look around. Only when Cardinal Peretti took a seat behind the desk did Pearse shift his focus.

Peretti looked much older than he had on television, older than Pearse recalled from the one or two times they had met over the past few years, large functions, little chance to remember a young priest. He was dressed in simple clericals, only the purple shirt beneath to distinguish his office. Pearse saw a kind face, gentle features, olive skin with a hint of a tan. The eyes alone betrayed the strain he was under.

"I'm sorry for all the precautions," Peretti began, "but we had to make sure that you hadn't been forced to wear a wire, that sort of thing. You understand. There's so much going on right now."

Pearse continued to stare at him.

Peretti nodded, then said, "Something to drink, Father? Or eat?"

Pearse shook his head slowly.

Peretti let out a long breath. "You're wondering what's going on." He waited, then said, "Maybe I'm not the best person to do that." He looked past Pearse to one of the men at the door. A quick nod. Pearse heard the door open, then close. Peretti tried a smile. "You've been put through a great deal in the last week. I know. I wish . . ." He seemed genuinely concerned. "I wish I could have stepped in earlier. But until I knew you had the scroll—"

"I'm going to give it to Blaney," said Pearse, no emotion in his voice. "I thought you might want to know that. I don't really care what he does with it after that."

"Yes, you do."

The voice came from behind him. Pearse turned.

There, in the middle of the room, stood Cecilia Angeli.

"You know you do, Ian," she continued.

Without thinking, Pearse stood and moved to her, their embrace immediate, her viselike grip around his back enough to begin to shake some life into him.

"It's good to see you, too, Ian," she said.

Pearse spoke. "I wasn't sure if you—"

"For a little while there, neither was I." Letting go of her, he returned to his chair, while she sat on the edge of the desk, arms folded at her chest. Same old Angeli. "The cardinal was nice enough to come and get me." Before Pearse could ask, she pressed on. "Actually, the men at my flat were quite pleasant. A little threatening at first, but after that—or at least after you called—they let me get down to my work without too many distractions. Having them there actually forced me to take the time to finish that piece for the English journal. I really should thank them. Of course, I wasn't allowed to leave, but I sometimes stay in for days anyway. It was rather nice to have someone to cook for." She looked at Peretti. "Of course, there's still the matter of those broken windows. And I'm going to need an entirely new front door."

"Yes. I know," answered Peretti. "As I said . . . we'll take care of all of that, Professor." He leaned across to Pearse. "So I take it Blaney doesn't have it."

"Of course he doesn't have it," answered Angeli, waving her hand to quiet Peretti, her eyes on Pearse. "Ian's too smart for that." The glint in her eyes was growing. "So . . . what is it?"

Pearse's gaze, however, remained on Peretti: "How did you know to find me at Blaney's?" he asked.

"Trieste," he answered. "That's where we caught up with you."

"You were at the airport?" Pearse said, his head clearing. "Then why didn't you just pick me up? You could have gotten your hands on the scroll then and there."

"Yes, but we wanted to see where you were going, whom you were getting in touch with. We needed to know who was involved."

"And if *I* had been involved, I would have been delivering it to them."

"By that point, we knew you weren't."

" 'By that point?' " Pearse repeated.

"About three days ago, we began to link you to what was going on: a priest missing from the Vatican, his name on a ferry manifest to Greece a day before the theft on Athos, then at a camp in Kosovo. We tracked down your friend Andrakos a day later. He was rather surprised to hear you were a priest."

"I'm sure he was."

"He told us about the professor, whom we found two days ago and brought here. It was only then that we realized the extent to which you had been involved. Even then—"

"You thought I was one of them."

Reluctantly, Peretti nodded. "You never answered the notices we placed in the newspapers. And, given the way you handled the men at Kukes—men who we'd sent to help you—yes."

Pearse thought for a moment. "The boys with the yellow boots."

Peretti nodded.

"Salko must have known," he said to himself.

"What?"

Pearse looked back at Peretti. "Nothing."

"Not to mention," Peretti added, "we'd pieced together your connection with Blaney back in the States."

"So you knew he was involved?"

"Yes and no. We had our suspicions. We knew von Neurath and Ludovisi were meeting a great deal."

"Who?" asked Pearse.

"The link to the Vatican Bank. Blaney's name had come up as well, but there was nothing substantial."

"So you must have known about the Manichaean connection?"

"To tell the truth, no. The most we knew was that the 'Perfect Light' prayer was floating around, but we had no idea what it meant. That information, unfortunately, died with Boniface. At first, we assumed it had to do with the bank. We thought that maybe von Neurath was using the specter of the Manichaeans as some sort of diversion while he ferreted away the funds to ensure his election. We had no idea that this was something far more . . . I don't even know the right word to use."

"Mind-blowing?" offered Angeli. "I've added that one to my list, along with 'minor-league' and 'boonies.'"

Peretti nodded somewhat distractedly, then turned back to Pearse. "Your visit to Blaney was the confirmation we needed."

"But I didn't know Blaney was connected until I got there," said Pearse. "I went to him for help, and I didn't take the scroll in order to protect *him*."

"We took the chance that you wouldn't have left yourself that vulnerable coming back to Rome."

"That was quite a chance."

Peretti looked at Angeli. "The professor can be quite persuasive."

Pearse seemed ready to accept the answer. Instead, he began to shake his head. "That still doesn't explain how Blaney knew it would land in my lap?"

"How what would land in your lap?" asked Angeli.

"The 'Perfect Light.' None of this happens unless I get hold of that first scroll."

Angeli slowly looked over at Peretti. The two of them shared a glance before she spoke: "He might talk to Ian, help us understand the scope of this thing."

Peretti said nothing.

"Who might talk to me?" Pearse asked.

Peretti continued to look at her; he then turned to Pearse. "There was . . . an inconsistency in everything the professor told us."

"I don't understand," said Pearse.

Again, Peretti looked at Angeli. "It's worth a shot, I suppose." He nodded, then stood. "Why don't you come with me." Before Pearse could ask, Peretti was out from behind the desk and headed for the door. Pearse had no choice but to follow, Angeli at once behind him.

They made their way along the corridor and up a short flight of steps at its end. A single door awaited them at the top. Peretti removed a key, unlocked the door, and opened it. He led the way in.

There, by the window, sat Dante Cesare. He continued to stare out as they stepped inside.

"The one inconsistency," said Peretti.

Pearse stood dumbfounded. "I . . . don't understand. You saved him?"

"Hardly," said Peretti. "We were equally surprised that the 'Perfect Light' scroll had conveniently fallen into your hands, so we decided to check on that. The professor said that you had told her that the men from Vatican security had visited Cesare, and that they had spoken with his abbot. Imagine our surprise when we found out that the time sequencing you had described wasn't quite right. According to the abbot, the Vatican men had visited Cesare, but only *after* Ruini's funeral, not before."

Pearse stared at Cesare. "After?"

"Which meant," said Angeli, "that everything he'd told you was pure fabrication."

Pearse needed a moment to respond. He moved closer to the monk. "He wasn't in any kind of danger?"

"Not in the least," said Peretti. "We found him digging away at San Clemente. He's refused to say anything."

Pearse turned to the cardinal. "But I thought von Neurath's men—"

Cesare quietly laughed to himself as he gazed out the window.

Pearse stared at the monk, then turned again to Peretti. "I want to talk to him. Alone."

Peretti waited. "All right, but I'm not sure you'll get any response. My men will be outside." He took one last look at Cesare, then followed Angeli out into the corridor.

Pearse waited for the door to close before moving to the bed. He sat. It was only then that he saw the handcuffs attached to a rail on the wall.

"Don't worry," said Cesare, rattling the metal, "they've taken every precaution."

"I thought you weren't speaking to anyone."

"None of them have read the 'Hodoporia.' I'm assuming you have. I envy you that. Which means you understand what we're trying to do."

Pearse continued to stare. "You were with Blaney all along."

"Very good."

"No chance meeting in the park."

"No."

Pearse nodded slowly. "Amazing performance."

"You missed a better one that last night for von Neurath's men."

"I'm surprised they didn't kill you."

Another smile. "The Father took care of that. You became far more interesting to the cardinal rather quickly. Blaney saw to that, as well."

"He told me he was trying to protect me."

"Oh, he was. But he also knew a little fire under your feet would get you to the 'Hodoporia' all the faster. As long as von Neurath's men were always a few steps behind, no need to worry."

Pearse waited. "If Blaney knew how to find the 'Perfect Light' scroll, why use me at all? Why not send you?"

"*Knowing* how to find it was far different from actually *finding* it."

Pearse needed a moment. "Ruini."

"Funny little man." Cesare's gaze dipped for just a moment. "Boniface had him off looking for something entirely different, and he stumbles across the 'Perfect Light.'" Again, he laughed to himself. "Talk about bad luck. For everyone." He waited. "Once Ruini had the scroll, we knew von Neurath would do whatever was necessary to get it from him. And we knew the cardinal was going to be the next Pope." Cesare finally looked at Pearse, eyes devoid of all emotion. "Now do you understand?" When Pearse didn't answer, Cesare turned back to the window. He let out a long breath. "Allowing von Neurath to get his hands on the 'Hodoporia' would have made him uncontrollable. Who knows what he would have done with it? He's never trusted the Word. He doesn't understand its power. So Blaney needed someone who wasn't part of this, someone von Neurath wouldn't know, someone to find it for him first. Keep the balance. It's what Mani had prepared you for." Again he turned. "Any clearer?"

"So Ruini found the scroll, and you killed him."

"Von Neurath's people did that. We knew they would. It's why I was sent. To bring you in." Another long breath. "I suppose, for a time, he thought I might be able to handle it on my own. But then I didn't have

the training for the scrolls that you did. Plus, there was always the outside chance von Neurath might be able to link me with Blaney. Your
connection was far more remote. We knew it would take them at least
a week to discover it. By then, you'd be back. Or dead." He turned back
to the window. "At least now I never have to hear about baseball again."

"The sacrifices we make," said Pearse.

"Yes."

Unable to look at the smirk any longer, he stood. "So Blaney went
through all of this just to keep von Neurath in line?"

"He did it to make sure that the power of Mani's Word would remain
pure."

"Purity at its finest."

Cesare waited. "I'm surprised. I'd have thought after reading the
'Hodoporia,' you'd be less hostile. You really think we're some group of
fanatics, don't you? I find that very . . . odd."

"Why should I think that?" he said, turning to Cesare, his tone now
matching the monk's apparent indifference. "The church bombings, the
Vatican, the bank, the hysteria over Islamic fundamentalism. Am I missing anything? Oh, and of course the one true and holy church for the
initiated. Do we all get to be Manichaeans now, guided by those of you
with the gnosis? No, that doesn't sound like fanaticism at all, does it,
Dante?"

"Ten million Manichaeans is more than enough."

"Impressive."

"We've no interest in converting the masses."

"Just leading them around by their noses."

Something seemed to change in Cesare. He turned to Pearse, a
decided contempt in his eyes. "Unlike the Catholic church, Father?" He
didn't wait for a response. "What if I told you we've got child-welfare
initiatives, drug-abuse programs, planned-parenting centers, all set up by
the hundreds, both here in Europe and in the States? Would you think
differently? We're simply removing the darkness to free the light. In the
abstract, I suppose it does sound like fanaticism. But not when it has a
practical face to it. We've pumped millions of dollars into those areas
and others so as to establish the base we need to put our cells to proper
use. The Catholic church isn't capable of making that kind of difference
now. You're an outdated and impotent monolith. You won't even go
near half those areas because of ancient doctrine. Well, we're going into
them and doing something about it. Fifteen hundred years ago, we

wanted to destroy you because of the corruption of certain theological truths. Now, we simply want to put you out of your misery, turn the church into something that has real power, and that can make the world whole again."

"Those are two very different objectives."

"Not if you understand what we're trying to do."

"You mean like creating raw panic? I guess there's nothing more practical than that. I'm not sure that's what the 'Hodoporia' has in mind."

"I agree. And it's not what we have in mind, either."

"Not from what I've seen."

Cesare seemed ready to press on. Instead, he stopped. The lazy smile reappeared. His gaze drifted out the window. "That will all be corrected."

"Oh." Pearse nodded. "I get it. Blaney's the good Manichaean with all the programs. It's von Neurath who's been the rogue all along." When Cesare didn't answer, Pearse continued. "You really expect me to believe that Blaney had no idea what von Neurath was doing? Do *you* actually believe that? Unless I've missed something, you need to eliminate every other church out there before your true and holy one can make its appearance. Which means von Neurath is every bit the committed Manichaean Blaney is, and every bit as crucial. Maybe more so. Blaney needs this violence and hysteria just as much as von Neurath does."

Cesare looked again at Pearse. "He needs the 'Hodoporia' for the reason you've just pointed out. Are you that dense that you think there haven't been Manichaean Popes before now? Benedict the Ninth, Celestine the Fifth—but they were as devoted to the 'Hodoporia' as we are. And not just to its destructive force as von Neurath is. They refused to do anything—in fact, they knew they *couldn't* do anything—because the promise of the 'Hodoporia' isn't just about destruction. It's about rebirth. You more than anyone know that it explains what the unity is meant to look like beyond the corrupted church. Without the 'Hodoporia' and its full promise, those Popes had no choice but to keep their power in check while they served a corrupted church. A man like von Neurath doesn't understand that."

"Really? Or maybe those Popes realized the greater paradox. That in order to achieve the triumph here on earth—your one pure church—they had to unleash a darkness that would have tainted any consequent light, no matter how pure. Blaney's just convinced himself that the 'Hodoporia' can rise above that. How convenient."

Cesare had lost the smile. "You really didn't understand it at all, did you?"

"I guess not."

Silence. Cesare again turned to the window. "Well, then, you've missed your opportunity now that Blaney has it."

"Oh, he doesn't have it."

Pearse thought he saw the slightest crack in Cesare's expression. Just as quickly, the monk regained his composure.

"Then he will soon enough." He slowly turned to Pearse. "How's the boy? I meant to ask. He has such a good mind for the prayers."

The two men stared at each other. Cesare then returned his gaze to the window. "Such a lovely little soprano."

Pearse stood there, his eyes fixed on Cesare. Once again, he felt a rush of violence. With every ounce of restraint he had, he slowly turned and headed for the door.

"Good-bye, Ian."

Half a minute later, Pearse watched Angeli rise from her chair as he walked back into the library. "Well?" she said.

Pearse said nothing as he moved toward them.

Angeli sensed something. "What is it, Ian?"

"Did he tell you anything?" asked Peretti, once again seated behind the desk.

Pearse drew up to them. He continued to hold Peretti's gaze. Finally, he spoke. "I can't give you the scroll."

The cardinal leaned forward. "You have to believe me that we're not involved—"

"That's not the reason," said Pearse.

"Then it's the scroll itself, isn't it?" said Angeli. Pearse started to shake his head, but she was already taking off. "I knew it. What's in there, Ian?" The glint was back. "Why all the fuss?"

He started to explain; again she pressed.

"What have they been hiding all these years?"

Pearse saw the anticipation in her eyes. He knew she wouldn't let it go. Very quietly, he finally said, "Q."

"Q!" Her knees nearly buckled. "You mean to say it's . . . Of course."

Ten minutes later, she was pacing the middle of the room, a cigarette in one hand, waving wildly as she spoke. "That's remarkable. Unbelievable. The Resurrection bits alone . . ." She stopped and looked at the two of them. "No wonder the Manichaeans wanted to get their hands on it. Out with the old church, in with the new. It's perfect. This whole Islam business finally makes sense."

Angeli's enthusiasm was having a very different effect on Peretti. The lines on his face seemed to deepen as he spoke. "Something like that would be dangerous in anyone's hands. I can understand your hesitation."

"No, you can't," said Pearse, now seated in the lip of the desk. Again, with no emotion in his voice, he said, "I'm giving it to Blaney."

"What?" Angeli blurted out. "Giving it to . . . If those passages are in there—"

"I know," said Pearse. "I don't have a choice."

"I'm afraid it's not your choice to make," said Peretti.

"I think it is." Pearse waited before continuing. "My son's life depends on it."

The room fell silent.

After several uncomfortable moments Angeli said, "I . . . had no idea."

"Neither did I," said Pearse, again no emotion.

"How did—"

"In Bosnia, during the war. Before I took the cloth."

After a long silence, Peretti finally spoke. "So you never knew about the boy?"

Pearse shook his head.

"But why would Blaney have him?"

"Because he's known about him from the beginning. He made sure that he was raised as a Manichaean. And then made equally certain that I never found out. Probably with this very moment in mind." Pearse waited, then said, "He has the mother, as well." He saw the look in Peretti's eyes. "No. She's not one of them. She was as much in the dark as I was."

"You're certain of that?" he asked. Pearse continued to stare at him. Peretti nodded. "I'm not sure that changes anything."

"I think it does," said Pearse. "I have the scroll."

"You can't be serious," said Peretti.

Pearse stared back at him.

"Actually . . . I think he can," said Angeli. It was clear her wheels were spinning. "You say the scroll is unambiguous about the Resurrection business?" Pearse nodded. "But you also say it's equally clear on individual responsibility, autonomy, and women?" Again, he nodded. She looked at Peretti. "That could be very helpful to the church right now, Eminence."

"Where are you going with this, Professor?"

"I think that's pretty clear, isn't it?"

Peretti shook his head. "No. You can't have one without the other."

"Why not?" she said.

"You can't simply write out the things you don't like."

"Why?" It was Pearse who now asked.

"'Why?'" Peretti seemed surprised that it was Pearse who had asked. "Because, Father, we're talking about the Holy Word of Christ. You can't overlook that."

"The Gospel writers did," said Pearse. "They had Q and chose to take what they wanted from it." He waited. "Maybe that's what the church needs now in order to survive in the next millennium. Another dose of selective editing."

Peretti stared at him for a moment. "From what the professor tells me, Father, you're the last person I would have expected to hear that from."

"Things change." Pearse waited. "Look, my own reasons for you to do this aside, without those forty lines of Resurrection text, you'd have a very powerful document, something to take us beyond the brick wall we've all been running into since Vatican Two. Modernize the church without losing touch with the Christ we've always known. Q might just be the answer."

"It's the Word of *Christ*." Peretti let the phrase settle. "I can't permit that. And neither can you. You know that."

Angeli jumped in. "I've worked with hundreds of scrolls, Eminence. None I've seen has ever come close to the one he's describing. We're lucky if we find a few strands of parchment here and there. The fact that this one hasn't disintegrated makes it seem almost . . . unreal. You might have to lose a few bits just to make sure it looks authentic." She stopped him before he could respond. "All right, I'm being a little facetious, but you do understand the point. It might be the one time when you can have your liturgical cake and eat it, too."

Peretti slowly began to shake his head. "It would raise too many problems with the canon, even from the little you've said. The Eucharist *is* the liturgy. A document like that would have to confirm its pivotal role."

"Not if those were the sections that were missing," she answered. "I have a rather nice reputation when it comes to filling in gaps in scrolls like this. As long as the incisions are made with a bit of finesse, I don't think it would be all that difficult to leave the right sorts of holes, ones that would clearly imply the existence of whatever liturgy you felt was essential."

Peretti thought for a moment; again he shook his head. "What you're asking—"

"What other options do you have?" said Pearse. "Keep it hidden? Who would be overlooking the Word of Christ, then?"

From Peretti's expression, Pearse had hit a nerve.

"You're both missing the point," said Angeli. "Without the Resurrection passages, Q would be the very thing to pull the rug out from under the Manichaeans." She had retrieved her cigarette and was taking two quick puffs before crushing it out in the ashtray. "Q is their grail, correct? It's at the core of everything they believe in. I assume Blaney and this monk believe in it that strongly, too?"

Pearse thought for a moment, then nodded.

"Well, here you have a chance to tarnish the grail and place it in their hands. Show them that it's no threat to the church, that it would actually strengthen her. A thousand years searching for it, and their one great hope turns out to be an empty promise. Whose foundations would be shaken then?"

"Somehow, I don't think Erich von Neurath needs a grail to sate his ambition," said Peretti.

"Fine," said Pearse, an ultimatum in his tone. "Then it goes to Blaney, as is."

Again, Peretti waited before answering. "You know I can't let you do that."

Pearse looked directly into his eyes. "Then you have a problem. Because if I don't pick it up by tonight, it goes to Blaney anyway. Instructions in the package. It seemed the logical choice at the time."

Peretti continued to stare at Pearse. "You really think Blaney would make that exchange and then let you go?"

"Yes." No hesitation. "He owes me that much. And he knows it."

Peretti was about to answer, when the phone rang. He picked up.

"Yes." For several seconds, he listened intently, unable to mask a moment of surprise. "We're sure on this?" Several nods. "Do we know who she is? . . . All right, fine . . . good." Still listening, he looked across at Pearse as he spoke into the phone. "No, I think we can do better than that. Wait for my call." He hung up. Finally, he said, "Von Neurath is dead." Slowly, he shifted his gaze to Angeli. "How long would you need to . . . revise the scroll?"

She thought for a moment, then said, "I don't know. Two, three hours. It depends on the—"

"Then do it." He looked at Pearse. "When you're done, you'll call Blaney. By then, I'll know where I want you to make the exchange. Acceptable, Father?"

Pearse simply nodded.

▲

The Villa Borghese at dusk has an almost ethereal quality to it, especially in the Pincio Gardens, the area just above Piazza del Popolo, where the long promenades—most named for saints and Popes—lie under vaulted rows of pine and oak, each dotted with benches and lampposts. The sounds of Rome disappear, replaced by the occasional footstep on gravel, fewer and fewer of them as the sun dips down and the glow of lamplight begins to make itself known.

Pearse listened to his own footfall as he made his way along one of the wider walkways, Viale Leone IX his destination. As ever, Angeli had been spot-on—two and a half hours to alter the scroll, the offending passages removed with expert precision. It was only when it had come to disposing of the unwanted pieces that her hand had hesitated. Both of them had looked at the strands lying in the small bowl on the table. It was Pearse who had produced the box of matches.

The conversation with Peretti had been short. The location and time. The call to Blaney hadn't been as easy, although it was clear he'd been expecting it. Pearse would be coming alone? Yes. Who had helped him? All he wanted was the boy and the woman. Blaney had to trust him on that. An hour.

He had then spoken with Petra and Ivo. She had promised she was up to it. Ivo had just liked the idea of another adventure.

He saw Blaney seated on a bench halfway down the path as he turned onto Leone IX. Another fifteen yards on stood Mendravic, Ivo by his side, Petra in a wheelchair. No one else. Pearse continued to approach. Five yards from Blaney, he stopped.

"Can she walk?" he asked.

"Yes," answered Blaney.

"Then tell them to come over to me."

"Let me see the 'Hodoporia.'"

Pearse opened the box in his hands. He tilted it toward Blaney so he could see the scroll inside.

"How do I know it's the 'Hodoporia'?"

"Send them over."

Blaney waited. "Hand me the box."

Pearse remained where he was, box in hand. "You know, von Neurath's dead."

Blaney showed no reaction. "Yes. And no, it wasn't me, if that's what you're wondering."

"Send them over," said Pearse.

Blaney waited, then looked at Mendravic. He nodded. At once, the Croat moved out to help Petra from her chair. She refused. Very slowly, she stood. She took Ivo's hand.

"All right," said Blaney. "Now give me the box."

"We'll wait until they're past me." Blaney looked as if he might say something. Instead, he took in a deep breath, then nodded again to Mendravic. Petra and Ivo slowly started out. Both men watched as the pair drew nearer.

"Am I right in thinking it was Daly who was trying to help you?" asked Blaney. "Kukes, this afternoon?"

"Peretti," answered Pearse. "Cesare sends his regards."

Again, no reaction. "A little more obvious, but it had to be one or the other. One of them will no doubt be the next Pope." Pearse had never heard Blaney's smug side. "I assume he has men scattered about the park."

"I said I'd come alone."

"Somehow, I doubt that."

Pearse remained silent.

Petra and Ivo moved past Blaney and drew up to Pearse. She grabbed ahold of his arm. He immediately held her at his side. Ivo gave him a quick wave.

"Hi, Ian."

"Hey, Ivi."

Under his breath, Pearse said to Petra, "I need you to keep going. The bench across from us. Can you make that?"

She nodded once and took Ivo's hand.

When they were far enough off, Pearse turned back to Blaney. Without any prompting, he moved to the bench and sat. "There's no one else here, John. I took you at your word."

"Then you're more naïve than I thought."

"Maybe," said Pearse. "Maybe not." He handed him the box.

"You should go," said Blaney, his fingers busy with the straps. "You have the woman and the boy."

"Still protecting me?"

"More than you realize."

"And how's that, John?"

Old fingers were having trouble with the knot. "Several of von Neurath's men are here," he said. "Not my choice. They've been at a loss for what to do for the last few hours. They weren't that keen on this exchange."

Pearse let his eyes wander casually to the surrounding trees, seemingly unaffected by the news. "So why the charade?" he asked. "Why didn't they just take it from me when I got here?"

"Because I'm sure several of Peretti's men are also here. No reason for anyone to do something foolish. I'm not sure, however, how long they'll wait. I don't have quite the same sway over them as Erich did. You should go. Now."

"No," said Pearse, eyes still on the trees, "I think I'd like to see you read through some of it."

"And why is that?"

"It might not be everything you thought it was."

"I see." Blaney nodded. He was finally making progress with the knot. "Then you obviously didn't know how to read it."

For the briefest of moments, Pearse thought that perhaps he'd let himself forget the fundamental rule with the Manichaeans. Hidden knowledge. Had he missed something in the verses, something even more profound than the Resurrection segments? Was there a final word game that he had somehow overlooked? He quickly remembered that there couldn't be. Q had been written by Menippus, a first-century Greek Cynic, two hundred years before Mani's birth. Even the Manichaeans didn't reach that far back.

"There are breaks in the text," said Pearse. "I can tell you what's no longer there."

Blaney was starting to roll back the parchment. He stopped and looked over at Pearse. "What?"

"The missing text. The stuff to threaten the church. It isn't there any-more."

Blaney started to answer, then stopped. He went back to the scroll. "You wouldn't have done that. I know you, Ian." Blaney had reached the first gap in the text.

"That doesn't look like natural decay, does it, John?"

Blaney scanned the sheet of parchment, his expression more and more uncertain.

"Don't worry," added Pearse. "Angeli tells me she'll have it looking authentic enough by the time Peretti presents it to the Biblical Commission."

Blaney rolled deeper into the scroll. He found another gap. Again, he stared down at it. Almost in a whisper, he said. "Why?" His face was etched with confusion. "Why would you do this?" He slowly turned to Pearse. "You always believed in the sanctity of the Word. I *taught* you to believe in the sanctity of the Word. How could you have done this?"

Pearse continued to gaze out. "If you had time to read the entire scroll, you'd see it's not a threat at all. In fact, it's—what did Dante call it?— a rebirth. It's all in there. Except it's the Catholic church that will be using it now. Peretti wanted me to pass on his thanks."

Blaney stared at Pearse a moment longer, then looked back at the scroll. His fingers began to trace over the gaps. It was as if he were caress-ing a wound. "It's the Word of Christ. Who are you to say what can be taken out? I chose you because of your faith in the Word. In the *Word*."

"It's the denial of the bodily Resurrection," Pearse said offhandedly. "That's what's missing." He turned to Blaney. "Dangerous stuff." He watched as Blaney stared at the scroll, only a slight shaking of his head. The rest of him seemed frozen. "It looks like you have a choice, John. You can either let Peretti get his hands on the scroll and use it to inject new life into the church. Or, you can destroy it, and hope that the church eventually runs itself into the ground. The problem is, if you *do* destroy it now, you won't have the 'Hodoporia' to guide you at that point. You won't have the one piece of scripture that every good Manichaean looks to as his ultimate guide." He waited. "I guess that's not really much of a choice, is it?"

Blaney began to roll the scroll again, his eyes darting back and forth, searching for something to tell him Pearse was wrong.

"You won't find anything," said Pearse. "We made sure of that. Trust me."

Blaney's arm began to shake, his grip on the scroll weakening. His head suddenly spasmed, a jolt that forced Pearse to reach over and take the scroll from him.

"John?" Blaney's entire body began to shake. "John—"

He started to gag violently. Pearse had wanted a reaction, needed it, but not this.

At once, Salko was moving toward them. Pearse dropped the scroll and reached out for Blaney. Instantly, six men appeared from the trees some twenty yards off, one of them the titan Pearse remembered from his escape from the Vatican, all of them descending on the bench, guns drawn. The first shot rang out.

But not from the men racing at him.

Utterly confused, Pearse spun around. It was then that he saw Peretti's men emerging from another group of trees, guns firing, the clipped sounds of volley and return. Pearse dropped to the gravel, pulling Blaney down with him. The old priest had stopped shaking. In fact, he had stopped moving entirely. Pearse lifted the head and looked into his eyes. Blaney was gone.

Only then did he hear Petra's scream.

"Ivo! No!"

Pearse spun around. She was forcing herself up from the bench, trying to pull Ivo back. But he was too well trained, too intent, the sound of the shots telling him to find an open space, lie facedown. Pearse watched as his little arms pumped in the air.

Everything seemed to slow, Pearse dropping Blaney to the ground, grabbing at the gravel to force himself up, Ivo too far from him, endless shots ringing out. All around him, men were falling, and still Ivo ran. From the corner of his eye, Pearse saw the last of von Neurath's men nearing, firing wildly, the gun aimed directly at the boy. Pearse leapt out, a sudden tearing pain in his own leg forcing him to the ground. For an instant, he couldn't see a thing. Only the gravel, images of Ivo, his son, once again unable to protect him, the chance to lose him now. Again.

A final shot. Ivo screamed.

Pearse looked up.

There, lying in front of the boy, was Mendravic, his chest covered in blood. Ivo was crying wildly as he pulled at Mendravic's arm.

"Get up, Salko! Get up!"

Unscathed. Perfect. Pearse breathed again as he saw his little man standing over Mendravic's shattered body.

Even so, the Croat was doing all he could to calm the boy. Pearse pulled himself to his feet and hobbled over. Petra already held Ivo close to her chest as he continued to scream. Now at her side, Pearse took them both in his arms for several moments before turning and dropping to Mendravic's side.

The sound of Ivo's cries seemed to vanish as Pearse took Mendravic's head in his hands. Barely focusing, Mendravic looked up at him.

His breathing was erratic as he spoke: "I taught him how to run out like that." He coughed several times. "'Out in the open, Ivi. Out in the open.'" His neck arched for a moment. "He's all right, yes?"

Pearse nodded. "Yes."

"Good . . . that's good." He tried to swallow. "I never meant to . . ." He squeezed Pearse's arm, the grip powerful. "You have to know that, Ian."

Pearse nodded, tears beginning to roll down his cheeks. A final act of redemption. "I do."

Mendravic tried to nod, but his back suddenly constricted. He stared up at Pearse, an instant of clarity in the eyes. His grip then released. And he became still.

Pearse held him there, gently pressing Mendravic's head to his own, unwilling, for the moment, to let go. His body began to shake, tears flowing for the man he had known. The man he would always know.

Slowly, he laid Mendravic's head on the gravel. He brushed away his own tears, shut the Croat's eyes, and made the sign of the cross. Then, as best he could, he made his way back to Petra and Ivo.

Four men lay dead, the rest in the hands of Peretti's men. The scroll was where it had fallen, Blaney's arm cast awkwardly over it.

None of it mattered, though. Not as he reached Petra and Ivo and wrapped his arms around them. Again he cried. They pressed into him, all three quietly cocooned within themselves.

⚠

Two hours later, Pearse was still holding Petra's hand, Ivo on her lap, the three of them seated across from Peretti in his library. The stars outside the oriel windows were holding Ivo's gaze, the first time since the Pincio that he'd stopped shaking. Angeli sat as well, the scroll in its box at her feet.

The doctor had left twenty minutes ago, Pearse's flesh wound handled easily, more attention for Petra's side. She was doing fine. A little less activity would be good. She had refused the sedative for Ivo.

"And I can't convince you otherwise?" said Peretti.

"I don't think so, Eminence," Pearse answered.

"It's an extraordinary opportunity, Ian," said Angeli, no small degree of hope in her voice. "And I could use the help."

Pearse shook his head.

"It's not because you're worried about the instability in the church, is it?" asked Peretti. "Because if that's it, you might want to know that we've decided to make von Neurath a martyr in all of this." He saw Pearse's reaction. "Oh, yes. The woman who killed him has an interesting enough background to make her and Blaney the perfect models for a fanatical movement within the church."

"Hard to believe," said Angeli somewhat playfully, "but they were actually going to destroy a recently discovered parchment, a very sacred scroll that, some say, may shed light on a whole new, liberalized church. Can you imagine that?" She smiled. "Luckily, we caught them in time."

"Sounds reasonable enough, doesn't it?" asked Peretti.

"So no Manichaeans," said Pearse.

"No," answered Peretti. "Something that well entrenched wouldn't blow over so quickly. This way, we defuse the current situation much more effectively."

"And then?" asked Pearse.

"Then . . ." Peretti bobbed his head from side to side. "Then we publish Q and tell the world that it's actually something called the 'Hagia Hodoporia.' That should send a shock wave through the Manichaean cells. Impotence has a tendency to undermine even the most powerful of heresies. I imagine it might even make your friend Cesare a little more talkative."

Pearse nodded.

Peretti continued to stare at him. "But it's not the instability, is it?"

Pearse waited. "No, Eminence, it's not."

"Then why?" When Pearse didn't answer, he continued. "I realize the priesthood might not be what you want now"—he glanced momentarily at Petra and Ivo—"and I would certainly understand that, but you have the chance to take the church someplace it's never been."

"But built on what, Eminence?" Again, Pearse waited. "A few hours ago, we had the Word at its purest, and we decided to alter it to protect the church."

"True," countered Peretti, "and if I remember, you were the one who said we had no other choice."

"Fair enough. But that's always the argument, isn't it? Protect the church, keep it strong, no matter how much we might need to change the message."

"It's still a very powerful message."

"To a point, Eminence. I suppose taking a match to the 'Hodoporia' helped me to see that."

Peretti's tone was slightly less inviting "And how is that?"

Pearse waited. "I always thought that if I found something pure enough, everything would fall into place, no matter what the expectations surrounding it. But that just isn't the case. Nothing stays that pure when it has to fit into a man-made structure. And Christ knew that. That's why He designed the message with each singular spirit in mind. That's His infallibility, His power. To know that everyone brings his or her own faith to the table, purely individuated, purely isolated, and yet, it's in that perfect singularity that the message makes sense. It defines a relationship built on one brutal truth: that it's our responsibility to find connection with the world outside us. No one else's. And certainly no church's. In a strange way, the Manichaeans brought that home to me." Not even aware of it, Pearse pulled Petra's hand closer to him. "It's that connection that lies at the heart of purity, and makes clarity possible."

Peretti continued to stare at Pearse. "You realize, of course, that it's the church's sole purpose to enhance that connection."

"I'm not sure I agree anymore."

Peretti was about to answer. Instead, he held back. "Well," he said, nodding, "then we'll be sorry not to have you."

"So," said Angeli, clapping her hands together and standing, an attempt to diffuse the moment, "you're leaving me with His Eminence." She laughed to herself as she looked at Peretti. "I'll tell you, I'm not easy to work with."

Peretti smiled. "I'll keep that in mind."

"Ashtrays," said Pearse. "I'd recommend them as a peace offering."

"Very funny," said Angeli. "So, now it's back to the States, then?"

Pearse looked at Petra. "We'll see."

"I have some very good friends at the Biblical Institute in Boston. They'd love to get their hands on you."

He smiled at Angeli, then turned again to Petra. "I think the first order of business is to get this little one to sleep."

"Of course," said Peretti, immediately on his feet. "We have rooms for you upstairs. And please, the villa is yours for as long as you need it."

Pearse stood as well, then Petra, as Ivo hopped down to the floor. Pearse waited until he had Peretti's gaze, then said, "Thank you, Eminence."

"No," said the cardinal, "thank you . . . Father."

Pearse turned and picked Ivo up. He then took Petra's hand.

Before they had taken a step, Angeli was on the move. "Wait, wait." She darted in and kissed Pearse on the cheek. "I've always liked doing that. I suppose I'll miss it." She smiled at Petra and Ivo, then looked back at Pearse. Before he could reply, she was already bearing down on Peretti. "Now, the way I see it, Eminence, we have two choices. Well, one, really, if you understand how the . . ."

Her voice trailed off as the three of them stepped out into the corridor.

"She speaks very fast," said Ivo.

Pearse and Petra both laughed softly. "Yes, she does, Ivi," said Petra. "Yes, she does."

Epilogue

Brewster, Massachusetts

The sun hovered on the horizon, more yellow than orange, dipping ever faster into the perfectly still bay. No wind on the beach, the heat gentler than an hour ago, every breath suffused with the taste of salt. Late September on the Cape, the days grasping desperately at what no longer was theirs.

Pearse stared out, the easy rhythm of the tide lapping at his feet. Three weeks home, and he was only now beginning to have a sense of where he was.

Blaney had been right. The papacy had gone to Peretti a week after the first news stories. Special circumstances. The *novemdieles* had been cut to six days, eight cardinals and a healthy dose of bishops called on to convene the conclave. They'd elected him on the first ballot.

More interesting, though, was the piece of scripture—"The Book of Q," according to the scholars—that Peretti had been so instrumental in saving from the clutches of the so-called conspirators. Guarded more closely than the Dead Sea Scrolls, Q was helping people to regain focus in the still-raw aftermath of the bombings. Angeli was making the news, always fun to see. And important people were beginning to sit around tables. A first step. It would be some time, though, before a sense of normalcy—whatever that meant—might return.

There were positive signs, though. A group of Methodist ministers in the States was claiming that the Vatican was hoarding Q for itself—rumors of Catholic scholars having pieced much of it together for their own purposes. The internal bickering had started.

There was hope after all.

And, of course, no mention of the Manichaeans.

A splash of water hit him in the back of his head. Pearse turned to find Ivo, his little hands pulled up to his mouth, a look of anticipated retaliation in his eyes. It was only in the last few days that he'd begun to act more like himself, Salko's death still so close.

"Uh-oh, Ivi," said Pearse, "I think it's beginning to rain."

Another burst of laughter, a quick run to the water's edge, then back. "It wasn't rain! It wasn't rain!"

"Hmm." Pearse nodded seriously. "Then what could—"

He didn't have a chance to finish as a bucketful of water streamed down onto his head. Chilled for an instant, Pearse jumped to his feet, Petra quickly retreating out of arm's reach.

Howls of laughter as Ivo ran to her side. "We got you! We got you!" he screamed.

Pearse bent over, hands on his knees, eyeing his prey. A mischievous grin rose on his face.

"I think we made him crazy, Ivi," she said.

Ivo's eyes went wide as he ducked in behind Petra. "It was Mommy who did it." He laughed. "Mommy dumped the water. Not me. Mommy."

Pearse began to move toward them. More shrieks of laughter from Ivo as he and Petra slunk backward. She, too, was laughing. Pearse was within striking distance, when Ivo bolted away. Pearse looked at her, the smile so inviting. He then darted after Ivo, more howls and shrieks until Pearse caught him and picked him up, charging wildly into the water.

"No!" Ivo screamed in laughter.

Deep enough out, Pearse tossed him in the air, waiting to see the doused little face reappear.

"Do that again," Ivo chortled after he'd wiped the water from his eyes.

"Time to get Mommy," said Pearse. He turned and began charging out of the water. The look on Petra's face was almost too perfect. A moment of panic, then utter capitulation. Ivo was cheering.

Pearse drew up to her, arms outstretched, ready to hoist her onto his back. Instead, he slowly straightened up and wrapped his arms around her, the heat from her body pressed against his chest.

She held his gaze for a moment, then kissed him.

"You still don't look like a priest," she said.

"I'm not anticipating that's going to be much of a problem anymore."

She smiled.

"Have you told your family?" she asked.

"They knew the moment I stepped off the plane." He suddenly picked her up and began to walk toward the water.

"No, Ian. No. Come on. The doctor said I can't go into the water—"

"Until today. That's what he said."

He was up to his knees, Ivo now at his side.

"Boy, you're going to get it, Mommy." He giggled.

Pearse whispered in her ear. "Or we could wait for the midnight swim?"

"Yes, we could," she whispered back.

He gently kissed her, then placed her feet in the water. A moment later, he was after Ivo again.

"So I'm going to get Mommy, am I?"

Ivo howled as he tried to escape. But to no avail.

As one, they fell into the water. Pearse grabbed him and pulled him tightly to his chest. They floated there, heads bobbing together.

Far from insignificant in a seemingly empty sea.

 **Author's Note**

It would have been impossible to attempt this book without taking advantage of the truly extraordinary scholarship that is now available on early Christianity. For their work on Gnosticism, I am greatly indebted to Elaine Pagels, Kurt Rudolph, Hans Jonas, Robert M. Grant, Charles W. Hedrick and Robert Hodgson, Jr., Geo Widengred, David M. Scholer, and Bentley Layton. For their studies of Q, John S. Kloppenborg, Christopher M. Tuckette, and Burton L. Mack were invaluable. And for their more general overviews, John Dominic Crossan (whose *Jesus: A Revolutionary Biography* is simply a marvel), Leif E. Vaage, Jaroslav Pelikan, Robert W. Funk, Roy W. Hoover and The Jesus Seminar, and, of course, Peter Brown provided the strongest of foundations on which to build my own Q.

The world of the Manichaeans was a bit tougher to dig into, but the research there is, I discovered, equally rich. Iain Gardner, Luigi Cirillo, John C. Reeves, and Paul Mirecki and Jason BeDuhn have put together some of the most intriguing collections and commentaries on Manichaean scripture. Peter Brown's chapter on the Manichaeans in his *Augustine of Hippo* remains essential reading.

I would also have been hard-pressed to imagine Greece and the Balkans, both during and after the war, without the exceptional books of William Dalrymple, Michael S. Sells, Sabrina Petra Ramet, Misha Glenny, Laura Silber and Allan Little, Noel Malcolm, and Peter Maass.

Together, they made my own research a genuine pleasure.

About the Author

Jonathan Rabb is the author of *The Overseer.* He lives in New York.